Daughter
Mine

Daughter Mine

———◆▶✕◀◆———

HERBERT GOLD

Thomas Dunne Books
St. Martin's Press ⁑ New York

1- 7/78

For Leo
old friend, fellow young writer

THOMAS DUNNE BOOKS.
An imprint of St. Martin's Press.

ISBN 0-312-26306-6

First Edition: July 2000

10 9 8 7 6 5 4 3 2 1

According to the sages, forgiveness is required. However, if a person who has sinned against you apologizes, you do not have to forgive. If he makes up for his sin, you are still not obliged to forgive. But if he then changes his behavior so that he will not sin in this way again, you must forgive him.

*Daughter
Mine*

One

On a day like any other, which turned out to be like none other, a telephone call came his way. The caller was a young woman who spoke in the drawling layabout accent of late adolescence. In his office he heard mainly from lawyers, defendants' distraught families, and legal-aid volunteers; usually it was the Spanish-speakers who needed his help in court, translating for Your Esteemed Honor their optimistic explanations of how the lady's purse happened to jump into their hands as they ran down the street to get home in time to feed a sick child who would miss her papa even more if he were convicted on a third so-called offense. The addition of ALSO FRENCH AND ITALIAN TRANSLATION & INTERPRETING SERVICES looked good on his stationery and on the frosted-glass door, but these days there weren't many Parisians or Neapolitans picked up for shoplifting, assault, or drug-dealing; or if they were, they seemed to be adequately bilingual, not needing his services.

"Mr. Shaper?"

"Speaking."

"Mr. Shaper?"

"Yes. I hear you."

"Mr. Shaper, this is your daughter. My name is Amanda."

After he waited for the kook to just go away, after a pause

for a crazy kid giggle and the click of hanging up, he said: "I
don't have a daughter."

Her patience was equal to his. Just as calmly she replied,
"Yes you do. Margaret Torres is my mother."

Margaret Torres? The screen continued blank. For a moment he knew nothing, then he recognized the name but still
had no image of a person. Then, in sequence, he remembered
a film shown at the Mexican Consulate nearly twenty years
ago, during the days when certain adventures came more easily. Little bundles of toy food were passed around, wrapped
in corn tortillas. The director of the film made a long-winded
talk in what he fondly thought was English; he said he was
inspired by the great auteurs, Godard, Kurasawa, and El Indio. Margaret Torres said she was a painter. She liked it when
he said she had the right eyebrows, powerful like those of Frida
Kahlo. Had she gone home with him? That part was still vague.
No, he went to her loft off Capp Street in the Mission. He
was lazy; it was one of those evenings in San Francisco; he
spent the night but probably left before breakfast—didn't
recall breakfast. He never saw her again—oh, right, one more
time—but sent her a check when she telephoned to say she
needed an abortion.

A San Francisco kind of guy, all heart: didn't try to make
sure he was the responsible party, sometimes called "the father."

The young woman on the telephone was saying: "Let me
make an appointment, okay? I'd just like a look at you. You
think this is a crank call?"

"That's right." And then, surprising himself, "Can you
come right over?" And heard himself adding as a reassurance
to them both: "This is my office. 1061 Market."

"It's in the book," she said.

He sat with his hands folded, chin resting on his hands, in

a theatrical position of waiting. He left the door ajar. He did not straighten the papers scattered on his desk. It was mostly junk mail, but this stage setting meant to suggest he was busy, he had things to do, there were routines a person of his age liked to follow. He would decide what he needed to do when she appeared. After awhile he went to the sink, brushed his teeth, that was one of the routines, and took up his position again. He sat in an attitude of dramatized patience for an audience consisting, so far, of himself.

He heard rapid footsteps down the hall and locked his hands together.

She pushed the door wide and made her little prepared speech: "This had to be, it had to happen, I couldn't wait forever. You left the door open, so I thought it was okay. . . ." She was standing there. She had wanted to make a more impressive entrance.

It was strong enough for him. "I left it open for you." He studied her, the mouth, the wide forehead, the shape of the head—the particular shape of the head—and stood up, steadying himself against the desk. "You're right. You are. You are my daughter."

And they both stood there. This person who looked like a young woman, resembling Dan Shaper as a boy, did not throw herself into his arms. He did not reach out to take her shoulders and draw her to him. She said: "I suppose you don't want me to smoke."

"Come in," he said. "I've given it up."

She walked past the shelves with their legal texts and dictionaries in various languages, the metal filing cases, a print of Notre Dame on one wall, next to a print of the Prado, next to a tortoise with a man sitting on it from the Boboli Gardens, and asked, "What's that?"

"Comes from Firenze, Florence. Please sit."

This sort of thing, a daughter invited to settle into a chair just as if she belonged here, just as if she really was his daughter, could have consequences. Shaper was certain he ought to be suspicious. Doubts were called for. Amazing offers were frequently bogus. What if she were only a so-called daughter? Alarms were going off. There was a clanging in his ears. His tinnitus had gotten much worse. He was too old to be a new father. He could express certain doubts and act upon them with sensible demands for blood tests, DNA tracking, all the benefits of modern paternity-checking science. But instead, having looked at her, gazing upon this young woman whose eyes were trying to decide if he measured up, he was overwhelmed by awe. There could be no mistake about the shape of the head, the wide forehead, something in the mouth, even his cowlicked hairline, although her hair was dark and glossy, a young Latina's healthy hair. He had never been able to imagine what a female version of himself might look like. Now, despite the inevitable static—chromosomes courtesy of Margaret Torres—he knew.

She settled like a familiar client or like a daughter into a chair, her clumsy shoes with their stomper heels and soles extended, but then he had another idea. His tinnitus was screeching. "Is that comfortable?" he demanded. "No! Why don't we get some lunch?"

"Mom told me you might turn out to have a keen mind," Amanda said in the easy, drawling, false style of her telephone conversation. "I can light up in the street and maybe that'll be my last one ever. Hey, might even throw the pack away."

As a father, he had the right to advise against smoking, but as a cautious man, he had already committed his rash admission of the day and it was too soon to offer good counsel about health and hygiene.

"Or maybe not," she said.

She was a first-year student at San Francisco State who had almost finished the year, almost gotten her credits, when she decided she needed some time off right now, no more fooling around with nonessentials. Understand: there were issues. Finding her father was an issue, right? And that normal California issue: getting a life? After a screaming fight with Margaret Torres—odd how she repeated the entire name of this person who happened to keep house for her, didn't say Mother—Margaret Torres gave her the other name which she never meant to give her. She always said it wasn't important, a mere detail left over in the total embryo picture which happened to contribute a blotch of protoplasm material to Amanda's making. For sure Margaret Torres had done the real work; some daddy stuff had done the playing; but even as a child, Amanda always felt this wasn't the complete story. She moved out, rented a room. She moved out before she found the room; it was that kind of fight with Margaret Torres.

Then, after a few months of considering things while waitressing at Ti-Couz, a crepe restaurant in the Mission (various other career options not to be put into the information pot just now), she decided to telephone the mere detail name that Margaret Torres had blurted out. It was an idea this D'Wayne (never mind about him) enthusiastically supported. Having decided, she took a little more time. And then, when it seemed to be exactly the right moment, she waited a little longer to make sure. And then one morning she woke up and said to this D'Wayne: "*Now.*"

But she needed another quiet period for drinking coffee and meditation. She kept her hands warm on the cup. Having grown up with the blotch-of-protoplasm concept, it took certain procedures to get used to a different idea. "And so I just did," she explained. "I knew eventually I was gonna find you. For a ton of years I used to say to myself I'm just gonna, like it was a new language, you know?"

"The future past conditional subjunctive," said Shaper. "A grammatical shift."

She puzzled over this and then suddenly grimaced, full of pep. "You got the joke. 'New language.' You tried to improve it, even if you couldn't."

"I'm a language professional. I do the Romance languages. Four and a half of them."

She didn't pick up the logic here. She'd only been his daughter on active pedantic bantering duty for an hour or so. She was prepared to laugh if necessary, if he was making another joke, because courtesy required appreciation of attempts at humor, no matter how stupid.

"French, Spanish, Italian, and a little Portuguese."

"That's only three and a half."

"I was counting English."

She sliced from the bar of Monterey Jack. She tasted. She crunched the ridiculous Saltines in takeout packets which were all he had. He realized it would have been a better idea not to walk around the corner to his flat, but the entire situation was new to him. She shrugged. "So already," she said, "the embarrassing silence. We just met and already nothing to say."

"That's not the case and you know it." He wanted to add: *Amanda,* but speaking her name aloud seemed too forward. He took a deep breath. She did the same and they realized they were sighing in a similar way and they both shrugged in the same way and then they both laughed. "Maintenant que la glace est cassé," he said.

"Huh?"

"Just something I say sometimes."

"Your mantra?"

He would never use that term. Maybe her mother's Wicca friends—why not just say witch?—used their special vocabulary. But it was too soon to be critical of the daughter he had enjoyed, if that was the word, for such a short while.

Sometime halfway down the bottle of wine they were sharing, this young woman who was a complete stranger to him except that she happened to be his daughter mentioned that Margaret Torres had also used the word "snot" to describe his part in her conception, and although her Wicca colleagues thought it was about right, by the time Amanda learned a more kindly word, "sperm," she decided that Margaret Torres wasn't telling her, and perhaps didn't know, the whole story. At a certain age a girl realizes that her mother doesn't know a fuckin' thing. The same revelation might come to pass concerning a father if the girl happens to have one.

He stared at this unidentified flying object with clunky shoes who seemed to have travelled the astral plane from some outer space on the San Francisco peninsula and coasted to a landing in the middle of his life. He didn't know what to do with her. He didn't know what she might do with him. Any precedents applied only to others. He didn't know what they would do together.

"Oh man, do you look bugged," Amanda said. It was not a question.

"Why should I be?" Shaper asked.

"This happen to you a lot? You find a lot of your old kids popping up here and there?"

Another joke together. But only Amanda was smiling.

Shaper listened and decided not to contribute to the discussion just now. Amanda looked at him with eyes narrowed by red wine, previous late nights, current fatigue, and suspicion. Listening in silence seemed to be his best option at this time.

The Monterey Jack was gone. There were a few white crumbs of salt and Saltine on the black plastic plate. The bottle was empty. It was a wine so fine that it didn't require a cork; a screw top sufficed.

When she stood up, he said she shouldn't be driving after drinking half a bottle of wine and she looked at him as if he were truly ignorant and said she had a Fast Pass for the Muni, had he forgotten she had no automobile? and he offered to drive her someplace and she said: "You had more than half the bottle, you're wobbly, Dad, and I won't be responsible."

Later he thought about it and decided she was being sarcastic or maybe just funny. But he guessed he really was a little wobbly. When she said that word *Dad*, a term in a language that had never been applied to him, a sudden heat broke through his belly, something like queasiness and dread and maybe something else, too. Pride? Was that supposed to come with paternity? *Now that the ice was broken.*

The next time she came to his apartment, she began by asking, "I know mathematics isn't your strong suit, talk and blah blah blah seems to be, maybe that's why you found this little career of yours—"

"Thanks," he said, thinking: Okay. Okay. He could explain that it was a useful job, providing simultaneous translation for Latin speakers—well, Spanish mostly—ensnared in the justice system; also it was his living. He stored up the explanation, a remark or two that she would not appreciate at this stage of her resentment. It would be no fun to be called pompous by a new daughter. He nourished himself with unspoken self-justifications and wondered if there was a normal stage for the father of a nineteen-year-old daughter.

"—but I've been thinking?"

"Yes."

"You said you know three and a half languages and I've been counting on all my fingers and what I get is—"

"Hey, Amanda. Knock it off."

She fingered the pack of Winstons which her fingers wanted to open. Her fingers wanted to extract a cigaret. She said, "Right. It gets old real quick, doesn't it? Could we go someplace, do something? Maybe you'd like to buy me a present?"

"What I thought," he said cautiously, "is I'd buy us a good meal, someplace nice."

"Getting to know you," she intoned, trying to remember a song. As soon as they hit the street, she expertly flipped out the cigaret, glanced at her father (*dare you*), lit it. A panhandler asked for spare change and she took the cigaret from her mouth and gave it to him. Somehow, to Dan Shaper, this seemed unsanitary, even though it went from her to him and stopped. His daughter was confusing him.

"Hey Dad, you got a girlfriend?"

"At the moment?"

"Any time you want to mention. We got to start someplace."

"At the moment, nothing special."

She took that in, gave him a brief respite, and then said: "What's her name? Tell me about Miss Nothing Special."

"I don't think that's any of your business right now."

"Uh-huh. Okay. So what is my business, Dad?"

He didn't know. He knew less than anyone. One of the nice things about his long bachelorhood was that life could be anxious, boring, empty, a person slipped into hypochondria, anhedonia, all kinds of Latin diseases of the soul; but the person could still cling to a sense that everything was under his own control, the routines of his diminishing life, his own chaos. Now that the ice was broken, the old familiar way was shattered.

It was the first of several meals shared by Amanda Torres and Dan Shaper. They were making progress, he thought, in a difficult courtship, one for which he had no model. It was not the usual seduction, in which the goal was defined by novels, movies, songs, and hormones. He took her to restaurants a step up from the ones where he ate alone or with his pals from the courthouse. Women appreciate waiters who are deferential, offer tasseled wine lists, recite the specials of the day with half-closed eyes—this was his opinion as a long-term bachelor. One evening, having made progress, he said: "Shouldn't I meet your mother?"

"You have met her."

"Come on, Amanda. We're in this together, but I told you, I barely remember, it was a long time ago. I don't know what she looks like, I sort of remember the sound of her voice—" Amanda winced at this; was she imagining the cry of pleasure or pain or a grunt of indifference at her conception? "I don't know anything. I only know what you tell me and . . ." He decided not to say that he didn't trust her grudges against her mother. "She's an artist, but what else?"

"She wears," Amanda said slowly, "when she has to go out for some reason, a migraine headache. *Sort of* an artist."

"When I knew her, she was ambitious, I think."

"Fucked you? And she was ambitious?"

Shaper raised his hand. Objection. Slow down, please.

Amanda let her head waggle loosely on its neck hinge, not apologizing but recognizing she had gone too far. "She's changed," she said. "Single mother raising the obnoxious brat and stuff. Okay."

Heading into this unpredictable ride with his daughter, he needed to know about Margaret Torres—that was his opinion. (Gather evidence, reveal concern to all involved parties,

try to be informed, allow for possible misapprehensions.)
Amanda spoke of her mother with a range of emotion from
casual irritation all the way to bitter irritation, but Shaper had
read about the tendency of daughters to pass through stages
with a parent. Around the time they develop a taste for salsa
and curry, adventures in dining and sex, adolescents also find
nourishment in a little fresh family spite. Margaret Torres was
a painter; she used to follow some Goddess religion; was she
a nut? Or was she a California seeker, a questing young
woman—oh, like him, less young now—raising a child in a
difficult world?

She had never approached him for help. She had dropped
off the face of the earth, though Napa wasn't all that far.
Maybe she was simply brave, determined to take what she
wanted on her own terms.

It occurred to him to hang around Napa, to go look at her
cottage ("shack," according to Amanda), but stalking the lady
seemed impolite. From Amanda, he heard only bad news. In
this matter, learning about the mother of a man's only child,
it would be better to judge for himself.

Amanda found his curiosity entertaining. Why should he
want to know anything about such a boring person—"Trust
me, Dad"—with her boring single-mother friends, conning
county social workers for benefits because no sane person in
Napa, and not enough insane ones in Mendocino, wanted to
buy her woodcuts or quilts or her thing collages?

"*Thing* collages?" Dan Shaper asked.

"She sticks junk to other junk. Crazy-glues tin cutouts on
old motors. Once she stuck nails point up on typewriter keys
and somebody bought that one. It was a joke."

"Pardon?"

"Excuse *me*. It was like a statement about the agony of
temping in a word-processing pool."

Shaper tried to imagine the years of this artist and single

mother, taking dead-end jobs and hustling food stamps and doing her best.

"I'd like to see her again."

Maybe Amanda's conscience was struggling out of the ooze, struggling to be born, and maybe not. Maybe Dan Shaper could live in the same world as this person, Amanda Torres, and maybe it would be difficult. She might be too young to have a conscience. She was considering her options. She looked into her father's eyes with a cool and challenging gaze—eyes probably like Margaret's, not like his—staring until he turned away, and then said, "I don't know what I think about that. Of course I can't stop you."

"But you'd rather not see us together?"

"Not yet."

"When?"

"You should pay, Dad."

There was no kindness in this foreign word, *Dad.* Her healthy little teeth scraped the artichoke leaf; she dipped it into a vinaigrette sauce, scraped it again. The snarling smart-girl style disappeared as soon as her smart mouth ceased uttering its smart-ass words. She was working toward a new subject and it gave her trouble.

She said: "There's something you could do."

It was time to do something for others. In general, Shaper thought he was an adequate friend. He bought the *Street Sheet* from the homeless who congregated near his office. He wrote checks at holiday time to the people on his list. He liked chowing down, going to movies, enjoying an occasional misdemeanor joint with Harvey, the undercover detective, and Alfonso, the black sergeant from Central Station he'd known since beginning in the court system. Sometimes the three of them exchanged news, views, and any sympathies that happened to turn up.

Somehow he had taken on the sentimental habit of wiring roses to a former woman friend on her birthday, and he planned to keep this up as long as he still had an address for her. Making the phone call to the floral agency, then a week or so later getting the thank-you from Veronica, was a little ritual he enjoyed. Also he had come to the time in his life when he noticed a shortness of breath despite his workouts, and he got up to pee at night even though he cut out the evening coffee, and sometimes he felt dizzy if he jumped up when there was no good reason to jump up. His doctor said heart and circulation were fine for a man his age. The phrase "for a man your age" seemed ominous. It was more ominous for a man his age who had no heirs, no one to carry on after him, and certainly Veronica, the flower recipient, wouldn't do.

Well, now he had someone. Maybe he had someone. Shaper could hold the flag high, be a painstaking counselor to the Latino clients whom lawyers and the court sent his way, and hope to be taken quickly if fate decided that he would, after all, not be forever young. He preferred to spin, fall, and crack his head on the marble floor of the courthouse rather than stand around his late middle age with dandruff on his shoulders and conjunctival eyes.

Or he could hurry up and have a family now.

"You were right to do so. Call me. To call me," he said. Margaret Torres hadn't let on; asked for a hundred dollars for an abortion and had taken it, gone off to Napa, out of sight, and used his hundred dollars to raise a child. A hundred dollars wasn't enough, even wisely invested, but since she had just disappeared . . . Feeling righteous wasn't the right way to go just now.

"I feel very validated," said Amanda.

If he had raised her, she wouldn't have been named

Amanda. If he had raised her, she wouldn't have said "very validated."

"Margaret Torres didn't want me to know your name. She let it slip when she was deep in a headache about me. Like I gave her migraines, but you started them off. That was the opinion she got from this Wiccan therapist in Napa. She dressed me in her old clothes till I got too big—"

"When you were a baby, you must have had kids' clothes."

"Garage sales. Church sales."

A hundred dollars doesn't go all the way, Shaper thought.

"She dressed herself to go out mostly in a headache. If it was a special occasion, like parents' night at school, she dolled up in one of her best frontal-lobe migraines."

"You told me already."

"I get to nag. I'm practicing being a kid with her daddy."

Whatever she seemed to be working up to asking or telling or punishing him with—no rewards planned—she didn't let it just roll out on wings of chat. He noticed a slight overbite when her mouth was at rest. Amanda was not at rest now, but she closed down for a moment. Silence. Then she said: "Could we go to your place?"

He didn't like the question. He thought of the mess. The cleaning woman was due. The unmade bed, the wadded towels. But what the devil was he thinking of? This was not a date, this was not a seduction, this was not a case of needing to worry about the right music on the antique KLH player, splits of champagne in the fridge, clean linen and fresh soap. It was only his daughter, wanting privacy for a difficult moment in her life.

Only his daughter.

"What's those on your walls?" she asked.

"The paintings?"

"Yeah, paintings. You could do posters at half the price, less, plus spend the money on something worthwhile." She winked. "I can think of someone. Let's get real, Dad."

She may have added, "Hey," but he wasn't sure. He moved to distract this line of father abuse. He hoped she could see it from the other person's point of view, although he'd heard that, in general, nineteen-year-olds weren't skilled at the procedure. "Is there something you need?" he asked.

"Wheels." The answer came quickly. She had given the matter previous consideration. "Something nice, what I'd really like is a Miata convertible, but probably you wouldn't go for that. A little Fiat or something Japanese? At least with a sunroof?" She studied the freezing on his face. "D'Wayne says wheels is a good start."

"Who's D'Wayne?"

"I'll compromise. Doesn't have to be new, how about that? You could come kick the tires with me, pick it out together. Accommodate your budget, okay? A father-daughter thing, buying the used transportation vehicle."

"Come on."

"You want me to get real? Doesn't fit your budget?"

"Okay, put it that way. Get real."

She let her eyes survey the walls, the furniture, the towel on the floor left over from his back exercises. Her silence wasn't what Shaper considered getting real; it was only a pause. "The trouble with drug abusers, D'Wayne always says, is they got no finesse." Shaper tried to predict what was coming. "We use a little, but we got fuckin' finesse, so it's just recreational and creative purposes, like relaxing." Amanda appreciated his discomfort. A small smile played across her small plump mouth. She was not exactly baiting him, but seemed contented with the direction of their conversation. She was taking control. She was baiting him.

"Sometimes when people cross me, I get in a . . ." Paused,

considering how to describe her frame of mind. "Indignant, so a little herb cools me out. You smoke a little herb sometimes?"

"When I was your age, I guess I did."

"And now?"

"Drifted away from it. Didn't really change anything."

She shook her head disapprovingly, as if she had heard that this stringy older guy used to perform the Royal Canadian Air Force exercises on a towel in his apartment, something macho swingers did in those days, the seventies, back then, but now he was just drifting along with advancing age as it worked to mistreat his body. "Try smoke," she advised. "Or in brownies, that's good. Mellow you out, Pop, you look nervous."

She smelled of soap and salsa, not marijuana. She must have come from a burrito breakfast, carbo loading to keep herself sturdy. She may have been influenced by the weight-training culture of her generation. "So I have this boyfriend, D'Wayne, he's a percussionist, gonna be, at least. When he gets his set of drums, learns how to set them up. Doing something else for the time being." Stopped, waited for interruption. Okay, none, went on: "Margaret Torres thought D'Wayne was just a stage, but I'm still in it."

Shaper wasn't being invited to critique her boyfriend.

"D'Wayne says I'm wasting my time with you. He has no father and he's just fine. What do you think?"

Here too Shaper thought it best to express no opinion.

"Hey, are you talkative today," said Amanda.

"I'm listening."

Then they were both listening and neither was speaking.

"Kind of boring?" Amanda asked. "You often like this?"

He couldn't remember if Margaret Torres had been a talkative woman. He thought Dan Shaper might be considered a talkative man, within the range of normal civilized urban blabbing. But where did this generation of young motor-mouths come from? Did television close-ups and laugh tracks teach them to leave no thought unexpressed, no lack of thought unvocalized?

He said, "If you want something I can really do for you, I'm ready—"

"To *consider* it?"

Stopped him. Didn't even wait for him to give her what she asked for. "Do you just want to fight or could you let me be your father?"

She stared, grinning. "Does it have to be one or the other?"

Shaper wondered how she had come by this boiling temperament. Maybe a daughter, for her own balance, learns to knock a father ajar; especially an ignorant smug father, of which he might be a shining example.

"Ready to do it if I can, what I can do for you." He felt like putting his head down, but he didn't. He hoped stubborn, bumbling persistence could match sarcasm, turbulence, the edginess of this person with waxy purplish lipstick covering the chap marks and staining her teeth. What kind of couple do we look like? he thought, and then remembered: we're not a couple. He wondered if he had a right to be proud of her and decided maybe not that either; no rights or privileges here.

Fathers often have pleasant obligations on Sundays and national holidays, other than picking from the special brunch choices and reading almost every word in the newspaper. Was it too late to take his daughter to museums or ball games, or just to pick from each other's plates at the special brunch?

At her age she would have better things to do—her boyfriend, D'Wayne, whom Dan Shaper already despised, even the name. . . . Already he was like a father.

He said: "There's nobody you have to impress around here. We're not in a public place. It's just you and me. It's between us, Amanda. Okay?"

She shut down her side of the chatter. She sat crosslegged, looking at him.

She was smiling, he was smiling, they were each carefully smiling at each other. He wasn't sure if this was courtship or diplomacy and if there was a difference. It might be hard to have a daughter, and harder still to have one born to her father at age nineteen. He had evaded the diaper and snotty-nose times. He had avoided other negotiations in the deal between a father and a daughter. He hoped it was not too late to make the deal between Amanda and Dan Shaper.

She fingered her pack of cigarets, alert for what he would try next. She was a woman keeping her finger on the trigger. Fortunately she found something better than taking out a cigaret and smoking it in his face. "Okay, never mind the wheels," she said. "That's just something I really need. It was just a good idea."

"You don't know my finances. We haven't gotten around to discussing them."

"I don't even know you," she said, still sweetly smiling. "But there is one thing, won't cost you more than coffee and a muffin, coffee and toast if she stays the night."

"Pardon?"

"Excused. I've changed my mind. You're so persuasive, Dad. I want you to meet Margaret Torres. I didn't tell you—she's been living in San Fran. I want my mom and dad sitting right here in front of me."

She lit her cigaret, dragged deeply, exhaled luxuriously, and enjoyed her little double-reverse twist on previous positions. Next move, his.

Two

Ferd Conant, young Pascual's court-appointed lawyer, took Dan Shaper's arm in his smarmy fashion, with many a squeeze, just as if they were friends, while they walked past the sheriff's orange-vested work detail, a flock of losers outside a jail shed. The sign hanging from a branch said NO BEEPERS. Shaper wanted to shake off Ferd's fingers, which seemed to be living a busy life on his arm. What was Ferd doing, protecting him from the brigade of street-sweepers lined up in a lot on Bryant, next door to the Hall of Justice, picking up their bag lunches, tunafish on white plus an apple, no choice about the mayo, while a stentorian sheriff's department sergeant bellowed out the names on her clipboard? "Ramirez! Washington! What-the-hell-is-this? Bok Choy?"

A sullen young man stared at her with the desire both to kill and to be polite to his jailer, a difficult emotion combo, leading to conventional Asian inscrutability. He said: "Bob Choy. *Bob.*"

"Okay, Bok, you move your butt behind Diana Washington there and wait till I finish the roll."

"*Dina,*" said Ms. Washington, a street-walker now committed to a session of street-sweeping.

Ferd released Shaper's arm in order to reach up and rearrange the hair pattern over his scalp. He was briefing Dan

Shaper on the client, a sweetie accused of firing a shotgun at a party from which he had been turned away—"didn't really shoot at them, just happened to be driving by and the shotgun sprayed in their direction, due to the fact that he had it cradled against his shoulder, and the vehicle (no registration) hit a pothole and his finger was resting on the trigger. Could happen to anyone, you know? Not you or me, but ethnics—"

Pascual's English was limited, which was what brought Dan Shaper into the picture. He was a legal resident, green card, had one for seven years, and kept so busy as a roofer, mucking in tar and shingles, smoking so much grass, that he didn't require the local language, not even when he was in court, thanks to the services of our cowboy interpreter Gaucho Dan here.

Shaper preferred Pascual's Spanish to Ferd Conant's brand of Hall of Justice, court-assigned, full of himself American. Ferd's fingers, finished with his hair, squeezed Dan's elbow. Stop a minute to watch the SWAP program draftees; stop and gloat.

Behind them on the sidewalk, a tall transvestite in spike heels, the strappy look, slapped a black person on the back. The black person whirled, saying, "Don't ever come up on me like that. I don't know what I'm gonna do."

"Goodo! Can't do nothing here anyway. Hey, so where you been?"

"Away. Got myself messed up again, girl." The black hooker was wearing a shamrock pendant for luck, a beeper for business, and that was the end of the jewelry she wore, unless you counted the glow-in-the-dark chain tattoo around her neck and the needle scars in the crook of her elbow.

On the street outside the Hall of Justice, clusters of visitors to court and jail and future inmates of the jail ambled, smoked, discussed, mixed. The hookers of all sexes seemed

comfortable in their alert boredom; the street kids cultivated
the middle-distance stare of grownup hoods (cool, cool, cool).
Ferd Conant advised Dan Shaper that their client spoke your
basic street English, but needed an interpreter for the subtleties of legal terms of art, since the roofer-mugger-shotgun
wielder preferred to spend his down time with his homies
rather than boning up on American jurisprudence. And Pascual could use the extra translation pause for framing his answers. "And you gotta have a job, too, Cowboy, keep you out
of the welfare system, am I right?"

Puccineli Bail Bonds stood across the alley from upscale
Cafe Roma, near Sidebar Cocktails with its traditional neon
Frisco symbol, the purple martini glass, presiding over the sad
lies and sadder truths of the bail-bond traffic. It was more fun
to borrow money for, say, fresh wheels than to stay off the
county farm until the trial.

Ferd Conant wore a wide tie down his chest and pouter
belly, emphasizing the bulge of long lunches, a man with time
for pleasure on his hands. He wasn't all business. Other lawyers at the Roma were dapper and shiny, especially the young
African-American ones, for whom the shaven head had succeeded the Afro, dreadlocks, the James Brown Conk, and ponytail styles. A beefy Latino lawyer was escorting a colleague
for a soy chai drink, a petite Filipina with loud spike heels to
tell the world she was strong, proud, and her tinkly voice,
darling smile, and fragrant hair should delude no one. Except
it deluded Ferd Conant, who murmured, "Like to fit that one
right over my lap, wouldn't I, Cowboy?"

Dan didn't answer, since Ferd should know his own mind.

"Those ethnic-type lawyers, they're really intent on doing
the right thing," said Ferd. "Start at the bottom of the wrong
things and then reach for the stars. I was like that once. Just
once, a moonlit night in June it was, but the whole episode

passed like a burp, you know what I mean, Cowboy?"

It didn't take much effort to discern Ferd's meaning; seldom did.

"Hey, wanna onion macaroon before lunch?" Ferd asked.

Dan Shaper looked startled.

"Good, so you're listening. Nice pointy ears. Just testing, see if you pay attention, Cowboy."

A segmented truck was maneuvering up to the loading dock of the Hall of Justice, its backup warning beep surprisingly timid. The truck was delivering tons and tons and tons of paper to wipe the dirty behinds of the guilty and the innocent alike; enough for the jail, enough for the courts, enough for jurors and judges from all walks of life, enough for a great city fed on taco salads and burritos-a-go-go. Maybe some of the paper was for Xeroxing.

A motorcycle cop pulled up in front, his keys, flashlight, baton, gun, handcuffs, and wireless equipment around his waist, weighing down his chassis. He unstraddled himself. He wasn't here to testify. His seat was well shined from sliding against leather. Ferd bumped Dan's elbow. "Bet he gets a lot. . . ."

"Probably deserves it," said Shaper.

On the steps of the Hall of Justice there were enough cellular portaphones hooked to belts, or in left hands, or at ears to fight a major war of words. Every cop, security guard, full-of-himself lawyer, or dope dealer needed to punch up his or her beloved to ask what's for lunch. For some reason or reasons, the streets nearby also contained enough skinny Persons Living With AIDS to move even the heart of Nancy Reagan. Some were panhandling, some were hobbling with canes, some were just there for the sunlight and the company. Folsom Street, the traditional leather and S&M village, was only a nice stroll or hobble away. Strong men would weep at the sight, but Shaper decided there weren't any strong men in the vicinity, because no one seemed to be weeping.

Oh-oh, there was one, Harvey Kurtz, the giant undercover cop, with his shaven head, black tee shirt, and cheap black pants, the better to show off a muscle-builder's knotty and veiny bulk—the most obvious undercover cop in the Western world. He wasn't weeping and no one would think he carved out those muscles through prison-yard weight lifting. He waved to Dan; no time to talk now. One finger curled just a tad; was he giving it to Ferd Conant? These were actual working hours for Harvey. He mouthed the words: *Later, man.* Yes, that little flip of finger was aimed at Ferd.

The Polk 19, the Downtown Loop 42, the 27 Bryant; a lot of buses converged here to bring families (grieving) with kids (solemn or fidgeting) to look on during the travails of defendant significant others. Ferd dug his elbow into Shaper's flank. "Hizzoner Rufus," he said. "Rufus" wasn't the name of the black judge pushing toward the elevator on flat feet, no sense of rhythm, heading up to chambers. "My clients call him the race-traitor. And right behind him, that's Hizzoner Hyman Pastrami—" Ferd suddenly remembered something about Dan. "Hey, no offense meant. People call me a Wasp all the time, what do I care?"

Ferd Conant usually had a bad taste in his mouth when he argued a case, but who could blame him? The lawyer assigned by the court to an indigent defendant is usually defending someone below Ferd's station in life. Perhaps he should have made an effort to hide the taste or, absent beverage, sucked on a good strong mint. The tradition of sportsmanship in the Anglo-American system, descended from the teachings of Moses and Jesus, plus the Magna Carta, fortified an American ideal of fair play for guilty assholes. Absent mint, or perhaps parsley for the deeper gastric emanations, Ferd might have felt better if he brushed his tongue. Naw. Needed to remedy diet, character, and selection of beverages.

"Dan," he asked, "ready to try to make sense of this hombre, Pascual Ramirez?"

"Si," said Dan Shaper.

Shaper plugged himself into Pascual Ramirez, testing, testing, one two three four. He whispered into the mike uno dos tres cuatros, he made sure the batteries were tightly tucked in, he stretched and straightened the cord, he adjusted the earphones over Pascual's head in a finicky professional way, wanting them to fit nice and snug, still murmuring, murmuring, and asking if Pascual heard him okay. Pascual nodded. Shaper hoped he wouldn't have to replace the batteries in the middle of a mendacious paragraph. He hoped the client, who was accused of spraying shotgun fire in the direction of partyers, with intent to do harm, would not rip the equipment off his head and begin shouting. Indignation, as with his daughter, Amanda, was always a risk.

Dan Shaper had studied Spanish language and literature in college, did a summer program in Cuernavaca in a time of favorable dollar-peso exchange, fell in love with Cervantes, Unamuno, Lorca, and a part-Indian herbalist. More useful for his job than the heroes of Spanish literature (or the herbalist, who went back to her husband) was his technical training in Interpreting and Translation at San Francisco State University. In the Legal Interpreting course he practiced handling the mike, battery pack, earphones, while overcoming jitters about doing justice to subtleties in another category from the analysis of symbolic layers in *Don Quixote*. For example, it would not be fair to a client to translate "bathroom" as "shithouse," as in, "She came at me with her knife, so I pushed her into the shithouse," when what he had said could be more delicately translated as "crapper."

Shaper hated to make errors. If he did, he stopped the proceedings to go back and change the record. He sensed an entire courtroom breathing exasperation at him when this happened. He was finicky about the job, tried to keep up with advances in the field, took his cases home with him and sometimes had trouble sleeping. He was careful to say Latino, not Hispanic, because some of his clients were from Spanish-speaking Latin America and disdained a label which disrespected proud Aztec king or West African chief origins. That was during certain years. During other years they treasured heroic Conquistador roots. If ultimately Shaper couldn't keep up with the linguistic shifts in multicultural okayness, he would have to take proud senior citizen, valiant golden-ager, or distinguished old fart status, whichever would be correct at the time.

Paid by the court, hired as an independent contractor, Dan Shaper was requested by lawyers if they liked his work. Ferd Conant knew that Shaper needed him to be on his side. The job was like dating instead of marriage, a quick intense encounter and then the client goes away for awhile or returns to the street. Ferd Conant would wave him adios until the next loose-tempered roofer, rug-cleaning dope runner, wife beater, or purse snatcher came along.

When Juan or Jesus ("Hay-suss") or, in this case, Pascual Ramirez was on the stand, Shaper stood alongside and buried himself intensely in playing all the parts, very softly murmuring the questions in Spanish and then interpreting the responses, such as Yes, No, or how the fuck can I remember I was high all that week . . . in brisk, clear, unjudging tones. While Pascual sat at the table with his court-assigned lawyer, Shaper sat next to him with his microphone, his battery pack, and the soft headphones fitted over Pascual's ears. At this point, foam earpieces were the kindest elements of Pascual's life.

What went through Pascual's mind as the courtroom cacophony washed into his ears could not be translated; surely it was a confusion. "At this point in time, out of the presence of the jury, Your Honor . . ." "I will express my discretion, Counselor . . ." "I will call to the stand—state for the record that my client—direct your attention to . . ."

Once a new judge explained a ruling by saying, "That's a metaphor," and the attorney asked, "What, Your Honor?" and the judge said, "A simile, a phrase of art, a form of higher analogy—you went to college, didn't you, Counselor?" and as Shaper worked, he saw this previous Pascual, who happened to be named Pedro, moving his lips to try to follow a Spanish that meant no more to him than the English dialogue meant to most of those in the courtroom.

Barry Schrecker, the D.A. assigned to dispose of Pascual's case, an easy call, had a killer's intention although he was just serving his time as a prosecutor in the District Attorney's office until he could get the connections and rep that would make him a rich defender of drug dealers, money launderers, and what would be the Mafia if this weren't northern California, where there is no Mafia. Now, poor baby, he had to waste all his hormonal and metabolic ferocity sending idiot gang bangers, purse snatchers, crack or heroin street retail dealers, runners, lookouts to jail or prison, depending on how many strikes they had struck. Grunt work. It was soon to be far, far beneath Barry Schrecker.

He got some of his exercise moving around, doing his little stiff dance for the judge, jury, and those in the various other boxes—witnesses, gawkers, seniors for whom this was better than a matinee during the long days waiting for something, maybe only dinner. He wore crewcut fratboy hair that went with the stocky, muscle-bound, heavy-thighed body. He was overage for the haircut, but his full cheeks were warranty for his continued right to it. Proud of his body, Barry Schrecker took care to move so that folks noticed, but wore built-up soles to give him an additional half inch. A fellow can always use an extra half inch.

Ferd Conant surveyed the jury, his yellow tablet in hand. The Asian grandmother of many, the black retiree, the kindergarten aid in walking billboard tee shirt, the activist-style woman in butch pants and vest who might consider all defendants victims of society with the exception of male defendants (both prosecution and defense took a chance on her). . . . "All rise. The Honorable Robert J. Wilson, Presiding Judge—"

"Good morning, everybody," sang your-honor, "sorry to keep you waiting." Was he running for something?

The steno sat at her table, punching boilerplate into the computer.

In a moment they invited the cop to the stand—trained expressionless demeanor except for the muscles working in his jaw. He was sworn in, nimbly reciting, "Yes, I do swear." And then to business: "We had the defendant, Mister Ramirez, pulled down, proned out like an airplane, double-handcuffed for safety reasons, he was laying facedown like that—"

Dan Shaper interpreted for Pascual at high speed, in the interpreter's trance, that state where two languages flash between ganglia in the brain and come out the mouth, with enough brain cells left in operation to note that the cop had said "laying facedown" when he meant "lying facedown," as if he didn't want to pronounce the word "lie"—

"That is correct," stated the cop.

Ferd liked the word "proned out" and kept using it on cross. "Were there other people proned out at that time? Is it your custom to double-handcuff a proned out suspect? Did you search his vehicle after he was proned out and double-handcuffed? Do you remember, are you aware, of the other officers who assisted—were they known by you?"

The usual.

The cop stepped down, his shoes crunching loudly as if there were tin cans in them to improve his posture, his extension upwards to fill his beat, his presence, his official persona. Shaper could take a few breaths without English-Spanish and Spanish-English sparking in the parts of his brain assigned to this work. Sometimes he thought the frontal lobes were bulging like burritos, spilling out sour cream and guacamole. Someday, if all went well, he would invite Amanda to visit the court to see what her father did for a living.

Shaper had a moment to study the jury, that all–San Francisco agglomeration of retirees, Asians, blacks, housewives, the subemployed—these were not parallel categories and the jury was, of course, not representative at all. Those who wanted to get out of jury duty found reasons to do so; those that one or another side thought leaning in one or another direction were eliminated. The "jury of your peers" had become an imaginary construct. "Jury Nullification" was becoming a popular local option. Evidence, like a stop sign or a pedestrian walkway, was taken into consideration when convenient. Lawyers scratched their heads, or hired professional head-scratchers, to decide who leaned toward freeing or not freeing, rewarding or sending away for a good long time. Sometimes expert evaluators could tell by the race, ethnic affiliation, age, occupation, or look in the eye. Often the expert evaluator could tell wrong; that's what makes ballgames. In the case of Pascual Ramirez, there wasn't enough at stake for anyone except Pascual to call in the experts.

The next witness approached the stand, wearing his orange sheriff's department clean-up vest, excused from sweeping the streets in order to testify in the interests of Justice. Since Justice is blind, the iridescent orange vest would not dazzle Her. The witness sat there bewildered while bulldog Barry Schrecker barked: "We stipulate that People's Exhibit 2-B does not pertain to the scene of the incident on the very afternoon of the event."

The orange-vested SWAP-program witness, confused, would readily have so stipulated.

But then Schrecker asked: "So it's your testimony that the shirt the defendant was wearing with the campesino mark on it, that was the same shirt?"

Huh?

At the end of this line of testimony, the judge sent the witness back to his street-cleaning detail, along with good wishes that he not be hit by a truck. A lot of peculiar bullshit was being expelled in Judge Wilson's courtroom. It was a real score in bullshit for connoisseurs like the orange-vested witness and percipient seniors on the democratic benches.

When it came to the defense's turn, Ferd Conant, he of the pink scalp but surviving lock of hair and the steel-trap mind, proposed a surprise alibi for consideration by the court. "The Defense would like to call to the stand Mister Lorenzo, uh, de la Gloria-Gomes."

After the proper gloating, shuffling of feet and papers, murmurs of approbation, and swearing in, Lorenzo de la Gloria-Gomes ambled to the elevated chair. He emitted a big smile and bombshell news: Pascual was at his house watching

TV, romancing his sister, and drinking a beer when the so-called shooting took place! Take that, Mister Prosecutor! And Lorenzo could prove it—the TV was still warm! He had the Dos Equis bottle with Pascual's lip prints on it! How's that for DNA, guys?

Lorenzo's testimony was no better than that of the preceding witness. Dan Shaper, in civic-employee mode, doing his job, kept a straight face. Lorenzo wore an ancient but clean Snoop Doggy Dog tee shirt and low-slung diarrhea pants, crotch nearly to his ankles. Did he inspire confidence? Not a bushel and a peck. But as a dude of integrity, probably called cojones, he dressed to please *his* posse, the Capp Street Federales, not *their* group, wherever Anglos lived with their Range Rovers and their kids in tuition schools where the only Latinos had ophthalmologist daddies or affirmative-action contracts to cook asphalt for the city.

Ferd Conant didn't go for that sort. Ferd Conant was a different sort. Ferd Conant was the sort who was *there* for Pascual (Juan, Hay-suss, whatever), making objections, offering witnesses, drinking his variety-pak of beverages, collecting his court-mandated fee. He was a caregiver, with a license to give care.

Too bad Lorenzo, whom Pascual wanted to present, couldn't change the general drift of things. The problem with Lorenzo's compassionate and well-meaning sworn testimony was that it had already been established, admitted and so stipulated, that Pascual was, in fact, on the scene when the alleged shotgun seemed to fire itself. Also, Lorenzo's sister was in Guatemala at the time and Pascual wouldn't have romanced her by e-mail. Also, they didn't drink Dos Equis in Lorenzo's house—a blatant appeal to ethnic loyalty, in case there was any such in the jury—but Budweiser because of a deal with the corner store. However—Ferd Conant tugged at his forelock—Lorenzo was not a total loss, since he was a living demonstration of the warmth of Pascual's allegiances. That should count for something. Ferd aimed a significant long gaze at the jury to make sure they got it. "Thank you, Mister de las Equis, and perhaps the time line is a little revisable."

Sure. Some people, honest agrarian societies, live by the sun and the flow of the seasons. Others are slaves to mere digital chips and shotgun powder-burn evidence.

In due course Pascual himself was again presented for the contemplation of Justice. He fidgeted on the stand. Dan Shaper stood by his side, murmuring the words of others to Pascual and firmly enunciating the responses of Pascual to the world.

"How long was it after the gunshot that you ran into the alley?" asked Barry Schrecker.

The question was easy enough to translate. The answer was: scared, fled, didn't stop to check the second hand on a watch.

Then there was the question about the powder on hands and clothes.

Here the response of the defendant was a little more complicated, to wit: those things probably happen in the laundry because clothes get mixed up; seven brothers not counting my sisters and the cousins who sometimes sleep at our house; my mother goes to Church almost every day, my uncle lives with us when he doesn't live with his wife, now he's in Nicaragua; we buy a lot of clothes at Goodwill and they say the hitman shooters donate at the store on Mission to help people with AIDS and they didn't launder the fockin, excuse me, the mother-fockin vest because that stretches the elastic—you know, Your Honor?

His explanation emerged in sections, interrupted with objections, admonitions from the judge about respectful language, consultations at the bench, repetitions for the sake of getting the court record down accurately. Shaper felt he performed his role without serious error. He had a veteran's experience with Central American forms of Spanish.

There was a short recess. Folks peed, folks telephoned, folks smoked. Then Barry Schrecker began a new line of questioning with a dramatic impatient sigh. "You *said*," he said. "No, strike that." He paused to offer the jury a premonitory touch of ominous. Silence can do that. Every good prosecutor knows about the value of ominous silence in the courtroom and Barry Schrecker was a good prosecutor, in Barry Shrecker's opinion.

Pascual secreted one kind of logic, that of fear and evasion; Barry Schrecker another, that of ambition and bloodlust; and the judge tried to fashion a fair linkage of the two, just as Dan Shaper tried to interpret the words of Pascual for Schrecker, the judge, and the jury.

"Do you have a reason for wearing the colors of the Capp Street Gang?" asked Barry Schrecker, having given the close, tight courtroom air a full charge of expectation.

"I know nothing of that."

"The Capp Street Posse?"

"I thought you said 'gang.' I'm just wearing the colors of the Capp Street Posse."

"Is there a reason?"

"When I open my closet, those clothes come out."

Shaper imagined apparel leaping from the dark at Pascual's throat.

What they had here was not Socratic dialogue. Distinctions between the words "gang" and "posse" were important to the client. Entrapment in logic fault was important to the D.A. A time-out occurred while the bailiff woke up a sleeping senior, attending just another street-shooting trial. Schrecker was annoyed at this break in his rhythm, insult to his dramatic technique. In Barry Schrecker's eyes the gleam of appetite was on the verge of gratification. Being guilty was like being in love; not everyone revealed it to the world. But Schrecker smelled a conviction, he was going to get a conviction, he was sure of it; Pascual would be found guilty, would go away for awhile, would enjoy the blessing of love only from men bigger and stronger than Pascual Ramirez.

For a moment, across Barry Schrecker's meaty face came a look of peace and contentment, that of a man given a surprising glimpse of heaven on a fine spring day. His new bout of silence was intense and controlled, filled with frowns and lip-pursings. It was wind-up time. Schrecker was ready for the pitch. "You said you saw the smoke from the gun, the shotgun, but didn't see the shooter? You said that?"

Si. Yes.

"It is your testimony that you never turned after you heard the shot to see the shooter?"

Si.

"You are so familiar with nearby shotgun blasts that contaminate your clothes with gunpowder residue that—no, strike that." A contemptuous little kickstep lift of one leg. "That's all, Your Honor."

And like a tugboat he triumphantly docked himself at his table, threw himself into a chair, extended his legs, enjoyed another moment at the center of the universe. Ferd Conant had his work cut out for him. Procedural challenges, recapitulations of time frames, discussions of how shotgun blasts often fly randomly through the air of the Mission district, and winsome thin locks of forehead hair might not be enough to do the job.

Shaper wondered if Pascual was misunderstanding the proceedings. It seemed that he was listening to some other language, attending some other event, a cockfight perhaps, because the defendant bounced happily in his chair, beamed at his friends in the courtroom, winked at the jury, and was that a kiss he blew toward the judge? And now Pascual Ramirez did rip off the earphones which had been dripping language into his head and began to shout in English, a conversation with spectators, with nobody in particular, with everybody in the courtroom and the universe: "Fockin lies! Fockin liar! Fockin get off my back!"

So, after all, he did speak perfectly functional American. Still, Dan Shaper would be paid for his labors, for the workman is worthy of his hire. But no one could pay him for the knowledge that Pascual was dazzled, blinded, made articulate by his fate, and therefore Dan Shaper and he were both incomprehending brothers, linked by the wires, earphones, and microphone. The sudden flame of misery in the body of poor lost Pascual made cool Dan Shaper feverish; instant contagion infected the man who had achieved immunity. Pascual, rent and destroyed, shouted words of clear English adequate to his purpose but understood nothing, nothing, just as Dan Shaper understood less and less as his life took its new turn. Pascual would go away; Shaper would stay. Shaper too was a member of the immense family of the confused, not even knowing his own daughter.

"Fockin worl', get off my fockin back!"

Bailiffs twisted plastic shackles around his arms and chest. As they dragged him off, Pascual Ramirez neglected to thank Dan Shaper. In this world, a person has to do his best without expecting gratitude. He may even not be doing the right thing.

Three

It was not as if they knew each other. In that time of the early seventies, when the ghostly strays of the Summer of Love still danced through San Francisco, they had barely reached the stage where the word "acquainted" might apply. All they had done was met, bumped, shrugged, agreed—gone back to (Dan Shaper seemed to recall) her place.

The only unusual part of the incident was her call saying, Thanks for the tip about seeing that old black-and-white *Seven Samurai* movie and oh, by the way, I'm pregnant. He sent her a check for a hundred dollars to take care of the problem without fretting about who was the responsible party. At the time it seemed easier, as hassle-free as dumping a hundred dollars could be, when he was about to head to Cuernavaca with his main squeeze. Decent and practical Margaret Torres got the picture, cashed the hundred, and never bothered him again.

But didn't have the abortion. Wasn't so practical after all.

Had the child instead.

So now he was looking at this kind of sturdy, pretty nineteen-year-old who would have been a perfect stranger if she didn't happen to be his daughter. While awaiting the arrival of Margaret Torres, Amanda's mother, he showed Amanda photographs of his own mother at her age. He had studied them often. There was a resemblance across the years, across the generations. These things were uncanny.

Amanda examined the photographs carefully, especially one in which Shaper's mother was dressed in a tuxedo with a corn-cob pipe stuck in her mouth. "Could I have a print of that one?" she asked.

Neither Amanda nor Shaper needed to say: looks just like me, looks just like you. They both knew what they were thinking. Next time he saw Amanda, would she be gripping a corncob pipe between her teeth? He was getting on to her tricks, as she was on to his.

"I didn't know they had unisex in the old days," said Amanda. "Your mom was really hip about gender. Wow."

"It was Halloween," said Dan Shaper.

The entry buzzer sounded. He didn't listen for the crackle of voice, buzzed the person in. He worried that Margaret Torres might judge his apartment with its monkish accumu-lations of nothing much—he had vigorously cleaned house in preparation for this occasion—as unworthy of a man who had visited her once in late-flowerchild digs. He worried that he might blurt out something nervously sarcastic about Goddess festivals, the Wicca religion. He had already lined up his pos-sible gaffes by asking Amanda if her mother would ride in on a broomstick.

"Not very funny, Dad."

This brisk knock at the door would be Margaret Torres.

While he was trying to fit the clear image as she now came into focus over a vagueness which he strained to bring back, she too was observing the stranger who inadvertently con-tributed to the advent of her daughter. There was a narrow-ness in her eyes of intense judgment of his gray hair, his shiny high temples, or of his being there. He wondered if the evident critique hid something more sentimental, perhaps even (too much to hope) in the vicinity of tenderness: Yes, this guy is gray, with receding hair, but it used to be dark and glossy. Yes, this guy's spine may have settled on its discs—is he an inch shorter or had he worn his boots to bed? Yes, the spaces in the front teeth are a little wider, probably spreading due to a failed root canal, an extraction.

Dan Shaper now remembered a detail from that misty evening of the early seventies. She had said she liked gap-toothed guys and he was almost gap-toothed enough; he had decided there was a sense of humor someplace in this Frida Kahlo devotee; too bad (or maybe thank God) they hadn't videotaped the encounter. Unrecoverable now. The raw past lay in leaky memory vaults. The fully edited version was Amanda, a silent observer to their observing of each other.

"Did Amanda tell you," Margaret Torres abruptly asked, "did she tell you I'm a member of the Natural Law Party?"

Shaper wondered where this was heading. He suspected small talk planned in advance.

"And a graduate of MU?"

"Michigan?"

"Maharishi University," she said. "Fairfield, Iowa. They gave me a graduate fellowship and I taught levitation, assisted in the workshop, stacked mats and towels. But then I missed Mendocino, so I did my exercises by mail. That was before we moved to Napa because Mendocino got expensive. Meditation didn't help with the rent. Amanda doesn't remember this stuff. It was hard. It was a struggle—that was before fax. Now you can just run stuff through the computer. But I got my degree."

"You can levitate?" Shaper asked, thinking, *Whoa.*

"Can't you tell?"

He wasn't sure about the correct answer, so he said, "Amanda didn't mention about Iowa."

"A lot of things she doesn't mention. You notice she talks mostly about herself? It's not having a father."

"It's her age, I think."

Heavy sighs from another corner. "Shit," said Amanda, "I guess I'm not even here."

Margaret Torres firmly corrected everybody in the vicinity. "It's not having a father. I was everything to her. Now she comes up with this idea she had to find you, instead of just riding the flow? I didn't have a father and you can see *I'm* all right."

Shaper expected her to levitate then and there, but all she offered was a little happy hop, a goofy grin and a shrug. An almost flirtatious sidelong wink which made her look both like Amanda in her occasional fun-loving moments and like a woman who was starting, almost, wait, there it was, to remember the night they met at the Mexican Consulate—the prelevitational Margaret Torres, aged about twenty-five at the time, invited to the screening of a film by the director called El Indio, a true artist who had shot dead one or two of his wife's lovers and also worked with John Huston.

Margaret, like Amanda, seemed to have a load of questions for Dan Shaper. "Have you noticed," she asked, "I'm not cutting you any slack?"

"I've noticed."

"How observant." For Margaret Torres this was developing into a nice social occasion involving both popular genders. But reminiscence of the past wasn't going to turn a strong woman mushy. "You know," she said, "if you and I met under other circumstances, say we were the only Americans caught in a rare snowstorm in Nepal, I bet we'd have hung out together, maybe changed our lives."

"Did that anyway," he said.

Glad to assert the upper hand for an instant.

"Until I found out what a slimy shit you were," she said.

How nice and polite of her to put it in the past tense.

"Hey, I'm sorry," she said. "Maybe I shouldn't have said that?"

"It's okay, never mind."

She looked amazed. "You're used to people talking to you that way?"

"No, but, uh, you're a special person."

Amanda laughed. Margaret Torres laughed. Dan Shaper decided to join them; Dan Shaper laughed. Margaret Torres said, "Hey, aren't you easy to please. Might have changed my whole life if I knew a man could take it when I leveled with him."

"As I said—"

"I know. I'm a special person."

Amanda went off in a renewed fit of the giggles.

While Margaret Torres was chattering in this nostalgic way, Dan Shaper had to blink because he began to see a monkey with thin lips and tiny sharp teeth and a tongue flicking stuff at him, shells and saliva and disdain. After a blink or two, during which time her voice faded out, he again saw a somewhat worn woman of a certain age with bones that used to be good and still were, beneath the stained envelope of skin and of organically grown carbohydrate turned flesh. She lived in a country where there was weather. Too much sun roughening the cheeks; lines of stress around the eyes and mouth. This sort of marking doesn't happen to monkeys. She was a normal human woman who had been dealt (dealt herself) a harder time than many. In northern California the winters are long and wet with, in the world of single mothers, a vast loneliness.

"We can go over what I did and then what you did and then what I didn't do and what you didn't do right now or at your convenience or at some future date," Shaper said.

Margaret Torres said: "Huh?"

"I guess that was too much to handle. Let me phrase it another way—"

"No, no, please." She put up her hands to protect herself, making the sign of the cross, about to cry Sanctuary. "Not again, I got enough. Wow. You're some explaining type of person, aren't you?" She looked him over and he blinked rapidly to keep the monkey vision at bay. "Have you ever tried a little counseling for that explanatory thing you have? Doesn't matter what school of therapy they're from, just so she has sympathy for you. I'm sure you can do something about your vocalization issue."

Dealing with Margaret Torres—not the Question of Margaret Torres, but the Actual Human Person Margaret Torres—was more vital than a whole bunch of religious holidays all bunched together in one big blowout observance. This wasn't a really pious comparison, since Shaper had his doubts about religion ever since the time he stopped calling the Christmas gift-giver Sanity Claws. (Also couldn't believe in human levitation as practiced in Fairfield, Iowa.) But Margaret Torres, brought home to him by a sudden daughter, that was something to reckon with.

If she was the mother of this daughter, she was the mother of Dan Shaper's daughter. No getting past that; sticking point; every exit blocked; deal with it. He didn't have total control. Already he could feel a little stirring of affection for Margaret Torres; not exactly any tender melting, but kind of liking her—*interested*. So: might as well go all the way. To a collegial, colleague like familiarity; nothing sexy, of course, not that. They just happened to find themselves parents together who were never together. Oh, goddamn Amanda, what an intrusion.

Dan Shaper was a father who hadn't signed on. He preferred to leave mom off the team, but since she was sitting here, saying No every now and then, a pretty good naysayer, right up there with the best of them, single-mom naysayers, a Gaia-type seeker with poetry in her soul, complicated beyond the hegemonic imaginings of a male victim of the traditional patriarchy, he couldn't forget about her even if she wasn't his pick. He breathed deeply, an answer to the problem of panicky hyperventilation which he had worked out in the wisdom of age, experience, and familiar melancholy. He tried to make it seem like mere breathing, not sighing. He considered Margaret Torres. He was too shy to imagine her dream life; it would be rude to get into a condition of empathy. It would be a commitment. She was terra incognita, unexplored. She steered her own course. Had they lived together and raised their daughter, he would have dined on low-fat products, not much red meat, but ample fish, fruit, fresh vegetables, heart-friendly grains. Much stir-fry and soy had been bypassed. No lactose-tolerance discussions. But at the end they had salsa in common, they had met at last.

Margaret and Dan were only at the earliest stage of sociability. "So how is it, spending a whole life in San Francisco?" she asked, and he hesitated before answering, even though this was a merely gracious question. She was meeting him halfway. Hesitation saved him from making an incorrect or incomplete reply and she seemed to forget the question—a habit of nervous urban sociability—and went on to a more specific declaration: "Yeah, wouldn't mind a burrito or some Korean barbecue, haven't had any since the last time I came to town. That kim chee is a garnish to remember."

He remembered it, too. The taste of cabbage, pepper, and

garlic buried in a bog and watched over by otters. He could easily spring for Korean; it would be a pleasure. At the time of Amanda's conception, it came back to him, Margaret Torres wore a ponytail tied with a ribbon and looked younger than her years. Now her hair was short, curly, and she looked older than her years, but still nice and agreeable despite her doctrines. The doctrines showed on her face but not to the extent of entirely wiping over the good bones.

A lot of Shaper's life had been devoted to negative turmoil, the stillness of untouchability, single-occupancy care. His span on earth seemed to be shaping up in one of the classical ways, including a beginning, a middle, and an end. (At some future date, yet to be determined.) He was a helper of the troubled in the criminal justice system who didn't speak the language, but personally, he himself, he spoke the language and knew how to sidestep difficult events. He practiced a busy waiting for what came along. These women, mother and daughter, caused positive turmoil, not the kind he liked. And they were hungry. He had thought that Amanda was supposed to hate her mother, but now she was hungry, also. It wasn't even two against one.

"Or Mexican?" Amanda asked. "D'Wayne and me had Korean last night."

Already they were whipsawing him. Well, he longed for a nice juicy burger with French fries.

Jalisco 2, second in an ambitious line of Jaliscos, was just down the block. Shaper would impress them by ordering at the counter in fluent Mexican. Anticipating, he sniffed the spicy oniony smell of salsa. Okay, forget kim chee. He transferred all his yearning to burritos. As they strolled, memories slid into place. He wondered if Margaret was still enraptured with Frida Kahlo. She had shown him her beat-up Corvair back then, long ago, in the seventies, an emission-emitting heap with an image of tragic Frida stenciled to the door on the driver's side. Wherever it rolled, that particle-spraying Falcon, not Corvair, was a below-book-value reproach to patriarchal hegemony.

"Wow, has the cat got your tongue," Amanda said. She had been watching, ping-ponging back and forth between her mother and father.

"You talking to me?" Shaper asked.

"No, just flapping my lips. Course I'm talking to you, Dad. Have we overpowered the poor guy?"

He was hungry for burrito, taco, guacamole, refried beans. Screw kim chee. He was concentrating on his hospitality duties and that's why he fell silent. Amanda muttered something about takeout, doesn't this Jalisco deliver, but they were already on their way. What he was beginning to feel was that, besides her ideologies, Margaret Torres also possessed, the more he looked at her, the more he sneaked little peeks at her, a worn, creased, weather-bruised, middle-aged prettiness. Wicca worship didn't ruin it. He was revising all his assumptions.

Margaret Torres said, "No sir, no way."

This gave him a jolt. What right did she have to pick on him by reading his mind? Maybe Wiccans were on to something. If she passed the time with other single mothers dancing by the light of the moon at midnight in piney forests, maybe there was a reason for it. Who was he to judge? All through history, folks have gotten useful stuff from strange stuff. Take the Druids, take the little brown elves who probably had beriberi due to Vitamin B deficiencies, take group marriage communes of the pre-herpes, pre-AIDS Sixties. . . .

"Hey!" Margaret Torres, interrupting his silence. "Knock it off."

Sort of an exploded nuclear family strolling a downtown

street on their way to an ecologically sound lunch. Kind of a modern small affinity unit, heading out for tasty but thrifty chow. Mom, Pop, and Their Big Girl, each locked in his/her own thoughts, but fully aware of the presence of the others. Bachelordom had been distracting in its own way, but Dan Shaper could understand why married men and women sometimes felt nostalgia for the old days of freedom. He remembered why children dream of orphan status. A crowd of ghostly considerations circulated above them as they trudged toward sharing in the holy ceremony of brunch.

The Tenderloin churchbells rang, summoning the southeast Asian immigrants, the homeless, the transsexuals who called themselves the transgendered community, and those who didn't give a fuck what they were called, call them Susie Sixpacks; the spoiled by Vietnam, the alcoholics and drug addicts and the recently discharged from custody, summoned them to grateful noontime worship. It was time for the prostitutes and the pimps to thank God for all His blessings after the morning commuter drive-through blowjob rush and before the evening tourist trade. The Tenderloin had been a convenient home to Shaper for years (secure building, plus walk to work). Now a kind of suspense hung in the air, a stillness around the tolling bells, and although he realized that boredom must have been aging him—comfort, convenience, regularity, and boredom—he wasn't ready for this tightening in his chest. He was no longer a smoker, showed no previous symptoms of emphysema.

Greedily Amanda watched. Amanda was judging, measuring, calculating. Probably as a child she had dreamed of an entire family, mom, dad, and daughter; and, better late than never, it had come true. Wearied by the struggle, Margaret must also have imagined the possibility. And now that Shaper had encountered this stirring, inciting young woman, his daughter, he found himself stirred and incited. His state of mind reminded him of horniness without the . . . oh, without the horniness. He had not diapered the child, he had not wiped the nose, he had not read the stories and helped with the homework. What he found instead was a creature with a curled sarcastic lip and a taste for variety ethnic eating.

Margaret attended to his silence as if it were a movie, listening to the tape of his thoughts. "No," she repeated.

"You said something?"

"Not what you're thinking. Give it up, Mister."

He didn't know what he was thinking, so she was unfair. His cheeks felt hot. There was no point in denying an accusation which she had not specified. She had a deep inner intelligence and charm, but that wasn't relevant. He liked women of a deep inner beauty and charm and also, if the truth were told, of a shallow outer beauty. As he moved through life, this limited his options.

When Margaret Torres confirmed that Dan Shaper was, just as Amanda had reported, in the business of translation and interpretation, she remarked that some men nowadays were looking for fulfilling lines of work. She knew a man in literature, up in Mendocino, wrote mysteries, and she knew one in healing right at home in Napa (he did aura work, no actual touching, no latex gloves), but they were gay guys and you could expect things from them. She also understood the need for Shaper's profession, given all the worthy undocumented future citizens sneaking across the borders to the south, as was their right. So she wouldn't judge. She had empathy for whatever augmented his self-esteem. Some Napa-Sonoma shamans might consider her a collaborator with the patriarchy, but as far as Margaret Torres was concerned, a man had the right to Carte Blanche or Visa or whatever, until, inevitably, he proved himself a slimy shit.

"Ensues the consequences," she pronounced in the judicial tones of someone who had seen it all and suffered fools gladly. She would cut a little slack for him or anybody. While she was doing so, slicing away, Shaper was leaping at the proffered opportunity to put off a final decision about her. Margaret Torres was, in a sense, a close relative.

Yet he suspected conflict, though not between Margaret Torres and himself. It was between Dan Shaper in late middle age—back problems, interruptions at night to pee, discovery of a previously undiscovered daughter—and the Dan Shaper he often thought he was, with the aid of an extra cup of coffee and of not looking in mirrors. He was unencumbered. This was a person with glossy dark hair, no root-canal jobs, and the ability during a certain historical period to insinuate a suggestion and find himself in bed with a stranger who might, for all he knew, turn out to be the girl of his dreams or at least pleasant company. He had been one of the many San Francisco persons of this sort. This person he had been was the father of Amanda and so was the other man here present, full of regret, nostalgia, and cross-purposes.

During this period of Dan Shaper's abstention from entertaining conversation, cat got his tongue and wool being gathered, while Amanda waited for something to come of their meeting—at least a bit of entertainment, that was the least they owed her—Amanda scuffled, turned her ankles, and gazed admiringly at her clunky shoes, Doc Martens knockoffs, just as if they were dress-up pumps with shiny straps. They were her dress-up for this and most occasions.

Shaper's daughter was calling, he recognized that. In some ways, both Margaret Torres and Amanda were pains in the ass. Oh well, they weren't the first.

"Dad," said Amanda, "how can I say this?"

"What? Just say it."

"Are you listening?"

"Yes. Say it."

"Okay, this is like . . . Okay, all my friends, they gave their dads, ones who had one, like a hard time off and on. I didn't. So now I owe you all the hard times I didn't give you. Can you take it?"

"I'm trying to, Amanda."

He thought he detected a look of friendliness on her face. There it was, there it went. She was about to tell him the things a five-year-old, a ten-year-old, a fifteen-year-old tells, and all the ages in between, the bedtime confessions, the dreamy sleepytime confidences, but of course they had disappeared into the history which had not taken place. She was about to speak and all she could really say was that she could not speak.

"Amanda, I'm trying."

"Okay, Dad. Credit for that. I'll tell D'Wayne."

"D'Wayne?"

"I'll tell him."

And then she closed that door. All doors were dangerous around here. Time for food; sometimes it helps.

He wondered if Margaret might like dinner sometime in a more upscale ethnic restaurant. It could be a social experience without a whole lot of money committed—not a real contractual attachment. She wouldn't have to feel patronized. Plus, it would unobtrusively demonstrate that his stomach was as efficient as ever, despite the years under his belt—he could handle Korean, Moroccan, Indian, even Ethiopian, although for some reason the subvarieties of Chinese, Hunan and Sechuan, gave him a little afterburn. Maybe it was the garlic or the ginger; could be the fried onions, if there were fried onions; Dan Shaper didn't know, wasn't a dietitian, although he had learned about après-repast seasoning with Tums.

"Dutch," she said.

"Pardon?" It wasn't one of his normal cuisines. Did she go for some kind of Hollandaise sauce?

"We'll split the check."

It seemed that, while musing, he had spoken his invitation aloud and she was accepting with her own ideological qualification. It was mealtime, time to think about other mealtimes, insulin merrily pumping away; Shaper's tendency toward hypoglycemia was set off by excitement. Many people who live alone, not just Dan Shaper, take to thinking aloud, trying out their thoughts by speaking them into the air. This was a different procedure from that of the crazies who wandered the Tenderloin, jabbering at nothing, chimeras, spooks from the past. Dan Shaper fit a different category. When he talked to himself, he was carrying on an intelligent dialogue.

"Hey, man . . ." A veteran panhandler, beefy and roadworn, glared into his eyes and demanded both payment and respect, the dynamic duo of spare-changing, the variety-pak of street hustlers. ". . . I got my needs, man." Shaper touched the arms of Margaret Torres and Amanda to move them along, giving the man with the styrofoam cup extended like a dueling sword his best keep-your-distance warning look. He was the guardian of this nuclear family.

Margaret Torres fumbled with her purse. Shaper muttered, "Just keep walking." Margaret Torres, equipped with theories, 'perform random acts of kindness,' 'they do what they have to do,' all sorts of theories in opposition to Shaper's, existed in the actual present in addition to the dreamlike distant Seventies of his younger manhood and her conviction that a woman does whatever she needs to do in order to become Frida Kahlo, Joan of Arc, or a free-range animal of the Aquarian age. Margaret's noble calling obliged her to ignore the styrofoam cup, put the dollar directly into the spare-changer's

hand, make the human gesture of touching him, highly sugared Thunderbird meat against doctrinaire vegetarian meat.

Put it on a bumper sticker, Shaper thought, and then corrected himself: She does what she has to do. Why criticize a
random act of kindness, just because it made him feel small?

"He had bad vibes like a juicer to me—the smell, I can still
taste it. Dope doesn't bring out the evil that way, but hey,
whatever works. Probably there's a reason. How close you
ever get to homeless, Dan? Could happen to anyone, you
know."

Evidently Margaret wanted to create propaganda for the
styrofoam-cup guy, felt Dan needed it. She didn't always talk
that way. When she was nervous, she fell back into Northern
California soulspeak (whatever works); when she was worried,
she invoked her sisters, her spirit guides, her theories. But
when she was straight with herself, and no one snotting her—
Dan Shaper, for example, not snotting her—she gazed
thoughtfully and acceptingly out of her gray eyes at the confusions surrounding a woman of her time.

Shaper was threatening a mother's entire history. She cut
bravely into the edginess he imported, this shadow invited
back by his daughter, unasked and unneeded by Margaret
Torres. She had won her calm and her certainties through
hard living. She survived. How she viewed things worked for
her.

Being with others involved slippage, messy clamberings,
strangers throwing her off balance. Dan Shaper had resolved
the same problem by keeping his distance except during working hours. The structure of his role here could be limited;
send a check or break the deal off. Or be unlimited: blood
tests, rancor, lawsuits. So he understood Margaret's problem

(no, he didn't). He had the same one (like hell he did). With the risks she took, bringing up the sturdy daughter, even providing Amanda with the power to fight back at her—smoking the hated weed, spiting her mother, longing for her father—she had taken more chances than Dan Shaper had. She survived by means of triumphing. Margaret Torres, valorous woman, tripping through the time warp. About himself, in the matter of bravery, Dan Shaper wasn't so sure.

"The chopped steak is chopped on the premises," he suggested confidentially, expert in the cuisine at Jalisco Número Dos. "I watched them do it. I advise you to pick anything you want."

"Wow, the big spender," Amanda said. "I had a guy come on to me like that once. He called me 'babe.' I hope you don't do that, Dad." But by the way she peered over the glass into the food bins, he could tell she approved.

They finished their ordering at the counter, Shaper sneaking casual looks at his daughter and her mother to see if they noticed his excellent Spanish accent, dipping ingratiatingly into Mexican for the occasion. He ordered extra trimmings, avocado, sour cream, carbo-loading for discreet emphasis on linguistic prowess. They sat at rough plank tables, like outdoor picnic equipment, under papier-mâché parrots perched and hanging above them. A mariachi tape skipped merrily along. On the wall a poster showed a girl dressed in winter clothes, charging down a beach with the legend SKI ACAPULCO. Someone around here had a naturalized or resident alien sense of humor. "Sometimes real mariachis come in"—urbane Dan Shaper, sophisticated denizen of the Tenderloin—"usually on Fridays at lunchtime, if they get up early enough."

"Frida," said Margaret. "You remember?" She was pointing to a young woman, probably a defendant's girlfriend, with a portrait on her tee shirt, the emblematic and unmistakable dwarfish body and the long dark caterpillar line of eyebrow.

Shaper sighed. "I do. On the door of your Falcon."

Margaret grinned and so did her daughter, two happy young women ready to dig into comfort food, and Shaper remembered Margaret Torres with the ponytail tied with a green ribbon. "Now I'm a licensed Gaia Consultant."

"What's that?"

"Licensed by my school in Mendocino. We don't use the word Shaman anymore—upsets native Hawaiians. I'm a trainer."

"So they train, then you train, sort of a franchise deal?"

"Sarcasm is a typical control mechanism, Dan. Amanda tries the same thing, I don't know where she learned it."

"Patriarchal genes."

"Bullshit," said Margaret Torres.

"Okay," said Dan Shaper. Okay to breathe, too, go for the big one. "Margaret," he said, "let me tell you frankly. We're really different now, we think differently. We both went on with our lives. It wasn't a time for thinking about the future, was it? But those times come back to me very strongly when I see you. You know? We must have really liked each other."

A struggle, an extreme wrestling match, a major-league wrestle, took place all over the creases and folds of Margaret's face, which knew soap and water, knew scrubbing from the chill seaside salt air, but had very little acquaintance with emollients. She had gone from Macramé Power to painting to levitation to Gaia Consulting without much time out for applying makeup. This stranger, Dan Shaper, was asking her to deny truths she had earned in favor of impulses she used to have. He hoped she wouldn't fall back on Karma.

She took her time. The mariachi music, the fresh guaca- mole worked their spell. "I remember that night pretty good," she said. "We saw that dockimentary and you gave me your Come Hitler look."

Well, thought Shaper, if a person is an artist, a seeker,

maybe a little nervous malapropism only operates to spur the person on. I gave her the Come Hitler look, she went thither, and now we have the results—Amanda plus this social event.

"I can't say I didn't go along with it. So I did. But it's not a real fun ordeal, raising a little charmer like Amanda. Hey, are you listening?" Margaret Torres asked.

"Yes."

"You never did listen much. Though how would I know?"

He was lost in turmoil. Who said he wasn't listening? But it was better that she couldn't read his mind every time. She didn't seem to hear the heys, groans, and dramatic sighs Amanda was tossing into the discussion as her contribution. He was listening so hard the friction was making his ears burn.

In sunny California both gloom and years were crowding him. They were among San Francisco's less-acknowledged risky behaviors. Long ago, amid the stragglers from the Summer of Love, Shaper had embarked on the familiar adventures of the time. Now that foggy night at the Mexican Consulate with El Indio's forgotten movie—it wasn't a dockimentary— was returning with full consequences yet to be seen.

Shaper felt quite certain, despite Margaret Torres' nice squinty gray eyes which reminded him of Amanda's, that this meeting wasn't going to turn into a case of the lonely aging guy finding his long-lost love after the conversion of years into wisdom. That kind of hopeful recycling wasn't in the cards. No sir, not for this veteran court translator and interpreter. Muchas gracias, he was comfortable enough already worrying about cataracts, irregular heartbeat, C.R.S. (Can't Remember Shit), and the dreaded dribble which a retiring judge had confided in him was the inevitable fate of both the justice and the defendant community if they live long enough.

Dan Shaper was practically certain he was growing shorter

every day. On his birthday he marked his height with a pencil on the bathroom door, twisting his arm (ouch) to get the pencil level with his still-hairy crown. Next year he would see if he measured up. He had found middle-aged ways to augment the excitement of breakfast, the thrill of the second cup of coffee, the news of the world as filtered through the *Chronicle*. ("Again this morning the world failed to come to an end. Nevertheless our wire services report disaster and tragedy everywhere, including the gala opening of the San Francisco opera season.") He had taken to reading the obituaries, fearing to be surprised by notice of his peaceful end, surrounded by no loved ones. Sometimes he would dream over an innocuous death report, feeling he knew the person, and if it reminded him enough of himself, he attended the funeral services. Well, he did this once. What stopped him was that the other mourners might think him a pickpocket or a sly wooer of widows over the wake snacks. Also he had a job to perform, helping some juvenile explain that he wore gang colors and carried a shiv only because it was a cultural pattern inherited from his Aztec ancestors, who invented the Walkman and the Saturday night dancing Buick Skylark. The reality of the grieving family at the funeral—a former person had died—was a shock, though not so much a one as if he had discovered his own obituary in his breakfast scan at the New Dawn Café. Facing up to his own selfishness was another project that lay ahead of him.

"A-*huh!*" Amanda was clearing her throat, darting quick looks around, forming judgments and interrupting the deplorable lack of attention to her. "I like this place." Shaper appreciated her approval of Jalisco Café Número Dos. Fluorescent tubes buzzed and clacked overhead; mariachis plinked; papier-mâché parrots perched with cocked heads. A Cost Plus Tiffany lamp stood unlit, cord unconnected, next to the condiment rack on their ranch table. Jalisco 2 was charging full speed ahead in the direction of charm. Amanda's words may have been a hint: would he spring for dessert?

For his daughter, anything; let's upsize the meal. "Have the flan," he said flairfully. "They make it the way it's supposed to be made in the Mexican countryside—sugar fried in condensed Pet milk, recipe goes all the way back to the Nestles conquest."

"I've cut way down on dairy," said Margaret Torres, "and custard's the worst."

Amanda got up, shoving the bench back, saying, "Sounds good to me. I like lifting off that brown stuff on top, it's like a scab." Shaper didn't think he could hand her the money for the flan, seemed rude somehow, or indiscreet—he was an inexperienced dad—so he got up to go to the counter with her. He would have one himself.

"Bring an extra spoon," said Margaret Torres.

Shaper harbored a little secret. He was going to order three of them. If Margaret didn't finish hers, that was her business. His own business was a cautious threading through events as tricky as a funeral or a birth.

At the counter Amanda bumped Shaper sociably with her hip. "Hey, you two getting acquainted, you forget about me? I'm still part of the deal too, remember?"

"We were talking," said Shaper. "You weren't left out."

So here came a little light chat from Amanda. "I should sue you for support my first eighteen years, those blessed years of childish innocence which were taken from me by a deadbeat dad. It's payback time. Somebody told me"—*who?*—"I'm a victim of Abandoned Orphan Syndrome."

"Who said that?"

"D'Wayne."

"Who's D'Wayne?"

But for the moment she had nothing more to contribute.

"That's three flans," Shaper said to the guy at the cash register, adding, "Sue your mother." The register guy looked startled until he realized Shaper was talking to the young woman.

"No use, she doesn't get it, she thinks she did what she had to do. We haven't determined yet whether you get it."

He took a calculated risk. "Maybe I do. Is that the way you want to go?"

He felt good about his question. He was certain this would be the beautiful moment when she cried, "No!" and threw herself into his arms. Instead she winked, hip-bumped him again, extended her hand, and said, "Shake. Dad, I kind of like you. You're not a deadbeat, you're only an absentee. And now you're not anymore."

He carried three ancient Aztec desserts in paper cups back to the rough plank table, food-bringer, hunter, alpha male. He asked Margaret Torres: "So who's this D'Wayne?"

"You brought one for me, too?" She cracked the caramel crust with her spoon and lifted it to her lips. "I really crave flan, it's a favorite. You're all heart, Dan. They say some assholes, not that you were ever a *total* asshole, because how would I know, turn into genuine nurturing human beings as they grow older and find their powers fading."

"Thanks, Margaret." With such flattery she was distracting him. Who D'Wayne was, that was a matter for grownup Amanda to explain. Instead, she was explaining: "I really mean it, Dad, you got some ketchup to do. The money is like a start. I mean, you could get off the hook. Dad? I need it and I'm way sure you owe it. I'm thinking dollar amounts, cash or check. I hope you can take a hint."

"I get the general idea. I think we have to work this out."

"*You* do, Dad. I'm the receiving party. What the general

idea is, is you owe. So you gonna work it out?"

"Who's this D'Wayne?"

"You have to come up with it, that's what you have to do. Dad." Something in his face must have shown her that he didn't like the way she leaned on that word, so she said it again, still leaning on it: "*Dad.*"

Above the mariachi tape he could hear a rasping noise, that of his peace of mind leaking away.

Four

'Thou shalt not steal' was a pretty good saying, nice ring to it, and certainly prudent advice for a large part of the clumsy-fingered population, but Gyro Brown was explaining to Dan Shaper that it didn't apply to him, his family, his traditions, his rights. Therefore, by virtue of tribe and family, it also didn't apply to his darling daughter Shari. Shaper, doing his job in helping her through the legal justice system, needed to understand the background of the gypsies' blessings and curses.

They had always been ironworkers. Rom artisans made the nails which were used in the Crucifixion. Poor Jesus, dragging his burden through the city of Jerusalem, looked up under his shaggy locks, caught sight of a gypsy, and lost his temper. "Because you made the nails for my cross," he said, "you will wander the earth until I return." But then, because He was a forgiving soul, a rabbi, and a future Christian, He added: "But because you made them sharp so they will hurt less, you may live by your own sharpness."

"I think," said Shari's dad, "my fathers before me lifted some purses in Jerusalem that Friday. It was an exciting day. Everyone was thinking about something else. You know the expression, Thank God it's Friday?"

Even in times of political correctness, even in San Francisco, Dan Shaper doubted that an ancestral curse and repentance from Jesus would stand up in court as a defense for Shari Brown's chronic shoplifting. Shaper was not Jesus to make an appearance on behalf of his client; for one thing, Jesus died the first time at age thirty-three and Shaper was going on twice as old. Mercy, he felt, was a great concept, and mercy plus the distraction of overcrowded jails might combine to keep Shari out of confinement one more time. "I'll do my best," said Shaper, "but it's really the lawyer's problem."

"Now it's everyone's problem," said Gyro Brown, the grieving concerned father.

"All I can do is help with her interpretation, but it seems to me, Mr. Brown, your family speaks English quite well."

"The shit we do," said Gyro Brown.

"If Spanish is your primary language—"

"Romani is, then Spanish. Then whatever comes next, wherever we wander, doing our job, just like Jesus said we should."

"In that case, sir, I'm not sure you need me. You've already got Someone."

"Do you think the City and County of San Francisco appreciates the big picture? Don't you notice how the system is crazy about details?" Gyro asked, brow wrinkled, eyes rolled upward to appeal humankind's fate and the destiny of his people, the Roma folk, gypsies, whatever. The eyes swiftly rolled back again, not to miss anything. In his pious posture, the whites of Gyro's eyes were those of some suave urban forest creature; then the eyes were other than that—alert, entertained, heated by internal charm giving himself pleasure. "Isn't it your job, help with the details, Dan? The words, the good English, the swift explanations? Anyway, making it easy for you, Shari's already in a better line than boosting, that was just a youthful stage—"

"In her career search," Shaper interrupted, trying to staunch the flow.

"Right, right, right. So non es problema, hey?"

If Shari Brown, Gyro's daughter, whom as an attentive father he led through the perils of childhood (unlike some fathers Dan Shaper could name), had now passed into the stage of serious shoplifting, pockets in her coat, pockets in the pockets, pouches everywhere on her person, then this loving dad appealing to him here must be the broker, retailer, or fence with impeccable tagged women's clothing in the trunk of his roomy old Cadillac and access to the device that deactivates the little chip that goes *chip-cheep, chip-cheep* and brings the store dicks running. They pay no attention to Jesus. Annoying *chip-cheep* like a shriek of displeasure. Someone forgot to snip the extra tag the fuckers put in the 34-C cup of a Maidenform bra.

Would a real booster do that? Only a mere girl with poor language skills, like her father, omitted such an obvious precaution.

"Counselor Conant appreciates I might forget on the stand, slip my mind, brain damage due to being hit by this Mission-14 bus—now that was a good case, Mr. Shaper. Concussion and C.R.S."

"You're pretty fluent for brain damage, Gyro."

"Got the doctor's certificate—Can't Remember Shit." (Yeah, heard of it.) "Ten percent disability for logorrhea when my glands act up. You ever been hit in the head by a Mission-14? You'd appreciate my agony. So anyway, I told Counselor I want your aid and willing assistance to express myself. The normal fee to you, of course. We sue Legal Aid if we have to, plus the court has to make provision for the one with loose bowels, no kidneys, blind, deaf and dumb, or the person who is linguistic-challenged like me and my ethnic subdivision. *Far-staysh?*"

Far-staysh meant, Understand? Shaper got the reference. He would go along for awhile.

"—and truth to tell, these mutual friends." Gyro didn't want to go too far, so by way of going just far enough, he lowered his voice. "Counselor Conant. And, you know, D'Wayne and his lady."

It rang a bell. Shaper said nothing. D'Wayne and someone. Shaper spoke English and a selection of the Latin tongues, but at this point a little silent logorrhea was in order.

Ferd Conant, the young woman's lawyer, had called to say she needed an interpreter because she was rejected for juvenile division on the grounds that she wasn't a juvenile—

"Is she or isn't she?" Shaper asked.

"Well, that's under dispute. Her family says she is, she distinctly remembers being born quite recently, but unfortunately the chicken shit indicates—"

"The what?"

"The official records, but she's a gypsy—maybe—and they work on a different calendar. Dear little Shari spoke English well enough when it was a juvenile matter, but now she and her family, the cat's got their tongue—actually, it's Judge Katz—"

"Haha," said Shaper.

"Hey, they're Romani, might be, you know? I'm like you, I take what I can get," said Ferd.

Ferd had graduated from Lumumba Law, a chartered school where he married the Miss Night Extension Homecoming Queen, after a previous career as a doorman at the Joystick Club. First he moved up from cowardly bouncer, and now he had moved up, dreg-wise, to taking the legal leavings in difficult times for advocates and defenders. One adult in seventy-two was a lawyer in San Francisco, which meant a fellow had to hustle if he didn't want to go back to wrestling cockeyed tourists from Stockton back out onto the street. Miss Night Extension Homecoming Queen dumped him when he took the temporary work most of his fellow lawyers finally found, driving for Veterans, the non-Yellow alternative.

"I don't speak Romani," said Shaper.

"She speaks juvie. Just doesn't *hablo* the adult felony-type English, buddy, okay?"

Shaper sighed. Okay. The court would pay minimum and he could communicate with the young woman in her own street-smart, purse-snatching, shoplifting, palm-reading, geriatric-handjob American. "It's a learning experience," said Shaper.

"I knew I could count on you, buddy. A boy's gotta do what a boy's gotta do."

True for boys and girls. Which was why Shari now had been picked up on her sixth shoplifting charge when the store dicks happened to shake her and a bunch of small but pricey items clattered down her pant legs like impacted turds. She should have stuck to Nieman-Marcus and Nordstrom's; the lower-ranking establishments, with their buzzers, surveillance cameras, equal-opportunity security hires, alarm chips attached to hems, and suspicious nature were inhospitable to a lonely girl out on a little expedition with her dad. She was just keeping her hands in.

The two of them, dad and daughter, companionable, an example for Shaper and Amanda, arrived fashionably late for their appointment, surveyed the general shabbiness of Shaper's office, took disdainful positions without regard for small objects of value in the vicinity. There were none. Their scouting routine was the habit of long discipline, probably

inappropriate for this consultation. The lateness was explained by means of "stuff to do, shit you wouldn't believe."
Dan Shaper's normal role as translator-interpreter was being
given a stretch here. El Famiglia Brown claimed a right to
syncopate their response (defense on grounds of tradition,
faith, alternate vocabulary, and Rom rage?) while the justice
system was in the process of learning to avoid rude behavior
toward ethnic, color, and gender minorities, majorities, whatever. Applications had come in for Ebonics translators. Folks
were feeling his/her/their way around here.

Gyro blinked at the daylight, filtered and gray, soiled by
Market Street, as if he had never noticed a city afternoon
before. Were there many of these, all the time? Gyro travelled
through the day on business, but this didn't mean he had to
see it. He used it, he saw visions, he made his own tropical
festival.

But when the sky made a mucky gray of things, with the
help of traffic and history of course, the sky could do a pretty
complete job of it. Gyro was very interested. This sky streaked
with yellow and the other colors seeping in through Shaper's
askew Venetian blinds—interesting. Gyro completed the
spectrum with his own bright energy. Shari was lucky to have
such a father. Shaper hoped someday Amanda would feel
lucky to have the father she had.

"Lemme see that watch," Shari's dad commanded.

Shaper raised his wrist. "About a quarter after twelve."

"No, let me. Take it off." And he reached for Shaper's
wrist.

Shaper pushed him with his other hand, jabbed him in the
shoulder, not hard enough to be a punch and too hard for a
joke, so that in his confusion the time-seeking dad said,
"Hey!"

"I'm not taking it off."

"I'll trade you. I'll get you a better one."

"This one does what I want it to do."

"How does the word Rolex sound to you?"

"I understand the word Timex. Can we get to business?"

The guy was used to teasing folks, scaring folks, facing them down. Shaper didn't want to play, he didn't even want a quarrel or some sort of symbolic power match. He would settle for a time-out.

"Okay," Shari's father grumbled. "You're no fun, are you?"

"Used to be. Not anymore, Gyro."

Shaper stared. Shari was just sitting there comfortably, enjoying the contest. Shari Brown radiated a warmth, an amazed joy, after the genetic exercise of making her way from some mountain fastness, perhaps in India, across Europe, through Hungary and Romania, somehow to Spain, somehow to the Atlantic, somehow through seasickness and a generation or two of fortune-telling, tinkering, used-car dealing, and palm-reading, until here they were, here were Shari and her father. She looked strong, full of tender resolve, ready to deal. That flush in the cheeks was not embarrassment. Her deep, healthy, florid glow sent waves of heat toward him. "Now we're both having fun, aren't we, brother?" asked Shari's father.

Gyro's mouth was pursed, making little kissing sounds to the air. Shaper had seen experienced cons do that, meaning This one's a pussy, you're a pussy, but he was just cleaning his teeth, sucking his tongue against his teeth, trying to get rid of an unwelcome shred.

Somehow, he knew not why, this family made Shaper nervous. They didn't just want to hustle his intervention with the court system. They wanted to hustle him, dangling this ancient child in front of him. He already had his own daughter to get used to.

"Would you care to let me know what you have in mind?"

Shaper asked the dad, who answered indignantly: "Now why would I even think of such a thing? What a rotten rotten idea to hint, you rascal. She's a big girl, she makes her own dates. Joke, understand and forgive, my friend—it is Gyro's way, the way of festival. Life must always be a festival because it is so short, are we right about that?" And then he leaned forward, lowering his voice, in case the walls had ears. "Love is a strange thing, not like the old days. You can't tell a daughter what to do anymore. She sees a cute older man, balls hang kind of low, she goes for it. It's the thrill of that veteran's overhang."

Shaper stood up from behind the desk, went to the door of his office, and opened it so that the traffic in the hall could witness their conversation. Gyro and his daughter observed this action of a timid man with pleasant amusement. They hadn't done anything wrong, just talking, had they? There was no lawsuit in the offing, was there? Shaper returned to his desk, felt unusually alert, rapped his knuckles on the blotter, and asked, "Are you really a gypsy?"

"Depends," said Gyro Brown.

"Depends?"

"Depends on who you ask."

"I'm asking you."

Gyro Brown wrinkled his brow, searched his memory. He cleared his throat. The truth was heading Shaper's way, nearer, nearer, growing near. Here it came. "We prefer you call us Romany people. I walk the walk," said Gyro Brown.

He looked at one of the devices on his wrist, not the watch this time, and lifted his wrist to his ear. This was a man who marched to the sound of his own beeper. "Now that you are acquainted," he said, "I leave you to business. Shari, answer straight with our Mr. Shaper, no fooling around. Mr. Shaper, this is a precious person to me. So I'm outa here."

Shazam, almost like that. He kicked the rubber stopper and the door shut behind him. Shaper stared at the image of his name inside-out on frosted glass. In the breeze of her father's departure, Shari looked bereft for about ten seconds—Gyro was so important to her!—and then cheerful and robust again. Resiliency was a part of her emotional repertory. The powerful know how to honor, and that meant a generosity about putting others at their ease; Shari sought this sort of power, along with getting what was rightfully hers. Her ten seconds of nostalgia for her father's enveloping strength and love were about enough for the procedures of bereftness to play out and make room for joy. Like Gyro, she knew there is only a brief span on earth allotted to each of us, although of course some folks enjoy a more extended briefness than others.

She smiled at Shaper, she shrugged with the shrug of a sturdy slip of a girl, indicating that her father was too much (in the strictly positive sense, as in 'He's too much'). She had learned the value of smalltalk to ease the way in social intercourse; it worked like certain distilled petroleum products of a proprietary nature, sold under various names in spray cans for squirting into rusted locks or joints to cause a general easing and loosening. (Do not swallow or allow to remain in the eyes. Call Emergency if ingested.)

Shari applied her own version of this unlocking remedy. "I'd like something to drink, maybe a beverage," she said.

Close inspection of the client time. She didn't squirm as Shaper gazed, she wiggled, which is a different proposition altogether in a young woman like Shari—dark (could be a Spanish gypsy), long straight black hair and flashing eyes (bring on the castanet and flamenk away the smokey hours), a nose that quivered when she suppressed the nonembarrassed giggles (no evidence one way or the other on the gypsy question). Shaper concluded there was as much chance that she was of Romany heritage as that she was a Finn. Wasn't a Finn. Shaper didn't know about the Rom people, but Finns don't inquire about future events by asking, "So wha hoppinin, man?" Nothing that Shari may have planned for Shaper was gonna hoppin, however, if he could keep to his tradition of watchful waiting and general bystander caution. He was a father now, too. He needed to think about the future beyond the night's or sometimes the afternoon's distraction.

A spice-laden curry breeze wafted from the pink cavern of Shari's mouth when she finished a sentence without quite shutting down. She left things open. She contributed to the warmth and meat steaminess of things. She rolled her eyes skyward, a trajectory interrupted by ceilings, and seemed to be thinking a few noble thoughts; seemed to be; or maybe just waiting for Shaper to make a move. Exotic girl aromas, pink cavern of mouth, sweetly patient brooding upon the rooftop, ceiling, or sky usually caused normal men to make moves.

She shrugged. Not normal? Oh well.

"Why I'd like a beverage is because I'm thirsty," Shari declared once again, in case he had forgotten, looking around for a refrigerator, dispenser, pitcher, bottle, or rock to strike like Moses with her staff. "Isn't that what I heard a waiter say once? 'And for your beverage, Miss?' I was with a guy that time."

"You don't need a Spanish translator," Shaper stated.

"Do you speak Romany?"

"You don't need that either."

Her eyes were so shiny, gleaming under their coating of youthy shellac, the deep black of them, they looked like Indian goddess doll's eyes. The Spanish gypsy story certainly worked for her.

"So are we getting a beverage outside someplace or do you have something right here?" She was staring into him. The already clear enough was being clarified. He cut short any other thoughts: This crazy little dose of poison—not crazy at all—is conniving at full speed.

"You just sit there and look at me and say things," Shaper said. "Isn't that nuts?"

"You're nice too," she said. "Plus, I like your aftershave."

"I don't use aftershave."

"You mean that's *you?*"

"I don't think I want to get into this discussion."

"You're paid by the hour, aren't you? So what do you eat, then? Something smells nice."

He was pretty sure, with the curry on her breath, she couldn't smell whatever she was smelling. He ought to get her out of here. "Why don't you stroll nicely away?" he asked.

"I don't stroll nicely, Mister. Do other things nicely though."

"I'm sure."

And he was. He had neglected to prop open the door again after Gyro kicked the rubber stopper away. Maybe he should just lumber off, scamper, flee the hell away from this neat, boiling, spicy-smelling little trouble-bringer with the nice tight rear end that lots of young women have before the years of cheeseburgers and french fries do their work. When they're older, they have to tend themselves.

She might be the sort who would tend herself, but he'd never know. "You're bad news, Shari."

"Right on! Now you got your groove. You had nothing but previous good news in your life, Mister Shaper?"

She caught the flick of his eyes. He was examining the goods. There was still a chance.

"What I do," Shari said, "guys ask me for something, I just say no, they like it when I say no first, but then sometimes their charm gets to me."

"Smart girl like you," Shaper said, "what I do with smart

girls like you is I open the door"—he stood up, crossed the room, and did so—"and I think about trouble every minute of the time I spend with you. Not that it's likely, since I'm not a Civil Service, this is my own business, and also I don't have a wife to worry about. Would you like to discuss the problem you already have and not make new ones, Shari?"

"Okay, Mister."

"I'm all ears."

A beatific smile came across her dark face with its sharp long nose and deep deep eyes. "All ears, that's what you all are. Take your time, Mister Gadjo. This what they call fore-play?"

A late career as muddled older guy was turning out to be more complicated than stamp-collecting, golf, or worm-raising for organic gardening. He'd be feeding the worms in due course anyway. One thing he believed about becoming a new father was that dignity no longer permitted the pursuit of young women. He was feeling his way in the proper-father-with-proper-dignity department, a whole new area of endeavor. If a woman didn't respond to a single charm-soaked but needy telephone message, he gratefully withdrew from the field. It was now the rule. Amanda was absorbing all the energies of neediness, yearning, something very like desire.

Dignity summoned him to do nothing, no flowers, no candy (candy? In San Francisco? Amid all this tooth and ar-tery health?), and especially no whining messages asking why, oh why don't you want to see me again.

He wouldn't even wait for the answer. He'd go out to the movies with Harvey or alone to eat Chinese food under-ground by fluorescent light, and at any hour he chose, sending hot sugared pork fat sliding down his chopsticks—he treasured his freedom. It was a gift beyond price. Of course, he'd keep the answering machine on in case an agreeable person happened to call.

Or Amanda.

Not long ago, a spell with a young woman named Monique was so bad, so full of deceit, chagrin, failure, and jealousy— she visited him once smelling of kum, didn't even have the courtesy to bathe before their reconciliation dinner of shell-fish and other cajoling toy foods he had sent out for. . . . How bad was it? So bad that he wanted to marry her, so bad that he asked her to marry him, so bad that in her own despair she accepted to marry him. And the next day came straight from her office, again smelling of kum. The boss was unhappy with his wife, but didn't believe in divorce. It was a matter of faith, morals, and community property.

Monique and her employer, who was a partner in a down-town law firm, suffered a lot. Dan Shaper would so stipulate. Poor Charles, Chip, had all his kiddies to consider.

For a time, when Monique left town, left the state, gone to start all over in Manhattan, Shaper couldn't bear the smell of his own bed because she had been in it. Her cologne, her sighs and groans, her invisible mites. He bought a new mat-tress. His heart pounded when he heard hard quick heels on the sidewalk outside that sounded like hers. He felt nauseated if someone ordered clams on the half shell, one of her little pleasures, sometimes feeding him a clam with a vinegary lemon sauce on it, saying, "See? I share." Tipping the clam juice into his mouth.

First her body went away, and then the smell of her, and then the ghost of Monique was gone. But sometimes, when it was cold inside (inside him; the weather was irrelevant), the ghost came back to haunt him, her sharp high laugh, her teas-ing, her impeccable recall of anything he said which amused her. She made him feel humorous. She remembered. She was the book of part of his life that had been fun until it stopped being fun.

He heard she was in London. Great. After awhile, he noticed that the morning muffins at the Roma across from the Hall of Justice tasted good again. He was on his way back to appetite. He put extra nonfat milk in his coffee to build a healthy body because his mother used to tell him to do so if he insisted on making himself nervous by drinking so much coffee. He was calm as the calcium kept busy circulating, precipitating away, building strong bones for the calm mature person.

He still couldn't eat clams. Then one evening, on a stool at a raw bar, he ordered clams and sat there triumphantly sucking the little shells, with a goofy smile on his face. He would remember Monique and her clams, but he would also remember enjoying a vinegary spicy lemony taste alone at the Nob Hill Raw Bar.

For a time he persisted in the habit of damp and anxious sleep, alone in his bed, awakening to make a face at his body's spiteful fussing; he balled up his sweaty pajamas and heaved them at the closet door. Later he put them in the laundry bag. Nowadays he slept pretty well, the dampness a normal exhalation, a night and morning metabolizing enterprise, and wouldn't be ashamed to share it with some agreeable new friend, should one appear.

In an early attempt to recover from Monique, he approached a lovely skinny young cigar-smoker—all in black, of course, a pants suit—in front of Dunhill's on Sutter; he offered to help; but probably his timing was off, because she was busy throwing up into her cellular phone, hiccuping dry heaves, green of face (nice eyes, though). "I suggest not inhaling," Shaper said, "although it's tempting with one of those Uppmann Modero Número Dos because they're so tasty."

She went on barfing, turning to the Dunhill window without an answer. In his benevolent way Shaper hoped that next time she would remember to sniff, roll, lick, taste, and savor, but not to draw the smoke into the lungs; and perhaps he would have better luck next time, provided she didn't recognize him.

The day wasn't wasted. A homeless guy squatting nearby held up a sign saying I HAVE "CANCER" and the quotation marks gave Shaper something else to think about. Was it to differentiate himself from those who had non-quotation-marks cancer? Was it for emphasis? The homeless guy picked up the barfing anorexic model's stub, about five dollars of cigar left on it, when she staggered off to clean up her cellular phone and call Stars to see if she had any appointments. (By this time, Shaper had decided she was a model, not an ordinary anorexic, who had failed to study her cigar-lover's instruction manual for cool contemporary bulimo-anorexics.)

Shaper resolved to practice his social skills, if any, elsewhere, certainly not on the street—past that age—or perhaps just settle into the easy times of a veteran.

Once in a while, just for sociability's sake, he sniffed a bit of cocaine, expecting no miracles of it. Under coke, a North Beach acquaintance, brains boiling, confided in his dearest buddy Dan ("Hey, what's your last name again?") his genius business idea—dated toilet paper! sold only when fresh! Maybe flavored! Why should Adwalla juices monopolize the field of timely home products? Treat your asshole to the best!

"Shaper, Dan No Middle Initial Shaper. I'm not a businessman."

"Makes no never mind! We can go into it together! With your business savvy and my creative touch, we'll wipe out the competition! Scott and what's it, Kimberling Clark, playing catchup, man, but we're out there ahead of them, aren't we?"

Occasionally Dan used to join his colleague, Al Manion, in the big drafty Victorian he called the House of Charm on Vallejo in North Beach. Al, a lawyer, specialized in victimless crimes, such as narcotics, and sometimes called on Shaper when a Colombian client overstayed his welcome in the U.S. while carrying condom-loads in his belly or bricks of it in his rental car. Usually when Al and his friends breathed their lines through rolled-up paper money, not pretentiously using hundred-dollar bills—they didn't care, a crisp clean G. Washington or A. Lincoln would do—they went giggling to the closet to put on funny clothes and head out South of Market to the Giga-Byte Dance Club. If Shaper was sleepy before, he no longer wanted to sleep but stayed behind by the fire, wide awake, sometimes with the person he had shared the lines with, if there turned out to be one. He and the person made love sleepily, negligently, and lay there toasting, listening to the crackling oak logs, confiding that they both liked the smell of hickory. That was all. Not Monique—Monique was history. No big deal and no great leap forward in toilet-paper marketing.

He had drifted off the high life, just floated free. Partly the times had changed, mostly his own time had moved on. He was no longer fighting middle age. He wasn't fighting. He had given up on perfect love, taken a pass. He was at peace, a better friend than he used to be. When his buddy Alfonso said, "I got some good stuff," he said: "Maybe some other time. Got some work on my table at home."

At home he had a bed, fairly clean sheets, dreamwork to do on them, that was all. Sometimes, without shame, he rinsed out yesterday's tee shirt and let it dry in the morning sun at the window, where anyone passing on Ellis could look up and see it.

Five

Gyro Brown kept a branch office upstairs at the hank Hotel (formerly Shank, but the S fell off), where he used to do sidewalk auto repair at the curb. He no longer needed the room on the street floor for his wife Elmira's business, palm-reading and expertise on matters of love, health, and finance (I can personally bless your money, put it in this here spiritual box), but the space helped in the storage and sale of portable electronic equipment and items of clothing which fell off delivery trucks in that stop-and-go downtown San Francisco traffic.

During the hard times which followed the Crucifixion, an entrepreneur like Gyro had to ask his entire family's help in keeping body and soul together—sad but true. The last two thousand years had been turbulent ones. A wife couldn't just sit around drinking flavored beverages, tending her fingernails and passing on the secrets of cuticle trimming to the daughter. Shari was destined to build her own successes. Such would be the case, the proud father realized, ever since she learned at the age of five—great round black eyes, a flirtatious thing she did with lashes and general mobility in the eye sockets, an avalanche of pure childish cute—to nail the attention of shopkeepers while Gyro scouted the shelves for small items of food or apparel. What times they had together, father and daughter!

A few hours before the unfortunate Crucifixion, lumbering

past on the Via Dolorosa, Jesus had promised Gyro's iron-
smith ancestor a longterm vacation from routines, and his
family wanderings proved that Jesus told the truth; this wasn't
just another divine parable. Now Gyro was a man of property
and optimism, his own optimism but the property of others.
Elmira, his wife, pitched in and kept her nails bright, besides.
She was diligent. Shari inherited the good qualities of her
parents and the blessings of the Son of God.

Dan Shaper liked winners. He admired a man who was not
a plodder, not a victim, two vulnerable points in his own character. Gyro was a man who took arms against a sea of petty
regulations. Gyro stood solidly on his two legs as if they were
four, and walked with the gait of power, loping along not too
fast, unhurried, in control. In response, Shaper tried to correct his own stance, turning his feet out and bending the
knees an invisible fraction so that it didn't look as if he had
only temporarily touched down on earth. Here in Gyro was
a whole man, an entire fluid operator; even his rear slid sneak-
ily sideways when he strolled. He stole a step when he
climbed a stairs. His flesh fit sleekly on his bones, not jiggling
like a fat man's, not tight and blue like a thin one's. He could
move forward while moving in several simultaneous other directions.

Also the person Gyro was not a man of small aim. His
ambitions were generous—big shoplifting (especially during
crowded lunch hours), dynastic palm-reading (especially during the difficult period around national holidays, when the
lonely need to have the murky future deciphered out of their
clouds of melancholy). He was a tycoon of swift moves. "I
used to could steal things pretty good, when I wasn't so honest. I shake your hand, your freckles are gone. Shake it again,
no more knuckles. Now I'm more into family, friends." He
poured his warmth down upon Dan Shaper. But sometimes

he still liked to test the clerks at Tenderloin convenience stores. "Let's go seven-elevening," he would say to Shari, because she knew how to distract a pimply underpaid horny kid.

Here on the downhill slope, rent-controlled in Floating Mote Arms with its plaster gargoyle cornices at the bottom of Nob Hill, Shaper was ready for risk, an adventure, even something wrong—yes, why not really wrong? The years ahead were too short to squeeze in fatal troubles, but a few stimulating ones would help make old age more than a mere way to pass the time. Given his choice, he might have selected true love, for example—that would be chaotic enough—or a lottery win, some irrational exhilaration, engulfing in nature, if Amanda had not come to surprise him, if she had not also brought Margaret to resurprise him. If trouble came in the form of pain which he then passed through, gaining a family along the way, well, others found satisfaction there. A person could go for it.

He was going for it. He had been distracted by the repetitious easy-come easy-go of his days, which were far from heartbroken but in the neighborhood of bored, the vicinity of sleep too much. Since Monique, very quiet. Now he was cocked for trouble. He thought he was reading himself correctly; understanding might be too much of a claim. A person complete in himself isn't thrown off course by others.

"Okay, ready," muttered Dan Shaper. He spoke aloud. Talking to himself was evidence that a man of a certain age has decided to shake things up, kick the works, put the mechanism in the way of helpful injury. He could go along with a limited Gyro Brown program, today meaning he found himself climbing into a generation-old Cadillac, classic sweep of fenders, classic rust, grand fins pointing where the vehicle had been and where it might be heading, a frequently battered rear bumper with deckled edges rubber-hammered out at curbside by Gyro's rubber hammer. Shaper recognized the deal. One of the Brown famiglia's little sidelines must have been sudden stops, whiplash settlements; Ferd Conant, Esq., doing the legal stuff. Jesus on the Via Dolorosa, crowded with pedestrians, gawkers, souvenir peddlers, and donkeys, may not have had this form of fraud in mind. He issued the pass before Lloyd's of London invented insurance, but isn't anticipation the business of prophets? What good is a Messiah if He doesn't get it right the first time?

It wouldn't hurt to go for a nice ride in a floating big old gas-guzzler. So Shaper was nicely settled on a spacious front seat, wooden beads dimpling his back, when suddenly the door creaked open and a small, intense, sturdy, hot body flung itself alongside his less small, less sturdy, less intense one. "Hey!" was all that came to mind.

She was beaming and splendid in her new blouse accessory, a button she must have boosted from a tourist shop on Grant: KISS ME, I'M CHINESE. "Going with you today," Shari announced.

"No you're not," said Shaper, "or at least . . ." If Gyro said she could ride along, Shaper was getting out. This was panic. No enclosed spaces with Shaper and the young person pressing herself against his thigh (it tingled, it had a mind of its own).

Gyro understood. It was a job for a father. "Scamper," he commanded.

"Annh!" A wail of protest, head jerked around, thigh even closer.

Gyro grinned at Dan, comprehension overflowing so early in the afternoon. "Carmencita, Chica, darling daughter, por favor . . . fuck off."

He would do anything for a friend, even putting his daughter out of the family vehicle in both English and Spanish if she made the friend uncomfortable.

Shari heaved herself out to the sidewalk and with surprising strength heaved the door back shut, rattling loose parts. Velocity was her theme for the day. She didn't have to say anything. As far as she was concerned, her dad and this old fart could lounge their way in the Cadillac straight to hell (or to a salad bar). From behind, as she ambled fiercely around the corner, she renewed Shaper's memory of her origins in the land of Wiggle. Only after she was thoroughly gone, had jostled him and departed, had lifted her paws hard and brought them down harder, did Shaper realize that the turbulent little animal bumping against him had been wearing nothing under her blouse. Her body was gone, the breeze of her departure was invisible, her shadow no longer streaked across the sidewalk. His thigh stabbed. Her father grinned.

Gyro shook his head, doing the dramatic presentation of *that's my girl*. Why did Shaper get the impression that maybe this incident was as planned as the rear-endings to which the Cadillac's bumpers were witness? That Shari didn't go scampering and wiggling down Ellis as a regular thing?

"So I ask you something," said Gyro Brown. "Stead of a salad bar, how about the same thing, makes no difference, a rib joint I know? Look at it this way. You get the healthy coleslaw and I get what I want, too, some barbecue, how you feel about that? You know what I'm saying, Dan, like a compromise between what we both need?"

Gyro had a proposal to present for consideration in company with some nice red sauce, sugar, pepper, and tomatoes cleverly transformed into a ketchuplike deal, covering the meat. His teeth were prominent, his eyes dark and gleaming, his smile a fulfillment and endmark of smiles; but these were not the proposal, they were only the sauce of it. He wanted to go into business with Shaper. He felt limited by what he called his ham-and-eggs factory of traditional tinkering, his variety-pak. He was larger, he saw Mr. Shaper as larger, together they could be big. "You understand me yet?" he asked politely. "*Huge.*"

What Shaper could do was mostly what he always did, help lead the speakers of Latin-based languages through their legal problems. Dan had once dated a woman who thought German was a Romance language because so many romantic stories were told in German, such as the operas of Ludwig von Wagner; once dated her, but not twice. Now he referred to his trade as the Latin trade, not the Romance language business. As a beginning, Gyro suggested he could find the people who needed Shaper's help. Prove himself as a scout; inevitably lead to greater trust and gain. Gyro would do more than merely help—he would *assist.*

"I don't need—" Shaper began. "The lawyers—"

"Want!" cried Gyro. "Want is another matter, my friend. You want!"

"I think you've got the wrong man and the wrong business," Shaper said, and from his courtroom experience, he knew how unconvincing was this denial.

Both Amanda and Gyro had awakened him. Comfort wasn't everything, even during the closing years. Gyro was smiling deeply into his eyes; they would both pretend he needed to be convinced.

Gyro's spirit levitated in a previctory celebration. "I will never say I am King of the Gypsies, far be it, that's too much responsibility, but, my friend, I am a prince. Ah, perhaps not even a prince, who knows in these times? But a captain! A man! I am a man, sir!"

"So stipulated," said Shaper.

Gyro would not take offense at legalisms, not at present. "My dear friend, you sit at your desk playing solitaire when you could be prospering." This was not true, Shaper did not play solitaire, although he sat a lot, doing very little, reading the newspaper, cleaning his nails with the blade of a knife. Yes, he could afford to prosper more than he did. But as far as he was concerned, lacking responsibilities until recently, organized for the quiet life until recently, he prospered sufficiently for his means and needs. His nails were clean, his cuticles pushed back. His desires were modest.

Gyro observed Shaper's thoughts keenly as they were expressed by silence and twitches of the face. So Shaper was being cagey, okay. Cagey was an option under average circumstances. Gyro explained about family, how important it is for everyone, an enduring value; a blessing, sometimes a surprising one. Of course, enduring values can be exaggerated, since they don't always endure. In Gyro's thought, the Rom people had a correct view of family, but others needed to understand—he had seen a book which inspired him—*The Family of Man*. He had carried a whole box of those books from a parked delivery truck to the trunk of his Cadillac for selling to a bookstore which specialized in bargain gifts. He had lifted the Family of Man onto his own shoulders. At holiday seasons there was a nostalgic market demand. The experience taught him respect for the back-stressing weight of compassion in the face of human diversity.

For Gyro, Shaper was a fellow person of family; like him, a man with a daughter. A mist of saliva and eloquence made Gyro's breath visible as he convinced, convinced, was sure he could soon convince. The open road lay before them. They could travel together down the sun-dappled route. Did this make sense so far?

Gyro was alight with explication. Shaper thought the best program was to listen. Gyro told of the difficulties in dealing with large quantities of goods which spilled out of delivery trucks or leaked from the windows of warehouses at night, in the dark and damp, when alarms were disabled by water main breaks or an electric prod. . . . A person like dear Dan Shaper could have an important role to play, friends among the police, in the justice community—Harvey the plain clothes weightlifter, Alfonso Jones the smiley black sergeant who smiled too much and was too smart to have any fun with, Ferd Conant the jerk-off lawyer they both knew—in total, a position in the social structure and a fluency in language which poor Gyro Brown, himself, unfortunately lacked. It was his great sorrow, along with the back problems which were a consequence of advancing years and midnight toting.

Shaper wanted to be elsewhere and was as happy as he could remember being at his front-row seat for this performance.

Gyro said, "You are thinking. I like that. We are intelligent people, but we, my people, we don't think. You may not be so intelligent, but you think all the time. So it works out even between us, am I right?"

He had left out a few middle terms in his analysis. Shaper was not planning to offer logic lessons to Gyro, who had further items which he urgently wished to impart.

"So therefore, sir," he said, "if people say I am Romani, gypsy, why not? You are Gadjo—what the fuck? If people say I am Spick, Hispanic, Latino, Undocumented Dark Person, then I can also say I am Romani, if that's what gypsies call themselves."

"You're not?" Shaper asked.

"Of course I am." Gyro turned up his palms in victory, nothing to hide. "You see? Already there are doubts. This is the beginning of knowledge. Everything depends on where you look. So there are questions, Dan?"

"I don't need to make these decisions about you."

Gyro took this statement under advisement. Cagey; he liked cagey. He was thinking along the same lines, and suddenly moved closer to Dan Shaper, put his face near Shaper's, mingled breath, exchanged food smells, and asked, "Aren't you a Jew?"

"Yes," Shaper said.

"Well," commented Gyro Brown, "I just wanted to make sure." He removed his face from the closeness which made nonethnic persons uncomfortable. He waggled his hands, palms turned down, in a generic gesture. "Makes no different to me what the fuck a man is, even myself. Who I am is of interest sometimes, nothing better to explain with, but as wiser heads prevail—what the fuck. Again I say. So let me clear up something else. I have a reason for asking. Do you like sex, is that an interest of yours?"

"Okay," said Shaper. He didn't intend to explain further. He could go along with it on a quiet afternoon, and there were other details, such as the dream of perfect understanding, but they were not relevant in this context.

"So do I," said Gyro Brown. "It's like finding the back door unlocked at the Good Guys—"

"Pardon?"

"—and the alarm turned off. It's like finding a new shipment of laptops just waiting to be forklifted into the vehicle. You know, deliveries? When it's good, a sweet young thing topping off your lap is like driving through the night with a carload of stuff."

Shaper had never thought of it that way. Of course, it had been awhile since Monique or anybody important. When Gyro spoke of the carload of laptops, a dream of deep consummation enveloped and flushed his face. He sighed.

"We don't have to get into the particulars—" More sighs. After a moment, Shaper realized what particulars he was about to get into: "—if you like to bite or be bitten, make your peepee on someone or they shower on you, or even the dirty stuff some people like. That's personal. That's between her and you. You don't need to treat me to personal stuff I got no right to hear unless you really want to say."

"Thanks," said Shaper.

"You don't want to say. Okay. But I want to help, I have the experience, am I right? I can help."

"Thanks again," said Shaper. "Muchas gracias."

"Do you like ones called Mary or Jane? Or do you prefer the Thalimas, the Sharis?"

"Depends on the personality, Gyro." Hey, he was being drawn into man-to-man discussion. "Shari, your daughter, on an individual basis—she's your *daughter*, Gyro."

Gyro Brown chewed his upper lip, taking this in. He appreciated a thoughtful person, if it wasn't just the reluctance to put forth energy. "What's," he asked, "what's the longest love affair you ever enjoyed?"

Shaper didn't keep track. Time-length measurements were more appropriate to auto trips, it seemed to him. Most often it was the other person who remembered exactly when it started and when she started to end it. That was how it ran. For him, things seemed to fade out imperceptibly until a sudden long evening of minimal conversation when she said, if she wanted to be kind, "I don't think you care for me anymore," or if she wanted to be less kind: "You're a selfish rotten lover, I don't like it, and give me back the keys."

"Enjoyed?" Dan Shaper asked Gyro Brown. "I suppose enjoyment . . . It does end." Monique had been a little different. "Unless, of course, it's true love."

Gyro showed he was a good listener, a helpful friend. "And that hasn't happened."

"Right. Haven't found that. For me, it ends."

The new true friend persisted. In order to help, he needed

the facts. "And so sex, it's good, it's hard to explain, it happens, it's better than the big deal about love?...We discussed that already."

"I recall."

"You *remember*," Gyro corrected him, "because I said it. Funny how I forget things I tell folks sometimes, but they don't. Maybe I'm just an attractive person."

"Charismatic," said Shaper.

"Hey! Watch it!" Gyro Brown warned him. "You don't have to call me names. The thing is, I've got plans."

"I figured. Would you like to tell me what?"

"Of course! Without full knowledge, how can you be a true partner? But not yet."

"So I'm an untrue partner just now."

Gyro was delighted by his friend's educated flow of logic. "For a little while, Dan. Then, not. Less so. Okay?"

"No."

Gyro was as happy as he could be. He still hadn't said what he had in mind for Shaper.

So then he talked some more, but he didn't say about what.

Finally, with many a smile, sigh, shove, wink, he continued not to say, he did not tell. "Aren't you hungry?" he asked. "Shouldn't we celebrate, my friend?"

Gyro wielded his Cadillac as if he were captain of the line of traffic; his scouts had secured the terrain; he was in charge. In one rapid placement, pausing for a reverse snap and then a sudden stop, he parallel parked with a prideful little sidelong glance at his passenger. No fussy maneuvering; Gyro ruled vehicle, road, and the meal to come.

They were walking down Third. Gyro took his arm. Gyro looked around, a searching glance at very little; that is, at the bodegas, the car repairs, the empty and boarded up stores, the undershirt drying on its hanger at an upstairs window, the rainbow flag indicating gender activists colonizing the neighborhood, the hitch-hookers smoking and lifting their hooves like ponies and smartly saluting the passing motorists.

A lady pulled at Shaper's sleeve. This isn't done to strangers on an American street. Shaper pulled away. The lady said, "You got the time?"

Shaper said no and pulled away. The lady may not have been a girl; she may have been a boy, dressed in girl's clothes, with torn mesh stockings, holes linked by string, over long legs which needed a fresh shave.

"You got the inclination?"

Shaper shook his head.

"It's just hanging down there?"

Shaper shook his head.

"You got a cigaret?"

Shaker said he didn't smoke.

The person moved close and declared in an operatic alto: "Well then, fuck you," and stretched the borders of street repartee. She was not all talk. She spit on Dan Shaper.

Gyro grabbed the person who was neither girl nor boy but evolving on its path through the hormonal maze toward a future result; Gyro spun the person around; Gyro twisted the person to the sidewalk and, venturing with careless curiosity, kicked the person between the legs. Who knew what anatomical target Gyro explored? Only the person, who yelped, squirmed, folded into itself, yelped some more. Gyro turned his foot as he thrust so that it would sting when he spun the person to the pavement; he gave his foot a little twist; in sport this is called follow-through. The person screamed. Gyro observed.

A man in a wide-shouldered gray suit, a gray Borsalino knockoff pulled low toward his ears, ambled out of the doorway of the Patek Arms Residential Hotel, Rooms by the Day, Week, Month, & Hour. Gyro shoved the squirming body aside and greeted the man coming toward him. The man's knees were bent. It was a struggle to be fly and graceful, like a loping panther, while also picking up speed and keeping the Borsalino stable. "Willie," said Gyro, "you got someone here doesn't know her . . ." Peered at the person on the sidewalk with hands between legs; shrugged. ". . . his manners. Whatever. You got to deal with that unless you got some other idea."

Willie seemed to know Gyro, although Willie wasn't his name. He said: "Spit on you, that what happen? *Delbert*."

"On my friend," said Gyro. "*Delbert*."

"I tole her not to do that no more."

Okay, so the gender pro tem was determined. "Did anyway. Tell her again, Delbert."

The person on the sidewalk rested there, hands between her legs, curled uncomfortably, watching for further developments. Gyro removed a pack of cigarets from his pocket—he hadn't been smoking, as far as Shaper knew—and dropped them on the person. "Here, but it's not good for you," he said. "Need a light?"

"Lookahere," began Delbert, and having begun, didn't seem to know where to take it from there. He stood with a furrowed thoughtfulness on his face as the person on the sidewalk gazed appealingly upward.

"Delbert?" said Gyro. "You got a crazy out here, you know that? This one's a crazy." And he took Dan Shaper's arm, steering him forward. He called the man Delbert like an old friend, and didn't cover his back as they walked, pacing really, Gyro matching his step to Shaper's, toward the oasis of Louis' A-1 Bar-b-cue No. 1. "What a demographic we got on these Frisco streets, am I right, Dan?"

"I don't think—"

"You don't agree?"

"—I don't think you're a gypsy, demographically."

Gyro squeezed Shaper's elbow. "I saved your ass, and this is the gratitude I get—misgratitude and mistrust. If you'd of been in real trouble, not just a little mucus on your sport attire, I'd have saved you, too. Whatever might could happen, you needed me, I was there. And this is how you treat me."

But there was no deep reproach in the air. There was a fresh Bay breeze of supercilious reproach, salty, invigorating. Gyro was happy to have been of service, so why did Shaper feel less grateful than he should? Gyro was percolating with all the friendship progress brewing, history in the making; air vents were hissing. It would be a shame to spoil an era of good feeling.

Gyro pulled a flaglike handkerchief from his pocket, unfurled it, dabbed at Shaper's shoulder. "Let me just, no offense, wipe a little," he said. He looked stern for a moment, grave, a spit-wiper. "Here a little, and here." Pursed his lips because, yes, he wanted to do an okay job for his friend. Then he stood back, grinned, thought of something funny, and said it: "*Lookahere*." Then shook his head at the general amazingness of the world.

There in the San Francisco yellow-gray noontime light, it was time for a bit of meditation, about thirty seconds of it, before they entered the neon and metal and frying grease friendship culinary universe of Louis' A-1 Bar-b-cue No. 1. During this pause, a barely perceptible syncopation, Gyro may have been thinking about the responsibilities of making a new close friend in midlife, the heavy burden of the goodwill of Jesus on the Via Dolorosa, the escapades of his daughter, all the charms of the struggle for existence. For his part, Dan Shaper was thinking about washing very carefully before eating and taking a paper towel to scrub the place on his shoulders where the irate hooker may have landed his/her microbes. Gyro had done his best, but Dan Shaper didn't feel totally clean.

Gyro's treat. The choice of Louis' A-1 Bar-b-cue No. 1, down on Third, was his; the pleasure to be shared. They would break cornbread together. No need, just because they were working out a few business matters, to avoid a chance at good eating. No need for good eating not to be accompanied by good beer, good noise, the jovial companionship of strangers, who often made the best kind of friends.

"Don't you just go for that 'cue?" Gyro asked, and without waiting for Shaper, offered a hint of the correct answer: "I sure do. Uh-*huh!*"

Although Gyro was treating, Shaper wondered if Dan was paying. It might work out that way when a man has a license from the Son of God, plus plans for Dan Shaper he wasn't yet ready to share.

"On me," said Gyro, not only treating but reading Shaper's mind. And added instructionally: "Always pay small checks! You're not a big eater, are you? Watch your diet? Keep fit because who knows what the future may bring?"

"Right."

"I knew," said Gyro.

"This dark power of yours must be used wisely." If kidding was in order, Shaper would try to keep up.

Without asking, a passing waiter slid a paper cup of cole-slaw toward Gyro, who rubbed his hands together. "Here, try this—you must! Really creamy. Kills that vegetable taste."

Risky listening was a change for Dan Shaper. "You want to tell me something?" he asked.

"Maybe. Got to work it out in both our minds first, don't I? Relax, my friend."

"What is it?"

"*Not yet.*"

Other older guys fell more happily into sexual adventures than gastric ones, since AIDS is a disease which takes time to develop but gassy stomach, heartburn, and acidic backflow are only a short interlude away. In most cases, a person lives long enough after partaking of richly barbecued food to suffer its retribution. Nevertheless, Shaper was willing to follow Gyro into the rib joint, partake of the slabs of nutrient heaped onto his paper plate, smack his lips and wipe his mouth with the back of a hand while emergency napkins were rushed to their table by Louis himself of Louis' A-1, asking "Good?"

"Not bad," said Gyro.

"What," Shaper asked, "what does Shari have to do with all this? You don't need me to defend her."

"So how do you think and feel about that? You can't trust me in some way? Is that what you feel, Dan?"

"Yes."

"See, I don't just ask what you can do, I don't just tell what I think you can do. See? I'm the sort of person, first I ask what you *feel.*"

He trusted Dan Shaper to appreciate that. He expected Shaper to appreciate Shari because she was young, robust, dark-eyed. He intended him to appreciate Gyro because Gyro was just a wonderful person, fundamentally blameless, thanks to a nice improvisation on the Via Dolorosa, and also Shari's dad. He invited Dan Shaper to ride along, filling the hours, because appetite is more enjoyable than boredom. A smile kept Gyro's generous lips parted, his large square yellow teeth innocently bared, forgiven in advance, and his breath a complex of ingestion, exhalation, meats live and cooked.

The coleslaw, creamy, dripped itself between the prongs of the fork. Keep those napkins handy. The soda, an off-brand version of Coke—caramel coloring, sugar, an extra shitload of caffeine, comes with your order at Louis' A-1 Bar-b-cue, the Heart and Ribs of Third Street—made sure the charred pork with its accompanying fats and spices went down with no fuss. You can never go wrong with cola-type beveraging, but designate the driver in advance and be careful not to pee on any delicate suede or fabric.

Gyro talked. Dan talked. Gyro talked a lot, Dan talked some. At intervals, Louis himself came by and asked, "The best, yunnastan what I'm sayin?" Confidently wiping his big hands on his apron, he waited by the booth until they expressed full agreement. It was a kind of capitulation; that was how Louis liked it. He kept a clean 'cue joint. He changed the apron almost every day. "It's good, good," said Gyro, a communicator. "It's good," said more restrained Dan.

Louis Himself moved on to the next table. "Is it the best, you hear what I'm askin? Yunnastan what I'm sayin?" And the chorus was trained. The eaters at the next booth said, "The best! More sweet potatoes!" And Louis said, "We don't give them sweet potatoes with the plate no more, you got to order à la." It sounded like Allah. Dan Shaper thought: Allah Cart. "The price of them sweet potatoes went way up, they was drivin me into the groun," said Louis. "But hey, I'm bringin you a special order, cause you ask so nice. You like yams?"

A host like Louis, a place like Louis' place, with company like Gyro's, was an antidote to the noise of the world, the threats of living a certain number of years, suffering damage. Shaper was sensitive about the subject. He could imagine submission to age, and had sampled that; now he was being offered a chance to fight back. Gyro was confiding in him: "When my family lived in England, Ireland, that place, we lived in caravans—that's what we called the wagons—and ate apples made our lips pucker. My whole mouth puckered up, Dan, they were so sour. That was all we had to eat in the winter. But now my mouth can relax. I look at you and my people can smile again."

Dan Shaper thought it wonderful that the sight of Dan Shaper could cause a whole people to relax, a happy turn for them after their journeys from the Holy Land to Egypt, Romania, Hungary, Italy, Spain, and points between and beyond. It was one of those compliments, like being charged with having a sense of humor, which few can deny. Jesus, the previous guarantor of the fate of Gyro's people, had remained silent for two thousand years. These days Shaper also kept his own counsel.

And despite his self-expression, Gyro also looked like a person who kept something in reserve, such as what he really intended. Shaper admired a man who knew what he wanted; wished to become such a person someday. It was a final ambition for a man who otherwise had been seeking sunlight, good digestion, regularized sleep, and a peaceful descent. Nice of Shari Brown to have a few careless troubles which brought her father together with a new best friend—just when the person found himself off balance, due to the sudden grown daughter.

"We called them caravans," Gyro said. "The English called them lorries because they live in houses, no wheels. Shit, now we all call them trucks, so what?"

"It's a small world."

"Check, my friend. Sometimes I need someone to load the stuff on the lorries. I forget about my Cadillac because I'm back to there. You ever do that, your age? Sometimes I'm looking for the wagon I'm riding."

"Looking between your legs," said Shaper.

Mirth took over. Gyro's laughter exploded in their booth. His new friend Dan Shaper had a sense of fun! Oh, boy, and Gyro slapped his thighs. "Giddy-yap, giddy-yap!" he managed to choke out between cries of pleasure. "Looking . . . for the horse . . . you're on!" he sobbed; he tottered. Although the leatherette of the booth contained him pretty well, he reached for Shaper's arm to keep from falling.

Dan Shaper waited, smelling coleslaw cabbage and onion, feeling glum. Abruptly the storm subsided. Gyro wiped his dry eyes; the act symbolized a flood of mirthful tears. Then he leaned across the table. "So we're in business, right? Those ass-holes burn down buildings for the insurance, don't even own them but do them anyway, hired by some smart investor. . . . I'm too old for that shit, Dan. I'm sure you understand how it is when a person grows weary of the routine."

Gyro had a way of drifting. Dan would see what came. At least arson wasn't child-molesting, you could say that for it. And you could say that Gyro glowed like the beginning of the world. He had the optimism of a pickpocket who might negligently dip his hand into a passing handbag and find trea-sure beyond his fondest dreams. The next score would forever be the best. He had appetite. Somehow the meat on Gyro's plate had disappeared and the last of the red sauce was being sopped up by cornbread and none of these procedures halted the flow. He gazed longingly at the streaks of crimson and crumbs on his plate; all good things must come to an end, though there might be exceptions to this rule. As his saliva ran for barbecue, so his hopes ran for riches and fun. He looked warmly into Dan Shaper's eyes and sought a colleague. How could Dan turn down such an offer?

Dan Shaper's familiar griefs did him no good. Gyro could make him forget unease. It's comfortable when life passes by; comfort can be a good thing. But it would never happen to Gyro. He would tote pleasure in his stomach, not comfort on his back. He was inviting his dear new friend Dan to come along on the journey. Onions and garlic powder in the red sauce, too, judging from the ardency wafted toward Shaper by Gyro's breathing.

While packing up for their ride together, Gyro decided about dessert. "The pie, that brown nut pie," said Gyro. "That lumpy juicy sticky stuff is so good, isn't it? Crunchy?"

"I never eat it anymore," said Dan Shaper.

"Today you will. To celebrate, am I right? You've come all this way? It's the best, my friend, I guarantee. Louis!" he cried, crooking not just a finger but his hand, his entire arm.

While Dan tasted the thickly oozing sugary brown slab on its paper plate—more like a crusted pecan pudding than a pie—Gyro gazed upon his face with great tenderness and delight; he gleamed upon his lovely pal, freebasing fellowship. Why? Simply put, he liked having a friend. Friends are good, but they don't just fall off the truck or creep out of the warehouse at night. Gyro needed a friend and here one was, handy for use if properly instructed.

How could Dan Shaper not answer friendship with trust? But even in his relief at having something that got the blood going, it occurred to him that he should keep trust out of the deal.

And if Gyro cheated him? Oh, worn old Dan Shaper needed to quell his doubting spirit. "What if you do me harm?" he asked.

"Yah?"

"Use me to do something . . ."

Gyro considered the possibility. "Yah," he said, breathing with a careworn sigh, a man who had wandered the earth, across bridges and seas and entire continents, including hostile invented states of Europe.

"—get me in trouble?" Shaper asked. This was one of those embarrassing silences between them.

"Ah, ah. You should forgive. What are friends for, my friend?"

"So what precisely do you want from me?"

"Good question."

"I haven't got money to be a good deal in any way for Shari. Even if I died fast—assuming—there wouldn't be much gain."

"For me, a son-in-law, that would be an honor." Hand on heart, eyes uprolled, banners snapping in the breeze above an invisible parade ground.

"Come on, Gyro, this is not a proposal and you know it."

Gyro looked winsome. Gyro's friend had said Gyro's name. "You're nice," Gyro said.

"Fuck off, Gyro."

"You're learning!"

Dan tried gathering his strength. He called upon the smells of cooking, the heat of bodies, the strength of Louis' clientele of drivers, security guards, bristled old folks, eaters with appetite. "Then what is it?"

Gyro made little milky designs in his plate, pushing shreds of coleslaw into patterns which creamed and bled into other patterns. "I just want to help," he admitted finally.

"Your daughter? Yourself?"

"You and us," Gyro said. He gazed deep into Dan Shaper's eyes. He was so happy he just could not stop smiling.

Modestly he bent to the post-pecan pie scraps of slaw. He could leave a plate alone while he shined upon Dan Shaper and then catch up with him, eat well ahead of him, dripping a little with loving appetite from the corners of his mouth; and in a few instants of darting fork, sparkling knife used as a pusher, come back into position to shine and reshine. The paper plate was now clean; only crumpling could extract a few more drops of mayo. Gyro was sucking juice and fiber from between his teeth. His tongue wiped. Silently he observed how other people ate slowly, inefficiently; in this case, Dan Shaper was the guilty party.

"I also wrote a song," said Gyro, "so if I had a band, I could sing and play myself to fame and fortune, hit records—used to fiddle a little, like some of my people. But in the meantime . . ." He cleared his throat:

"When you're dead you're done
So let's have some fun—"

"See," he explained, "What that mean, it means ain't no use in stewing around, stalling, cause it don't make no never mind, know what I'm saying?"

"Now you're trying to say it like a black man?" Shaper asked.

"You want to sell a song, less it's country western . . ." Gyro grinned. He liked to get good at whatever he was doing. "There's two kinds of girls, Dan," he said, "the right ones and the right now ones. Shari is a right now girl, don't you think?"

"Mature beyond her years."

"That's what I mean," said her father. "We got to make sure she capitalize, not just picky-yoony shoplifting crap. This is a young person of quality."

It was rare for Gyro to avert his eyes. Usually he counted on his gift of hypnotic gaze, which may have been one of the privileges Jesus had in mind: dark liquid eyes, focussed and intense in man-to-man situations. But Jesus, not being a father himself—except perhaps to the world—had not considered all the riddles of paternity. Gyro coughed up a little cream and family sensibility, red sauce and sugar-stimulated phlegm, but swallowed it again, not wanting good nourishment to go to waste. "I don't necessarily think you have to believe everything I tell you," he said.

"Thanks."

"Are you calling me a liar? You have prejudice in your heart about Roma people?" Gyro asked indignantly, happily.

His way with mood had always served him well. If a man is in balance himself, he can get more leverage if the adversary, or in this case, the dear friend, is out of balance, teetering, in danger of bumping himself in his own face where the middle organ, the nose, part of the breathing apparatus, contains a whole network of sensitive nerves and delicate cartilage, not to mention the denseness of tiny capillaries. "As the saying goes, it's my way or the wrong way."

"The saying doesn't go like that, Gyro."

Gyro beamed upon this slow learner. "Now it does." His alert gaze swept over the wall, catching the mirror, and quickly passed on. Gyro snubbed his reflection. He didn't need a mirror to tell him any lies. When a person can't know others, or his own child, or even much about Jesus except that a dispensation had been granted, what was the point of trying to know himself? It was only a reflection anyway. Gyro lifted his head and Shaper could see his Adam's apple throbbing like a pulse, like a scale-covered heart. The guy talked. The guy used words. But the guy was a word man for concealment, not for revelation; not enlightenment but endarkenment.

Shaper hadn't let his own soul run free, either. It wasn't supposed to go that way in California, in San Francisco, where a person was invited to take whatever name, whatever history, and whatever future he could get his hands on. Yet there came emergency times in a person's life and here in Dan Shaper's were several.

"Do you ever faint because you want someone so much?" Gyro asked.

"No, but I used to get pimples. That was a long time ago. When I wanted something so much."

"I still do," Gyro said thoughtfully. "And dizzy? Do you get dizzy?"

"Not from wanting something," Dan Shaper answered. "Are we having a heart-to-heart talk?"

Gyro's grin was happy, his lips wide. "More soul-to-soul, like that, Dan. I personally have an old soul and so do you. But I think mine is a *leetle* bit older than yours, if I may say so."

"You may say so."

"I did."

So they had completed a phase in their life together. Now they could pay the check in silence and depart. Dan paid.

Within the peristaltic contractions of the criminal justice system in San Francisco, just as in the human digestive apparatus, occasional surprises bubbled up and sought egress, but generally what seemed destined actually took place. This was different from real life in the world outside the cells and corridors of 850 Bryant, known to the police as "downtown." The jails were decrepit, the prisons were packed, the county farm grew organic vegetables in a soil of mercury, tar, old batteries, PCBs, and clumps of human waste, for sale to arugula restaurants, cuisine dining destinations. The county farm wasn't the place for a lovely postteen shoplifter (sexual abuse among the zucchini by lonely inmates and guards). The probation officers were overworked. The criminal defense attorneys were wearily cynical, except for a few ponytailed ideological radicals, who were energetically cynical. The dockets were backed up. The courts were disorganized and the bailiffs, stenographers, and clerks usually didn't speak Tagalog, Arabic, Spanish, Cantonese, and Ebonics; often they had trouble with English, too. Generally speaking, the computers were down.

Shari was just an innocent young person, a child at heart

although not in the true sense a juvenile (a lost nonexistent birth certificate situation going on here). As a possible gypsy, Roma person, free-spirited member of a free-spirited ethnic persuasion, she had earned special status and consideration. Wasn't black; *probably* wasn't. Dark a little, swarthy a little, lovely, of course, but not, you know, not what any strict construction could name "inner city person." Psychopathy, not as visible to the naked eye as skin color, often looks like charm. She boiled with her charm.

After due consideration, the charges against Shari Brown were dropped, dismissed, filed, put aside, although there remained the question of why her father claimed she needed a Latin interpreter, Mr. Shaper, just because, when the store detective grabbed her arm and twisted it behind her back, she pronounced the word of legitimate self-defense as "fock." Who speaks clearly when flocks of butterflies are going off in the stomach, the goods are under the coat, and the dick is yelling, "Hey, hey, hey," as if fighting for breath. "Fock," had said Shari, "tua madre." She didn't even get it right.

The kindly obese black lesbian Municipal Court judge with a Star of David pendant hanging outside her judicial robes, Her Honor Raychella Jefferson, stared at Shari and sighed heavily. This was a love that was not to be; this was the strictly business part of the day. "Proceed on your way," pronounced kindly Judge Jefferson. "As the Judeo-Christian ethic states . . ."

Shari was already moving. Her Honor showed a flash of unbusinesslike temper.

"Young lady! I was counseling at you right chere. I was mentioning the rule of religion in the dominant homophobic paradigm, not my roots in the True Israelite faith, because some facts from history happen to tell it like it is—"

Shari turned her lovely heart-shaped face toward the bench.

"—so go and sin no more. Which meaneth: Do your darndest to augment self-esteem, girl."

"Been there, done that," murmured liberated and grateful Shari. "You're wasting both of our time." To Dan Shaper she now turned winsomely. "You were beeg help, explaining to the folks what I mean when I struggle to express myself in the language of the dominant paradigm."

"You've learned a lot," Shaper noted.

"Got to move fast in this highly competitive mondo. But I'll never understand a man who gets a terrific offer from my dad and still . . . like to tell me what's wrong with you?"

"When I find out," said Shaper, "I'll be the first to know."

From the bench the looming shadow of Justice stirred, aggravated. "Clear out my courtroom, hear? You ain't the only stupidass perpetrator I got to send on their way, some of them deserving a heavier punishment. Don't make me think again, girl."

Shari and Dan continued their discussion elsewhere. The smells weren't the best at 850 Bryant, and the long-haired and the tattooed awaiting judgment were looking impatient when they weren't nodding out. A senior couple, here daily for the free show, impatiently rattled their *Chronicles*, waiting for the next act.

With a father's solicitude, Gyro remarked about the judge: "Beeg womans. Put a freezer compartment on her tits, make one helluva refrigerator."

The stale air of the hall outside the courtroom was at least moving. "Wanna ride down with me and Dad? We're all going the same direction," Shari said.

Down, thought Shaper, saying, "Por favor," while Gyro stood by, still contemplative, wondering how the hell Jesus put up with His world.

Six

There's a Place Between the Living and the Dead, and It's Open Twenty-four Hours," Gyro intoned. "You can guess what that is, I bet not?"

"Wong's Donut Shop?" said Shaper. "Down on Bryant near the Hall of Justice?"

Gyro's large yellow teeth expressed appreciation. "Not Wong, *Wrong*. Bad guess, but you win anyway. The Yerba Buena Foundation, my friend, serving a hungry minority of the people."

Shaper waited for explanation.

"Mostly, but not exclusively, men. Equal Opportunity for women available upon demand."

Gyro had a feel for people and Dan Shaper qualified as an example of a human being. On a basis of need-to-know, Gyro Brown needed to know what the people he could use could be persuaded to need from him. He was ready to provide for the needy, so long as they were ready to let currency or other fair exchange fall from their hands along with the attractive risks falling upon their own heads. Dan filled the bill.

This could be a deal. Gyro opened his arms and his heart and revealed the palms of his hands, pink, ridged, in all honesty. His nostrils flared, showing a few mature hairs. He understood what Dan Shaper needed—it was obvious! A little romance, an interruption of the long slide toward oblivion. Amanda might nag and telephone, Margaret Torres might disturb an old forgetfulness, and they both did; but Gyro was here with him now, bringing promises of further distraction. Gyro was turning his vanishing comfort into a surprise party. Hadn't Amanda already done enough?

Aging men appreciate fresh smells and fresh flesh; this is a known fact. Gyro knew where to find vibrant bundles of charm, suitable to every taste. He was prepared to point Dan in the right direction. In fact, Gyro was only here to serve. All he needed in the way of thanks was the creative satisfaction that Dan's spirit and body could come around to good order. He wanted to add to Dan's store of memories in case he lived into advanced old age. What he suggested in return was that Dan give Gyro what Gyro wanted. Was that too much to ask?

Fuck no. Not when a person is profoundly enriching a fellow human person's existence in this brief period before the Second Coming.

"So," Gyro explained, and what a total explainer he was.

"I don't know."

"Of course you don't. Take a chance, hey?" (Gyro on the edge of winsome.) "Please?" (Falling off the edge.) "So what is it, my friend?"

"I'll go with you this afternoon."

"Of course you will," said Gyro. "On a fine day in this most beautiful of all cities, what harm could befall?"

He had a talent for reading minds, which was sometimes helpful in doing business. The day was warm, sunny, dry, in a way unusual to San Francisco, and it made Shaper think of country summer days when school was out and adventure consisted of riding his bike out for a cheeseburger at a drive-in; the bicycle had balloon tires, a wire basket, and a bell to protect him from cross traffic. Now, not tottering yet, still secure in his balance, he tended to feel the daylight was safer than the night; he didn't eat cheeseburgers; balloon-tired Schwinns had gone high fashion and were called mountain bikes.

It was generous of Gyro to take into account the yearning for prudence which contradicted Shaper's other yearnings, such as to be young again. Maybe he was finally at the right place at the right time and about to get lucky. He wasn't discussing his recent paternity.

"So come, we're going," said Gyro. "And you don't have to do anything I say," he confided with an encouraging little smile, "because I'm just thinking out loud on your behalf, so don't even follow my advice. Unless you want to make your brief hour on earth worthwhile, my friend."

His large yellow teeth beamed their high glow in the direction of Dan Shaper. "Y'understand what I'm saying?"

"It's in English."

"I hope you understand."

But it was not pretty clear at all. There was something in the smile; there was something about the teeth, the gracious spirit of Gyro Brown offering him a world of joy and interest. It was somehow not nice.

Was not nice the word for it? Just because the teeth were yellow, heading in the direction of orange unless Gyro took time out from fulfilling the will of Jesus to see a dentist? (Too late for brushing.)

Dan Shaper wasn't sure he understood his own thoughts. The part that was most unclear was not Gyro but himself. Gyro was offering pleasure at a time in life when lonely men had poor choices. What pains could Dan suffer at this stage? Even AIDS takes a while to develop. A senior citizen might well die of heart, tumor, prostate, Alzheimer's, jaywalking, or repetitive routines before the sneaky virus had a chance to work its will in him.

"Got nothing much in my calendar today," Dan was saying.

Gyro hummed to himself as they drove up Pine, a one-way canyon through the center of San Francisco, reciting to Shaper: "The therapist is in. The therapist will see you now, big boy," and then the sign appeared:

> ## THE YERBA BUENA FOUNDATION
> ———•◦•———
> *The Therapist Is In*

Hand-painted in curvy psychedelic letters, like the ones that used to say Good Karma Café or Light-Sound-Dimension Gallery, it hung from wires at the entrance to a fine old Victorian mansion which dated from the era when Pine had seen better, two-way days. Some of the rusty spears on the metal fence which kept the overgrown garden from being eaten by goats or rabbits were blunted, like teeth that had bitten down too hard on nuts, grown tired after much use, or maybe attacked by playful homeless folks with nothing better to do. "Shari," said Gyro, "don't need to go boosting anymore. Got a half-dozen therapists in her stable, we don't call it a stable, and this summer she had two students saving up for concert tickets for the school year. Two Eastern college girls"—he shook his head—"surprised me by swinging both ways, just like anybody else. That part kind of, didn't really surprise me—made me think. From an institution of higher tuition, you understand me?"

"Executive Planning Director" was Shari's title for her role as owner-manager of the Yerba Buena Foundation; she hoped it didn't sound cold and distant. Proud Gyro had never dreamt, as a careless young man pounding away at the steaming fragrant body of the girl in the trailer next to his truck, that their firstborn would grow up to be an Executive Planning Director, graduated from shoplifting, with many therapists counting on her to protect them from wackos.

"This is a surprise to me, too," said Dan Shaper.

"You've got lots to learn," said Shari Brown, "like every guy I ever met."

Gyro relaxed tensely. "Good. Great. So now that you're old friends and understand each other, how's about helping our new friend Dan here understand us even better? We already understand him, so that's only fair. This here is the real estate, Dan, but we're only renters. That could be a problem, the building. And then there's staff, always you got to take care of staff. Medical, panic attacks, female things. And advertising when you got to go easy about too much publicity. And that brings up another matter . . ."

Shaper was not a lawyer, he was not an experienced investor—his money in Golden West Savings—he was only here for the ride that Gyro and Shari were taking him on. They seemed to think he was a species of virgin with court connections plus available cash.

So they understood him? What did they mean by that? Since he was still engaged in the lifelong struggle to understand himself, it didn't seem fair that they could come to knowledge so quickly. Perhaps it was another benefit of that malediction on the Via Dolorosa that seemed, in general, to be Gyro's ace in the hole.

The Browns led Shaper on a tour of a house built with what used to be a ballroom (cut-glass chandeliers), a breakfast nook, maids' rooms, bedrooms for children, adults, and guests—now a clinic devoted to advanced surrogacy. It was pretty clean, considering. The towel bins were emptied regularly.

Running a therapy center required much coming and going of bulk laundry. It would have been more efficient to install industrial boiling, churning, detergenting machines, but Shari concentrated on therapy, not towels; she sent the laundry out with union truck drivers who came grinning and abashed or solemn and businesslike to the back door to pick up the linen and sometimes a stained pillow. Everything was organic on the premises.

"You have to meet our therapists," Shari said. "Your normal dopefiend hooker can't do the work. We keep files; we fill out forms. They have to make notes like under the category Special Needs or, oh, Eck-cetera."

Secretarial skill was essential. This would protect them when the inevitable tragic bust came, the police wanting distraction, breaking into Shari's program for patients with unassuaged desires that led to anxiety, insomnia, allergies, murder, rape, and cigaret smoking. It was a therapy research center with detailed files; for a brothel investor, it didn't get any better than this.

The parlor was decorated with a homey New Orleans sensibility, appropriate to a clinic offering treatment not covered by your HMO. Shawls with fringes, brocades with scenes of dogs hunting. Non-Tiffany Tiffany-style lamps glinting their fractured multicolor lights, courtesy of Cost Plus. Tchotchkes. For some reason, probably sentimental, a Buddha celebrating the opening of the Asiatic Gardens, "Best Cantonese," according to the legend across Buddha's bronze knees, squatted on an end table between the lamp and a bronze frog with an out-of-proportion gold-painted circumcised human penis. Things to occupy the mind and heart besides the worn copies of *Modern Maturity*, *Penthouse*, *Hustler*, and *Spanking Mamas* during moments of waiting for the therapist to finish her douche.

Oversized couches from Goodwill facilitated sociability;

overstuffed Goodwill chairs in shadowed corners facilitated irritability for patients who treasured their loneliness, seeking no premature human contact.

And there was a client sunk in one of those armchairs. Bent over his crossword puzzle, he looked up as he noticed Dan Shaper. "What's a four-letter word for cunt?" he asked.

Shaper, court interpreter, said "I don't know," but then professional noblesse oblige checked in. "Maybe twat."

"Come again?"

"Twat," said Shaper, adrenaline pumping, "cooz—that's Southern Appalachian."

The client snapped his finger. "Oh Christ, how could I've forgotten? Shows how stressed-out my wife—well, never mind. Down in the dumps. Uptight. Jitters." He seemed to be a tester of his stock of synonyms. His finger snap wasn't what anyone could call a real snappy snap.

Shaper didn't want to intrude, yet he was curious, from a lexicological point of view, while telling himself not to dip into what really, truly, deeply was not his business. . . . "What kind of crossword puzzle is that?" he asked.

"What's a five-letter word for genital blisters?" asked the man in the armchair.

This should have ended the discussion, but Shaper had another thought buzzing over his head, not like a fly but like a half-forgotten obligation. "Are you here to get? . . ." he began. (Noise of buzzing fly.)

"What?"

"For therapy?"

A thin smile tightened the puzzler's mouth. "Not really, but sometimes Shari lets me come work the puzzle because other people are too . . . what's an eleven-letter word for 'preoccupied?' I like the atmosphere. She gets them—the crosswords—from an outfit in Canada—Vancouver. Everybody deserves a social life, you know. . . ." Voice trailing off, back to puzzle matters.

The Foundation provided his social life. Who needed rubbings, oilings, lubrications, cries and murmured treats—the complex erotic ramble—when a person could spend his downtime expanding his vocabulary in a discreet environment?

"Anal intercourse, six letters, verb," muttered the crossword man.

Helpful Dan Shaper was about to contribute—this was easy—*bugger*, when from down the hallway he heard someone emit a long keening wail, followed by a short shriek: "Shut the door!" and Shari made a little smile, a little shrug of satisfaction. The wild command echoed through the house; curtains shivered in its breeze; even the puzzle-worker paused, pen lifted into the vibrating air.

For an experienced interpreter-translator it was a moment of chagrin. Shaper had misheard the French guy, a sentimental wailer-shrieker, crying out, "*Je t'adore!*"

At the same time, an enormous yellow-and-red bumblebee came motoring at low level through the parlor, also looking for sweetness. The bee broadcast a small silken switching noise. Where were the flowers, where the hive? This bee was a work-of-art creature, tattooed just above the knee of a young woman in a short shimmering wrap, hastening from the Frenchman with labile emotions to wherever she now wanted to go. The bumblebee strained upwards, condemned, unlike the Frenchman, never to reach its goal, always near, always far, embedded in the thigh of an industrious young woman. Poor bumbling bumblebee, forevermore watching from below.

Shut the door, shut the door, Shaper thought, isn't that the truth? How hard it was to express our deepest feelings.

The crossword person bent back to his labors, pen tracing

through the sets of boxes. He wore a smile of postacrostic satisfaction. "Cytomegalovirus," he murmured, "fifteen letters, retinal complication, that's in the eyes, due to immune disorder . . ."

Bumblebee there was, bumblebee there had been, with all the suggestions of a rose garden, of a thorned rose, but the lady left in her wake a slight scent of, what was it, gym? Not exactly, but close. Of locker room. Of socks and undies. Shaper shook his head and said to Shari: "The business is working out okay, I guess."

"Working," she said. "That girl, the one you liked, you probably still thinking bout her, she's a hummer."

Ignorance challenged him to say nothing and he rose to the challenge.

"The busy bee girl. Hums while she works, gives a thrill all up and down."

Shaper, seeing, said, "I see." He thought of an organic power stem, an entire spinal column transmitting vibrations.

Shari leaned close. "Asks folks to call her Pammy, but her real name . . ." She whispered into Shaper's ear, her breath warm and soothing. "It's okay to tell you since we're so close. Her real name . . . suspense, suspense . . . long story short . . . her real name, Dan, is *Pam*."

As far as Dan Shaper was concerned, Shari could go on whispering into his ear as long as she liked. There was validated biological tradition of comfort in a young creature's breath on a person's sensitive and needy parts.

Shaper wondered if he shouldn't save himself for Pam the Hummer, aka "Pammy," but it was time to abandon the quest for perfection. He had not been mature enough for prudent making-do during the period when the song advised, *Love the one you're with*. But oh, he wished that bumblebee vehicle might again come sashaying past. Surely she was headed for the shower. Shaper imagined careful mutual soapings, up and down, in and out (a leap of imagination putting him also in the shower; conspirational giggles).

Instead, Shari was saying, "While it's fresh in her mind, filling out the cards? You know, the medical form? What Frenchie likes best and how to serve his future needs, based on serving his past needs?"

Shari had that California way of making a statement into a question, her voice rising, sharing. The green-carded French resident alien emerged, eyes downcast, less frisky, in a hurry now, no longer in the grip of troubador passion, muttering, "Merci, Madame, à bientôt. Eet ees launch hour, I must to my shoppe."

"Then to your shop," advised Shari. He looked well-launched. "Same time next Wednesday, you rascal?"

She waved him out. She confided that he was prospering in the profession of urban haberdashery, whatever that was. How a man earned his daily bread and weekly blowjobs was not her concern.

Shari, her father's daughter, was speeding through youth toward maturity. She respected her clients, even during times of exaggerated Gallic emotion, promptly shutting the door when a voice reverberated through the house, shut-the-door, O shut-the-door, aieee! "I know what you think, what you think you think, Dan, but it's not all just dirty stuff, you know—golden showers, enemas, yucch, laxatives, double-yucch—it's about Helping People. Why do you think the Foundation has lasted this long? We've been here eight months, we've survived, Dan—soon it'll be our first year—"

Time to put up a bronze plaque. As far as Shari was concerned, the Yerba Buena Foundation went back into the mists of time when horny landlocked dinosaurs took to flying in order to meet their beloveds high in scary, carnivorous, giant ferns. Love bites changed everything. Humanity evolved. The Yerba Buena Foundation kept track on three-by-five cards instead of a computer because kindly Shari preferred not to embarrass therapists who weren't computer literate, didn't consider word-processing to be part of the arsenal. Muscular contractions were the rock-bottom stone basis of their talent.

Fanny Funkybutt's shrill telephone voice penetrated the office wall. "Yerba Buena! Foundation! So what can we do for you, big boy?" All fell silent. Fannie (not her real first name) Funkybutt (not her family name, either) only did fill-in telephone duty. Her specialty was being scrubbed in the oversize tub by men who liked to swab down a really funky person. It was surprising how sanitary many men have gotten to be. "So be happy!" cried Fannie.

"We'll have to review telephone manners," Shari murmured.

"Write it out, she can read," Gyro said. He turned to Shaper. "I buy these family-size bars of Ivory. We got one client comes in Saturday night without fail, even shampoos her, you know, *hair*."

Gyro turned finicky at the oddest moments.

"Yerba Buena! Foundation! So tell me your sad story, honeybunch."

Shari winced and jotted a reminder to herself on a yellow pad. Not clear on the concept of electronic etiquette, Fannie would need a script.

When she came out to meet the new friend of Gyro and Shari, Fannie stood up for herself against an imagined criticism (she had imagined correctly). "I'm a person of whip," she said. "Why should it just be 'person of color' or 'person who happens to be gay?' "

"Fannie de Fouet," said Shaper. "Bastido."

"You talking Latin at us again?" Shari asked.

The person of Romance languages lowered his eyes. Gyro was having a splendid afternoon.

A Delancey Street Movers truck in low gear wafted a soft

smell of exhaust, a humid and swamplike urban breeze, through the drawn curtains. The folks inside, getting to know each other, were adjusting to cities full of consumable strangers instead of the jungles full of prey from which, eons ago, they had evolved.

"That Fanny," said Gyro admiringly. "The voice knocks trucks into the bike lane, but she's so fine—her ass is as big as all outdoors."

"Tell you what. You can call me names," Fannie said, "while I pee on your face. That a deal you like?"

The person of teasing was outwitted by the person of whips and water sports. For Gyro, letting things run their course, the day could not have been brighter.

A man in a shiny green summer suit, fabric of a petroleum-derived product people wouldn't normally wear in San Francisco even if there were a traditional old-fashioned American summer in San Francisco, slipped through the front door during the absence of the dog and security technician. Initial telephone screenings couldn't eliminate all wackos; there needed to be protection in depth, a kind of moat and drawbridge, which was the duty of the German shepherd and D'Wayne. So that was D'Wayne.

The polyester-clad visitor was explaining to the dog and D'Wayne, back from wherever they had been, "I don't want to like what I liked then, when I was young. I want to like what I like now, when I'm sophisticated."

"I can dig it," assented D'Wayne.

"I like today, not tomorrow, not yesterday, I like *now*."

"I hear what you sayin, man,"—D'Wayne getting a little closer with heavy shoulders, moving into the personal space of patience fast running out. So this was the D'Wayne whom neither Amanda nor Margaret Torres was willing to explain during their family conference with flan at Jalisco Número

Dos; a gleaming person with a gleaming pet companion who assisted him in security duty at the Yerba Buena Foundation. Dan Shaper busied himself with trying to process two kinds of information, that which he was now receiving and that which he did not yet have.

"God wants all His sons," the green-suit guy was saying, "but let me finish, to walk the walk and talk the—*Jes*-sus."

He had been here before. He was known. D'Wayne had him by the green polyester collar. "Out, my good man, *out*." In this brief hustle doorwards, German shepherd confident but playing backup, no one was hurt; one was insulted. The green-suited, born-again, fun-loving person went quietly, miffed. Some dudes didn't mind their manners during an opportunity not to catch herpes, chlamydia, gonorrhea, or AIDS. They took advantage. No time for that, man. Period, full stop; stirring and flanks heaving of dog, who was also salivating heavily due to unfulfilled herding instincts. D'Wayne shook his head and massive shoulders.

Fuss and fidget within the premises were nipped in the bud. A clean delineation of parameters was D'Wayne's responsibility. The drooling German shepherd, a honey-beige animal with glossy black undercoating, a seeming designer mix of German shepherd and pet hamster (Shaper was not expert in zoology), sniffed Shaper's crotch. With D'Wayne in full control, there was little else for a good dog to do that D'Wayne couldn't do better. D'Wayne wasn't into drooling and sniffing Shaper's crotch. D'Wayne was more into talking cool and then, if necessary, erupting fearsomely while wearing a strictly business broad smile.

Pam the Hummer returned, face aglow after soap and water, makeup gone, hair brushed and gleaming, to say, "God, I hate those cards, that file. They're worse than the fucking Frenchman."

"You've *got* to," Shari said.

"Wanna check I did it right?" asked Pam. "Reason I didn't go to secretarial academy is I don't really prefer office work—"

"I'm sure you did it right. Pam, you're always putting yourself down and you shouldn't. You're a terrific person."

"—just like the reason I didn't finish cosmetology school, where I was first in my class, is why in shit's name should I spend my time on other people's bodies, shampooing and small-talking some housewife, when I could . . ." She trailed off, a little lost in the thought.

Shaper finished it for her, ". . . spend your time on the Frenchman," but not aloud. Pam had self-esteem issues.

"Get better recompensulated with men, even if there's no medical or pension, but who the fuck needs benefits in a world where people could die, pffft, tomorrow? Or like even yesterday?"

Pam could easily hum her way through philosophy school, too, thought Shaper, glad he wasn't given to interrupting people.

While he stood there, greedily noticing—the Tiffany lamps, ash-scarred coffee tables with magazines from which the subscribers' stickers had been unstuck but the bar codes remained, an office-surplus metal wastebasket dressed up with ancient Aquarian flower decals—a first-timer poked through the door ("Welcome to the Yerba Buena Foundation," said D'Wayne, dog purring). The first-timer was trying to erase the wariness on his face and to replace it with a seen-it-all look. He was wearing black pants, black tee shirt, black boots; he pranced toward Shari with the bounce of a person earnestly striving to walk black, walk ghetto. An orthodontist, Shaper decided, and Wednesdays were his day off. "You're the? . . ." asked the hepster.

"Therapist in charge," said Shari, finishing his difficult thought for him, "and you came to the right place at the right time, I see," letting her gaze slide to the tightness of his pants. He should have been wearing Dockers, not straight-legs from the Young Man's Boteek. "Pammy, no, Darlene might be about your size, maybe. What do you think? Since you're up to speed already, you'd like Black Barbara?"

"What? Who? *Black?* No!"

"Just thinking out loud," said Shari. "Actually, we like the clients to sit around, have a cup of tea—herbal? how's that sound?—whatever, get acquainted. This"—tugging at Dan Shaper's sleeve—"is one of our financial people—"

The orthodontist hepster cracked his best knowing smile. Perfect teeth, probably a courtesy treat from a colleague, performing mutual orthodontia during previous Wednesday downtimes. "*Investor*," he said, "that's a good one, I'd like to buy in myself. What's the deal? Freebies for investors?"

Gyro, Shari, and the good folks of the Yerba Buena Foundation surrounded Dan Shaper with their studious regard while he wondered at how a man's life can change even if he doesn't deserve the change. Then they left him in D'Wayne's big hands while they departed for unstated business. Shaper didn't mind. The humidity of Shari's consideration, like the heat of Gyro's, made him long for a little silence, a little rest. While silence and rest were not D'Wayne's strong points, he was still a distraction from the Brown family.

D'Wayne, security guard, dog master, valued employee, appreciated showing Mister Shaper the real estate. It deepened an acquaintance which might, who knows, someday bear issue. The ardent smile in D'Wayne's eyes, the swift revelations of teeth, made it seem he had his own business with Dan Shaper. He did. But first, with kindness and cordiality, he prepared the way.

"I make sure folks behave as to being one of the guys and

gals around here," said D'Wayne, "so please to meet you. It's D'Wayne with a doohicky between it, Dee Doohicky Wayne. Duh-Wayne, see?"

Shaper heard.

"People look at my driver's license, they get all confuse. Same thing with my checks, when I have a account. How you spell doohicky? they like to ax. I tell them it's not a straight line, it's like a little piece of jism hanging out there, if you get my drift."

Shaper did.

"I can ascertain from past-type situations when some dude is gonna get, you know, need to get eject. Difference from police work, I don't need no further information, the probable cause, the search warrant. Burden of proof bullshit is on me but ain't too heavy, see. What I pronounce, excuse me, is my magic words, 'Eighty-six, asshole!' Maybe they go quiet, maybe I have to eject, that convince them a little, head bouncing on the sidewalk and all."

Shaper planned to regulate his behavior up to the standard of D'Wayne's burden of proof.

D'Wayne was shaking his head. "People are funny. My line of endeavor, you learn that—gotta. Otherwise it's just too aggravating."

"What makes you eject someone?"

"Sometime," D'Wayne murmured, frowning, playing events back through his head, "it's like a case of bleeding, you know, runny herpes. The girls don't like that. Or they get obstrep. Or they fill out the cards, enjoy the treatment, and turn out it's a cash flow problem. That one, severe. They got a family, they got a car, I wreck the car. I don't like to wreck the person, but cash flow problem—"

"You've got to think on your feet," Shaper said.

"You can say that," said D'Wayne with a touch of pride.

"One of them runny herpes, I recommend a doctor—derma-skin guy. Not that a doctor can do shit, you know what I'm sayin', but I get to authorize."

"Speak with authority," said the court translator-interpreter.

"Don't need to repeat what I say," said D'Wayne. "I hear me."

Some folks might think doorman at a whorehouse was a comedown from other professions, but how about Security Consultant for a Medical Therapy Research Foundation? D'Wayne walked Shaper through his theories about life, career choice, and destiny. "I'm playing backup here, which is good. That's my whole basis."

"And Gyro backing you up?"

"Got it! Plus the dog, Fella. I say, Rip, like that, Fella rips, so I don't like to say it all the time."

D'Wayne, like many large crafty men, liked to keep his interlocutors on the defensive. "Drunks or perverts come in here, they say, 'No problem,' and I translate for them, just like you do: *No, beeg problem jerkoff*, or sometime: *Asshole*. Tell it like that, real close, nose on their nose, usually they hear me."

"I'll bet."

"Even if they in a mood to not listen, they hear me. I take them upside the neck, they hear me. I whistle for Fella, they hear me."

Shaper heard him. No problem. "You ever let them back, once you put them out?"

"You ever put your toothpaste back in the tube?" D'Wayne asked. "Well, once I did, it was that Michelle, come in with her husband—Michelle's a girl's name, y'unnastan what I'm sayin?—and this Michelle wanted to watch, got herself a little overexcited. So next time, she promise to be good, I give her another chance. I'm a sucker for a pretty wife."

"It was okay the next time?"

"Fine, fine. That Michelle just so fine, this time her husband wanna watch. So that Michelle and me, we would let him, but I got my own reason why I don't do that. But you want to give people a chance to take their pleasure in this world. My mommy raised me like that."

"Right, right," said Shaper, this always being a good remark to offer a large man with hands bearing swelling and scars at the knuckles from use in combat rather than age-related arthritis. D'Wayne's hands contracted into fists, expanded again into huge slabs of striated meat, then tightened in a fight-or-fight reaction, no real choice. He was on edge and standing close. Shaper said: "Absolutely on the nose," and hastily added: "You're clear on this, I see."

D'Wayne relaxed, tried to do so. He beamed his toothy victor's smile. His great hands opened one more time, and one of them slapped Shaper at the shoulder. "You're all right, man!"

Shaper regained his balance.

"Amanda said that, you all right to the max, she say, and I got to agree."

"*Amanda?*"

"Hey, didn't she mention?"

While Shaper assimilated this fragment, using silence as a time for learning and study, Doohicky Dwayne, D'Wayne, filled the idle moment with information in the form of words. In his own way, like Gyro, he knew that words help people understand each other, and the beauty part was how they could also serve to increase the stock of ignorance. Sometimes a person could finesse the deal with words.

"I picked myself up some esteem just cause I was born relaxed," D'Wayne admitted. "It give me the strength of ten, plus my medicaments to build my muscle mass and get me an edge. Plus I don't just *rely*, I work out. Plus that's what I'm here for."

Having the strength of ten helped him to make a living. Self-esteem was overflowing D'Wayne's massive container. As a court translator, Shaper felt he was exaggerating the ghetto speech—it swung this way and that—and his purposes were yet to be disclosed, and it was better not to try to hurry him, and his purposes were sure to be confusing for Dan Shaper, the person he was now confusing. As D'Wayne intended.

As D'Wayne and Amanda seemed to intend.

Gyro crooked a long finger (all his fingers were long, blunt at the manicured tips, the knuckle hairs black and long) and then pulled down the corner of his mouth in what may have been some kind of highly syncopated Rom gesture, all of it to emphasize an obvious point: the orthodontist client there alone with Shari, come here, come here, no business of yours, come here right now into this other room, buddy.

Shaper went where indicated. D'Wayne had had his way, maybe not all of it; time for Gyro to continue the program. They were standing at a doorlike French window which grandly opened out over crumbling molding, ants hurrying hither and yon, in and out of little passages under crusted layers of cream-colored paint. They looked out over a tangle of alley plants, a tree of heaven, ailanthus reaching for the light, much random greenery, sprouts segmented like bamboo, very long grass with rat trails through it. The Victorian next door was boarded up. Across the alley jungle, the similar Victorian was streaked with scorch marks where someone set a fire which evidently didn't take because the juicy bodies of termites extinguished it. Or conscience struck the arsonist and he peed it down. Or the ratshit at the foundations dampened the flames.

Gyro and Dan stood at the window, appreciating the ecology of a San Francisco alley, communing silently until one of them would interrupt the stillness. Shaper noticed a scatter of gray feathers on the rat trail. A gull or a pigeon had met its fate. Shaper was the first to break into this moment of meditation, reverence, brotherhood. "You look like some actor, let's see, only younger. . . . Anthony Quinn."

"Sometimes people say that," Gyro said. "But I don't look like him and I don't smell like him."

Nevertheless, Gyro wasn't displeased. It was a law of the twentieth century: no one ever minded being compared to an actor. In a few years Gyro might carry a noble banker's belly, but so far there was only a muscular forward pout of his navel. Although now it was his turn to offer a compliment, Gyro often moved matters out of turn for his own purposes.

"Do you know what it means to be a gypsy?" Gyro asked, the answer ready. "To have anger. Have bad righteous anger. And to have permission."

"Right. Jesus said."

Gyro was grinning. Ah, this man appreciated conversation, the meeting of the minds. "And Roma folks like to shuck and jive. I like to do that, too."

"But you're not?" Shaper asked. It was time to listen past what the man repeated too often; past the fleshy confidence. This friendship was ripening. It was time for Shaper to be shrewd. "You're *not* a gypsy?"

"Are you getting smart, man," Gyro said. "You must be my kind of Rom person."

Shaper stared. Who was he to worry about others' truth or lies? People made out the best they could. He wished the world were other, he wished it were different, he wished . . .

"Care to share your thoughts with me, as a brother?" Gyro asked. "Like a brother I been sharing my thoughts with you, even my trying-out thoughts which you gaje call—civilians . . ."

"We call them lies," said Shaper.

The shadow of the swaying curtain moved across a sun-blasted strip of light. Gyro was changing shape before his eyes. Gyro, becoming something else, was already someone else, just another American, fully multicultural whatever he was, a city-grown player, as good as native, almost real, better than genuine. He liked the sodas, the cars with angry animal names (Jaguar, Fury, Leopard, Tiger); he could be deeply aroused, blissful eyes shut, nostrils distended, inhaling profoundly of the blessings of the earth and chemical technology, at one with the universe, when a no-smell deodorized armpit was presented to him for a test-drive. Not for Gyro Brown anymore the old North Indian, lost in the mists of time, the wander across Hungary and Spain, the caravan travel; no shoeing of horses and tinker-with-motors rough life, close to nature, with pitchfork-armed peasants standing sullenly by the roadside to threaten his passage. He was becoming gaje to the max. He was learning to deal with impulse-control issues. No open fires with mystery stews, no knife-grinding or chicken-abducting or setting up the daughter in a live-in storefront to tell fortunes and read palms. Palm-reading was for losers who couldn't pick a pocket for shit. Similar critique for even the more refined advances in shoplifting. A millennium therapy resort was for a winner like Gyro's daughter. Didn't Dan Shaper also want only the best for Amanda?

His eyes came barreling in on Shaper, speeding down with the high beams on, crossing the center lane and heading straight toward him, and even his voice rumbled with excess octane. "You know that saying, an eye for an eye and a tooth?

There's a Roma vow, my friend, like a malediction, and what it means isn't you insult me and I flick a charm your way against my biter like this"—he flicked his nail, his tooth clicked—"no, no, my friend, it means you do what you shouldn't do to me and all your teeth, all your eyes . . . they are at risk. I can only say this in English. In Roma we do not say 'at risk.' In Roma we say: You will be buried in stinking unholy ground where the worms and rats eat until they are fat and farting and they eat each other. It's what you could call a curse."

You could. "Why are you threatening me?" Shaper asked.

Gyro grinned. "Insurance. In advance of any bad thoughts, a little fair notice." He wasn't sure how intelligent Shaper would turn out to be—maybe he was too much in need these days—so he explained with more soothing words. "A policy of insurance for a person like you, aware is what I mean, really wants to keep up, don't you think? Even if he's an older individual for what he's going through?"

How kind. Gyro really did understand something about Dan Shaper. Shaper could be led to enjoy a predicament. He had this in common with his new gypsy (or perhaps non-Roma) friend. It felt terrific to slip out of the years which had embraced him despite no courtship on his part.

"I'm a Golden Ager, Gyro. I've got a Senior Fast Pass for public transportation."

"But you're okay, still move on your feet. You want to hear what Shari thinks? Says you're toasted and honey-roasted. It's okay to be a man of experience, even not such fascinating previous experience, if he's ready for something new at the golden-age, senior-fast-pass, slow-fuck stage. You know what I'm saying?"

"You don't leave much to the imagination."

"Am I right?"

"I'm sure you'll decide."

Gyro leaned forward with concern. He was in an extended explaining mode. "You know how sharks do, my friend?"

"I've heard. I saw the movie."

It didn't stop Gyro. "A big tearing bite, then another rip, then another, till he gets the whole stupid swimmer? Well, that's not me. I *nibble*. You just keep on swimming, I keep on nibbling, and pretty soon you're still swimming but you're all gone. You're a swimming ghost! And I'm not nibbling anymore, but man, I'm *smiling*. You know what I'm saying?"

"I can guess. Jesus said you could."

Gyro grabbed his hand. "Raht! Gimme five! Am I one smart Roma dude or not?"

Shaper decided only one dumb non-Roma dude would let himself ride along with this good buddy who might be anything, even what he said he was. A man pregnant with the last trimester of his time on earth shouldn't need rebirth in the jaws of a shark.

"So when we are gone, our daughters will still be here. For a father to outlive a daughter, no, I do not wish for the worst person in the world. Certainly you are not that person. You are not the worst, no. Please take pleasure, pride, and take notice."

"Take notice?"

"Close close attention. Shari has many friends and now a new friend in Amanda, you understand me?"

The house was on a turntable, a carousel spinning slowly around him. Shaper was on that carousel, spinning along with the furniture, but the walls were still and that's how he knew he was moving. He was dizzy; he was not having a stroke; just having a little bewilderment. He inquired calmly: "What are you saying?" Unobtrusively, so as to alarm no one, he gripped the edge of a chair.

"Amanda."

Dan Shaper was willing to be stupid with Gyro, distracted from his long sleep by him, but now, when the man said this name, he asked himself for complete alertness. In due course the room would stop spinning and Gyro would make things come clear. Amanda could be any young person's name. Shaper decided the heat in his face was not visible because Gyro took no notice, his lips in silent whistling mode.

In fact, he moved the subject forward. There was a noise of someone being admitted at the front door, D'Wayne murmuring his welcome, the dog stirring. "Since this here is the best therapy money can buy," Gyro said, "we let money buy it. No valid patient goes away untreated. Then they want another cure, another, another. It's like food or God—needs regular attention, which is superior for a business. You know me, my friend, having someone to live after our time is the pleasure that is more than pleasure. Through history"—the carousel spinning again—"every race has always found this to be true, even before they die. Such is our nature."

He inclined his head in the direction of the man now being welcomed by Shari, passed along from D'Wayne and the growling, grumbling, muzzle-wet dog. "Who knows," Gyro asked, "if living after himself is not on his mind this very moment, filling his pants—?"

The client passed through the room, head lowered in the miscreant perpetrator duck. Gyro fell silent on the theory that he was invisible if he didn't speak. The client was carrying a plastic package that said L'eggs on it, some kind of sleekness for the thighs and knees; he had brought equipment for his special needs.

If you have some free time today, Shaper was thinking about Gyro, would you please continue to shut up? That, or get past the philosophy?

But it was not to be. Gyro had so much to confide.

"And me too, a tragedy. I am becoming"—his voice deep, musically anguished—"becoming a city gypsy . . . turning into an American, like you, Dan—just another gadjo."

Gadjo meant outsider, foreigner to the portage people, worthless but useful, sometimes good prey . . . well, just a gadjo. Despite the orange veins in his buttons, the streaks of color in his suit, Gyro might be a gadjo with a pinkish dick merely shadowed by sparse dry gadjo hair.

Shaper heard the hum of a small organic drill behind his ear, the hovering sound of insect hunger. Calmly he detached part of his attention from Gyro while continuing to listen with the other part. The mosquito anticipated its meal, prepared to land. Shaper understood about the temporary anesthesia, that he wouldn't feel the drilling apparatus until too late. He snatched a handful of air, opened his fist, and there in his palm lay a crumpled but recognizable gauzy corpse. It existed no longer to grow frantic with hunger; it had sped rashly into oblivion and eternity. A look of triumph must have crossed Shaper's face. Gyro interrupted himself, asking, "Hey?"

"*Moos*-tiko," said Shaper. "That's what one of my burglars called it. He thought the word was—"

"Yah, moos-keet in some other language. Not mosca, my friend?"

Shaper felt invigorated by his victory over nature. The law of survival of the fittest applied to him. "Now are you going to tell me Jesus gave them permission to suck blood, too?"

"Hey," said Gyro, "speak up for yourself, right? I like that."

Irked at calling himself a gadjo, Gyro was ready to take any necessary recovery action. This had been fully authorized during that fateful long-ago afternoon in the village of Jerusalem. The necessary action lay coiled invisibly in the human interval between Gyro Brown and Dan Shaper, who needed to be cut down again, needed it badly. Gyro sucked on his lip and ready, aim, fire: "You know this little girl calls herself Amanda, good baby for a boy around here?"

The mosquito had vanished forever. Shaper wanted to stamp his foot on Gyro's instep, break tiny bones, a behavior studied during his military service. Hand-to-hand combat was misnamed; the point was to win without combat. The adversary screamed; healing was slow; a person ended up limping for a long time.

Instead, mildly, Shaper asked, "How do you know her?"

He wondered where tiny filmy biting creatures went after they were squeezed in a fist. Well, they were oxidized away, that's life and death.

"Right," said Gyro. "The age group, generation they call it, go to the clubs, the music, they get around. So does Shari."

"Okay."

"They're friends, you know what I mean, what they call, that generation, 'best friends?' Two girls together, just starting out in life? Meet a lot of people down on Eleventh Street, Folsom, the Mission, how do I know? You perceive the picture with your perception equipment, don't you?"

Shaper tried to stay awake and calm, and succeeded in doing so, because it was important to factor in the advice he heard next: "So if you got some idea about Shari, am I right? It could get a little complicated, my friend. But business . . . Shari likes you. We think you can learn."

Shaper succeeded in listening and not breaking the small bones of the man's instep. That would only provide temporary relief.

D'Wayne, gatekeeper, German shepherd at his side with its muzzle gleaming, D'Wayne's hand resting companionably on the dog's collar, was waiting at the door to usher Dan out. D'Wayne's smile was meaty and rich.

Seven

As far as Shaper could tell, the work he had done to bring Amanda into the world was worth doing—this conclusion about a common miracle was an astonishment. But who was he to judge what it was to be a father?

The toiling and sweating with Margaret had sent forward this vividness, now opening like a time capsule. Maybe Margaret and Dan had laughed and tickled. Maybe they had whispered secrets; he no longer knew what the secrets had been. He wished he could remember the lovemaking that created Amanda, the smells and stray hairs, the whispered secrets if there were any, but even without remembering, fragments came back to him; a Jefferson Airplane poster on the wall, orange crates with art supplies, brushes, smeared glasses, clipped photos from magazines, a young woman of the Aquarian time who admired William DeKooning, Allen Ginsberg, Janis Joplin. Probably there was a wet roach in the ashtray, a joint shared while they sat crosslegged on the mattress and discussed what people discussed before they crawled into each other. He wasn't a reliable witness of that season in San Francisco. He had not counted on the results. Here Amanda stood.

"So, Dad, you've been helpful. I mean, like those meals lately—nice casual dining. The advice spoils things, but that's okay. Now we get kinda real, you ready for that?"

"Pardon?" he asked.

"I mean, this is not a test anymore. We're not just poking in outer space, you know?"

"I'm not sure."

"What I mean, Dad . . . Wow. Am I shy." Not a factual statement on the part of the new daughter. "Boy, is this way hard, Dad. Okay." Arms stiff, head bobbing, a rehearsal of shy, modest, retiring, and diffident. "I need a normal child's regular income that I didn't ever get before, you know, for my normal, your daughter's needs? There."

A look of hilarity. Little hairs above her nose, between her eyebrows, which she didn't pluck; just a few crosshairs above the bridge, the same configuration as his own eyebrows, but sleeker, softer. And she was not shy about meeting his eyes now that she had spoken. "Does that mess you up?" she inquired with great solicitude. But the pupils, below those gleamy crosshairs, were sharp and glinting.

He took his time. They had already taken all these years, hadn't they? A heat had come up in San Francisco since Amanda came to stoke the furnace. Shaper's cold hands were no longer cold. Her hot heart had changed the weather, even the sky. None of this was expected. He had gotten accustomed to his personal meteorology, inner and outer, wearing socks to bed, putting a lotion on his hands and rubbing them briskly, getting along. When the fog swept in, as it did most afternoons, that was how it was supposed to be—no heat down here.

"I'd like to help," he said, probably too formally, so he stopped and then began again. "I want to help." And again: "For my own self I need to do what a father should do and I will. I want to."

"Within your means? Like that?"

"I'm not a rich man. I'm not all that prosperous, even. I'm okay, I can't complain—"

"You wanna complain?"

"How about if you tell me what you need and I tell you what I can do?"

He kept trying to do this right. She kept trying to help in her own Amanda way. "Why don't we do this real practical, hey Dad, is that the question? You'd like a budget?"

He would not respond with sarcasm just because an opportunity for it came up. "That would be a practical idea," he said. "Clothes, tuition, books . . ."

"How about I eat? How's about food, Dad?"

He waited for the weather to subside. "Amanda. We're both feeling our way. We're feeling our way in the dark."

"Oh boy, aren't we. Just like how a kid used to be made in those days. In the dark." She made little blind feeling motions, a spider with its many legs exploring the web it had spun. "Hey Pop, who's got the flashlight? Pop? What should we call each other?"

Eventually she would settle on whether he was Dad or Pop or That Asshole. Among these possibilities, he hoped she would choose Dad. He was afraid she'd start calling him Dan or Mister Shaper.

"Just trying to help you lighten up, so whyncha lighten up, okay, dude?" She grinned and extended her arms as if to welcome him into them without his needing actually to move—it was a gesture of general hospitality. "Take your time. This afternoon by five would be just fine."

His consternation.

"Oh Dad, just kidding."

So now, since he was a grown man, recent father of a nineteen-year-old, he took control in a grownup, mature, standing-tall-and-stretching-on-his-heels fashion. By a mighty act of will the discs of his spine opened up, so that he was nearly as tall as he had measured for his U.S. Army physical long ago. Her gaze as he mobilized himself was canny. Her father, bringer of chromosomes if not nurture, felt proud that she knew how to challenge him. It was something in the genes. It may not have been comfortable, but it brought furtive uncomfortable satisfactions. Flying motes like insects swarmed across his eyes. He was standing in front of her and saying, "I really want to feel you're not just *taking*. I really do need a budget."

"It's way spiritual, Dad. I really believe in religion—not!—but I hope you get that I wouldn't try to hurt you because I'm a very spiritual person?"

"I still need a budget, Amanda."

Dan Shaper had passed his career in the court system, the bureaucracy of justice, waiting for defense lawyers to ask their questions and rehearse the perpetrators. Lying, manipulation, and felony were part of his extended family business, like backyard barbecues in other families. One thing he did well was not rush incriminating details. Even if the perp was a moron, Shaper's job was to let matters unfold, follow the offered leads. Amanda was not a moron and probably the money from her parent wouldn't just go for stupid tattoos or studs in her nipples. Amanda was a serious person, possibly serious about getting high or inappropriate men. D'Wayne came to mind. She wasn't ready to say and Shaper wasn't ready to ask. About his response to the answer, when it came, he hoped against hope that he too would not be a moron. He wasn't sure if he could expect this much from himself.

He knew the face he was giving Amanda, grayness, cheeks eroded by age, remnants of pink streaked amid the slivers of beard, a pale stare, a squint, coolness, coldness, suspicion, out of warranty. That's what she had to see. Expiration date near at hand. If the eyes were the window of the soul, Shaper's windows were smeared with neglect and city silt.

She couldn't know that he wanted to reach his arms around her. He didn't know how different it would be to embrace a daughter. He must have embraced her mother.

Oh, confusion, and this person, this stranger who happened to be his daughter, about whom he had no intentions at all until she happened to manifest herself, was staring into his face with amusement, with impatience, with furious determination. She was watching him go out of focus and waiting for him to come back. She wanted something more from him. He wanted to give her something. He wanted a caring which he didn't deserve. That was his opinion, but he wanted it anyway. He had no idea of how to conduct them both toward that ordinary condition, a daughter with her father.

"Let me think," he said.

"Be my guest. I've never been contra—done it myself. Like maybe it's inherited? What's your opinion about that? Probably it's how I'm a girl who gets along someway, Dad."

"Young woman, I want you to be my daughter."

"Wow." She wasn't expecting a formal announcement. It sounded like a Municipal Court decision. "Wow," she said again. "It's not enough already? I have to be something else? Like prove something to you when you proved nothing to me all these years? How about a blood test, Pop?"

It had occurred to him. But she looked so much like him, eyes, Tartar cheekbones, small plump mouth, that he knew it would be a waste of time, money, and a prick in the arm. Truth to tell, he wanted her to be his daughter and knew she was. He had been contemplating the miracle since she first appeared, something smart, pretty, fresh, with smile crinkles when she blessed the universe with a smile, which had somehow manifested itself from his eroded, whiskered, aging body.

Did he need proof? He just shook his head.

The smart person with the smart angry mouth, a scrap of

spittle at the corners, said: "Listen, what if I had a lot of plastic surgery? See, I study these Polaroids of you, then I watch you on the street, hey, look at it that way, how about it, and I make a bigdeal *plot*, Dad—"

The smile crinkles with hilarious imaginings around her eyes. He'd have to try that one in the mirror. She even bounced on her toes a little when she walked, like him. How does someone inherit a thing like that? Shaper's father had done it, and now his daughter seemed to have it in her germ plasm, too. How far back do such miracles begin, how far forward would they reach in the procedures of birth, age, and birth again?

"—and so I got this student pro bone plastic surgery dude at University Hospital, needed like a guinea pig, to really practice on me. . . . Maybe like that? Showed him the Polaroids? What do you think?"

To say, You're running at the mouth in an ugly way, Amanda, wouldn't be courteous and fatherly. So he only said: "You're running at the mouth, Amanda. *Please.*"

He was present at the birth of conscience. She looked sad, almost stricken. Perhaps this wasn't the first time. She shut up.

She had a way of confusing him, his vision blurring as if he had cataracts, his knees turning unsolid, his back heavy— dazed, confused, fading—this must be what old age was like. She had a way of advancing him too fast into the place where he was anyway heading. Why the hurry? A child doesn't know about sympathy for the old, a young person only begins to learn.

Shaper thought: old folks get papery, too delicate to eat, but this working guy still had an appetite. His daughter looked as if she were hungry all the time, lips damp and glistening, that touch of spittle at the right corner. It was only appetite, not rage; it was disdain, not fury. Her sarcastic fun of a moment ago only served to delay matters. "Hey Pop, you hungry?" she was asking.

No, not really. This conversation was kind of filling.

"Forget about the day until tomorrow," Bob Dylan used to sing, and maybe that was the tune he made Amanda by as he romped above a stranger. It turned out tomorrow had been nineteen years away. When it came, his friends were growing older (even Harvey, even Alfonso), some had died; he was growing old; and one day a sneezing stranger would be assigned to clean out his dusty apartment, look for an heir, call Goodwill or a Tenderloin hauler. In his lair with the motes floating, the radio played an all-classics station to keep him company, keep the burglars at bay while he was off translating for other burglars—deep in his heart he was convinced that the flutes and violins of baroque music were anathema to burglars listening on the fire escape or at the hall door. They might think someone was home. Once again he was beginning to imagine, like a young man falling in love, having someone to tell his life to; someone who would tease a man who turned the music down when he was home, turned it up when he left.

Now someone had appeared to live after him and perhaps listen to his life while he was still present to tell it. Before finding Amanda, before Amanda found him, he didn't like thinking of how much time he had left. A promised sweetness had checked in to replace release by stroke, heart attack, cancer, or dissatisfied blade-carrying client, promises sometimes contemplated over fishball soup in the Vietnamese noodle place down the block. (When it rained, and the purple neon sign blinked PHO, PHO, and for under five bucks he could warm his belly before bed. . . .)

He had a daughter, sweetness unguaranteed, not the deal.

It wasn't his choice. Something was happening to Dan Shaper, something close and dear, like falling in love, like finding life worth continuing, explainable by metabolism, not logic; his biology, his logic, and he wasn't sure he approved of all the shifts in his previous steady submission to the years. He might yet live awhile. He might have someone to live after him. He had heard of the pains brought by children and here were a few of them all at once, crowding in on him, in payment for the childhood Amanda had suffered and he had missed.

He was not sure love, if that's what it was, maybe it was only metabolism, meant anything in this confusion. It could blow away like the fog in the afternoon winds. If he couldn't act on it, love meant nothing, it was not love. It left a drawing sensation in his chest, like the heart attack he was waiting for. It was not the heart attack he had made plans for.

Lilith, the she-devil, came to tempt men and curse them. The worst curse she could bring upon a man was to make him love her, for then he would do her bidding.

Shit no, this was only Dan Shaper's lost and found daughter, Amanda.

Shaper wished he could remember with her the front porch of the house where they had raised her, the swing he fashioned from ropes and a board which hung from the tree in the back yard (had the fond father first swung from it himself, to make sure it was safe?), and the tomato plants growing in the sunny patch, the two of them biting into the warm dripping fruit and the father shaking salt on his but only a dash of it onto the child's in her tiny paw, and the stories he told her at bedtime, the nightly saga of the whale, the seal, and the Esquimo . . . those matters this father hadn't attended to. The breakfasts with Shaper clumsily scrambling the eggs and buttering the toast and teaching Amanda to eat the crusts first, nibbling around the edges to make mouth sculpture of imaginary creatures, the mouth griffin, the mouth push-me-pull-you—the games with this child which this father had not played.

It hadn't happened, none of it. He felt the shadow of the warm little hand pressing against his as they walked barefoot at Ocean Beach, toes curling into the sand, and he said that was Hawaii out there, invisible, and that was Japan out there, even more invisible—Amanda giggling, understanding that the invisible doesn't have degrees, does it?—and here was a new story . . . The walk on the sunwarmed sand, that Hawaii, that Japan, they were all invisible, impossible.

The thin sagging voice of Bob Dylan blew out of open windows in those days. A high wind of forgotten origin blew across the earth, picking up bits of plasm from the genetic pool, then later, very late, blew this full-grown handsome creature into his arms. Except that both of them were too clumsy to touch easily. Except that her smart mouth was how she embraced him, if that's what she was doing, or exploited him, or looked for her rightful place in his universe, or her wrongful one if that was how it turned out.

In a break in the fog rolling overhead, the stars seemed brighter and sharper and more distant than ever, burning cold above him in the night sky of San Francisco. Somehow the day had turned into evening. He heard the words, *Let's go.*

Where?

"Let's go someplace, it's time," he said, "get something to eat."

"I'm not hungry anymore, changed my mind while you were thinking about whether you . . . Hey, I got someone waiting for me, so catch you later, okay? Work it out for yourself. I'll scamper now."

She was moving fast. If he was going to do so much thinking about what he owed her, she was going to make him do the thinking alone. Her butt was moving. She was gone.

Daughter of mine, he prayed.

I beg you.

There was a smell of fresh mushrooms in the air, clinging to damp earth. A city person who lived in the cement-bound Tenderloin, what did Dan Shaper know about the smell of fresh mushrooms in the dampness of root systems? Maybe it was toadstools. The smell was wafting from the noodle joint down the street with the purple neon sign that said PHO.

Eight

There had been a time in Dan Shaper's life when the ring of
the telephone was a promise of friendship, fun, or at least
company. There were also times when the noise was a threat
to peace, someone nagging at him because she thought he
had an obligation to her and he probably did.

This call, different from old times, interrupted him in the
old way. It caused dread and a perverse stirring of hope,
though there was no kindness in it.

"Amanda here. I need money. Been waiting. I need monies."

Monies?

Attending to the long space between her words and considering how to answer, he heard a voice drawling, "Just hang
up on the asshole, he ain't gonna come through." This wasn't
Spanish; it was a primary American language of infraction
which was familiar to him.

"Amanda, when can I see you? We have to talk about all
these things."

"All, these, things," she said. "All-these-things. Hey."

"Amanda, let's look at each other and talk."

"We've looked at each other. Hey, now we've talked."

"Amanda."

Silence, and then a soft voice answering: "At your convenience, Dad."

"Tonight?"

"Thanks for not putting this off cause of something else real important you have to do, Dad."

So Dan Shaper named the time and place where he and his daughter could meet. But Amanda had another idea, a private spot. Not his choice this time. A room with a sink with hot and cold water in case someone needed freshening up, towels, fresh commercially laundered washcloths. One of the extra bedrooms in the splendid Victorian mansion which housed the Yerba Buena Foundation.

In order to demonstrate her seriousness, she had not come with a budget for food, lodging, clothes, health, education, the matters a normal father might provide his daughter. Proving her seriousness, she was waiting with a friend.

"You worry I'm, like, using," said Amanda.

"I never said that."

"But bet it comes to mind . . . On drugs, owe some dealer? Or God knows what, Dad?"

"I don't think this is the way to approach things," said Shaper, trying to decide how to acknowledge the witnesses to a father and daughter settling issues between them. One witness, with a wet black muzzle and small, sleepily alert eyes, was a German shepherd, following the conversation but not interrupting it. Doing the same, at least thus far, was the dog's master, D'Wayne, at ease and unobtrusive, slouched in an armchair, long legs stretching out, as if he might go unnoticed because he was sitting, relaxed, and silent. Shaper decided it was really terrific of the four of them, German shepherd, Amanda, D'Wayne, and himself, to conduct the discussion at such a high level of courteous concern. In his state of acute attention to someone's next statement of position, Shaper heard the rumble of a pickup truck in the driveway, the sound of a flushing toilet, the click of a keyboard updating billings or records, and a soft murmur that might have been Shari Brown or someone else on the phone ordering takeout. Through these wooden walls, all sounds were gentled.

"So how do you suggest we get to it?" Amanda inquired. "Just curious. You've been a great dad, right? That your theory? Always like your gene pool, wasn't that what you called me?"

"Is it for tuition? Are you applying to school?"

"Whatever you want it to be for, Dad."

"I can't just hand over money. I apologize for the hard time you've had, but the solution isn't just gimme, gimme."

"Hard time I had maybe," Amanda said. "Actually, it was okay. You're a great negotiator, Pop."

"I've got to have a responsible reason."

"How about this?" she asked. "Send the mon, hon."

He didn't understand her.

"Come on. I need it. Don't be an asshole, Dad."

The word was like a kick. Shaper started, but didn't know where to move. The dog growled, a soft menacing rumble. D'Wayne sat up, cracking his knuckles, and then smoothed back the dog's ears.

"Sorry about that. Slipped out, Dad. Whatever was I thinking? What I meant is: If I don't get it from you, because I need it, I really do need it, well—" She shrugged. She was looking not at him but at D'Wayne. "Well, then Shari and Gyro got some part-time work for me. It's a safe environment, plus as a father I know you appreciate that. D'Wayne's gonna take care of me, too."

Shaper stood there. He couldn't walk out. He couldn't claim any ground. He fully understood what it was like to be powerless because he was powerless.

D'Wayne had finished with his knuckles, calmed the nervous dog. D'Wayne yawned. He said: "He ain't gonna go for it. Hey Amanda, just finish up with the . . ." Normally, D'Wayne didn't leave things unfinished, not even his sentences. But why repeat himself? The word *asshole* was still hanging in there.

Cheerful Amanda liked to make her own points in life. "I'll decide when I'm finished, okay?"

"Okay, okay." D'Wayne extended his pink palms. "Around this here little situation, you the boss, girl."

She turned a joyous face to D'Wayne, and there were the crinkly memories of it when she turned back to her father. "I'm not a blackmailer, threaten-type individual. That's not my style, Dad. I can earn my living. Far as Gyro's concerned, it's on my behalf." She watched for response, had trouble reading the strange father's expression. "Cat got your tongue? It's how we all think of it, Dad—Shari, Gyro, your special gene pool—"

"D'Wayne," said D'Wayne.

"So how do *you* think of it, Dad?"

"Wait."

"You've waited this long. I guess we can all just let you wait some more—you just take a little time, Dad—even if that's all you do, okay?"

D'Wayne stood up very politely to show him out. "Been nice talkin to you," he said.

Nine

His doctor tried to answer the question about why Dan Shaper couldn't sleep from three A.M. to five A.M. That is, he proceeded in the general direction of sleep like a normal citizen of his age and at a normal hour and pace. He flossed, brushed teeth, ran floss under his bridge, pulled eyelids, made a face in the mirror, inspected the results, quelled his disapproval of what he saw. Not having much choice in the matter, he accepted the gift which is supposed to provide wisdom, along with Social Security benefits. He poked his nose to test how much the cartilage was thickening, lengthening, and sagging under the influence of prolonged gravity. Pressing at the snout revealed hairs which could be snipped or not snipped at the bearer's discretion. Shaper fully accepted responsibility for having been born so long ago. And so to bed.

He fell as if struck on the head and slept until he woke, groggily stumbling to pee, and then returned to bed sweating, awake, unable to come fully awake, and terrified. He believed he wasn't scared during the day. He didn't know what he was scared of in those predawn hours. "Is it age?" he asked.

"I could give you some pills," said Marvin Feldstein.

"Why?"

His doctor shrugged. "You'd sleep. Of course, then you might be sleepy when you're supposed to be awake."

"Would it help?"

"Not too much."

They sat in Marvin's little office, staring at each other. Marvin told him he had the same problem. Yes, it was age, he said. "We're not really supposed to live this long. And now you have a new problem, like a young father. Of course, she's not a baby."

And they stared. Then Marvin sighed, it was almost a yawn, and said, "So if you're worried, I can tell you this—psychological pain doesn't last. Cut off a leg, smash a toe even, that'll hurt. But psychological pain wears out. It doesn't last."

He said this as if he believed it.

It only lasted until the end of life.

"I think you can't run away," said Marvin.

"I don't want to."

Was the good doctor humming to himself? Had he forgotten his patient? No, he was tuning up. It was like a hum, a low grumble and rumble in the chest, and it led to a little nostalgic song: "When you're about fifteen, it seems like your only problem—remember how you'd stand in front of the mirror, squeezing?—was pimples. Squeeze it out and you'll get sex, you'll get good grades, the whole world will be a welcoming place."

"It was more complicated for me," said Shaper.

"Me too," said Doctor Feldstein, and fell silent awhile. Then he seemed to wake from his doze and said, "Even then. So you don't think you could just squeeze old age out like a pimple?"

"Don't think so. Not Amanda either."

"I'm trying to be helpful," said Marvin Feldstein.

"Not succeeding," said Dan Shaper, "but thanks for trying."

"Geriatric fatherhood isn't an exact science. I don't know

of any cases of the deadbeat dad—not that you were really a deadbeat, but still—taking up the cudgels like that. Personally, I'd want to sleep all the time."

"Are you helpful," said Shaper.

Marvin liked to show he read something besides professional journals with their regular fare of new cures, reports of failures of the new cures, and techniques for improving fee collection, tax shelters, and malpractice insurance—insufficient nourishment for a philosophic temperament. Hippocrates never had to deal with the pros and cons of HMOs. "As our fellow tribesmen, the Hibernian guys, say"—oh-oh, one of his Irish proverbs coming—" 'you can't get there from here.' "

"I'm trying," said Dan Shaper. This was an old American proverb.

"You're not Irish."

"You can say that again."

"I believe you're of my people, Dan. As the saying goes—"

Even though he wasn't paying for his doctor's time, Shaper decided to escape Marvin's ruminations. Marvin seemed to be settling in, spreading his hams as he sat. "The gypsies think they're a lost tribe, too," Shaper said. "This Gyro does. He might not be."

"So share it with me."

So Shaper chose not to share at this moment.

Marvin stood up. "There's no charge for the visit. I'm afraid world-historical anxiety and newfound daughters aren't covered by your insurance. . . . But if you find a way to squeeze out the pimple, let me know your trick, will you?"

This pompous person with his mild chronic pompous despair. This kind man with his kindliness habit that required no consideration or preparation; it just happened, along with the fate that turned him into a doc. The daughter of one man was not the daughter of another man, even a kindly one. That's an immutable law of nature. It would have been nice to think empathy could make grief into nongrief—whole industries were based on this idea—but so far as Dan Shaper knew, no one else was Dan Shaper and the father of Amanda Who Should Have Been Named Shaper.

Marvin was not much help today, unless fellow feeling was a help. Okay, maybe it freed up a few endorphins. When he lay sweating and staring at the ceiling at three A.M., he could have the pleasure of imagining Marvin Feldstein doing the same thing. Oh boy, fun.

Marvin whistled for attention. Even his whistle was clumsy, spit-impaired, but it was better than invoking the word 'angst,' that all-purpose fog name for the inner life of certain bachelors of a certain age and education. They needed to explain why they slumped their aching backs into the wrong kind of armchairs, too soft for proper support of the lumbar regions, and read the wrong kinds of formerly advanced existentialist philosophy. Long evenings of solitary page-turning were easier on the liver than getting drunk, but less ameliorating to mood. The veterans in the purple-neon bars of San Francisco still called V-J Tavern or Ship's In Galley got to bed more efficiently. Even the late stoners from the Sixties with their stashes of medical marijuana knew that Owsley Blue was a better alternative to baby sleep than Jean-Paul Sartre.

Marvin was saying: "But you do have a specific problem, what we call a disfunction, I think that's what we call it . . ."

Yes, at night, when his head was thick and clouded, his legs twitching with desire to be elsewhere, or to be another body, or to run away, there seemed to be a problem. Or maybe he just needed to be in another body. Was that a disfunction?

"Sex sometimes helps," Marvin said, then shrugged, tapped

his pen on his prescription pad. "When it doesn't hinder."

He walked Dan to the door of the waiting room. A patient was waiting with his sleeve already rolled up and his Medicare card in his hand. "I'd like to meet her," Marvin said. "I've had some deals with my own kids."

Shaper realized he knew nothing about his friend's family, divorce, children. Marvin Feldstein was a sensitive doctor, your kindly old practitioner with bad posture who almost made house calls, but probably would make a house call if he felt real need.

Dan Shaper had no desire to run away from Amanda, did he?

"Hey, for blood pressure, heart, the whole shebang—the gestalt," Marvin said, "it's a fine idea to avoid excess angst."

Ten

"If your phone ain't ringin', it's me that ain't callin'." He used
to merely like that song—Mose Allyson at the On Broadway—
but as the years went by, it became the description of his life
except for business from Ferd or some other lawyer, or maybe
Harvey offering company for a movie. The silence in his
apartment was a case of everybody fascinating, lovely, and
kind in the whole wide world not calling.

Lately the phone took to ringing more often. Sometimes
Gyro, once Shari, sometimes Amanda. It was ringing now.
This time it was the old friend of whom he had lost track,
another new stranger brought back into his life, Margaret
Torres. She was saying: "I'm a modern woman, I'll come for
you. Do you usually get a corsage?"

"I'm allergic."

"Okay, did you used to be a joker? Let's just decide: We
were sort of friends one night. We have a daughter. Now
that's settled, so what next? How's about lunch?"

"It seems to have gotten complicated."

"Beautiful," said Margaret Torres, "we can agree on that.
Now get on with it."

Did she mean get on with his life? Get on with something
else? Get on as if Amanda hadn't happened?

Confusion was embarrassing for Dan Shaper. Under the

circumstances, he wasn't sure she should be inviting him, or even that he should invite her, or that any partaking of food together at all was appropriate. They had gone many years without breaking bread. Yet what was history had now become current events. It did not give him an appetite for a good home-cooked meal.

Nevertheless, she invited and he accepted.

It was like a date, she said. She would swing by and drive him there; no corsage, however; it was not a formal occasion. "Just you and me?" he asked, and she answered: "Do you always make the conditions? I'm the hostess around here."

He accepted anyway, thinking: It was the least he could do; thinking: What a guy.

She rang the buzzer and he came downstairs. She was grinning, slightly disheveled, hair blown this way and that, like a person who had driven a long way, and she smelled of soap and some light perfume. He seemed to remember, in the distant past, patchouli; no patchouli now. The grin suggested that this was all a good joke. She opened the door for him and then ambled around to the driver's side. "Seatbelts," she said. He obeyed.

Their business together was a long time developing and now, she seemed to be suggesting, was as good a time as any for Dan to deal with it. He didn't know what she wanted to deal to him. He did not take offense. He did not defend himself.

For their date, in this time of changed women's relations with men, so different from the time when he shoved her into the bathroom and leaned her up against the wall, and later pushed her down in some sort of backyard-slum city garden, so that there were twigs caught in his hair and scratches on her back, and maybe neighbors spying from their windows upstairs. . . . Well, now she just nicely drove up in her eight-year-old Honda Civic, so practical they are, to "call for" him.

"We have to do something about Amanda," said Shaper.

"We have to eat, too," said Torres.

This can't be, thought Dan Shaper, none of it is allowed. It can't be. It was.

"Yes, sure, let's have a bite," said Shaper to Margaret Torres.

"You always did like being fed by a friendly person."

"Did I? Doesn't everyone?"

She must have fed him twenty years ago. The memory had long been digested away.

Margaret now lived on Diamond Street near Market, a few steps from Castro but in the state of being called "the Castro," the urban village of gay high life and AIDS. She parked in a driveway—"Hey, there it is, not that you really need to know"—to give Dan Shaper a chance to say, I wanted to see your house, as if he had been waiting to visit the lady with an ailanthus tree in the alley, dusty shopper newspapers piled up at the door, and baby pictures inside of the daughter.

Margaret looked up and down the street. She was giving him a chance to take things in. "You can get hepatitis in Mexico from licking your lips, they use shit for fertilizer cuz they don't know what else to do with it and the dust blows and you lick your own or someone else's face . . . The dust blows around here, too. See that guy on crutches, sometimes he can walk holding his partner's arm—"

Shaper said, "Yeah."

"I used to see him on his way to the gym. A really hot body—buffed. That's our neighborhood, still cruising along. They're my buddies. . . . So you're ready to come inside? It's a mess in there."

"You don't know me," said Shaper.

"Yeah, but my mess. Your mess is *your* problem, Dan."

He knew he had to do this and there was a point to it. He

expected dust, unhung paintings leaning against walls, and Amanda's room, one she had recently been a child in. There was a stringy fuzzy-wuzzy bear, the puffs and wool knotted and crisp from kisses, dried saliva and who knew what else. There were sketches by Margaret of Amanda and other drawings, stick figures in crayon, called "My Mommy." There was a bed with a sideboard and cartoon paintings by Margaret in red, yellow, green, blue. There was evidence of a mother and none of a father; perhaps that was Margaret's point. The piled pillows, the closet door ajar, the red-painted stepladder; ancient history, recently finished.

In this house another past had left its shadow. Margaret said she awakened in the morning early, on Wall Street time, no further explanation. Then she coughed, shrugged, found no good gossip or fidgety business to make her friend more comfortable than he already was not. Because it was on her mind, she asked: "So what's your expectational backdrop about Amanda?"

This was not the flowerchild speaking. (*Wow, you're a really spiritual person.*) Shaper imagined a guest in the form of a stockbroker, someone heavy and noisy, and noticed a corncob pipe above the fireplace, a trophy left behind when the personal investment counselor account was closed and he was sent off for good. "I'm finding my way," Shaper said.

"Okay. You don't know what you're doing. You're becoming a normal parent. And?"

"I don't know what she wants. I know what she *wants*, but I don't know what's right. She wants money."

Margaret looked too happy for what she was saying. "You didn't do what was right for me—"

"How could I?"

"Yeah, that's a point, but you didn't. Financial-wise is only part of it."

This complaint from Margaret, and she slipped it at him

like a joke with no punchline or a punchline with no joke—
not really a complaint—needed to be set aside just now in
favor of the actual business before him. "What should I do?
To try to keep her away from the Browns? What about
D'Wayne? Is there coke or speed or—"

"LSD, Ecstasy, peyote, grass, *banana* peel, didn't we play
with them all? Maybe not all."

Shaper said soberly, trying to call her back, "Probably not
all, though some people did."

"You didn't know about me. I had a kid, couldn't just
go out to the Fillmore on weekends unless somebody baby-
sat. . . . You want to help her now, Dan?"

Margaret watched for a proper answer. Shaper thought it
obvious and for once he didn't speak the obvious. Margaret
looked to the Frida Kahlo poster on her wall, crippled Frida
Kahlo with the eyebrows like a caterpillar—"Mrs. Diego Ri-
vera, Victim of the Patriarchy"—and murmured, "Okay, she's
a big girl now. She's what we call an 'adult,' Dan. In fact,
Dan, when I think about it, Dan . . . Hey, she's about how old
I was when you . . ."

He knew what they did.

"And I not only had my eyes open but I was responsible.
Didn't think I was, but actually—look, she's healthy, great
teeth, she's tough enough to survive and find you even if I
wasn't too hot on that idea—she's *alive.*"

So she was. And Margaret too was alive and laughing,
laughing, saying, "I must've known what I was doing, otherwise how stupid would I be? And I'm not, am I? Would you
have knocked up some stupid chick, Dan?"

He laughed, too. He guessed he'd better, but in fact he
liked her and it was easy to like her, just as if they were old
friends. Nothing like a shared child to establish a link between
two strangers, more effective even than a shared joint.

Unfamiliar with the rules of engagement for a newly commissioned parent, Dan Shaper considered how to ask Margaret Torres what she felt about prostitution as a career choice for their daughter. Okay, sexual surrogacy with cardfile records, but put Gyro, Shari, and D'Wayne into the equation and that was how it added up. Okay, part-time. But still! He just blurted it out, emotion surging up, having no precedent for tact in the matter.

Margaret listened. She waited for him to finish. She said it was a poor idea, in her opinion, limited tenure, no long-term future, unless you considered it sexual surrogacy, in which case it was helping others plus raking in taxfree income, the IRS not being hip to what one of her fellow Wiccans called "fuzzy logic," a matriarch kind of thing. . . . And then there was the question about whether the Yerba Buena Foundation was a proper environment for therapy. Margaret noted that the factor of taxfree income could fuzzy down on your definition of "proper environment." That was a plus, but it could also be a minus. But then, for a young woman just starting out, with so many opportunities to explore her roles in life as she went along . . .

"Do you hear what you're saying?"

"I'm saying it, am I not? So I guess I can hear."

Margaret was bored with the niggling detail of this discussion. She had confidence in Amanda's ability to make her own decisions because, after all, Margaret was the parent who had raised her. Amanda was raised to be a warrior. Amanda was Diana the Huntress.

"I wouldn't mind being on different wavelengths," Shaper said, "except I do mind. This is our daughter."

"*My* daughter. A grown woman you don't even know. Not in common, there's no comparison, Mister."

At this point Shaper could not find the right words, if there were such.

Margaret came to his rescue. She wanted to be helpful.

"We can agree, Dan. . . . D'Wayne is a bad idea for my daughter."

My, she said. *My* daughter, said the woman with the canoe she liked to ride like a bronco out among the tides and breaking waves of the Golden Gate.

It occurred to Dan Shaper to ask Margaret, "You disapprove of D'Wayne?"

She fidgeted. "I just *indicated*. I'm a mother. What a silly question."

"So you could answer it."

She stopped fidgeting and grinned into Dan's face. "You get monotonous sometimes, you know? But he is kind of cute, isn't he? A big strong dude like that, wouldn't get monotonous?"

He remembered the wildness now. The file was open and things came back. He remembered the beatnik mess of her room, the sweat and glow of her forehead, the fun which was more than he counted on, so that he called a halt after their last tussle and scramble together on a bare mattress with mattress buttons bruising his elbows. And her canoe, she liked to paddle it out beyond the Golden Gate to watch the sunset and fuck in the rocking boat. Death by drowning, he thought at the time; icy ocean, crabs attached, still eating their eyeballs as their bodies washed back toward land.

"Do you still have the canoe?"

"Different one—aluminum. It's my kayak. I take it out sometimes. It's so quiet and lonely in the Bay. The waves slap me around, Massage by Neptune! Did you ever go out with me?"

"I don't remember," he said. "No."

"Taking chances didn't used to be your strong suit."

"But it was yours, Margaret."

She let a space of silence wash between them. She was giv-

ing assent to something, agreeing with him and with herself.
"Didn't make too much difference in the end. We're both
here now."

Dan Shaper was at the age of taking chances. Maybe it was
only the age of not giving a shit. There had been changes
since he first met Margaret in the final flush of that happy
Aquarian goofiness. If he got AIDS, he would probably live
as long as he was supposed to anyway. If he drowned in Margaret's canoe, it would only be a clean way to go. The busy
rustling crabs belonged at their place in the great chain of
being, in this case at his eyeballs. If his life became unquiet,
it had been quiet too long. "I want to do things for our daughter," he said, "do it right. I was sure I'd never be a father."

"So you want to start by doing something about
D'Wayne?"

"And Gyro's place. That life."

Margaret's eyes filled; something shifty about the tears and
the cool gaze behind them. "You got some catching up to do,
Mister."

He wished he had agreed to paddle out beyond the Golden
Gate twenty years ago. It was odd to remember what he didn't
do, a vivid flash to what didn't happen, their managing to light
a joint in the wind, his rolling thumpily onto her in the narrow bow, not even thinking of the trouble if a paddle fell into
the sea; and the effect of the memory was a pressure in his
crotch, a young man's imperative now, *now.*

He had some catching up to do. Down, old buddy.

There was no smell of casserole bubbling in her house, no
steam rising from ancestral soup pots; there may have been
takeout sushi from Ta-ke Sushi waiting in the refrigerator,
but the evidence was not clear. Glasses of white wine from
an already opened two-quart Eden Roc bottle were poured.

It turned out that the plan of Margaret Torres, once they

were inside, didn't center around a meal. Dan Shaper presented his suavest exterior and slapped his belly to quiet the rumblings therein. "I guess you don't eat a lot of lunch," he said, genial, bogus, and she answered something she thoroughly believed: "Yes." Then he apologized for the implied criticism of her offer of lunch, or in this case "lunch," by imparting some of his learning in popular biology; to wit, that rats who starve live longer than the sleek fat ones, it was a scientific fact.

"And fart less," said Margaret Torres.

Small talk, each of them seeking a zone of comfort in the other's company.

Then they were again discussing their daughter's career choice. Recently, previously, they had been discussing their daughter's apparent or suspected choice of pimp.

Something else was happening which they did not discuss.

Factors and elements and complications were not brought into the picture, but they were present anyway.

When she took hold of him, with a gentleness that confused him as much as her anger did, he let and they let their bodies make love to each other. Just as in the past, there was no judging of consequences; had they learned nothing?

She seemed to have learned something. Sweetness.

"This doesn't mean . . ." Margaret remarked sleepily, and she was not going to ask if they were a couple, as they had not ever been in a past which was so trivial they could hardly remember it. It had turned out not to be trivial. "This doesn't mean, dear, I'll do anything to help you solve your problem about D'Wayne."

D'Wayne? The problem was about D'Wayne? It was only Dan Shaper's problem about D'Wayne?

Someplace in the universe, even during the age of Aquarius when Margaret Torres and Dan Shaper had planted their time capsule, some folks must have had a better sense of what real problems were.

"You got to admit, dear. He's a hunky guy. To coin a phrase. . . ."

Shaper paused to seek a reply or comment, but then he heard soft snores and they were not his own. The great chain of being was clanking and rattling. Traditionally it had always been, hadn't it? the man who indifferently fell asleep after lovemaking, selfish or at least self-indulgent, while the woman lay awake, staring morosely at the ceiling. The world had turned topsy-turvy. Her breath warmed his cheek.

Eleven

850 Bryant, receiving and transmission depot for the justice system and intricate police workings. Here was the emission control center of a great city, where disinfectant fought nervous sweat in the elevators and would win the battle of noxiousness if reinforcement didn't arrive like the triumphant Marines, piss blaring. Sometimes a perp in custody would let go as a statement of protest against the system, or because of withdrawal from medication, or simply as a witty comeback against nitpicking accusations of chickenshit felonies. Occasionally more exotic aromas floated through, women whose hard use of their bodies interfered with taking care of their bodies.

Over there, detained at the metal detector, probably just dropped by to deal with a couple dozen parking tickets, lounged the renowned Harry Harness (not his real name), DJ at the Tray Frisko-Disko, an all-star retro joint in the Folsom leather district. Security loved to strip-search Harry. And alongside, muscle-swollen arms crossed in the language of superior contempt, stood Harry's keeper with Harry's saddle, stirrups, and straps folded unobtrusively out of respect for the sensibilities of felons who might not be free to disco for awhile. Essenemma, Harry's keeper, wore a tiny pinched smile at the ignorance of these security wage-earners, who were so unclear on the concept—Harry *liked* being strip-searched.

And now Ferd Conant, Esq., ambled into Dan Shaper's vicinity with his toes-out gait, like a fat man although he wasn't really a fat man, not what you'd call obese, greeting his court interpreter colleague with a most cheerful: "Hey, Danny-boy!"

Shaper winced. Sometimes one trivial annoyance could be as bad as other trivial annoyances—paper cut, stubbed toe, sand in the lettuce, *Danny-boy*.

In most of the world, money ruled. At 850 Bryant, the Hall of Justice, a special power was granted to those who lacked money, but this power only gave them the right to fart, piss, and shit in public, and to be knocked around for it, occasionally to knock others around—but only when nobody was looking—and to wear their tattoos, ponytails, and prisonyard muscles with abject pride. *Take no shit, then die young and punch-happy* was their philosophy. Don't tread on me any more than you feel you must.

Ferd Conant, Esq., attorney with a specialty in court assignments, was one of those who fed on the power that came of powerlessness, and when he said Danny-boy to Dan Shaper he was indulging in his right to annoy, play the living paper cut against a man who had been recently in his employ for a Guatemalan burglar with poor language skills. Crafty Ferd well understood, having been called Ferdinand the Bullshitter in chambers by an irritable judge, how a denigrating nickname could denigrate and therefore give pleasure. "So hey, Danny-boy," he repeated, having noticed—shrewd legal mind—that it made Shaper pinch up around the mouth and tighten around the eyes. Ferd considered his role in the court system several steps above that of some worn schmuck who happened to speak a couple of the perpetrator languages;

among the dregs down here on Bryant, Ferd was a dreg aristocrat.

Did crime pay? It paid Ferd Conant (it also paid Dan Shaper). Ferd made a steady living, even if the Chinese or Korean chicks, trotting around on their lovable waif legs, the Cindy Lees and Brenda Kims, fresh out of Golden Gate Law School, scorned the court-appointed advocate role and only competed with veteran Ferd until they could be recruited by a firm needing to beef up its equal-opportunity credentials. Sometimes Ferd tried to help a teenie-tiny Asian lawyeress by pointing out that to delay the trial, get witnesses to come downtown and then ask for a stay, usually tuckered out both witnesses and complainants, making it easy for their court-assigned asshole to get probation or even a dismissal. He would lean close and intone, "A stale offense is an unpunished offense, take it from the old tiger, Brenda," and she would lean away—"Thank you, thank you"—while he was thinking, Binaca, fucking Binaca, should have sucked on my Binaca. Plus: that was Cindy, not Brenda.

Was Cindy or Brenda grateful? Did they even care about good representation, the American way? Shit no. Just "Thank you" in that tinkly little voice of theirs, and then they wouldn't even trot across Bryant for a burrito, much less give him a chance at their cute Asian poonie-tangie.

"Danny-boy! Talking to you!"

Dan Shaper was watching the ruckus as his buddy Alfonso Jones, the detective, tried to bring a little order into the San Francisco headquarters of Blind Lady Justice.

Alfonso was playing shepherd to the band of prisoners coming around the metal detectors. It was a "Food Not Bombs" crew, arrested once again for illegal feeding of the homeless in Golden Gate Park, chanting "No, no, we won't go," as if we weren't already long out of Vietnam. Their

salt-and-pepper goatees, ponytails, and Mercedes hood or-
nament tattoos somehow failed to achieve the desired criminal
or homeless look—"Yes, yes, on the contrary, you're going,"
said Alfonso, winking and shrugging at Dan Shaper; no time
to chat now. Alfonso hated to spend any time but the oblig-
atory appearances with Ferd Conant.

Among the Food Not Bombs group were irate women
having their purses searched, another insult from the patriarchy. When activists carried methamphetamine—only a sup-
position—it was for purely medicinal purposes, to keep their
weight down; carbohydrates, a diet of Golden Gate Park
baked beans from the communal pot, tended to send the cal-
ories straight to the butt, no matter what some nutritionists
said. The noise of a mass arrest, remorse transformed into
fury and a swearing of revenge—like carbohydrates changing
into fat in order to embarrass diet experts—hardly interrupted
the steady beating of waves of fear, neediness, and civic control on the shores of 850 Bryant. The Food Not Bombs people, yes, they did have a look—Hell's Angels for Jean-Jacques
Rousseau. There was a Carlos the Jackal, there was an Ortiz
What's-his-face. Remorse was not detectable in this disturbed
air. Few normal San Franciscans around here. These were
citizens of the republic of distress.

The nonobese man who had hailed Dan Shaper, Ferd Conant, Esq., adjusted his sandy hair over the pink place on his
scalp with skilled fingers. He could do this without a mirror.
He was waiting for a lull. "The ones with the tattoos are
always, don't you love it, the defend-dance."

"So they say," said Shaper. "But then there are all the dope
lawyers."

"Money launderers," said Ferd, "future defend-dance. You
wait and see, buddy."

He was the expert. Ferd dwelled in the sheltering monolith

of 850 Bryant, if not in the building itself, at least in its shadow among the bail bondsmen ("Call Jerry Barrish, Open 24-Hours All Day Every Day Except Mother's Day"), bars with the traditional martini glass in purple neon, quik-chow joints, furnished rooms by the month, week, day, or hour, in buildings left over from erratic stabs at redevelopment—what more could a man want? Well, and public transportation was easily available, plus the church or other place of worship of your choice within easy striking distance. "I got my little burrito situation," he pointed out—literally pointed, tilting his chin in the direction of the Tecate Tavern, "I got my won ton situation, I got the other ethnic garbage down pat. The Arab place, love that hummus, a five-minute walk away, if it's nice weather, which it always is, 'cause this is California. What I need to find, like any other guy, what I really need is a twice-a-week regular little twat situation. Something in a Filipina would do, they're so clean."

"Shouldn't be difficult, Counselor." Shaper wasn't going to mention the Yerba Buena Foundation.

"But I'm hard to please, haha, get it? *Hard* to *please?*"

Shaper got it.

"So next time you're driving across town to the Foundaysha-roonie, how's about some company, okay, Danny-boy? No secrets from me, are they? Plus, I'll bring you a medal, a nice piece of bronze from Anthony Enterprises, where I get all my trophies. You deserve it—a daddy! First daddy there ever was, bet it feels like."

Shaper stared.

"Aw, don't mind me, I'm just grumbling. Probably wouldn't mind a nice little pretty daughter myself, aged about twenty, and miss everything comes before, the snotty noses, the hassle. Probably I'm just jealous. Probably I'm just a lonely downtown guy never settled for the basic truths make life worthwhile."

It wasn't Shaper's place to disagree with the attorney presenting his alibis.

But Ferd's eyes, oh, his eyes gave Dan Shaper trouble. Normally, interpreting for a client, Shaper looked at mouths and eyes to see lies forming, evasion, smugness in a street hood claiming he didn't forge the check, it was money correctly paid in a dope deal, or the little blond secretary whose purse he snatched was a regular client of his. Shaper listened deadpan and watched the lips grow dry, terror replace the Latin charm of a Mission-district creep who knew he might walk if the little blond secretary got bluffed out of appearing in court. But the little blond secretaries had grown tougher in the nineties; all that assertiveness training had infected victims throughout the Bay area, and the corner boys from De Haro and Capp Street and the Projects weren't keeping up with the latest trends in victimology. Shaper liked reading eyes and mouths; they even helped to find the correct English word, such as, Yo, I broke into her apartment to sell her stuff, besides it was raining on the street and I needed to dry off, man.

Ferd's eyes were a more difficult read, not because he was more sophisticated, a graduate of Lumumba Law (night), adequate speaker of American. Ferd's eyes seemed both lidded and lidless—Shaper hated to look at them. They gave nothing back. It was a wasteland in there, a scrub expanse of nada. It was a spiritual strip search that dirtied the searcher. The pinched mouth, a damp plump mouth, not diagnostically small, not clinically misformed or genetically compressed, snapped shut in the rest position after speaking. It gave something. When opportunity beckoned, it opened and issued spite. In fact, now that Shaper thought of it, reconsidered his peerings, the mouth amplified the spite veiled behind Ferd's eyes. Ferd Conant travelled on this fuel. He converted it into bile for longer journeys at 850 Bryant, in courtrooms, and in the noisy glassed jail spaces used for consultation between perp and legally mandated counsel. Ferd had the power of a creature in many ways like a human being.

Dan Shaper wasn't overly fond of Ferd Conant, Esq. Fondness was not a quality Ferd evoked in his fellow attorneys, in court officials, or in the lost, defeated, and probably guilty souls whom, in the blind search for justice essential to the correct working of a democracy, he represented. If Ferd had an old mother he cared for, a crippled sister he supported, no one knew about them. Perhaps Ferd was an anonymous saint. If such turned out to be the case, Dan Shaper would have been happy to cry, "Mea culpa."

After nearly twenty years of experience with Ferd, Dan felt safe that the guilty shouting of Latin expiations would not be called for.

Ferd grinned and commented on his most recent client. "So Danny-boy, the asshole offed his girlfriend, which maybe was his right, but then he killed the baby, which wasn't even his—how's that for no class?—also shot her dad when he yelled, 'Don't.' Closed down the whole family, but then didn't kill himself. That boy has no finesse. When I got assigned, I said, 'Hey, cop a plea, you're not nuts,' but no, he insisted on self-defense—against an eight-month-old? Shit, so now he's got a death sentence bothering everybody, tie up the system for years." Shook his head with appreciation for the folly of others. "No fuckin finesse, man. Least I'm out of it, some Cat Lick pro bono handling the matter."

Ferd looked as if he had been born in a back elevator at 850 Bryant, suckled in one of the burrito joints across the street where perps, jurors, and cops picked up extra salsa at the counter, schooled in corridors where negligent entry-level security people opened handbags and passed briefcases through metal detectors. If he'd ever seen a tree or a bird, there was no evidence of it in his expression; take that back—a gull or a pigeon had dropped beige poop on his shoulder. Like the rats and birds of the justice terrain, Ferd adapted for adequate survival. Though born Catholic, which he liked to pronounce Cat Lick, he was out of there. He had finesse. Sometimes, because man does not live by burritos alone, he took lunch at the Chinese joint he called "Numbah One," as in: "Hey Papa-San, bring me the Numbah One Special, okay Papa-San? And where's my tea?"

He would just sit down and yell for it.

Finesse.

Now he brought up the group murder case because he wanted Shaper's attention, curiosity always improving the tête-à-tête. This Hall of Justice person, who seemed to know about Amanda and the Yerba Buena Foundation, might also tell Shaper something he needed to know.

"Danny-boy—"

He hated being called Danny and Ferd knew it.

"Danny, so there's this story about your newfound baby, right?"

"Where'd you hear what?"

"Dad of the Year, am I right?" He brushed the flecks off his medium-weight summer suit. Traces of the really gray dandruff stuck hard, as did the gull poop, due to essential oils.

"Where'd you hear that?"

"Danny, you're asking questions," Ferd said. "S'like the secrets of the confessional, Danny, I don't have to tell you." Shaper waited. "How about we grab a burrito, practice your Mexican, we can fill our tummies plus have a nice comfortable two-way conversation."

Crossing Bryant, Dan Shaper sunk in morose desire to be elsewhere, Ferd Conant hungrily sucking from his Marlboro—

California's smoking regulations were hard on those who sometimes obeyed them—they were both trying to figure what they would be getting out of their burrito date other than a post-luncho drowsiness. In case words failed him, which they seldom did, Ferd's sour cigaret smell kept the universe at a distance. Dan Shaper walked and stood a long step away. Ferd thought it was timidity, quailing before the strength of a superior being; actually, Marlboros illegally inhaled in the men's room turned an ex-smoker's delicate stomach. "You don't like 'Danny-boy,' I keep forgetting, so how about 'Dude?'" Ferd inquired. "Cowboy? I gotta have a name for my favorite buddies."

The front teeth were jagged, needed repair, needed abrasive cleaning, were brownish. "So Dude, I was telling you, and I guess you want to hear, 'cause otherwise you would be elsewhere by now, about your little problem which you already have fully in mind except for being taken a jot and a tittle by surprise that your colleague Ferd is . . . cognizant, Dude?"

Clever Ferd, always looking to score. Since Ferd was often assigned to defend candidates for sanction to whom Dan Shaper was assigned to interpret, they had worked for years in a state of remanded collegiality. Ferd enjoyed their vocational association, closely resembling sociability; Dan Shaper, less so.

Therefore Shaper told Ferd, you're a little slow this time with your bad news; and Ferd responded to Shaper, so many datums to cover, Danny; and Shaper suggested to Ferd, wish you'd call me something else, say Mr. Shaper or even Dan. . . . "I keep forgetting, Dude. But if there's some way I can help in your family-type situation—"

"Lend me some money?"

"Always kidding around, aren't you, Danny? No, but advice, counsel, legal precedents, blood tests if you're into stuff, or a DNA or urine—naw, that's not relevant, though, hey, it smells like a pretty pissy situation. A deal I wouldn't wish on anyone, Danny, even if I didn't like you. Getting sued for all that past child support. Or the boyfriend—who knows?"

"I don't have any money."

"Yeah, but a judgment. Against future earnings. Your estate, if you care about that, Danny. For example, just talking legal: have you got an airtight will?"

Shaper was not making Ferd Conant his beneficiary, his executor, or his lawyer. Ferd knew that. He was just enjoying spinning the wheels and watching Shaper squirm.

"You got your little schvartzer situation—that D'Wayne. Plus . . ." Ferd's face contracted in the way of a man who wants to make his eyes twinkle. "Dark-haired gypsies have captured your home, but you must not flee. You must hide, then creep out in the night and strike back." He leaned closer as a security guard pushed between them, holding a cellular phone to his ear, hurrying away with his burrito in the styrofoam case. "Or you could let me find someone to strike back for you?"

"No."

"Suit yourself, so now you're stuck with feelings, Danny-boy. *Feelings.* Personally, I travel light."

Even the weight Ferd carried was no real burden. His clothes required no laundry because he found them at garage and yard sales (only buying the clean items) and then just dumped the woolen jackets and such when they got too dirty. What seemed to others greasy, frayed, and spotted with food didn't necessarily seem that way to Ferd. He saved a lot on laundry, which would cost more than the apparel. (His shoes and socks, however, were one-owner items.)

When garage sales petered out during the wet San Francisco winter, Ferd experienced what others called Christmas Depression because the luck of the draw created him not to be Robert Redford. Even without snow, sleet, ice, and arctic winds, Ferd's San Francisco winter was a time of deprivation. He felt remorse about the griefs of the ages. He felt poor. He would have dined on commodity food from the USDA if he could have stood in line for it without being recognized. Some asshole spots his lawyer eating from USDA cans of meat just one step up from cat food, that ungrateful asshole thinks he doesn't have top legal representation. Lady Justice, although blind, might smell something rancid in the Spamlike breath of an attorney explaining, "My client begs the court to acknowledge that he was fully engaged playing his guitar with the Mariachi Combo when the alleged purse was snatched." Endearing eccentricity took the Lumumba Law (night) graduate who was forever not Robert Redford only partway to a reputation for tousled charm and success.

Ferd had an offer and the offer hovered there in the grit-blown South of Market air. Dan Shaper sat over his styrofoam plate, poking at his unwanted lunch. He was at one and the same time a new father; a new father of a daughter putting herself forward as a therapist—the distinction between surrogate and working girl would be invisible to most fathers; a new father whose new daughter's significant other, his son-out-law, could be defined as a pimp (not that anyone was prejudiced, we were only dealing with facts here); a new father whose easy old life was turning hard. He didn't want the burrito, the sour cream, the guacamole. He didn't want the pains he felt.

Ferd Conant had a suggestion. Today was no different from any other day—he was full of ideas. Something could be done about Danny-boy's problem.

To begin with, D'Wayne could be taken out of the picture.

Arrangements could be made.

D'Wayne as a factor in the equation—no sweat.

Ferd was Dan's man, if only Dan asked. Favors, the providing of same, went with the franchise, so what was he waiting for? Not necessarily to take D'Wayne totally out, not to abduct Amanda and deprogram her (anyway, whoring doesn't qualify as a cult), nothing necessarily fatal, but maybe, just a sec, follow me here, from D'Wayne's point of view . . . decisive in making a decision which would be a reasonable option, hey?

What *was* Dan waiting for? An Act of God when he needed an Act of Ferd?

"That browbeaten guy reaction of yours ain't sufficient enough," said Ferd.

Shaper took this under advisement. He decided on a sarcasm defense. "You mean insufficiently approaching a near-satisfactory level?" he inquired, pointing his chin a little, reminding himself of the times years ago when he used to get into fistfights (late adolescent hormones, Basic Training with a bunch of bubbas). Now he was merely striking back at redundancy.

Ferd crossed his eyes. It was another of his favorite tricks. He used it to get laughs from the courtroom, followed by shy downcast winsomeness when judges reprimanded him (Ferdinand the Bullshitter). It was really grandstanding; it was lightening up, in his opinion, a stroke of that old-time boyish Robert Redford levity. But after tucking his eyes back where they belonged, he added, "Don't fuck with me"—heavying up a tad—"I'm not some ordinary night-law ethnic goofball here, Mister Tourette. I dated the Extension Session Homecoming Queen, got to marry her for almost a year; I think I might have an insight. I'm operating on your behalf as I could do, Danny."

Shaper interpreted regularly for Ferd's clients, drunken pickup drivers without licenses or insurance, purse-snatchers on PCP, shoplifters, "the crème de la flotsam," as Ferd like to call them in his elegant mode. No use tipping over a source of income with harsh words or the poke in the face he deserved. Shaper had read someplace that unexpressed longings led to artery blockages; if this was true, it was Friday before a long holiday with all the freeways down in his swollen heart.

In the shadow of 850 Bryant, amid the muck and fumes of a great city, the wasteful exhalations of grief and chagrin, Dan Shaper watched a word unspoken by Ferd floating toward him like the motes in his tired eyes. Ferd avoided pronouncing the word, though it was one he liked to roll around in his mouth, exhale with relief, a cloacal gas over Ferd's justification for his life. *Monies.* A word of art.

It seemed that projections about the future could cause action in the present as stringent as actual events in the past, for now Ferd was saying, "In this life, there's likely a question of monies comes into things."

By what procedure did Ferd learn about Amanda's request for "monies"? He wanted to do good and do well, serving the history of the future. Ferd's desires explained why; it didn't explain how. Though only a lawyer (but with excellent pipelines) and destined never to be a judge (far be it from him), Ferd was a man who planned to finesse matters on behalf of his clients and Ferd Conant, Esq. "You see how helpful a person is willing to be," he asked, "if only the other party is willing to be helped?"

As a mere intermediary, a mere arbitrator, a mere ambassador of goodwill, a mere concerned observer, a mere close friend and colleague to Dan Shaper, a mere public-spirited citizen in general, Ferd Conant gave the client a choice from the menu: line one, take D'Wayne out in some way yet to be specified; line two, apply monies as a calming agent for Amanda and D'Wayne. He was prepared to be the executor of Danny-boy's will.

There was a darkness around Ferd's eyes as he waited for answers, oily smudges of fatigue. Maybe it was only a case of phlegm, inadequate kidneys backing up and pooling under the windows of the soul. Dan Shaper was finally learning to give no answer when he didn't have one. Even in late middle age, a diligent person can continue the lifelong learning process.

"You don't do anything, there might be trouble."

"Maybe it can't be avoided."

Now even Ferd Conant fell silent. He had never learned to do so, but sometimes he just did. He listened to what Shaper had said. Perhaps he felt some kinship, a fraternal yearning. In all his life of jabber and poke, grab and feel smart, he had been trying, trying to evade the trouble that came of doing nothing but these things with his life.

Twelve

The giant muscle-builder, six and a half feet of Angry White Male, shaven head, tiny ears flat and pink against the skull, thin hedge of beard clambering trimly around the jawline, black tee shirt, black jeans, black boots with black socks, tattoos on biceps with tee shirt pulled up to make viewing of tattoos more convenient, was called Mr. Harvey Kurtz, not Officer Kurtz. But he looked too much like a criminal enforcer not to be what he was—undercover cop. Obvious enforcer or obvious undercover cop, an assemblage of body parts from the mesomorph gene inventory. On the springy balls of his feet he loped toward Dan Shaper, drawling, "Hiya, Cowboy."

"Hey, Harvey! Didn't see you."

Harvey laughed. "That's a hella whopper, Cowboy. *Every-body* sees me."

"Impossible not to," Shaper admitted.

"Or smells me. So just walking around, being visible, olfactory on occasion, I'm like one of those plywood police cars off the highway. People notice me, they slow down." He paused, grinned, slid into his fake southern drawl. "See me, they go *real* slow."

Harvey did southern, Harvey did gay, but what Harvey did best was stroll the city, stalk the city, looking as if bullets would bounce off his chest, knives would turn into limp gobs against his chest, and somehow, so far, for inexplicable reasons, he was still alive. His rank was detective. He was not an equal-opportunity hire.

"There you were with your best friend," said Harvey.

"Who's that?"

"Ferd the Goniff Lawyer. Watch out for that lad, Cowboy."

Dan Shaper wanted to make the obvious unnecessarily clear. "Not my best friend—"

"Just asking."

"—and you know it. He's no friend of mine or anybody."

Harvey spread out his great slab hands in a gesture which started out to be explanatory, as in, *Hey, whatever*, but instead, because of meat and muscle, seemed threatening. In this case the exercise was merely emphatic, leading to one of Harvey's keen logical deductions. "So if he's no friend of anyone, ain't no reason why you couldn't be the bestest of the no-friends in our boy Ferd's entire life."

It was too complicated. Dan laughed, Harvey laughed, and they slapped hands, Harvey nearly knocking Shaper off balance; then strolled away in opposite directions without a backward glance. Just another incident of male bonding at 850 Bryant. People hurried past, some nodding in semirecognition, some balefully glowering, and some, like Shaper, working here, moving in the dense justice element like sleepwalkers in the dream-crowded city of infraction.

Had Shaper and Harvey just concluded a conversation? It seemed so to Shaper. But sneaky Harvey, his good friend, was back already—how'd he do that? It was like a wily surveillance. Not yet finished with Dan, he nudged him away from the elevator, which anyway was stuck someplace upstairs between Bad Female Notions and Felony Unprovoked Assault.

He had matters on his mind, burdens, and Harvey always found it best to unload his burdens. The shaven skull seemed to swarm with black ants teeming out of the scalp where bristles of hair were striving through. A similar situation prevailed at the sideburns, where sideburns would be under normal circumstances, and where the narrow fringe of beard traced the jawline. The bristles were striving through. The eyes seemed edged in black. The long creases down his cheeks were black, shadowed. The head was enormous, too, although muscle-building isn't supposed to enlarge a bony braincase. The skull with its heavy ridges would give a threatening impression of Homunculus Americanus when some future archeologist dug it up. Harvey's ears curled neatly against the head, small and pink, or perhaps normal-sized, misfitting this enormous man with their untoward delicacy.

Harvey's dark bristles, smudges, lining of eye sockets were warning signals. The delightful giant could be dangerous. Even if he seemed dangerous, as giant shaven-headed muscle-builders often do seem to be, he really was. The ants were not ants, the black creases down the cheeks were not knife slashes, the eyes were sharp, merely healthy and well-lubricated, very similar to other human eyes. Harvey was not like other human beings.

"About your son-in-law-equivalent, that D'Wayne—" His hand was on Dan Shaper's shoulder.

And it was shrugged off. "How'd you know?"

Harvey performed a massive rolling of shoulders. "Wanna be like that? . . . Word get around. Telemouth on the street, Cowboy."

"How'd you know I have a daughter?"

"You got a son-in-law-equivalent, you best have a daughter, don't you?"

Shaper had been trying to assimilate the facts of his life,

letting them simmer, get ready for the great world, but evidently Gyro, Shari, D'Wayne, Amanda herself hadn't needed as much time as he did. In a city, things tended to go public. At 850 Bryant, even what wasn't public was public, private sufferings along with private pleasures. Someone Dan knew had been found tied to his bed with his underwear stuffed in his mouth—straight guy, a judge, supposedly straight—and it had been hushed up all over town. It had been hushed up in Pacific Heights, Cow Hollow, it had been silenced on Russian, Nob, and Telegraph Hills, the word had been kept a secret from 850 Bryant at the hub of the circle. . . . Maybe the judge's wife, who was weekending at their house in Tahoe when the unfortunate incident occurred, didn't know yet. Although folks felt it their duty to deplore the matter in detail, they lowered their voices to whispers—"*and his underwear was, you know, unclean.*" They swore everybody to total discretion, close friends and relatives excepted, on a need-to-share basis.

So it was only logical that Harvey, as a good buddy, would know what Ferd, a bad buddy, knew. An experienced court translator should have learned not to be too surprised by anything. Shaper wasn't that smart, but at least he had learned not to show it by stamping his foot with frustration. A small advance toward the achievement of aplomb.

"You want to do something about this?" Harvey asked.

"You been talking to Ferd?"

"I asked you a question, Cowboy."

"I asked you one, Harvey."

Again Harvey rolled the massive shoulders in what normally passes for a shrug, *Dunno, whatever,* but on Harvey Kurtz it was a kind of Richter Scale humanquake. "He talked to me. You know, I don't prefer dealing with Counselor Conant."

"What's the business he's talking about?"

Harvey shook his head. Far as he was going to go just now. Maybe Ferd hadn't revealed the possible gain for Ferd. "Your turn," he said. "Wanna do something, want my help?" He squinted down at Shaper. Harvey was smart and he could bully, but in this case he couldn't read Dan Shaper and he couldn't bully him, either. He decided to try persuasion. "This sort of peculiar for you?" he asked. But then spoiled his stab at advanced California compassion: "Cowboy?"

Dan Shaper didn't like being called Cowboy or Big Guy or anything else he was not. He was trying to be himself for Gyro, Ferd, and Harvey, user, adversary, or friend; he was looking for who he was for Amanda. The past was not what it seemed to be, was not even the past; he needed to reconstruct it. The future was even more shifty and impermanent. He wasn't ready to explain himself to anyone; this included Harvey, whose good opinion he valued.

"No," he said to Harvey. "Yes."

Harvey sighed. "Well, that certainly covers the explanation part, doesn't it? Okay. Back there you asked about Ferd."

"Did I?"

"Don't tempt me, pal. I suppose Ferd's p.o.v. is he thinks he could work protection for Gyro and Shari, pick up a piece of it somehow, run the money down to Mexico, though he'd prefer Canada—hates the sun, gets rashes, pimples, you know—that Anglo skin, gets those little melanoma-type cancers. . . . He'd like some action and some money. How would I know? But I don't think you want to deal with him."

"So tell me something else new," Dan said.

Harvey, laughing, socked him hard enough to make him cough. "Pope's still dead," he said. "Don't matter which one, it's always a true fact."

Street level at the Hall of Justice was a nice place for a

private conversation. Squeaky carts were wheeling court documents to elevators that might arrive in due course. The wheels should have been lubricated, but like Justice, they required divine intervention or a little grease. Addicts stumbled by with their unlit cigarets in their mouths, heading for the outdoors where California law permitted them to suck nicotine. Dazed defendants, irritated jurors, bustling lawyers, grieving family members washed back and forth past cops, guards, bailiffs, clerks, legal aids. The crowd eddied around Harvey Kurtz, who had the ability to create a space for himself and his company. In the environs, many individual personal concerns sought relief; they kept the noise level high.

D'Wayne might listen to Harvey. Something about Harvey's shaven head, his mean eyes, the badge in his pocket, and his not giving a fuck when he wanted to lay something down might make D'Wayne pay attention to Harvey. But Harvey was saying, "I won't give you no high fives, Cowboy, if you off him in one of those irate revenge moments. Proud Father Shoots Boyfriend, Sells Story to *National Enquirer.*"

"I won't do that," Shaper said.

"Thinking about it?"

"Dreaming, maybe, like anyone would."

"Dreams don't mean nothing. I used to dream things about that Josie I liked—guy in tassel booties and a stolen fuck-ass Pontiac. A *Pontiac.* She left in a *Pontiac.* Like it adds to the disgrace."

There was the thoughtful silence of old friends letting a strip of cool air settle, letting them breathe and settle down. Harvey wanted to get things clear, which didn't mean they were clear. They weren't. He rumbled and cleared phlegm and coughed and said, "See what I can do, maybe."

Shaper felt something like love. He was learning about the matter from the bottom up, on the ground floor of 850 Bryant. He might not have had a lifelong daughter, but he had a longtime friend. Inevitably it happens that a person can use one of those. Harvey was composed of the essential ingredients besides their history together—patience, attention, willingness to waste time, but a strict putting of limits to how much shit would be taken. "Man, that Ferd, still gets me, you so lonely for company you have your lunch with him?"

He was embarrassed to nag a good old pal. "You lonely, Cowboy, feel the need to share your guacamole, impart a concern, you can always do business with me—don't you know?" The giant detective, Harvey Kurtz, and Dan Shaper, the less tall, less powerful, less imposing court interpreter, liked each other. They weren't exactly a Mutt and Jeff couple, or a Butch and Sundance duo, but they had their own shared ways of defanging the snakes of 850 Bryant and feeling better after a nourishment squat together in one of the neighborhood take-out/eat-in joints. When Shaper told Harvey he felt safe crossing the street with him, Harvey looked embarrassed and shy, as if he hadn't quite gotten through his head that now, fully grown for a quarter of a century, he was six feet six and not yet shrinking. "So what about the Tenderloin?" he asked. He prowled and sprang on his outside running shoes as if he knew enough; the bullet head, a projectile braincase, understood the necessary; the little tattoo on the right biceps ("Josie") and the earring in his left ear which balanced out the tattoo—they all seemed to indicate control of matters.

Yet Harvey, at least in the off-duty world, believed himself to be shy. Folks are complicated; go figure. On duty, he made up for his inner shyness with a smell-my-breath, pig-eyed, chest-poking way of posing a question to the suspicious party on duty; no one ever pitied the inner shy Harvey Kurtz. This Harvey was a plainclothes detective whom even the dumbest chief couldn't rationally assign to go undercover, but chiefs weren't rational. Despite tattoo, earring, prisonyard muscles, the ropy bodybuilder's stance in his black tee shirts from Gold's Gym, he was not a good candidate for unobtrusive slipping into taverns and insinuating himself into drug rings. As a massage-parlor bouncer, he might have done okay. Harvey was, citywide, a known quantity, fingerprints all over him, no place for wires. When he wanted air and space, it was freely offered.

"An intercontinental ballistic missile could stop me," shy and modest Harvey Kurtz admitted. "Maybe a runaway truck. . . . Dan, I'd wear a vest except I sweat too much. Come on. How do you want to handle D'Wayne? Brother Alfonso thinks—"

"Alfonso!"

Harvey beamed, eased, having gotten Shaper's attention, having thoroughly surrounded it, a three-hundred-and-sixty-degree encirclement, saying: "Alfonso—so relax. It wouldn't be racist for the schvartzer to take out the schvartzer. We could do it legally, sure we could find something on this D'Wayne, but then heck, there'd be all the paperwork, the local news at peoples' dinnertime."

"Everybody knows. I might as well be on the front page of the *Chron*."

"Didn't you hear me say relax? Your *daughter*, Cowboy. Think about being a good father, will you? So let's say we do it another way, it's clean, fast, definite—it's satisfying."

Sure thing. To break D'Wayne's leg would be satisfying. Just hearing the chiropractic crack would be music to the ears. Maybe giving a person's daughter drugs, getting her pregnant, never mind she wasn't under any obligation to get pregnant—

"How about the neck?" Shaper asked.

Harvey did a little prissy small-mouth thing. Considering his general looming in any space, he could get away with a

CPA moment. "N-no," he mused, "a bone or two, leg, arm, oh kneecap I suppose, definitely not the neckbone, though. Had all the burrito we can stand today, let's get a beer, except I'm on duty. Coffee okay with you?"

The redwood outdoor picnic tables indoors at Java-Java Jamboree shifted on the splintered floor as the heavy feet of beveraging masses trampled it down. JJJ's furnishings seemed to have escaped from a barbecue in a downtown park. Harvey spread himself wide to disinvite other company at the table, not that the jury-pool people, the bail workers, the relatives and beloveds of perpetrators were anxious to join him. He was saving room, and then Alfonso Jones came up, not as big as Harvey but big enough.

Alfonso's uniform, now that he had left the police, was a suit with the jacket rolling up above his high round butt, the seams stretched at the arms. Some men get thin with pain; Alfonso, after the death of his son, had put on heft. He ate. His kid, aged fourteen, had been hit in a driveby in Newark, New Jersey, where the ex-wife had moved to be close to her parents and far from Alfonso. He ate, he ate too much, he ate what wasn't good for his health, but he still worked out and there was avenger strength beneath the flab. He couldn't take care of his son anymore. He could insulate his body with oil, cradle it in starches, fill the time with grease meals where he might forget himself and stare at nothing or forget himself and let his mouth work at artery-clogging banter. Remembering his son, there would be many a smile before Alfonso could rest.

He had taken early retirement and hired out as a security expert, working alongside Richard Hongisto, the former sheriff and police chief who had gone into the growth industry of protection, defense, armor-plated evictions, and escort for celebrities. It was distracting and profitable; what could be better? "Hey Harvey," said Alfonso, taking in all the black, the tee shirt, the jeans, the general blackness of costuming, "you still trying for movie star image?"

"Don't need it, Alfons'."

"Which one? That old Bronson guy—"

"Charles."

"Yeah, Chuck with the happy face. Or one of the other white ones. Charles Norris—"

"Chuck."

"—yeah, one of those chucks."

Having signified, he slumped onto a redwood bench. Harvey was busy with the agenda for the meeting. "We know it's not a movie our cowboy's in, man. So—pass the cream and sugar, please."

Alfonso slid items including Heinz Ketchup and Gulden's Mustard on their lazy-Susan base across the picnic table; said, "How you doing, buddy?" to Dan; folded his hands in front of him. He had glossy grayish fingernails. It seemed they were ready to do business.

Harvey was busy bringing Alfonso up to speed. "So I was saying he don't want Ferd on his side, even if the alleged lawyer has a law degree—"

"Yeah, but the only higher education he was good at was watching *Jeopardy*, he studied with Perfesser Vanna White. Have I got that correct?"

Harvey grinned, stretching the black wrinkles in his ruddy skin. "Sometimes you're a upward-mobile asshole, may we stipulate? Now that you're in the private sector?"

Alfonso grunted hunh. So be it. "That's highly traditional among selected representatives of my background," he said in stately cadence. "Same reason I develop this"—patting belly—"department. Harvey and me been talking, Dan, you know what I'm saying? So you don't want to break the goniff's skull . . . D'Wayne . . . that's an actionable offense my former brothers on the Force might consider a felony."

"Threatening him . . ." said Shaper. "What if he's not rational?"

Harvey flicked a malediction at Dan Shaper, fingernail against front tooth. "So we break-a da leg widdout no t'reat, huh boss? Hey, let's get practical. Some things you got to do keeping up with the times—"

"And the Statue of Limitations," said Alfonso.

Harvey extended his arms to Dan Shaper. "You're a living Statue of Limitations, Cowboy—civil contract employee, no pension plan, not a heck of a lot of ambition."

"Sta-choot," Alfonso muttered resentfully. "That's so racist, Harv, making fun of my elocutionary skills. We gonna take care of business or not? Don't we want to make sure our new daddy here build a sense of trust with his new daughter?"

It was nice to have friends to consider solving a person's problems with a stroke of easy, forthright, illegal violence. All three of them, in their lines of work, had been impressed with the results of harming the body parts of adversaries. If you got away with it, okay, assuming no conscience; if you didn't, very complicated results could follow, conscience not entering the equation.

There was silence and the consumption of beverages. It was a silence filled with foot thumps, high-pitched laughter, whispers from a nearby table.

Dan Shaper was trying to feel grateful and eased by the presence of caring old friends, beveraging together.

Alfonso's breathing was audible, due to too much recent weight; Harvey's breathing was audible, due to little starts of insight, decision, and rejected alternatives. In the picture, besides D'Wayne, there was also Gyro, there was Shari, there was even the daughter to reckon with. Shaper's breathing was probably audible, but he wasn't listening to himself. Three pals together, two of them figuring how to solve one pal's problem, the one pal not certain it was a good idea to do what they might figure out, all of them feeling their way. Three pairs of shoulders huddling over a picnic table brought indoors, one skinny white guy no longer in the bloom of youth, one black hefty, and one sport of nature giant with ants rushing out of his brain, boiling in turmoil over his scalp.

Maybe D'Wayne needed something done to him, something serious, maybe that was the only way to get his attention, and maybe Gyro was heading onto the same terrain. Shaper had heard it said that murders didn't really solve problems. Would it make Amanda different? Would he feel differently about Amanda? Was that what he had to do?

Hey, not to exaggerate. A couple of hustlers who are treated to broken bones isn't mass murder. At most, if a failure of skill led to accidental death, it would be serial killing in the low numbers. And the fact that Dan Shaper knew them personally would take it out of your normal serial-killing mode, where blind rage tends to operate without any real moral direction.

Now, that felt better.

"Cat got your tongue?" said Harvey.

"Wandering off someplace in the haid?" asked Alfonso.

One of them had paid and they were in the street, crossing where there was no crosswalk, lawbreakers through and through.

"Maybe," Harvey said, looking at Alfonso, "we should just do what we're gonna do and this other party here don't have to know about it."

Dan Shaper heard Alfonso's labored breath, his grunted, "Do what's right . . ."

"Deniability, you hear what I'm saying? It worked for Richard Nixon."

Dan Shaper kept step with these bigger men. "It didn't work for Nixon," he said.

Alfonso seemed lubricated by the possibility of action, Harvey Kurtz getting history wrong, Dan Shaper being his usual stupid pedantic self and correcting him; Alfonso's voice had some of its old relaxed caramel ooze. "Takin' under advisement, my man, takin' under advisement."

They halted to watch the flotilla of black-and-white police Fords heading out to their posts across the city. It was like watching the Genovese fishermen heading out into the bay in crab season thirty years ago. It was a shift change. Shaper wondered why grieving women weren't standing on the shores of Bryant, waving to their men—well, the Fords contained grim or laughing or bored gum-chewing cops who required no grief from their wives. After the cars swept down Bryant, Shaper heard the scratch of small animals in the grasses a hundred and fifty years ago here on the flats where the Hall of Justice now stood. He smelled Yerba Buena, the pungent weed which gave the village its name before there was a San Francisco and an 850 Bryant. He saw the footprints of the Indians who wandered the scrub, this overgrown murk of marshland and sand washed in from the Pacific, blown from the dunes by ocean winds. Without dowsing, he believed there might still be a freshwater spring below 850 Bryant, cooling its way beneath the jail, heading toward the estuary. A father of the father of the father (and of a few more fathers) might have hunted on this place between sea and bay where now the son, drawn back from Baja, wailed in a holding cell, waiting for a Spanish interpreter to be assigned by the court. If his ancestor carried a dream-catcher, it had not caught the nightmare of 850 Bryant.

The sun shined on Dan Shaper, and Harvey Kurtz and Alfonso Jones, and on Amanda and her mother, too, and Gyro and Shari, and the worried and angry and officious who moved in and out of 850 Bryant, just as it shined on the Indians, the grasses waving in the breeze, and the small animals of the marshland a century and a half ago. But no matter what anyone said, trying to be easy, relaxed, open, and accepting in the proper new age oneness with the solar system, it was not the same sun. Not the same air, not the same earth, not the same water. Not the same web in the dream-catchers.

We're still finding our way, thought Shaper.

"Hold off," he said aloud to Harvey and Alfonso, but he wasn't sure they were listening to him. They may have been hearing their own histories echoing in the exhausted late-afternoon air of the Hall of Justice.

Thirteen

Munn hunn?

He wasn't sure he recognized the voice on his answering machine. "Where's the mon, hon?"

Of course he knew the voice. Who else could it be?

Dan Shaper had a problem, two of them. Problems came with company, increased and multiplied. Maybe Ferd Conant could help, or not; or Harvey and Alfonso, or not; or Shaper could help himself. Or not.

Why not, he asked himself, he told himself—it was not a question—why not accept the privileges of age and follow the threads where they led. Let the spool unroll.

She left a number, but when he called she seemed surprised. People telephone when they are ready; the recipient isn't necessarily ready. Harvey visited perps at home, at odd hours, hoping to find them in their underwear, surprised, therefore thoroughly available. Something hidden behind the debris of her history tumbled out of Shaper's mouthy daughter, just one word, part of a language others spoke and she herself was now trying to practice. "Dad."

"Yes." *I'm listening.* He was also practicing, trying to be more intelligent than he thought he was.

"Dad. I'm not a good girl. You know that already. Probably I'm a bad girl."

Don't be so quick to judge.
"But I'd like to be a better one. I could try."
One wrong move and she'd hang up.
"Thanks," he said. She too was afraid of wrong moves. He could hear her breathing. "I wasn't a father at all. Maybe we could study together."

She was laughing, not a bad laughter, an easy and full of complicity laughter, and he could imagine her thrusting her hand in the air and giving him five, like an acquitted client. Neither of them would have been able to say so little and so much except by telephone.

But he wasn't planning to give her money until he knew where she was going, what she was doing with it, why she asked him for it. Isn't that the responsibility of a father?

Gyro beckoned, Gyro invited. Gyro took pleasure in showing familiarity with the word he pronounced "oppa-tunity."

Opportunity knocked for Dan Shaper at six o'clock during the early nightfall of a wet November evening, bringing gypsy-cooked lamb bones with thick tattered chunks of meat, roasted potatoes, a cajoling man's cuisine for another man. Shaper saw nothing better than to ride along until he found where he was going. He needed to eat before bed anyway, didn't he, to help bring a night's good dreamless sleep into his life? He had fallen into the habit of preferring no dreams to good dreams, which tended to end in disappointment.

It couldn't hurt to hear Gyro out. Gyro demanded time to present his opportunities. It was near winter, the day turned dark early, and there was no overflow of fun in San Francisco, contrary to what people believed, unless you personally were having some. Such was the law of life everywhere.

At the moment Dan Shaper was not really old, merely

slightly soiled in middle age, a veteran. He had positioned himself to live rent-controlled, with Social Security, his IRA, his savings, and his freelance court work, and he would hurt nobody unless it was strictly called for. He could go from Spanish to English and back again as long as Alzheimer's held off and the market in petty crime remained firm.

At dusk on rainy early evenings in winter, when the streets were desolate and his spirits low in sympathy with the weather and season, it was true that he imagined a loving hand resting on his arm. It would have been reassuring at this stage in life, it would have been nice. But still there were always the noodles with mystery fish bits at the counter in the steamy Vietnamese joint at the corner of Eddy and Leavenworth, and the hooker whom he answered in the affable neighborly negative ("Not tonight, thank you") when she asked if she had what he was looking for. Mystery castaway flesh after mystery fish bits were too much protein for this man using his fork to twirl his hot noodles into his spoon.

He was embracing his years. What he sometimes preferred was to enact bachelor hanging out in a bar called Thank God It's Friday, which changed its name every morning, Saturday, Sunday, Monday, and so on through the whole of God's good week at the bottom of Nob Hill. Sometimes with Harvey or Alfonso, but usually alone. He could do his business and his relaxing, some limited beveraging, and not tire himself excessively or become a stumbling target as he stepped precariously through the Tenderloin on his way home to bed and no known dreams. Under streetlamps, oily spots gleamed on Ellis like little ponds; pokeweed in sidewalk cracks, ailanthus trees in the alleys, this was his ranch and homestead.

It hadn't worked out as planned. Amanda emerged from the nondream, followed by Gyro, followed by the Yerba Buena Foundation and its jolly crew—he had thought his path was marked. A person had a right to a normal devolution, that was the whole idea of Social Security, but surprises seemed to be smuggled into the program.

Dan Shaper used to be mainly lean beef, head to heels, with just enough added bilingual thinking stuff to keep the apparatus moving, minimal gristle and regret in the mix. Beyond his professional skills in Spanish-English and English-Spanish, he downloaded the meat computer in his head of its nostalgias, losses, and dodged responsibilities. He avoided country music. He preferred nice clean ganglia. He programmed himself for no more surprises. Personally, Shaper didn't want to be quick and responsive, but fate seemed to be demanding responsibility from him. He was no longer running the whole show. Now there came, as if a new daughter wasn't enough, business appointments with unclear purposes, plus lamb, olives alongside the roasted potatoes, a little dish of feta cheese, and the varied sodas.

Gyro intended to lay out the oppa-tunities. Just presenting options, no rush; but a little hurry was called for. Probably Jesus had given Gyro's ancestors the privilege of logic that slipped like good gravy down the gullet.

"Hey hey, big guy," said Gyro.

"Everybody's got a name for me these days—are you going to call me that?" Shaper asked.

"Only when it seems right. You want to get laid, big guy?"

Stony face was the ticket here, Shaper decided.

"You know I'm the pal you need—you know it." Gyro's forehead with its deep ridges seemed to lean off his skull; he could smile and glower at the same time, another gift of his inheritance. "You *know* it, Dan, but the problem is, you don't believe."

"That would be a problem."

"Beeg problem, chico. Also you need a change—" He

jabbed two fingers at Shaper's chest. "—in there, *there*. Only thing is—"

"You already said. I don't believe."

Gyro felt things were moving forward. The forehead creases loosened. "But you're here, right?"

And he was. What Gyro hadn't figured out, and Jesus in his careless generosity didn't provide details, was whether Shaper was going along because he really wanted to, he was ready to go along, or he was having age of maturity nightmares and the nightmares lasted all day. These were mere details. Gyro wasn't obliged to know everything.

Gyro's bulbous forehead must have frowned its way through history. Perhaps the Neanderthal look came of furrowing, deep thoughts with no easy resolution, rolls of bone and cartilage, dense flesh. Gyro's life was nonstop festival after that casual divine promise, a rash moment in His time of trouble, probably due to stress. There were also worries on Gyro's personal Via Dolorosa. "When the wind is right," he said, "I can hear your sighs, big guy. And if I just squish over here"—into shadow with a fringed lamp behind him—"I can see little drops of sweat."

They were lounging, conversing, in the family apartment upstairs at the Yerba Buena Foundation. Whatever happened elsewhere, this was the Brown place of retreat. Shari, barefooted, watched like a good child allowed among the grownups. Her father smiled and she deftly picked up a roasted potato, using the index finger and the opposable thumb. Gyro looked on with pride. She followed with an olive, then a piece of lamb. Not a drop of dripping fell.

One of the many things Gyro loved about his daughter, her career of pleasure-giving well under way, was that she had ambitions and dreams. She reached. She was her father's daughter, this always reassures a man. The Yerba Buena office files kept three-by-five cards of names, addresses, telephone numbers, pet names, favorite kinks in order of preference, favorite colors, favorite girls (facilitators, therapists), and astrological signs. Soon it would all be on computer. As a clinical and scientific institute, the Foundation both treated and studied the God-given dilemmas of horniness. Shari had suggested reserving an adjoining room to serve women, it was only fair, and her dad had an answer for that: "Not so fast." Neither yes nor no; the parental role is to urge caution upon the children. "Let's see if they bust us first."

Thanks to the tradition of science, freedom, artistic expression, and software innovation in San Francisco, Shari believed capable legal counsel was available at cost-effective rates. "Dad! Eleven fucking law schools in the Bay area!"

"I didn't know that. How'd you find out?"

"I guessed." And oh, the girlish giggles. She could just twist any man around her little finger, especially if that was his kink, and this was the case with her doting father. Let Dan Shaper learn from example.

A curtain was stirring, a gentle breeze blowing through the room. The curtain was a heavy brocade, so the breeze must have been more like a wind. Someone was there; then someone was not there. Shari had been wearing Farmer John overalls, stiff denim standing away from her body, nothing much underneath, maybe nothing at all, and in the instant of her disappearance Shaper saw nipples, a few hairs around one of them, bare upper arms, no shaving there. And then a moment later she reappeared through the brocaded curtain in a long white gown, mystical attire, transparent, a silken slip underneath. She was still barefoot. She was a fast-dressing and undressing, fast-moving person who seldom stubbed her toes.

Along with this virginal bride's wardrobe, further revelations of Shari manifested themselves: a smile with a little nick

at the edge, a kind of dimple, and it seemed as if her armpits
had been shaved in the ninety seconds of her disappearance,
raising the winsomeness quotient. Shaper thought: Women
are magic, and what men do with them is delusional. Here
was Shari, an immaculate animal, smelling of musk and female
fluids, not omitting sweat, and also a ghost of a girl, an idea
of one despite her mocking of Dan Shaper. It wasn't because
she belonged to the privileged Romany nation that she could
do these things. She was of the temptress tribe. Lilith was
Margaret Torres' name for her. She had that skill which
Shaper wished to resist, knew it was foolish not to resist, knew
an older man should learn to resist, of hanging in his sight
like the motes that hang dreamily in the eye after a hot light
has passed.

"I tell you what I'm after," said Gyro.

"Sure like to know," said Shaper.

"Can I construct a gypsy out of nothing much? Can I con-
vert a Gadjo to a Rom?"

"Not sure I understand you," repeated Shaper.

"Can I turn an accountant into the fartherest thing from
an accountant?"

"I'm a court translator, not an accountant, so I'm not sure
this applies."

"See?" Gyro asked. "The failure of song in your poor life?
A court translator and you don't know you might as well be
an accountant? See what I'm saying?"

Further argument would be insufficient proof of anything.
Fact was, Shaper needed to proceed someplace and maybe
where Gyro was leading would do. At this time, his remaining
time rushing at him, Shaper had something to get over: himself, what he was, what little he would be in future. And a
process they had in common: Gyro too intended to get over
something.

Not himself, however. Dan Shaper stood there as an irritating obstacle to Gyro Brown's being the Gyro he loved so well. Jesus and Gyro were ready to fulfill Gyro Brown; the forlorn Gadjo needed redemption. And then lo, Amanda came along, and she was an unexpected blessing, like Shari, like the other gifts in Gyro's life of festival. A person could never tell when things were suddenly ready to work out just fine.

While Gyro felt he was on the right road, a dizziness of times past and future was interfering with Shaper's smooth passage.

"Personally, do I get in trouble?" Gyro interrupted himself (Shaper just happened to be present while Gyro practiced the spoken language). "Liddlebit sometimes. Look at this Gadjo I disputed. They decided it was Misdemeanor Homicide. Personally, it was a good-riddance homicide, and besides—"

"You have a Friend."

"I told you. I'm a businessman, what they call individual entrepreneur, convince people of things. The manual jobs, the gardening, the lower classes got them all locked up. My Spanish isn't good enough to be a gardener. You could probably qualify, Dan, liddlebit younger. But today's yard work, don't you hate that leaf-blower noise?"

"I don't see you as a labor-intensive person," said Shaper. "Selling cars?"

"More like it. . . . You had a fight and somebody died?"

Gyro considered the question. Did he owe Dan explanations? Did he want to relive a sad involuntary experience? He sighed. He had started the discussion and he should wrap it up. "There's this mental condition, Gypsy Pride Sundrome. You don't treat me right, it turns just like that"—snapped his finger against a front tooth, spraying saliva—"just like that, into Romany Rage. And then everybody but Jesus got to watch out."

"I will," said Shaper.

"My good friend. I wouldn't harm a person, never, but this Gadjo when I was young, impetuous, you know? begged to differ when I was sure of my opinion. I hit him once. He begged to differ in our way of discussing something."

"All you did was hit him once?"

"The brain bucket where I touched him up didn't hurt. What tended to kill him was when the *pavement* hit him. All I did was beg to differ, same right he had, only who knew the pavement was down there waiting?" Gyro's eyelids fluttered shut in recollection of the impetuousness of youth, a time when accidental misdemeanor homicide seemed to be in the cards. Again he sighed.

Of the quest for understanding and absolution, however, there was no end, no statute of limitations. "Your person-type individual has a pain, it doesn't last, you get used to it and you die, but Jesus?" Gyro's shoulders sagged as he considered all the burdens Gyro did not have to bear. "Thinking about it for two thousand years. That must seem like forever."

Gyro appreciated spiritual things, such as a smuggled Cuban cigar or the little curve of a woman's back just a handprint above the ass. His misdemeanor homicide experience wasn't so much a spiritual thing as a golden oldie, a nostalgia trip. The stupid Gadjo stopped doing everything as soon as his head hit the pavement, period, that was all. Sharing the memory with Dan was part of getting to know a new friend and colleague. Gyro treasured friendship, loyalty, paternal pride and guidance, such as his for Shari, Dan's for Amanda—all the emotional stuff that can mess a man up if he's not careful. It was complicated. Gyro's renewed sighing took the different form of a deep relaxed breath.

"So what was it like?"

Gyro picked up the reference. He was pleased that his

breath didn't appear to the outside world like a yawn. Even relaxing, he stayed in touch. The wavelengths of Gyro and Dan were coinciding, sliding off together into the universe. You mention homicide, folks perk up, they get curious, and Gyro was ready to fill in the details. "It was like this bo-teek prison, see."

"Where?"

"Near . . . California! What's the difference? Wanna check on it? Should be called Abuse 'n' Stuff, for juvies, you know? Most places, I have a good time. That place, I didn't." He meditated upon the memory. "No, not a festival. Even a nice juvie joint isn't the best environment for a boy. I nurtured grief, Dan. I objected. Little did they understand my heritage—"

"Your permission," said Shaper. ". . . made the nails sharp."

"I told you? Well, then you know. So they tried to fuck me over but I fucked them over back, so to speak."

He had these finicky little ways of adjusting his speech. When possible, he avoided the fuck word. Even with Permission, Gyro chose to keep up standards.

He spread his hands wide, showed the dark pink palms. "Black is beautiful, white is beautiful, everything is beautiful, but Romany is beautifullest. And among the Roma people, who is the most beautiful? Let us say Shari Brown, let us say Gyro, because a princess and a king—"

"Today you're what do you call it, royals? Since when?"

Gyro gazed upon his friend from a great height of explanatory patience. "My friend, you have been chosen from those among us who might have been chosen but were not." He stopped to glance into the full-length mirror near the doorway. He was tall, he was grand, he was satisfied with procedures so far, he didn't want to push too hard. But the mirror confirmed his previous statements and implications. "Make yourself at home, Dan. Mia casa, sua casa—whatever."

Dan Shaper still needed convincing. He was of the skeptical, rational, materialistic persuasion, a victim of narrow ambitions and catabolism. He was a reluctant beneficiary of unmerited bounty. He was unready to see Amanda make her life with D'Wayne, Shari, and Gyro. He wondered what the ignorant father was doing here and why he felt as if he had awakened from desolate sleep into a different sleep of vivid dreaming, dread, and need. It was very like nightmare.

"To my apparent understanding," said Gyro, ready to admit possible flaws whenever foolish nitpickers pointed them out, thereby disarming his adversaries, "I might or might not be a person of the gypsy race or orientation. Does it matter? I get the folks' attention. I got yours, big guy."

"To my apparent understanding," Shaper said.

"All the evidence agrees. That misdemeanor homicide, frexample, who else but a blessing from long ago could put the fix in, get me a cell by myself? So can we get on with the program, okay?"

"If I knew what that is."

Gyro spread his arms wide; he opened his heart to Dan Shaper. "Let understanding grow like a flower," he said, "big guy."

"Please don't call me that anymore."

The deal-closing smile faded; the heart was instantly less open. "What? Why?"

"I'm not big."

Gyro looked puzzled. Between friends, what did bigness or nonbigness have to do with a name of art? People don't understand each other, even during moments of intimacy, and that's why they need court translators or Jesus.

Smells of sun-baked tar and wetness wafted from the roof of the Victorian; a brief shower dropping on San Francisco.

Gyro opened the window to the rain, took a luxurious breath, ahhh, and the rain stopped. He turned back to Shaper with a shrug. He had these powers, although this time the heavens hadn't interpreted his wishes correctly. He *liked* rain; oh well. He wiped his mouth with two broad hairy fingers, cleaning out any words stuck to his lips.

Wasn't it nice of Gyro (noblesse oblige) to give Shaper this space for regrouping?

"Jews, you know," he said, suddenly remembering something, startling Shaper, and then paused to let the point sink in. He had a way of bringing silence to bear, giving his words weight. "Jews are a lot like Travellers and Travellers are like us."

"Travellers?"

"They call them Travelling Men in Ireland, except there are the women and children, too, and they used to be tinkers, if you know what I'm saying, horse people, mechanics, like us. But Irish. So they're blond, freckles, red hair, blond hair, blue eyes, probably cancer if they stay in the sun too much, and they're really Catholic, Catholic all the way, my friend—not like us. I'm not blond. Maybe some of my kids might be."

"? ? ?" Shaper asked without speaking.

"Ones I never laid eyes on. Like it almost happened to you. Smell that little drizzle, love that fresh air." Gyro peered out and gestured to the clouds. "Fog," he said, waving it in. Then he explained that his family had left tinkering a generation or so ago, left the trading in cars and the sharpening of knives. They had not lightly ventured into the crowded profession of special therapies. Before founding the Yerba Buena Foundation, Gyro had tried buying commodity food from various Indians for cash, died milk—"

"Died milk?"

"Commodity milk in the big blue boxes. Beans in the sacks.

Tomato paste in the gallon cans, so they could barter over to the necessities, like six-packs. The BIA doesn't distribute commodity six-packs, so your Native Americans have to rustle up mucho wampum if they want a couple Buds. But it was too much hauling, man, carry the commodity shit down from the reservation—it's always in some miserable scrub-scrabble place—and then find a warehouse in town, open up, look for the retail single mothers, know what I mean? So now we sell commodity ass and the guys can haul themselves over to the Yerba Buena and I don't have to encourage alcoholism among a troubled indigenous people." He shook his head. "More beneficial to society, you know what I'm saying?"

"You've been busy."

"I got responsibilities, man. I did a smoke shop, I did diet pills—bordering on the illegal around that time—had to put soup and pita in the mouths of my family. That's what it's really like. We lived in a doublewide, Shari just a bundle of diapers those days, but I wanted something more sporty. Not just for her. For me, my family. Unscrew the wheels and you get a real house resting down on real estate. So she would grow up ambitious like her father. And I did it, separated the transportation from the housing. I'm proud of my people, the travelling kind, but that doesn't mean I'm not an American."

"Everybody is," Shaper said.

Gyro was on a roll and wouldn't be stopped. He needed Dan Shaper, he wanted him, he studied how to get what he wanted. He was busy doing so now. "This one patient came in, drove down from San Jose, Santa Clara, Pallid Alto, some-place like that, said he was a cyber something. Wanted to carry his surfboard in with him. We said the girls wouldn't go for that. What he need a surfboard here for therapy he's getting?"

"How'd it work out?"

Gyro was proud. "We got a therapist, told us she was a cyberbabe, kept records on her PC. I liked that, I'm not shy. Broaden my horizons. She knows how to word-process, compute, double-reverse back, but she's serious about work—let the client get that carpal tunnel syndrome in his cock." With the gesture that had brought the fog in from the ocean, palms open and wide, he welcomed new ideas, personal computers, a cyberbabe, carpal tunnel, whatever. "That's her preferred deal," he said.

Confusions crowded into the room along with Gyro and the breath of fog. Shaper's life had become a mystery which he didn't mind not understanding. Because of a careless and forgotten moment twenty years ago, a daughter had become a daughter to him. Even his own life was becoming interesting. There was a gain around here he had not expected.

Gyro knew he was helping things along. What gave a person soul was neediness, grief, that which is unuttered alongside the normal core of inaccessibility and privacy. When people fell in love, they embraced contradictions and they were a contradiction which was embraced. Shaper was in a fluid situation here with the Romany guy laying out his line of chatter. ". . . so we matched up the cybersurfer with the cyberbabe, and you know what happiness is, Dan?"

Maybe he did and maybe he didn't. For the moment (it seemed prudent) Shaper wasn't admitting anything.

"Like that black fighter said," Gyro confided, "you're alone at the time of doom. But like I tell you and tell you, keep on telling so you pay attention—you're with me and Shari at the time of oppa-tunity. Maybe your kid won't be alone at her time of doom, man."

Shaper wasn't ready to share Amanda with them. Jealousy had left his repertory of emotions years ago, after he kissed a woman who said she stayed home to do her taxes but her hair smelled of cigarets and then she said, well, a former boyfriend was passing through town and for old time's sake . . . Jealousy did no good work and he gave it up more easily than smoking.

Shaper could have continued at peace. If he had continued to do his job, sleep in his own bed, remember not too much and not be reminded by others, there would be none of this confusion. In due course he would be one of those who wore the bus pass on a shoelace around the neck. In due course his life might be lucky enough to be taken by a sudden sharp twinge on the Polk-19 and then nothing, nothing. Instead, he was moving around, things were moving around him, and events in the past returned to cause events in the present. It turned out that there were consequences, Gyro, Shari, and Amanda, her time of doom unimagined.

Gyro Brown was a studious conductor of the mental traffic crossing Dan Shaper's face. This is what Gyro talked about: Travellers, gypsies, and Romany people; repeating. Jesus; repeating. Grifting. Scams, cons, and unswerving loyalty to himself; repeating and presenting for further consideration.

Shaper thought about Amanda.

Shaper thought about Shari, Gyro, and D'Wayne.

Shaper, not unlike Gyro, repeating; thought again about Amanda.

"I can help," Gyro said. The skin of his face, pitted, formerly oily, reflected the light with a smoothness and gleaminess despite the marring due to previous hormones. He was engaged in product development, step by step. He raised his voice a little to break into Shaper's dream. "I hereby give you oppa-tunity," he said.

This was already established.

"You don't have to invest in the Foundation unless you want to, but contact with the lawyers and those judges, that's something you can do. Those cop friends of yours. We need a nice person around here."

Some might call such a person a front man. Shaper didn't think he qualified.

"Dan, your attention, please. Someone like you who can use a new interest in life, that's just what we need."

Shaper qualified.

"And besides the cash flow, my friend, the stream of income, I'm an experienced father. In my people we are loyal and devoted. I can help. Let me be of assistance about your child, and not hinder in any way, my friend."

All Dan Shaper needed to worry about were human problems, nothing more. He was a little rusty in the area of drastic developments.

"I assume you are listening carefully," Gyro was saying, but before Shaper could confirm his listening or his nonlistening—Gyro expected high-quality attention—one of those normal Yerba Buena Foundation disturbances interrupted them. The hall door banged open and no one said, Excuse me. A man was fleeing, trying to button his shirt, abandoning shirt, zipping fly, as he lurched toward the vestibule, his mind not made up, so that one hand was at the shirt and one at the fly and nothing productive was being accomplished. His reclothing instincts had gone awry. His flat-footed gait suggested a person who practiced isometric rather than aerobic exercising; passive isometrics under strict supervision. Black Barbara waddled in pursuit, her silence ominous. Silence was not a skill B.B. cultivated, but the door was open and shouting on the street, even high-pitched ecstasies in a room without sound-proofing, was a Yerba Buena no-no. Black Barbara's lips were compressed with her effort to obey the rules.

"You see our problem?" Gyro asked.

The face of the man thrashing his way down Pine was familiar. No grace, no finesse, no shoelaces tied.

"Look at him, embarrassing is what I call it," Gyro said.

Barbara, dejected, pulled her robe tight and retreated toward her room, carrying her whip close to her breasts in the parade-rest position.

"So if he runs to the police or the D.A.," Gyro said, and Dan Shaper was thinking, I know him, I know that bozo, hangs around City Hall, and Gyro was still making things perfectly clear, although it wasn't as if he had been merely hinting up to now: "We need someone can visit the Chief, the D.A., the people—someone got the friendly contacts, get in the door, say, 'Hello, what's doing, let's talk about your campaign fund. . . .' Someone on the order of, let's see, knows 850 Bryant pretty good, gets to City Hall, nice record of no personal felony arrests."

Oh shit not again was the thought that came to Shaper's mind.

"Someone I know he won't be wired, hand them the envelope, dust off your hands real nice and then go enjoy a burrito. . . . Hey, you could afford that Susie stuff, the Japanese raw fish, you can afford *cuisine* cooking for yourself and any number of guests, that be your preference, or just a nice relationship with family that needs a few things. That sound good to you?"

"I'm not listening to you, Gyro."

"With all my heart I believe you are."

"I mean this is not my line."

"You've got everything but the bad habit of you don't catch on to oppa-tunities. You got the knowledge and the need. Even a brain surgeon never did it before, the first time he cut a brain. But then he did. So you walk in, let's dream a little, to the D.A., you say, 'Hi,' you exchange the pleasantries, the Forty-Niners, the Giants, depending on the season—show him a picture you got in your wallet and he says, 'Hey, you got a real pretty little daughter there, so what's she up to in her life?' "

Before Amanda became Dan Shaper's daughter, she had been a friend of Shari, a young person Gyro took an interest in, a person who needed all kinds of care because she didn't even have the benefit of a disfunctional family. The founder of one of the world's great religions had personally guaranteed Gyro's winning passage through life. Therefore Gyro hoped for good results from his future colleague, Dan Shaper.

Outside, Barbara's dissatisfied client began a high-pitched keening, flapping his arms, his unbuttoned shirt snapping like a flag in the wind, as a tow truck lumbered away from the curb with his ticketed four-wheel-drive sport-utility vehicle. "Just picking up my medication, please! I'm a Commissioner! Fuck you! I'll sue your ass!"

The commissioner was pulling out all the stops, every known means of aborting an urban fire hydrant parking incident. The tow operator flipped him a backwards bird with a well-greased finger that must have enjoyed lots of practice in succinct response to verbal hot flashes. The Good Karma Towing Service, run by the mayor's wife's uncle, an equal-opportunity employer specializing in felons who promised not to do it anymore, was part of the machinery that kept a great city unclogged. So was the Yerba Buena Foundation. Gyro shook his head, trying to decide on a course of action, since the commissioner—actually, a *former* commissioner—had a right to expect no harm to his vehicle while he enjoyed a relaxing interlude of discipline and enema. Should Gyro pay the ticket? Was there someone he could telephone to liberate the four-wheel drive? "Sir," he said, making a point, "let me call you a cab." The point was that at present he couldn't be responsible for rogue tow-truck repentant felons connected by loving ties with the mayor. He hoped Dan saw the unfulfilled need here.

D'Wayne was on the phone to Yellow and Gyro was explaining to Dan Shaper that he could be helpful with little details like this, maybe using Harvey or Alfonso as auxiliary middlemen, but their overriding concern was a general bust on grounds of illegal massage parlor. Gyro would not expect Dan to eliminate all the nit-pickings. In American business, rough edges keep people alert while enough cash flow smooths away the deeper cuts. Just a nick or two in the knife sometimes. . . . Gyro was dreaming aloud.

Gyro was seriously dreaming.

Shaper was hearing a proposal about Amanda and employment, about himself; he wasn't sure what he was hearing. Gyro was content to let chaos fill the air, like the cry of a client caught on a bright afternoon in a double tragedy, disapproval from Barbara, his favorite whipper and evacuation-counselor, plus abduction of his vehicle by a tow enterprise in which he had no interest. What the hell kind of unclear on the concept tow service calls itself Good Karma?

Gyro smiling, nodding yes yes yes, a fluttering kind of encouraging nod while the process of understanding made its way through thick skulls and encumbering tissue. Gyro wanting to cap things off by suggesting that Shaper's share in the business would mean his later life could be easeful beyond his previous dreams. How about a little avarice on the horizon? Simple, wasn't it? Why did Shaper look for difficulties where none properly existed?

Poor fellow just wasn't used to being a father.

Gyro enjoyed everything about himself, including his Son of God-guaranteed gift of confident patience.

"I don't need another job," Shaper said.

"You're self-sufficient," Gyro said agreeably.

"I'm not inclined to do this."

"I can well understand that, friend. You don't prefer changes."

"I've gone along okay so far."

Gyro winced at the cowardice of it all. "And you didn't mind. You had your habits, but now you have other people to think about. So maybe things need to be done a little different. . . . I see you're listening. It's not going to be so easy."

"It's up to me to decide."

"Goes without saying! Free country!" Gyro stared down at him, amazed. How slow this fellow was. How dumb this smart court interpreter turned out to be, faced by new facts, facts which weren't new except to him. "Used to run so smooth," Gyro said, "Spanish, English, English, Spanish, then go to the Wells Fargo and cash the little check. But now—"

"My choice."

"Bueno! Muchas gracias!" Shaper's interruptions needed no acknowledgment, yet a generous person gave respect even when it wasn't deserved. "There will be rewards. But you don't get to wait and wait, Dan. How can you not do good things for your very own child and your very own person?"

The loss of prudence seemed to be part of the good things coming Shaper's way. He wondered if Gyro hurt people, did damage. It was a question. The question included subdivisions concerning different categories of damage—to the body, to the peace of mind, the soul, the future. Shaper was discovering something interesting about himself. At this stage in his expectations, the thought of damage didn't worry him. It was an older guy's version of a boy's idea—he was impregnable, would live forever. The new version was that life could end at any moment and it was no big deal. Concern for his safety was no longer a part of his repertory. He knew he was headed toward the end—so what?

The desolate former commissioner on the street outside was not cozy in the embrace of inner peace. His face wore the pout of a boy who needed to go potty. Distracted by his enema and his towed automobile, events which failed to bring satisfaction to a man who lived for suffering, he climbed into a Yellow Cab. Sometimes even masochists couldn't get all the trouble they needed. "Same time next Tuesday?" he called to D'Wayne, who had helped him button his shirt.

"I'll write it down, big boy," D'Wayne said, "and bye now."

Shari came out of the little room which used to be a break-fast nook and now served as her office, her hair up in a bun, a pencil tucked into the bun, her face clean of makeup. She had been doing paperwork. She hated to be disturbed.

"Anybody think of closing the door?" she asked. "Anybody else want to do some of the jobs around here?"

"Dan and me were having a discussion."

Shari figured as much. She forgave her father, she forgave Dan Shaper. She would have forgiven D'Wayne if she hadn't already noticed he was busy on the phone and didn't require acts of generosity at the present time. "So how's the discussion going?"

Shaper had no quick answer.

"You taking in some valuable information?" There was a brief battle of the silences. Shaper scrambled to say nothing and achieved his wish. Shari said: "Well, you know my papa. Hey, Amanda knows him even better'n you. Now you're part of the family, so everybody can do what's best."

All agreed that Gyro had plans. What the plans were . . . Shaper's head hurt where capillaries unaccustomed to swelling were swollen. He was learning that having a daughter could affect the sinuses of a grown man. Other people's undiag-nosed plans tended to impinge.

Shari pulled a wooden peg out of the bun so that her hair fell around her shoulders, this time not an action of girlish wiles, displaying gleam, conditioner, a recent shampoo. She was merely nervous. She trusted her father to manage things, but Dan Shaper wasn't entirely a known quantity.

And he was thinking: Even to myself I'm not.

The Browns might be a known quantity to themselves or not, and the question didn't really concern them, but they did want to know what they could expect from Amanda's father. They understood what they needed from him. There was a bottom line. They were sliding him into place. "Your expertise," Gyro said suddenly, pronouncing it *exper-ties*, "handle the contributions. I don't care how, your friend Harvey, your buddy Alfonso, the sweethearts I don't get to see on a regular basis of mutual respect, you know? Especially those ones dress like you and me, plainclothes. You're on good professional terms, am I correct on that?"

"That's not—"

"In case you wondered what you can do, that's what you can do. I see a headache coming on, I look for the aspirin. Take the pressure off *before* the headache, how about that? Like the condom, prevents trouble in advance for later."

One of Gyro's gifts was not that of finding the flattering metaphor. Human prophylactic was not the role Dan Shaper saw for himself as a professional man with a new daughter.

"What I mean," said Gyro, "I keep Shari out of difficulties at her young age, best I can, no more or less than you wouldn't want Amanda doing certain things and make trouble for herself. Best you can, I think you would do that."

"Is she part of the deal here?"

"Depend on you, young fellow."

Shaper didn't have the matter figured out. Shaper wasn't intended to have the matter figured out. Gyro was suggesting a business deal. Gyro was suggesting a way to keep Amanda out of their business deal. Gyro took pleasure in decalming a person like Dan Shaper, who had lived his calm life too long.

"How about you don't worry about a thing? Just carry the

money to certain people. Don't shove it at them, all you do is leave it on the table so they can find it, pick it up before the cleaners come in. They won't want to leave it on the table for some night janitor just spend it on harmful activities. No hassle, not complicated, and here's another part—not taxable to all concerned. That sound good to you?"

Shaper lacked a contingency plan for dealing with folks who had a repertory of proposals, all for him. His own plan had been to survive and do his best in areas where he knew the grammar and vocabulary. But now he found himself in this sparkly town of San Francisco with its distinguished bridges and its urban perfumes of animal and vegetable transactions, especially after a few days of steady sunlight—rinds, takeout cartons, unrinsed bottles, clippings from the garden, Domino's plantings and Uno harvestings left out for the dogs, cats, shy raccoons, and human scavengers, fallen fruit from the pizza trees; here he was at other times, if he left 850 Bryant early to drive to the Pacific at Ocean Beach, breathing a clean salt smell off the fog; here he slept with his faith in the endless procession of not too difficult days which might end in a not too difficult disappearance off the face of San Francisco and the earth; here he stood, suddenly interrupted. A stray woman or Ferd Conant sometimes tried to interrupt him and usually failed to do so. Even his friends Harvey and Alfonso tried.

Amanda was interrupting him. Gyro came along with a deal. Things were not so quiet as he had thought. Shaper was making the small noises of interrupted breathing, chest rumbles of cogitation.

Across the room Gyro and Shari were considering him with expressions almost like sympathy, and he was considering them, as people tended to do, with suspicion. Gyro and Shari were considering his usefulness to them, and he was considering their disturbance to his life. He didn't know what to expect. Someplace, wherever she was during this negotiation, Amanda must also have been full of consideration.

Shaper felt as lost as the former commissioner out there on Pine, flapping his arms while the tow-truck carried his vehicle away. So he said to Gyro: "All this is new to me."

"Take your time," Gyro said, "but hurry up."

Fourteen

He credited or blamed no one else in San Francisco. Out of the material he was given, he had made himself what he was, a distracted older guy, diligent in the routines of withdrawal. And an inadvertent father, in love with his child, his very own rightly messed daughter.

While deciding whether to avail himself of Gyro's offer of an interesting life, he might as well accept Gyro's invitation to the Yerba Buena Foundation's Anniversary Celebration. They hadn't yet decided whether to call it the First, Second, or Third Anniversary; that was a mere detail. There would be food, drink, good fellowship, and further information. Shaper was ready for some.

"You're pretty careless about this whole deal," said Shaper. "You're not worried about the police? Right, this is San Francisco—but you're not worried?"

"Don't get me started on that," said Gyro, and since no one got him started, he got himself started. "Something that's perfectly natural and healthy, and even the medicals say you need it regular, shouldn't have to look for it on street corners."

"Furtively," said Shaper.

"Don't get me started," Gyro said. "Why shouldn't we sell therapy, everybody knows it's good for people? What if you need a little discipline and you got one of those wives, just fuck and turn over? What if . . . well, everybody does blow jobs in today's world . . . but what if she's wearing braces on her teeth, like every hot young kid you meet?"

Self-starter Gyro.

"Not every kid has to wear braces."

Sounding like someone who had done a survey, Gyro said: "Every *hot* one."

Shaper didn't want to argue. "Okay, I'm with you," he said.

"What's not to be with? I think, personally, you're still . . ." He looked disdainfully at Shaper's furniture, eaten by use, sunlight, and dust; he took inventory of the stained walls where a drainpipe seemed to have run into trouble; he surveyed the nonworking fireplace with an electric space heater set into it and an extension cord snaking across the rug. "But that can be remedied," he said.

Gyro proceeded. He wanted Shaper's decision to issue from an open heart. Otherwise he would be no different from someone who had the cards read, the fortune traced, the palm scientifically analyzed, but didn't heed any of it. No benefit in that.

Is this a deal for you, is this a bargain? Gyro was asking. No hurry, no rush, take your time, let it grow in your mind, Dan, because we can wait as long as Jesus for peace on earth, goodwill toward men; but also come on, get with the program. . . . Gyro was feeling fine about the progress they were making.

A fun-loving crinkle or two appeared at the corners of his eyes, then lengthened into subtly tailing lines. "I never hear from you unless I do it myself, call you, what kind of a friend is that? I thought Jewish fellas are like us Romany, you know, fiercely loyal? To family, friends, and business associates? And to hell with everybody else?"

"I've got a job," said Shaper.

"And I don't? And everyone does? Listen, all the folks will be there, even clients—they can wear masks if they're shy, but this isn't Halloween. . . . Isn't the anniversary either, but what the fuck, you know? You're an important part of the whole family, Dan, not just Amanda."

"Why do I feel I'm not in control of things?"

Gyro didn't like to upset anyone unless it was necessary. "Because you're not, my dear friend."

Gyro's invitation was only to a party and a person needed dinner anyway. Probably there would be a buffet laid out. He could avoid the wrong foods, drinks, and pharmaceuticals. He could choose to go home early, or maybe not.

"Love any party, Gyro," he said. "By day I'm a court interpreter, by night a disco dancer. I'm your man."

Gyro appreciated Dan's light touch, vain attempt at it. Dan had nothing to be worried about.

Dan Shaper was worried. His stomach sent signals of turmoil into his brain. He didn't like his stomach telling him what to think.

Are you doing anything wrong? his mother used to ask when she was alive, and still asked when he remembered her.

No.

That's a pretty short answer. Are you sure?

Well, it depends on who you're talking to.

Whom, she corrected him. She used to serve him what she called her famous bread and tomato sandwiches, with Kraft's Miracle Whip dressing, while she pondered his evasiveness. Now that she was dead, he had to make do with imagined victories over her, along with the bread sandwiches.

So are you doing anything right, son?

Mom, you're prying again. I know you've got my best interests to heart.

"*At* heart. Eat the crusts, come on, put some meat on you."

These days he would ask her to slide off the pseudo-mayonnaise with the flat side of a knife; cholesterol. But she couldn't do so at this time because she was dead; also at this time he was older than his pretty Mom before she checked out, due to internal growths which would now be hooked off by microsurgery.

One day soon he would drive out to Colma, stare at her grave, think relevant personal thoughts. Later his daughter might do the same for him, on the well-known theory that what goes around comes around.

Not necessarily. There was no justice (this was Dan Shaper's expert opinion) and vibes were not all that reliable in causing correct action. If they were, California would be the paradise people came to find, since it was the natural home of vibes. He didn't ask for grave visitation from Amanda, and all his Mom really deserved was his pleasant memory of tomato, Kraft's dressing, store bread, and continual sincere advice. (Tomatoes didn't put meat on the bones; no protein. Mom thought she knew everything, but didn't.)

One bad habit Dan Shaper never fell into was letting so much flab accumulate at his middle that the shirt would stretch over it with the button unbuttoned and a hairy belly exhibited like that of other carefree older guys. Not him, not this carefree older guy with higher standards, including situps, leg lifts, and self-supervised eating. He also shyly kept a tee shirt beneath the outside shirt presented to the court system and the rest of the world. Plus, he didn't forget to button all the way unless in a hurry to answer the ring from the Domino's pizza kid, who was eager not to lose the penalty guarantee for late delivery to customers who had all the time in the world but were chickenshit about the rules. Becoming a new dad put all his good programs in jeopardy.

Time to celebrate. As Gyro said, life must be a festival and it was the Yerba Buena Foundation's time. Dan Shaper opened his closet, shut it, opened it again—was everything now in question, even his shirts?—and decided to dress bland, dress for a day's work in court or in some lawyer's office, translating a poor misunderstood crack dealer's deposition into serviceable English alibis. Heading for the anniversary which was not really an anniversary, he dressed as if it were just another normal day when he didn't see Gyro, Shari, Ferd, Harvey, maybe a guy who liked to be whipped, maybe a guy who liked to be peed on, or a guy who liked, oh, who knew what some men liked? And D'Wayne. And Amanda.

Let's go, thought Dan Shaper, then saying aloud to his only long-term auditor, the person he addressed most often, the man with the adequately buttoned shirt: "Let's go."

⊰ PRIVATE PARTY TONIGHT, PLEASE ⊱

Christmas lights winked at the windows, though the Christmas season—even the shopping part of it—was yet to come. For Gyro, the nail-sharpener of the Via Dolorosa, Yuletide was a year-round festival. Shaper parked a little past the stately Victorian, taking a short stroll to gather his spirit about him. The curtains were drawn; a Walgreen's Novelty set, peppermint candy lights, gingerbread man lights, reds, yellows, and greens, in melting candle and other traditional shapes, were both festive and ominous. Silver icicles hung from the electric cord.

The traffic on Pine was sparse, rush hour about finished. The wooden stairs to the doorway creaked against the weight of his steps. He did not find his spirit well gathered. He took a deep breath, absorbed a ration of urban nighttime ebb, quiet, and damp before pressing the chimes. They pealed out the first phrase of a traditional carol, "God Rest Ye Merry, Gentlemen" (Let nothing you dismay, he thought).

That "Please" after "Private Party Tonight" was another of Gyro's classy improvisations.

The door opened. A welcoming wide smile awaited him. In substitute receptionist mode, since the regular doorperson was just leaving to give a high-colonic treatment to a client who liked disciplinary nurses in white coats, D'Wayne quoted her: "The therapist will see you now, big boy."

The one who wanted punishment by irrigation, his clinic record tucked under his arm, trudged up a thickly carpeted stairway from what must have been the grand ballroom during earlier times. There were trudge marks from earlier clients. Tonight, a special occasion, the Foundation's portals were barred to those choosing succor on mere impulse. Only invited friends of the Yerba Buena family were welcome. It did the regular clientele good to know how special they were; self-esteem was a constant concern for all those who made the Victorian on Pine a San Francisco institution since some time last year. Unlike HMOs, the Yerba Buena Foundation offered full service in its single area of expertise. Absolute discretion, sound-proofing, and an understanding with the police department shielded clients from the prying world out there, where a loss of joy was endemic, due to the fatal drift away from our roots in nature and toward a dependence on microchips, superficial stimulations, shitty love lives. It didn't need to be Christmas to be the season of celebration in this better place of one-stop medical overhaul, strict discipline, and condom use for all in bodily fluid situations.

In the future, there were to be no regrets. You couldn't say the same about Yuletide in the harassed streets of a great city.

On these premises, in a permanent time of sharing, giving, and flocked wallpaper, the person you were finally permitted to love most, yourself, was given his due (in select cases, her due).

D'Wayne's large accompanying animal, its pelt as sleek as if it had been oiled, sniffed at Shaper, poked a muzzle at his knees, prodded, snuffled, made a wet spot. It beat its tail.

"Move sharp there, man," D'Wayne advised, his smile ample, his teeth like miniaturized appliances. "Damn dog, party gets him all excited up when he smell it on your pants."

He was talking to Shaper, who was dodging, and the dog wasn't listening.

"Shoo! Shoo there!" D'Wayne finally said. "Sit!"

The German shepherd sat. D'Wayne turned up his smile rheostat for Dan Shaper. D'Wayne was a person who meant to get his own way about things without hurting anyone unless necessary.

Now came a deep and happy bray from a dear, dear friend. "Hey, been waiting!" Gyro cried, grabbing Dan Shaper past D'Wayne—Gyro's spirits lifted, as usual, by all the surprises he had arranged. "But you know you're late?"

"Hi Pop," Amanda said. "You always tardy? I was that way in school—maybe an inherited something, how 'bout that?"

"He was late getting to be a dad, what is it, twenty years late?" Margaret stated. Margaret Torres, too.

He deserved no respite. Hello from Harvey (a little salute, a mere twitch of hand at the forehead). Hello to Shari, her moles shining in the reflected Tiffany light (hadn't previously noticed the dark moles, maybe sexy for some men, on bare shoulders and one on upper lip; had previously noticed the Cost Plus Tiffany lamps in this parlor).

Hello to goddamn Ferd. "So you expected me, cowboy? Some people think they don't need legal representation, but

I like to socialize and then later, *voy-la!* They already got my card in their ashtray."

D'Wayne wasn't really working tonight. He and Fella, his big pooch, were watching over events, pleased and relaxed, D'Wayne sure that Amanda's father had to be paler inside than he was white outside, or gray, or whatever damn colors they turn when they're nervous. As for himself, D'Wayne had that hairless gleamy kind of body, muscled, rippling with muscles, while old white boys like Dan here just slacked down from buffed on their trip toward scummy whiskery ape looks and then no looks at all. Daddies go that way if they hang around long enough.

Along with hellos, trays were being passed and other trays with meat and feta cheese, other cheeses and ground lamb, and marinated grape leaves wrapped around chopped bits of foodstuff were stationed on various flat surfaces, and light was falling from the as-good-as-genuine-Tiffany lamps and also shadows from the dark places, spilling haphazardly in moving patterns across the folks, the carpet, the parlor objects, in a summer squall of indoor light and darkness; and the voices were making party chatter, ha ha ha, and deeper har har har, and Ferd Conant was chirping at Dan Shaper: "I come for the food, don't you, Cowboy? It's this gypsy chow, don't you just love it?"

"We call it Romany soul food," said D'Wayne.

Gyro stared until D'Wayne lowered his eyes; it only took a moment. "I call it home cooking. Nobody I ever knew calls it anything but what we eat when we have a feast. Now are we planning just stand around here calling it things or are we gonna eat?"

"She looks like you, Cowboy," said Ferd, "except she's pretty." He twitched his head toward Amanda; was that a wink? He sealed the transaction with a quick up-and-down nod that was definitely a wink.

"Eat, babies, let's enjoy, should we?" Margaret Torres, bringing pacification.

D'Wayne picked up a coated green plastic plate, still distressed about losing his staredown with Gyro, and went out of his way to brush against Dan Shaper on his way to the table. D'Wayne smelled of ripeness and cologne, male grease and a minty chemical additive.

"As an attorney-at-law, a working lawyer . . ." Ferd slid alongside with a joint in his mouth, a singed turkey-skin scent of marijuana wafting off his breath. "What I like is a dispute to settle, a domestic trouble, a money debt beef, Cowboy, or nondomestic, somebody making difficulty for somebody else and me in a difficulty-type situation preferring to come to terms always nicer than litigate . . . Hey, all this good vibe around here really picks me up—"

Where? Where? Where was the cloud of good vibes?

"—all this fine and tasty eating, so what can I do for you? I can get loaded, that I can do, but who would hire me for that? Am I so charming, such an easy lay?"

"Okay, Ferd," said Dan Shaper.

"Man, I'm really really having a good time, but I didn't come on that mission. Came here for excitement, Cowboy. When is it? When does it happen?" He leaned closer and put his decayed-fruit (at this point, not singed turkey skin) marijuana breath so close to Shaper's face, so damned close. "So now we're dining together, you know him better, breaking pita as it were, you like him a whole lot better?"

(*Who?*)

Ferd's fingers flew toward his scalp, adjusting the combover which seemed to have a will of its own, moving a hair or two this way or that. The oiled hairs were not evenly spaced. "You leave me with nothing to do, Cowboy? You enjoy your son-in-law equivalent? Your son-out-law, Cowboy, ha ha ha, get it?"

Ferd was Ferd-on-the-spot, adjuster, negotiator, facilitator, an in-between kind of person, right, Cowboy? Ready to position himself between Dan and D'Wayne, in case someone around here didn't desire to be a happy family with this particular son-out-law?

"I help, that's what I do," Ferd was saying. "Let me, it's my field of endeavor. Please"—he knew enough to stop with the 'cowboy'—"so why don't you?"

Ferd held his hands at his chest, palms facing Dan Shaper and the universe. Nothing to hide; don't hit me; everything open and aboveboard. "Hey Cowboy, why you frowning like that? Already got yourself those unsightly wrinkles—you try a little adhesive tape, keep the epiderm smoother, while you sleep or drive?"

"I don't drive much."

"Well, you sleep, don't you, Cowboy?"

Not this court translator and interpreter. He slept a lot less these days. Just now his eyes itched; cannabis did that. And there had better be a better son-in-law equivalent out there than D'Wayne and a better remedy for him than Ferd Conant.

"Come along, come along, no business, not today," said genial Gyro. "Ferd, please, my dear friend Dan—if you're drinking, you can drink more later, but don't deaden your buds—" He ran on, he sprayed them with words, he offered pleasure most demandingly.

Gyro had assembled a Romany picnic, food carried in straw hampers, although he was no longer travelling in trucks or trailers, what he called 'caravans,' because that was part of the past—past contracts still held, of course—rolls of cheese, chopped vegetables, and spices, maybe fruits, too, in pita bread ("Hey, that's not Spanish"; "No, it's not"), wrinkled olives ("Why does it have to be Spanish?"), tomatoes, onions, cold roasted garlic, salami which he sliced holding the fat tube and pulling the knife toward his belly and belt, fresh-cut salami it was, yum, good; "Make yourself a nice pile of tastes, my friend, your own selection!" For lolling, in case Ferd, Harvey, or Dan wanted to loll with one of the women, he spread pillows and a crackling tablecloth substitute over the carpet. It was the colored comics from the *Chronicle-Examiner* Sunday edition. Gyro was riding high on hospitality euphoria. There were no children, unless you counted Shari or Amanda, who were daughters, no longer children. Since this was a parlor of the Yerba Buena Foundation, you couldn't consider Shari a typical child.

They stretched out on Esalen pillows. Survivors of flower times, they could still lounge with legs working like those of easy-folding kids. San Francisco flew by on one-way Pine Street outside, as if the city were a motor event on flatbed trucks. Shaper couldn't see it, but the low whir and stir through wooden walls sounded like his past whizzing down Pine, heading out to his future. Perhaps—was there marijuana in the rolled sandwiches?—his future was also oncoming, crossing, passing the present in its search through the years he had already lived. Shari was smiling. Gyro had the high beams on. Shaper was eating, Harvey was observing D'Wayne, and D'Wayne was watching himself, pleased by the sight, his eyelids half shut and purplish. A good time declared for all.

A bottle of ketchup on a chipped black plastic plate stood in the place of honor with the flowers at the center of the table (roses, sprigs of green, Heinz). Shaper didn't know what ketchup had to do with Spanish gypsy Arab food, hummus, pita bread, chopped onions which were red because they were red onions or because they were mixed with beets. Many questions yet to be answered. D'Wayne took a piece of pita bread, poured ketchup into it, folded it tight so that it oozed like a wound, and neatly downed the pocket of ketchupped bread in one competent gulp, getting sugar, tomato sauce, vitamins, salt, and maybe a smidgen of protein through swift action. Now he could proceed to further business. Ketchup was an appetizer for a person who defined it that way.

Others were eating hummus in the pita pockets, or the chopped beet-red onions, or drinking from the mugs that contained wine, or holding the necks of beer bottles, and glinting sideways at each other, waiting for somebody to do something, maybe just for the party part of the party to begin. Dan Shaper was in an earlier place of his life. It was a time he had absented himself from, but now he was there again and here was the woman he had slept with once, okay, maybe more than twice, pressed himself in, drawn it out, let it crawl snakelike out; and here waited the living emblem, Amanda, of what he had forgotten; and Shari and her own father; and Ferd Conant, the happiest man in the world, expecting profit to come fully into view.

Harvey, a look of concentration on his face, was chomping on something vegetable, pale, and crisp. He didn't like the company. He was willing to wait around anyway. Muscles bulged in the black tee shirt, the tight black pants, the martial arts costume he wore for formal occasions, not that much different from the gray absorbent pants and shirts he wore for informal messing with people's bodies and minds. The tense buffing of his body was not merely a gymnasium pastime. In Harvey's case it was relevant to his approach to problems.

The sign at the front door of the Yerba Buena Foundation

stopped a puzzled client, who stood there peering at what looked more like a family party than a merchandising of orgasms. D'Wayne's German shepherd poked his nose at the door, growling. The client saw no point in trying to talk his way in. Easily discouraged, he retreated.

Despite the confusion from known and unknown portions of his life, Shaper was not losing himself here. The heat of bodies, intentions, and hungry eaters left him fully alert and mobilized. Harvey was present to help, but he didn't need Harvey. He was awake. Being awake like this was a feeling he remembered, so much like being young that it seemed as if he were young again and would never need rest in his future life. His breathing was easy, his feet felt agile, he was ready.

D'Wayne held the ketchup like a bottle of somebody's blood.

Shari slipped next to Shaper, took his arm and then let it go, not to be too forward; she smiled into his face, moved on. She wouldn't waste words, though words were present to be wasted.

Gyro loomed tall. He was wearing thick-soled hightop shoes. He had a dainty smiley-face apron around his waist, but it didn't make him seem like a foolish backyard barbecuer. The dark lava folds of bone at his forehead gleamed with sweat.

D'Wayne twisting the ketchup top again.

Harvey mouthing something at Dan; he didn't know what.

"A social life at last, hey Cowboy?" Ferd.

Shaper didn't answer.

Off to one side stood a little sideboard with carved pawlike feet and cloth booties on them, so they wouldn't scratch the floor when someone lurched against the table. It carried fliers for remedies against late-onset circumcision, including word from a plastic surgeon who performed foreskin transplants. A placard leaning against the wall gave an 800 number hurried folks could call to order foam, "Anatomically Always Ready Dolls," and suggested, "Put Your Hand on the Problem." "Mister Slow'n'Easy Lotion (Not Novacain)" promised hope for the hasty. There was also a little box of candy-flavored condoms, free samples, and Shaper wondered about those who might have trouble swallowing them.

"Nice," said Harvey, speaking up. "There's an answer for everything."

"Wuh?" Dan Shaper heard himself ask.

"What's in this mint I been sucking? Candy from strange women, pal." Harvey shook his head disgustedly. "I ain't been dosed in years, but I should of known."

Shaper also.

"You like?" asked Gyro.

"You love?" said Shari, correcting her father.

"Yes, food good, good, mucho bueno," Shaper heard himself mumbling. No one was here to shame him for stoned pleasure with these two dear ones squatting beside him, partaking of the ceremony of fine dining, sprouts, olive oil, bits of cooked herb dropping from their lips. Ah, this is heaven, this is life, he was thinking.

It hadn't taken long. The stuff must have been strong. Acid, hash, something good, or maybe just the best grass. Indoors, snug at the Yerba Buena Foundation, all was right with the world.

The more Shaper ate, the hungrier he grew. Where would it end? He imagined swelling like a balloon, ballooning up, floating toward heaven, lighter than air, bumping his head against the ceiling, bouncing off walls and ceiling like a pinball, and then he started to laugh and rapidly descended to earth, to carpet, to patterned rug, to comic strip images in happy Sunday colors. He was thirsty. Before he could launch on another flight, be launched on it, he grabbed a bottle of beer by the neck, but it had no neck, it was a can of Coke, which he never drank, and popped the pop-top and it squirted in a great gas belch all over the comic strip picnic papers and also himself and he was bouncing up again, carrying the sweet caramel fizz in its can, he drinking, the can efficiently dripping, and . . . and . . . and Shaper was giggling.

A little dignity around here. Fortunately, nobody heard him although the sound was very loud, a sputtering and gurgling by a man famous throughout the world for never, never, never finding himself doing such in the air, soaring halfway between earth and sky; famous for not using his head to play pinball games; famous for gloomy sobriety; and patient for nothing in particular except what all men of his age were watching out for.

Gyro was a careful conductor of voyages who knew where the free ride should end. He took his cigaret out of a personalized pack—Shaper hadn't seen much of those since smoking became unfashionable—a greenish leather-trimmed item with little Florentine crosses embossed in it. Hadn't seen it since the times when men put Brylcreem in their hair. Just a little something Gyro picked up while crossing Italy on the Ponte Vecchio, his hair running with olive oil, as good as whatever he used now. Tapped tube against pack; spit out tobacco filament; lit with kitchen match, thumbnail flicking tip.

Gyro was a natural man, red in tooth and claw, blackened thumbnail. Ferd was not reclining on pillows with Shaper. Ferd was standing and considering. Ferd was recontemplating the hope of business. A hair was out of place. Ferd was deciding business was developing nicely before his very eyes.

Shaper thought happily: What the hell.

Margaret Torres passed by with a cloth, saying nothing,

leaned down and wiped sticky caramel beverage from Shaper's shirt.

What the hell. A mom's prerogative.

Dear Gyro, prince of the Romany nation or maybe just having fun, his heart leaking hints, was a person with determined moves. If he was a gypsy (Rom, Roma, Tsigane, Traveller), he was mostly pure Gyro, not needing Jesus to make out as best he could. "Here, try one of these," he said, and stuck a slippery-sheathed tube into Shaper's mouth. Shaper could feel Gyro's nails scraping his lips, he smelled sulfur from the match on the blackened thumbnail, and then grape leaves, chopped eggplant, spices took over. He wouldn't wipe his lips until Gyro got busy elsewhere.

He wiped.

Gyro turned back and shook his finger at him. The thick tangle of eyebrows knitted together so tightly, you'd expect a wince when he tried to pull them apart, and yet he was grinning. Shame, shame, the shaken finger stated.

Shaper felt ashamed.

Spicy food smells also emanated from Gyro's wet mouth, from the pores of his skin. He was eating heartily, as Shaper also should, must. With the meditative inward look this merits, Gyro hefted at his crotch, lifting his dick to another part of the dark. All over his body, matters were now satisfactory.

On her way to a shower, Fannie Funkybutt drifted through in a terry cloth caftan, leading a very fat man by one finger. She tugged at the finger to increase his waddle pace. At his age, he didn't like to trot anymore, but he cantered a little at her command. Fannie, removed from party duty, was treating a special client today. He was wearing matching terry cloth, and seemed torn between the temptations of flesh (Fannie) and flesh (chopped spicy lamb). Along with her caftan, Fannie was wearing strappy high-heeled shoes, the spaghetti laces reaching up and holding on to her legs for dear life.

"We're like the mergency clinic, open all night," Fanny was saying. "Only thing, we're not your HMO, so we're there when you need me."

"You already said," said the fat man.

"Make sure you know. At your age and weight, you start to forget."

The fat man nodded along with Fannie. Pre-Jacuzzi, his lips were already wet, as a greedy fat man's tend to be. He really wanted to get going before she turned cruel. There was an original oil painting on the way, a water and beach scene, two lovers walking in an atmosphere of damp and lonely affection. This did not apply to Fanny and the fat man. In this clinic for folks with personal issues, pensive beach strolling in terry cloth caftans wasn't the program.

"You're always there for me," said the fat man. "What's not to appreciate?"

After one pass through the room out of courtesy and to load up her plate, Black Barbara hid out in her bedroom, door aggressively locked—parties made her gloomy, they were as bad as Christmas. For company she had nobody and nothing but her pet weasel, her dildo, and the TV. She turned the sound down. The guests could hear occasional squeals, caused by her pet, her dildo, or a car chase on the screen, suddenly turned up. She also kept a couple of good books on the shelf and dusted them regularly. Closed for Private Party, Please, gave Barbara a holiday, a chance to meditate. She used to be an M.D.I., Mentally Disturbed Individual, needing to stand in line for her benefit checks at an office not far from Shaper's apartment, but now that she had found work she liked, a way through tribulation that people appreciated, she was just what one could call finely calibrated, needing Private Time like a sensitive child.

"Hey! Keep it down!" she yelled once, and used one of the good books to pound on the floor, but then gave up, put the good book back in its place, and flounced angrily downstairs to join the revelry. Not wanting to put a damper on everyone was a sign of how far she had come.

Barbara's ample buttocks flopped despite the underlying musculature. When that flood of buttock swept around a person—such as Rick Blake III, her most faithful client—it enveloped him in a catastrophe of pleasure, he was washed up and swept far away into dreamland, his entire life was a worthwhile enterprise. And then the flood ebbed and left him bereft. Rx: Repeat Treatment as Desired.

"You'd like Barbara, she's like this other one, Valentina, the part Russian one, she has the mysterious quality," Shari told Shaper. "Lubricates naturally."

"Some je ne sais quoi."

"You speaking Spanish at me because you think all gypsies are flamencos?"

"I was thinking about Valentina."

"She's a miracle. Barbara isn't the only one. It just pours out, Dan."

Barbara and Valentina had their skill in common. Young though she was, Shari respected talent in others.

Amanda stood alone by the table with the leaflets and advertising fliers. Maybe she wasn't hungry. Her father said her name and she didn't stir; it was as if she hadn't heard, though her eyelids flickered at the sound of her name. He said it again. Now not even that barely perceptible blinking; no other way to express this anger. She looked like all the women who had been let down, all the women who had been abandoned by all the men; not vindictive or raging anymore, merely departed,

"Amanda."

A negative, an absence. Silence. She was dead to him because he had not been alive to her.

Shaper couldn't justify his need and longing to awaken this creature who was a perfect stranger and his daughter. He had earned nothing, yet found himself in love. Anything he did for her now was a lunge, a speculation about fatherhood and his onrushing old age. She turned away what he had never turned toward her. Surely she must have grown up longing for a father, and now her father turned out to be this griefy, confused court interpreter who seemed to know little more than how to get from Spanish to English and back again. It wasn't enough.

As time goes on, the schedule includes a broken heart. "Amanda."

"I'm busy."

"I'd like to talk with you."

"I'd like you to see I'm busy."

Surely he should have stopped there. If this were a woman not his daughter, he would have known to stop and go elsewhere, get out of her sight. Instead he said, "Can't we talk a little?"

"Can't stop you, can I? I'm standing here. So go ahead, talk. I'm polite, but I promise I'm leaving as soon as you shut up."

He gave up.

She honored this wise decision. She met his eyes for the first time tonight. "Later, Pop, I'll be glad to hear your sad story. . . . You can make me an offer."

He said nothing. Silence also gained no advantage. She sighed, stretched, and said, "Well, time to take a leak. Later, Pop."

Everyone gets the broken heart he deserves. He must have deserved his. "Amanda," he said, but she was gone.

D'Wayne was gone, too, and the dog was nosing Black Barbara and she was saying, "Get off!" Shaper couldn't see either Amanda or D'Wayne, but clear as a nightmare he knew they were upstairs, whispering and laughing; he saw and heard them giggling and murmuring upstairs, out of his sight and hearing. This was powerful grass he had eaten.

Dan Shaper believed he had conquered the misery of awakening alone and remembering loss, that longing after a woman said no to him one morning, rising from his bed out of her own dream of love and thinking, Enough, not this bozo, he's not it, I'm out of here. . . . He had come back to life. He barely remembered the women who gave him grief. He barely remembered grief at all. On the day after Thanksgiving, when Harvey or Alfonso asked, What'd you do for the holiday? he answered: Celebrated.

Pride was departed. Longing he didn't need was in its place.

Ferd had watched Shaper not speaking to Amanda, Amanda not replying. Ferd sighed, breathing the word Hey, but not wanting to detract from a meaningful lack of exchange between father and now-absent daughter, gone upstairs with her stud. Hey, there was getting to be room for Ferd. Hey, there was getting to be more room for Ferd. Mediator, negotiator, counselor, go-between, bagman, what the fuck—call Ferd anything, but don't forget to call him.

"Hey," said Ferd, "can I help? I can't represent Margaret or Amanda because that would infringe in the conflict of interest category, you and me being old-time good friends, Cowboy"—Ferd stopped for whistling sounds, an emphysemic creaking in his chest—"but if you happen to need help in taking out someone like an inappropriate boyfriend, well, I can be a guide and counselor in certain quarters."

"Thanks."

"And then if Margaret remembers her overdue past child support, I could make recommendations, couldn't I? There's lots of lawyers, Cowboy, one adult per seventy-two adults in Frisco alone. But only one me."

"God's will," said Shaper.

Ferd beamed modestly.

Now that they were moving from mere palship to the client-attorney relationship, the go-between role which Ferd Conant had developed as one of his legal specialities, it was time to ease the strain Ferd sensed in Shaper's regard for him. Among men, talk of love, adventure, and casual fucks always helps. Ferd had found this to be so, especially when he was dealing with someone who didn't care about the Forty-Niners or the Giants. "What I like about these third-world foreigners, French, say, that part of the country, is it's breakfast in bed every morning and black lace lounge-erie every night—you don't find that in modern-day America. Okay, so I buy the lounge-erie, purchase at a good price. I got this connection at Victoria's Secret, I did her a favor once." He leaned close (oh, his breath); Shaper leaned away; Ferd didn't give up and leaned even closer (oh, the bacteria lurking in his teeth and throat). "A real good favor. Everybody should do something nice for everybody else, that's my philosophy."

As Ferd spoke, during this dreamy lecture, flecks of yellowish stuff that by all rights should have gathered during sleep at the corners of his eyes instead appeared at the corners of his mouth. Listening, Shaper could almost hear the rumble of the motors that carried the persons who carried the coke that caused the difficulties which, to Ferd's benefit, abutted in a credit with the manager of a Victoria's Secret outlet.

"And when I put my tongue in her mouth," Ferd was saying—whose mouth? Shaper was losing track of Ferd's life—

"she chokes up, just thanking me for the lounge-erie." He was doing backup eyebrow wiggles to indicate great sex without having to violate good manners toward either the Victoria's Secret person or the lingerie-wearing, breakfast-in-bed bringing individual.

Shaper thought of signalling understanding with a few eyebrow wiggles of his own, but Ferd didn't deserve that courtesy. If it were Harvey, say, Shaper would have eyebrow wiggled to beat the band. But Harvey would never brag in this way, he wasn't a sexual signifier; nor would he promote a deal with a Victoria's Secret manager that involved skating so close to illegality, except perhaps in hot pursuit of a miscreant. Having dealt with Latino miscreants, Shaper knew that illegality-skating was inevitable among police and corrections officers.

Like Gyro, like Shari, even the miscreants and combed-over Ferd with his incorrigibly pink scalp wanted what everyone deserved in life, intervals of happiness and a sense of being loved, the strength to love themselves despite thinning hair. Even if some folks expressed the universal desire by paying for the right to stick a tongue in a third-world person's mouth. Who, considering all he was going through, was Shaper to judge?

He also tried finding some peace along these lines about D'Wayne and Amanda. He did not succeed, except theoretically. He imagined D'Wayne's big grin and glint bearing down at him. Theoretically, yes. But actually, sincerely, he wanted to do harm to D'Wayne. To deter him by destroying him. A very sincere wish during his age of advanced, unexpected, and unprepared fatherhood.

While Ferd told his story, Shaper's attention was fixed on recent news of Amanda. She had gone upstairs with D'Wayne and this was an act of revenge. Ferd sniffed out something peculiar, tilted, in his favorite cowboy's attention. Ferd looked puzzled, his eyebrows cocked: older person's lack of focus? Parkinson's? First clue to Alzheimer's? But then Ferd, mobilizing his insight resources, a people person, realized he wasn't the only center of Shaper's life. The man had concerns. Ferd could be patient.

Dan Shaper felt as chilled and withdrawn as Amanda. It had been deeper than disdain, her turning away. They shared chromosomes, genes, germ plasm looping back through the generations; they both had the skill of going gray and silent. Even Shaper's thoughts were sluggish. Somewhere in this tundra he knew there was, he *knew* there was an answering signal from his daughter.

She had stepped back as if he had hit her. Maybe it was no deeper than disdain, but disdain for her father was sufficient to do the job.

Ferd stood there, watching. He held an unlit cigaret between his fingers. With all his heart he shared Dan Shaper's troubles. Surely this sharing deserved to be rewarded. Poor confused cowboy! Clients were often like that before a skilled advocate climbed on board. Ferd practiced his people skill of not pushing the folks.

Ferd had shut up but remained stubbornly in place. Before he could say Hey or Cowboy again, Shaper turned toward Harvey, another guest for what was as good as an anniversary, and finally Ferd slid off toward the table with bottles, ice, glasses.

Harvey's hands were clenching and unclenching, the black tee shirt soaked with sweat. It was cool enough, but he dressed as if he had just emerged from the gym. This was the kind of workout Harvey disliked, nonaerobic, fight-or-flight reactions, unlimited blood pressure. Harvey disapproved of situations which called for action and produced no action of the sort he liked. Instead, Amanda, Ferd, and his buddy Dan had produced action of the sort he did not like.

"This situation is off the book, pal. What're you going to do?"

Shaper didn't answer.

Harvey had lectured him irritably when he moved into the Tenderloin. Dan argued back. It was near cheap eating, walking distance from the Hall of Justice, suited him nicely.

"Huh?" asked Harvey. "That your style?" Okay, if he insisted on the convenience of living among the junkies, East Asian tribes-people (no problem with them), massage parlors, parolees, methadone drunks, transvestites, skinheads, panhandlers mumbling about Viet Nam (some of them may have been there), teenage hookers and dealers (these could be irresponsible); but if he didn't want to be taken for just another golden-ager loser in a Single Room Occupancy hotel run by a guy named Patel, with cash from a pension check just waiting to be lifted, he had better learn to take care of himself. Shaper was fast enough on his feet, so here was the procedure for survival in the Tenderloin. Harvey held him with hard eyes and stood him to a condensed lesson.

If your adversary has a gun, give him what he wants.

If a knife, don't stop to think, just run.

Berserker, get the hell out of there.

"Should I dress like you in that karate-aikido-ninja drag?"

"You ain't built for it, buddy. In your case clothes don't make the man."

"I have a history of handling myself."

"This ain't bilingual services. Listen, here's what you do—"

Dan Shaper listened to Harvey. As age encroached, it behooved him to become as a child and learn from his betters.

Everyone around Dan Shaper was offering instruction on correct behavior. There seemed to be new rules that he couldn't get straight. The recent father of a grownup daughter qualified for help. Ferd and Harvey offered and Gyro also, unasked, gave it.

"I used to want to grow up to be one of the Little People—one of them midget dwarfs, shrimpola fuckers—but being six feet and all before I stopped, just couldn't equal-oppatunity my way into the job. Street fairs, carnivals, travelling folks, too much prejudice against Beeg Peoples, man. So I found an opening in Romany, that's my present gig."

"You're not really?" Shaper asked.

Gyro shook his head at the denseness of his delightful friend; the eyebrows locked again, hairs crawling, intertwined, never to be untangled until pretty soon. "Plus cook, practically chef, in Gadjo-style cuisine. Try a handful of this moussaka, we passed through Greek on our way to Hungarian, Rumania, Spain, Finland, and Stockton."

Shaper dodged as Gyro pushed a handful of chopped onions, meat, and eggplant toward his dumb face. He politely accepted it into a napkin, though.

"I also got a spare gig or two, one of the others fall through," Gyro added, licking his fingers. Under the circumstances, he could push Shaper pretty far, but he preferred not to cross the line. He would leave that to D'Wayne.

And sure enough, D'Wayne was back, ready, and available. "Mind if I call you Pops?" he asked.

"Don't," Shaper said.

"How about Pappy, you like that better?"

So he'd been in conference with Amanda upstairs. Shaper just stared.

"Oo-ee," said D'Wayne. "Knew a boy said he was a Panther, give me that look, but he was nothin but a dealer try to tell me I owe him the money, honey. I said I didn't, pile a shit, yunnerstan what I'm sayin? So you can stop lookin on me like that."

Shaper smelled roasting lamb from the kitchen. While his long-range smell receptors went into action, his circulatory apparatus was sliding into emergency mode. D'Wayne, on an errand from upstairs, was doing heavy homeboy, making a point.

"So where's the bread, Ted? Mandie says you owe, even fuckin Ferd say you gotta pay some just for old-time owing, and rights be: we need some backing from the girl's daddy, am I right? So you up for it? Pretty quick, Dick?"

It was a barbecuing lamb turning on a spit, that smell. Plus some sort of basting sauce. Plus, nearby, aftershave and sweat.

Dan Shaper caught sight of Harvey in the doorway, bouncing on his toes in his big Adidas. "What for that smile on your face?" Harvey asked. "What you got to smile about?"

Shaper wasn't sure if he wanted to defend himself against D'Wayne or against the shame of Harvey's study of things. He moved slowly toward D'Wayne while D'Wayne stood there, his big teeth gleaming, even the dark space between the two front teeth shining in its darkness.

"Hey, don't be like that, I don't wanna pontificate on you, man"—drawling, dragging it out—"hey, all I want is two thumbs up."

D'Wayne looming, arms wide outstretched, casting a shadow from the lamp behind him: "So gimme a hug, Daddy."

Harvey used to suggest the Boogie Flick for a quick answer to muggers. Dig a big one out of the nose—most people breathing city air can find a hidden black-and-green morsel—

and flick it into his face. Even your low-I.Q. junkie has feelings, and he'll wave and dodge in disgust, which gives you the opening for Step Number 2, so called because it calls for two straight-fingered jabs into the finicky mugger's eyes, and then you're out of there before he can whine, "Hey, was that fair?"

In this situation, with his daughter and his daughter's mother in attendance, the Boogie Flick lacked class. He put the Boogie Flick out of mind.

He could announce in comicbook Japanese, "*I declare karate!*" and swipe the side of his hand against D'Wayne's windpipe, damaging his Adam's apple, his breathing apparatus, his self-esteem, and possibly causing stumbling, vomiting, choking, a period of disablement, but this required precision, and Shaper, a scholar of Spanish literature, art, music, and legal terminology, could anticipate wrath and risks if he flubbed the target.

So where to go, which way to turn?

Punching, good. Boxing ears, better, with cupped hands on both sides of the head at the same time, producing a concussion effect, immediate disequilibrium, a squeaking, popping, piercing pain to ears. But would he want to deafen D'Wayne permanently, give him an excuse to suck off the tit of public assistance for the rest of his life? Not the public-spirited thing to do. Adrenaline sent Shaper through his checklist at wonderful speed. Biting, hair-pulling, groin-kicking, all presented advantages. Hair-pulling: D'Wayne stands in line at his neighborhood Social Security branch and claims a pension on the grounds of socially handicapped patchy baldness. But his Ike Turner retro conk was heavily oiled and what if Shaper's hands slipped?

Then other options were . . . but he wasn't going to run through Harvey's entire repertory. It was up to Dan Shaper now.

Having weighed the possibilities long and deep in the space

of a second or two (rapid adrenaline response of outraged father), and also having considered the lessons previously imparted by Harvey, his true friend in ninja black (options for incapacitating street hustler holding daughter in thrall), Shaper abruptly decided upon a procedure under these unforeseen circumstances. He tensed his toes and heels, he isometrically flexed, to the naked eye seeming barely to move, except that at the doorway Harvey's hooded gaze detected the snakelike poise of incipiency. Harvey was still and waiting. Harvey liked a good student. Shaper stood a step and a half from D'Wayne, saying: "I have a winning lottery ticket."

"Man, you *won?* Some toy radio or something?"

And while D'Wayne was thus distracted, wrapping his mind around the concept that his father-in-law-equivalent might suddenly be a rich old lucky fart, Shaper pulled a bill— a scrunchy, furrow-faced Andrew Jackson twenty—from his pocket and dropped it to the floor. In general, human nature finds it impossible to look at anything else when money falls from the heavens or the grasp of a nervous dad. D'Wayne stared. An idea was struggling to come to birth, having to do with immediate cash flow. D'Wayne was thoroughly distracted. In this context, legal tender was another version of the Boogie Flick.

And then Shaper did nothing he had planned, such as the breaking of the knee, the smashing of the instep, the head butt to the nose, the groin or Adam's apple jab—Harvey looked disgusted—but said only: "D'Wayne, listen to me. I want you out of my life and out of my daughter's—"

"You got no right to talk about me," said Amanda—when did she come downstairs?

"Got no right to talk about her," said D'Wayne.

Harvey said nothing, just shook his head, all his lessons unheeded.

Margaret Torres, an engaged mom, offered cheerfully, "All

this good food going spoiled around here, too many bad vibes? Just asking."

Not spoiled but cold, running with olive oil, neglected except by those who were not neglecting it. Black Barbara was eating. Fannie Funkybutt and the fat man darted in for a quick snack to go, darted out again, plastic plates loaded. Even Margaret Torres held a grape-leaf roll like a cigaret between her fingers. Gyro serving, bustling, offered cups of red wine in the parlor of this grand Victorian which used to be the residence of a distinguished San Francisco family, before it became a place of harried conduct.

Shaper thought it best to start, not just blurt things out. Harvey could look as sour as he liked. It would take him awhile to appreciate the value of including Amanda as witness in these negotiations. Her lover was willing to make an exchange for her in legal tender, plain old familiar cash payoff.

Shaper saw himself doing this.

He saw results because it was his wish and no good alternatives came to mind.

He also suspected the good results were not likely.

It was still work in progress. He was feeling his way through a life problem. In recent times he had thought he had no more life problems, only a death problem at some future date. It turned out differently. He tried a combination of bribe and insult, risking damage to his spirit. "I'll help," he said, "if you'll just go away."

"Say again?" D'Wayne asked.

"If you take a good long trip somewhere, leave my daughter alone—"

"You got smoke in your head, man?"

"—if you'll listen. If you'll accept a benefit I'm willing to offer. If you'll—"

He didn't even know how to do this.

"That how you gone be, Pop? Like some stupid rich daddy think big D'Wayne here gone say yassuh, thanks for the tip, let me wipe dem shoes for you one mo time, massuh. . . . You shitting me, man?"

Dan Shaper got no credit on earth for being stupid and desperate. Only a lost lover could be as lost as he was now.

"How much? Give me a figure—ballpark."

D'Wayne stopped rolling his eyes, doing his little minstrel show for the company. He was calculating, eyes reddened, rolling up a little, but imagining. A response was due. Now he had the figure in mind. He reached down, unzipped, lifted his dick. He hefted it first inside his pants and then flipped it out, purple, engorged. Flipped it back, saying "That's all the look you get."

His pants were bulging, but D'Wayne was aroused only to laughter, a high-pitched giggle, overjoyed, as he called, "Mandie, man, Mandie! Your pop want to ne-go-tiate! here—he wanna ne-go-tiate!"

Still laughing, drawling out that long insinuating word *negotiate*, coughing. . . . He cleared his throat, held his side, said, "Woo-ee." And he had an idea. "You like to try some wrestling, know what I'm saying? But since you ain't a kid anymore, I won't tie my left hand behind me. I'm an honorable man, you hear me? I just won't use it. Promise—*word.* Just let my left arm hang there for duration and do it all with my other hand and I won't knee you in the balls, nothing like that, yunnerstan?"

It wasn't too complicated for Shaper at this level. D'Wayne was not amenable to an easy bargain.

"Since you ain't a stud no more, daddy, you an old fart gonna look out for his baby found herself a *man*—"

Shaper leapt. D'Wayne was ready for him. He was as good as his promise. Only one arm wrapped itself around Shaper at the chest and back—one long arm pressing and squeezing, pulsating, sinewy as a snake; Shaper struggling, having lost the initiative at once, having not ever had it because D'Wayne was ready for him. . . . A smell arose from the men in their embrace. Around them, pumpkin faces were grinning, except for Shari screaming, "No, no, no, goddamit!" That punk smell, that burnt-feather smell, Shaper knew what it was. How dare he? How dare he?

Gyro was bending and holding the dog by its leash. It was pulling this way and that and emitting excited barks.

Shaper felt faint, pleasantly distant from himself and all trouble, but just because his very own carotid artery was being compressed by a one-armed man and his brain was doing its minimum with diminishing oxygen . . . just because his daughter's smiling lover was determined to send him to his knees . . . was no reason to spill out unconscious before everyone; including Harvey, who for some reason, probably Harvey's reasons, thought it best at this time not to interfere; including Margaret Torres, who was daintily nipping at her roll of grape leaves wrapped around chopped lamb and olives; including Shari, who was yelling "Goddammit," but was doing nothing more to interrupt matters than asking God for a personal favor; including Gyro, who was curious to see how this might continue; including Amanda, who yelled a command: "Stop!" And again: "Stop! Stop!"

D'Wayne stopped choking him.

Dan Shaper had not fallen.

D'Wayne, tired, rubbed his arm.

Shaper standing, first sure he would throw up and then sure he would not. Another case of biology yielding to the will.

Harvey being whispered to by Ferd, but Harvey shrugging and saying, "So far so good."

Fannie poking her head in, finding nothing interesting going on, despite the noise, and poking her head out. Black Barbara hurrying after to tell her, yes, it was interesting, but you had to follow matters from the beginning.

D'Wayne and Dan definitely the center of what interest there was.

"Now it suppose to be Murder One if you think about it first and then kill somebody's ass. So I don't even think about it," said D'Wayne, too tired for his minstrel act, out of breath, kneading the used arm with the unused hand to relax a possible cramp. Shari looked at him with admiration for his restraint. Because he was personally chock-full of self-esteem, he was able to do this, thinking ahead in a positive sense.

"Not afraid of anybody," Gyro murmured in the softest voice Shaper had ever heard come out of Gyro. He was evidently drafting a recommendation on D'Wayne's behalf. *To Whom It May Concern: This fucker is not afraid of anyone.*

"You got a pretty bad symptom coming on," Shaper said.

"Wass that?"

"Gonna get hurt, man. You show all the signs."

D'Wayne looked confused, and that was when Shaper hit him at the knees, causing him to collapse like an imploding building, but even before any dust could rise, Shaper's own knee lifted hard into his crotch—there, there!—lifting D'Wayne momentarily, and then his wail of pain was succeeded by a gasp. He lay twisting on the floor, voiceless but choking. Amanda knelt on the floor beside him, cradling his head and crooning for his ears alone. The glance she directed at her father withered him.

Harvey was saying, "Shit!" and holding Shaper, who already stank of sweat and tears. "Enough," said Harvey.

Who was to decide whether it was right to leap like a much younger man at D'Wayne with a desire identical in all respects to a much younger man's desire to kill?

Dan Shaper was to decide. It was not right. He had done it anyway.

He stood there swaying in the middle of the ring of curious watchers, some of them frowning with concern, as if Dan Shaper might also topple before their eyes. He was not toppling, not throwing up, and not speaking. Gyro seemed puzzled about his true feelings; Shaper himself wondered, his bloodshot eye noticing a young woman who had pulled herself into an armchair and folded herself tightly to disappear, arms around knees, which in fact does not cause vanishing. He knew what this sharp pain in his eye meant—an exploded capillary which would leave him looking like a blurry old drunk for a few days until the busy little scavenger cells carried away the debris and the whites of his eyes would be nice and yellow again.

D'Wayne's dog stood over his master, muzzle poking, licking D'Wayne, wanting to join the game, asking D'Wayne to tussle or sit up and play.

Like passersby, the celebrants watched the accident and awaited further developments. Only the dog seemed fully awake.

Dan Shaper was a sleepwalker who had used up his dreams. He had been a sleepwalker with no dreams and now Amanda was his dream. All at once, it happened. A man with no dreams woke up and found there was a dream anyway.

Call yourself by our name, Amanda Shaper.

D'Wayne was climbing to his feet. He stood there, shaking his head and smiling again, shaking his head and just asking a question. "Man, you lower yourself, you hear what I'm saying? Hey, come on. That what you prefer?"

The dog found a spilled paper plate with olives and chopped lamb and changed its mind about playing with its master. It ate with snuffling wet noises.

Fifteen

Coulda, shoulda, woulda, but didn't handle surprises as well as some men did. Except that his Spanish into English was as limber as anyone's doing the multicultural intercommunications job.

On the street where he lived, Ellis, on the streets where he lived, the Tenderloin, error and delusion whistled at him in the evening winds—the transvestites under the streetlamps, the whores at the bus stops, the junkies in the doorways—and Shaper sat in his apartment, breathing dust and the steam heat that came on according to mysterious impulses by the landlord's thermostat. Shaper's breathing was slow and regular, although he knew breath was not permanent anymore and never had been. He cheered it on. He knew more than he used to know. He was still in error. He had a sore knee.

His daughter was on the phone. The machinery of fatherhood was barely unpacked, not fully functioning.

"I've got to talk with you, Dad. I don't think I'm just asking for money."

Then what did she think? Shaper's voice was high and strained, as he didn't like it to be. "You can ask," he said. "Ask away."

"Okay, so that's not the point. I'd like to come to your house."

"My apartment. It's not a house. I'm just here temporarily,

for the past thirty years." He breathed, he waited, he forced his chest to expand, he tried to slide his voice down to the register of a man in control of his surprises. "Come on over, but I have an early court date—"

"Tomorrow night. Are you in bed at ten o'clock?"

"You don't want dinner? Make it eight."

"Negative. See you, Dad."

And he stared at the phone. Now he had gotten his voice down, but she was gone. He hoped it wasn't for another ceremony of grasping and revenge (not necessarily the correct evaluation of recent events). She said she didn't think she was asking for money, She wasn't sure? Maybe she was just trying to figure out what her father was good for. Along the way, every daughter must do that. Not all people are sincere, even newborn fathers, so daughters study who their fathers are. . . .

Don't they?

Men who live alone laugh alone. Now was the time to laugh at the idea of pretending to be an expert and not even fooling himself. No more tricks, please.

So he moved speedily over the clutter, sliding a dust mop on dusty places, hanging up some of the clothes left on the back of chairs, even tapping a pile of unread magazines so that they lay with a flat edge on the table. He pulled back to admire the unread magazines; nice smooth job of tapping one clean edge.

Now that he had done a good job of cleaning up—what a fine housekeeper—he shrugged and said nothing aloud. What he thought was: I've gotten used to being who I am, I guess she'll have to, also.

This speed cleaning completed, this top to bottom redecorating in honor of his daughter, ten hectic minutes of dust mop, magazine tap, and wiping hairs out of the sink, he was ready for Amanda. Surely she would be touched.

The buzzer sounded. It must have been Amanda, a day ahead of time, just as eager as he was, knowing he had cleared the way. Without shouting into the broken intercom, since it would do no good anyway and he knew who it was, he let her in. It wasn't Amanda.

"Expecting somebody?" she asked.

He stared. Occasionally liking surprises, not liking this one, he put away the daughter-greeting plan in favor of the uncomfortable welcoming of a different stranger who was not a stranger. Readiness was 'all, but again he was not ready.

"Is that how you say hello? Not even a kiss for your old lady?" He put his arms around her, he brushed her cheek with his lips. "Old lover and the mother of all your kiddies?"

All? He was startled until he realized this was her idea of cute. Well, cute, now that he recalled, had not been Margaret's strong point even during that brief instant when they shared some kind of Seventies casual funning. It wasn't cute to have the child. It wasn't cute to have the child without letting him know. Sometimes cute wasn't the way to go.

Finally he found something to say: "What's up?"

"Good, good."

"What's good?"

"Well, Amanda's smart," said Margaret Torres, "like me and you. So the genetics are okay. But here's the thing. She thinks you're too solidly into yourself, which is not so smart, which is also my opinion—a kind of mother-daughter solidarity here—and so you need a little rattling."

"Let's stipulate that I'm rattled."

"Shook up. That was a stupid move about D'Wayne."

She wiggled and bumped. Lips pursed, she hummed the ancient Elvis Presley song which, for all he could remember, might have been current when he and Margaret... "All Shook Up," she sang, grinning. "So now that you don't know what you're doing, what are you gonna do?" The corners of her mouth pulled down in a look of maternal concern, *Aw, poor baby*, with a mix-and-match flash of amusement in the eyes. During the years since they had last met, Margaret Torres seemed to have taken on a load of cuteness.

"I see," said Shaper, not seeing, "what you seem to want here."

"Vocabulary isn't my field," said Margaret.

"Oh yes it is."

"I'm not good at talking, but you're really upset, aren't you? The word I'm looking for in my own inarticulate way, not knowing all those languages you say you know ... is it discom*bob*ulate?"

In recent times lots of talking had been everybody's field of endeavor, Margaret's, Amanda's, Ferd's, Gyro's; even D'Wayne explained himself. Only Harvey kept the peace. But that was because Harvey just hung around the outside of Shaper's trouble. Let him in and he might gab away like everybody else.

Shaper turned his palms out in an ethnic gesture of admitted discombobulation. Margaret Torres shrugged in response. So much for harmonious agreement.

In the street, Guardian Angels in their brown berets were yelling at a gathering of dope dealers and hookers who were yelling back that they didn't see no badges, so shut the fuck up. Shrillness occurred. Afternoon shadows seeped through the curtains along with the sounds, the inner city lullaby of Ellis; the curtains blew erratically, as if moved by anger and encroaching darkness. The Guardian Angels didn't stop the noise, but they pruned it, kept it moving from street corner to street corner. The nice southeast-Asian kids, brought to this refuge after the desolation of Cambodia, Vietnam, Laos, and other exotic sources of Tenderloin restaurant enterprises, were upstairs doing their homework, getting into American mobility while their parents worked in the kitchens. Tonight the normal evening distractions were not putting Shaper at his ease.

He asked if she wanted coffee; she said no. He asked if she wanted a drink or food and she said no, no. He kept offering her things; she was a guest. He said he had a joint in the refrigerator (actually, had several) and asked if she wanted to smoke. She paused, considering. No again.

As an aware host, trying his best, he fidgeted. It was just between the two of them here and this put a burden on him. There were some old LP's he could play. He had a tape of Bob Dylan's "Street Legal," but it seemed too late to proceed with a program of music appreciation.

So what did she want?

It seemed there was something she didn't want and she felt bound by some obligation to tell him all about it.

"I'm not going to go to bed with you this time," said Margaret.

"Then I won't go to bed with you either," said Shaper.

They both laughed, like old lovers, which in a sense, at least, they were. This too could be stipulated.

"So what do you want?"

"Do you think that's all I visit you for?"

"Well, surprises . . ." He had cleaned the place for Amanda, and been glad to do so; now realized he hadn't cleaned it very much. The pile of unread magazines was straight, but there was dust in the corners of the room, the curtains were grimy, a sock drawer was open. Her eye fell on that drawer. Yes, that was the drawer where he kept his stock of condoms, but it was open in live-alone bachelor carelessness, not in stud readiness. Surprises, he thought, not saying anything more, and waited.

It turned out that Margaret didn't do things, pay her visits, without a reason. "About D'Wayne, I'm gonna . . ." She stopped to mobilize for absolute precision. Meticulousness was not her everyday habit, but she could call it up when she wanted it. "I'm going to surprise you."

"You always do. You like him a whole lot?"

"I want him dead."

"*What?*"

"Woke you up, didn't I? I want her out of there. He doesn't have to be dead, I suppose—"

"Jesus, Margaret—"

"—but out of there. You know how mothers are."

He leaned toward her, looking for the signs that she was about to start laughing.

"Maybe you don't know how mothers are. No experience." She brooded on her several thoughts. "Okay, not necessarily dead, that's going pretty far."

"I guess so," he said.

"You guess you don't owe us that, but think about it, okay?" She had a cheerful, nonjoking gleam in her eyes.

"I don't know what you mean for me to think about."

Now she was really happy. "But you're learning, love, aren't you?"

She didn't need to repeat herself. He had heard her sufficiently. She was ready to move toward procedures. "In your line of work, you must meet some people, someone you can count on . . . Someone you know."

"I know myself is all. I don't even hire out my accounting. I do my own taxes."

"It's better that way."

The population these days seemed to be ahead of Dan Shaper. One of the new people in his life was asking him to take exceptional action. He had experience with resentment and grudges, but this kind of drastic action wasn't in his personal tradition. Raising a knee to D'Wayne was not the way to go, even if it was the way he once foolishly went. Crossing the street to avoid Ferd Conant was more his style. Okay, once he took a landlord to Small Claims Court—unrepaired flue leaking water into his closet—but a Small Claims judgment didn't prepare him for an act of murder upon the request of a woman who wasn't that close to him despite their shared offspring.

"She wants him out?" he asked. "Is he violent?"

"Oh, she's in *love*. But maybe she doesn't want to be in love. Don't you remember about that? I mean, a girl without a father, she needs somebody, anybody, some bad dude— don't you see girls on the street corners around here with their guys waiting in the cars, putting them out to farm?"

"Okay."

"Smart daddy. So far, you see that. And don't you remember what it was like for anybody her age, even a low-octane boy like you back then, when you fell for someone who was nothing but trouble but still you fell?"

"Wouldn't have missed it for the world," Shaper said.

"Well then," said Margaret, "smartening up, aren't you? Taking ginkgo biloba and remembering things? Now that's a good daddy."

But the mommy hadn't answered the question—*What did Amanda want?*

A howl came from the street, seeming to pull with claws at the curtain, which suddenly blew in, carrying its load of grit and madness. Margaret looked startled and Shaper didn't know how he looked, but guessed his expression reflected thoughtfulness about being a father whose daughter had an inappropriate lover. The bland stare of a father whose collaborator in parenthood was suggesting he murder their daughter's beloved. The pensiveness, the due consideration, the moral and legal complications, and what Amanda wanted against what Amanda needed—or maybe Amanda didn't know. Even Dan Shaper, who had so far lived longer than his daughter, a habit of fathers which disconcerts daughters and sons, could list a lot of disjunctions between what he wanted and what he needed. Others could probably think of more.

Giving him time, Margaret went to the window, pulled the curtain, unleashing its load of allergens, sneezed, dusted her grimy fingers, looked for the tormented cat. Peace had been declared on Ellis. Maybe the cat had only been exuberant, a lovelorn poet among cats, or expressing self-loathing because the rat got away into the sewer, a lurking rat metamorphosed by cat noises into a speedy grease-bodied son of a bitch—maybe the cat was just testing its howl reflexes in case a prankster set its tail afire.

Urban creatures bump against a host of unpredictable choices and decisions on life's road. On this occasion Margaret gave Dan as much privacy as her generous spirit could afford. When she decided she had given him enough, she left the view of Ellis, cat, rat, Tenderloin possibilities, Torres imperatives. "He needs to be done and gone," she said. "Is that English?"

It wasn't Spanish, either.

"Your family needs him gone, Dan."

He understood her. He understood the word "family," too. She had planted the word "low-octane" back there for a reason, to get him going, to let him know she could finally be persuaded that he was okay, a real man, even if she couldn't be persuaded—wasn't that the way?

But then she blinked. A memory of the man who had become the father of her daughter, of the accident which could not have been merely an accident, of her own time in life back then, of her years as a mother, gentled the gaze which met his eyes. "It's your job, Dan."

Across the street a couple of Vietnamese kids were playing hopscotch in a court chalked onto the sidewalk, carefree among the ammonia smells of piss and the local outposts of crack, heroin, meth, and alcohol. How quickly immigrants of goodwill become American! Dan Shaper, born in the U.S.A., hadn't been carefree for awhile. He stored up for the future a resolution to have a few carefree moments before he died. Playing hopscotch with a racially diverse group of happy Tenderloin kids was only an idea; if it wouldn't happen, it wouldn't happen. The thought was what counted.

There was no tormented cat in a sack, set up for a southeast-Asian dinner, not visible anyway. Margaret folded her arms. *Well?* she didn't say. But that was the question.

In this extremity, the mother of his child offering the prospect of havoc, Shaper saw more than he wanted to see, more than the fishy motes which floated across his eyes, dead cells like errant sperm; he saw the dust fly from her chair when Margaret stirred, waiting; he saw the besmirched air stirred up by the traffic on Ellis, the staggering drunks, the hookers, the crack pipes, the kids studying American hopscotch; he saw his body shedding its skin as it grew, not quite so skillfully anymore, new skin. His metabolism became visible. His catabolic breakdown became evident. He was frightened by the crowd of dreads which pressed in on him, not death first of all—by fear that Margaret Torres would classify the man she had selected to be Amanda's father as permanently . . . what was the word again? Low-octane.

Margaret tried to equal Shaper in expressionless staring, but didn't succeed—he was the expert. Silences hurtled to and fro in his head with its unshaven cheeks and chin invisibly growing more gray as they sat there in the dusty light. If Margaret still smoked, she would have inhaled deeply, reached over, stubbed out the butt, performing all those pleasant ritual fillers of time and space which she had given up. "Hum," she said—a poor substitute, a synthetic sigh. If she were one to hum music to relative strangers, she would have done so, but she was not that one.

"So it's up to you," she said. "You're the dad. You recognize it without the fucking blood test. You acknowledge it. Ask him in a nice way, Gyro might do something for you, then bury him in a basement, say, but—"

She shouldn't exaggerate. It would only bring much more trouble. Gyro didn't do favors without getting bigger favors back, especially since he seemed fond of D'Wayne.

"I guess it's just your first big responsibility, Dan," she said. She peered into his kitchen. No blender, no microwave, no fine electric helpers; a crinkled box of generic-brand shredded wheat on the sink. He didn't believe in complication or dining in; not even much eating in. She sighed. "Responsibilities sometimes . . . Hey, maybe you got a big vat of acid in there? Surprise me."

Being his lover for a moment back then and hardly giving him a thought ever since seemed to give Margaret Torres sufficient news of Dan Shaper. He had been busy all these years without knowing how busy he was, all his old unfulfilled responsibilities piling up into the big burden which now rested on his back. No carpooling, no food or medical or rent bills paid, no worries during afternoons with the pediatrician or late-night visits to the Emergency Room, no boring homework or bedtime stories, no fretting about inappropriate friends during those drastic adolescent years—no father's duties of care, attention, and protection.

So now just one big obligation and deal with it pretty quick. Deal with D'Wayne. Okay, big fella, deal with him.

"And hey, Dan?" Margaret was asking. "You said something before, but are you sure? You said you know yourself."

Did he say that? It was an interesting claim. She was right to question it. As Amanda's mother, she had a right. She was bringing matters to his attention. She was permitted to do so.

Was he capable of doing what needed to be done? Did he know himself as such a person? Margaret was asking if he knew himself at all and so was he.

Sounds of Vietnamese kids studying soon to be American teenagers. The music of Ellis—cars, horns, a city squeezed tight. The cat howling again, maybe sick or lonely, maybe practicing for midnight courtship.

"I want him gone and you want him gone. Someday Amanda will want him gone. But Danny-boy, I'm not sure we can afford to wait that long."

Margaret wasn't employing her resources of restraint and subtlety. She was offering words to the unwise, asking him to be foolish and rash. The important thing here was that she meant what she said and Dan, saying nothing, agreed with her. D'Wayne deserved his future. Dan owed a lot to Margaret Torres; he owed more to his daughter. The time had come, after considering all the alternatives, to stop considering them.

Metabolically optimistic, operationally merely hopeful, Dan Shaper avoided trouble, fuss, or muss.

God doesn't permit all this comfort to continue. Shaper didn't believe in God, but the universe had its rules. In his case, the law decreed that he deserved a daughter. If he had wanted change before the end, he had it now; and even if he didn't want it.

Listening to the street noises along with Dan, alert in the

way of an old lover to his thoughts, Margaret called a recess in the proceedings. The time had come to remove her own distractions by first offering them to the accidental father, and then handing them over for him to consume in privacy. There was a look of concern, something of both care and resolution in her acknowledgment of another soul out there, that of the living Dan Shaper alone in his worn flesh, and her voice was soft, raised only enough to express anxiety about whether she should speak or not, whether this was really the time, whether there was any good time for it. Despite his hearing loss (unprotected ears during basic-training marksman practice, rock and roll during the Aquarian convulsion, the normal calcification of age), Shaper understood without asking her to repeat.

"I have to say there were bad thoughts about you because you were having an easy time. Don't tell me I could have stopped it. Don't be dumb about it, Dan. I wanted Amanda for myself. She wasn't an accident, *you* were the accident. But I had a hard time anyway. So now, old lover, it's time for you to have the hard time."

It was about as close as Margaret Torres could come to saying she respected the sanctity of this other soul. When it came down to important matters, she was trying to give up that old-time California bullshit.

And so now Margaret Torres was pulling him toward the bed. Dan Shaper didn't always understand what people, including himself, were doing these days. This tugging at him needed no spoken language. She led him there, she made him to lie down, clothes and all, shoes and all, and then lay herself lightly down beside him, hugging him first, not very hard. Then she hugged him tightly, tugging at his shoulders, as if passing some secret to him, a message. "What—?" he began, but she put her finger along his lips, shh, shush.

They were still fully dressed, shoes too. Then Margaret Torres stood up and said, "Okay."

Margaret Torres, ready for public appearance, smiled down at him from the bedside.

Dan Shaper rolled off the bed, leapt up like a fireman hearing the alarm, not wanting to be lying down when she left. Evidently she had other chores for the day.

"So you see," said Margaret, and she opened the door herself, he hadn't expected her to hurry away, she was hurrying away, "old lover," she was saying, maybe she'd said it before, "now you see it wasn't just about a sloppy roll on the mattress, not even then it wasn't, and now too, even if we happen to be here—"

But she no longer was. He heard her footsteps pattering like a girl's down the stairs.

It wasn't an occasion of sentimental retossing of their bodies on twisted sheets. It was an occasion about consequences.

The visit from Margaret Torres didn't end Dan Shaper's busy day, either. Normally traffic was light on the stairway. Shaper stood at his door, thinking about Mr. Patel, the responsible East Indian landlord, who kept many of the hookers and drug dealers out of the building. Mr. Patel was no reader of crystal balls. He couldn't be expected to evict tenants whose troubles with the criminal-justice system were merely pending.

As the iron gate clanged shut, Margaret letting herself out, someone else slipped in with no interference from her and strolled up the stairs. Shaper leaned against his open door, sure he had another caller. Sprightly, showered, cologned, validated by Jesus, Gyro Brown smiled backwards at the memory of Margaret—approving, admiring—before giving

Dan Shaper all his attention. (What a coincidence to meet each other here.) "May I help? In any way?" Gyro asked.

What a coincidence and how thoughtful.

"I think I'd like to run my own life at this point," Shaper said, "but thanks for asking."

Gyro wouldn't upset Gyro's present sunny mood, an event always to be treasured in a world of toil and trouble, by insisting on the obligations friendship put upon him. If Shaper insisted on risking everything, risking himself like a careless young man, why, that was one of the privileges of a careless asshole with not one shitload of a future ahead of him. Jesus hadn't taken account of this question, or if He had, it would take a more genuine Roma than Gyro to find the proper reference in the Apocalyptic Gospels. He had learned to suspend philosophy, enjoyable though it was, during the dilemmas of real life.

Gyro extended the two open palms of friendship, nothing concealed in his hands. "I was just passing by. Saw the gate open. Margaret looks in the pink, Dan! Thought I'd say hello."

Figured things out. Didn't need to ask what was doing. Once again Gyro's life was validated as a festival.

Sixteen

Dan Shaper formulated a four-part plan for his negotiation with D'Wayne, inappropriate lover of a newfound daughter. Preamble: apologize for recent loss of temper, impulsive behavior, and admitted hurtfulness (water under the bridge, how about it, D'Wayne?). Then Step One: appeal to D'Wayne's good nature. Well, briefly acknowledge this possibility, leading directly into Step Two: offer D'Wayne money, suggest he use the cash flow for relocation purposes, perhaps a nice warm climate, someplace more like California than San Francisco manages to be. Or even better, New York, the Big Apple, with its many opportunities for an enterprising young man.

Step Three, in case Steps One and Two came to naught or turned into an unrealistic expense: point out that Harvey could surely find something on him, a warrant, a violation, a stash of weaponry or unprescribed pharmaceuticals (you know how cops are when they have incentive).

Step Four: hurt him again, more seriously. Shaper barely formulated this alternative; if it happened, it would be impulse, not premeditation—that was decided in advance. But what he noted in his heart was: *destroy*. He didn't feel comfortable with the concept "kill"; it seemed too much like murder, which was considered an offense even among his neighbors in the Tenderloin. For the linguist-translator-interpreter of the Latin-based languages, death by design, a contrived hit, was still terra incognita.

The four parts or steps depended on D'Wayne, how he responded.

No. This time it depended on Dan. It was between Dan and Dan, the guy sliding alone through the years in a dusty walkup and the newborn father of one. On life's path, D'Wayne was an obstacle to be moved or removed by any necessary means.

Shaper's hands slipped on the steering wheel. There was no miraculous sudden heat wave making his hands wet. The weather was gray standard winter issue. Driving down Ellis, one of San Francisco's great boulevards of the nonmillionaire group, Shaper noted this odd clamminess. It wasn't caused by an allergy. It wasn't the hobbling drunks and junkies to be avoided as they slipped or tumbled into the street. It wasn't even Harvey in plain clothes in an unmarked car, a drug deal confiscation with antirust underliner on the fenders, cruising slowly; Harvey who stopped only for the most entertaining crimes, such as a tripping Montgomery Street stockbroker on his break from studying 10-K filings, getting knifed by a transvestite hustler whose time he was wasting. Hey, Harvey!

Harvey raised a finger, not the bird-flipping one, in an undercover hello, and also raised an eyebrow to show that he picked up vibes of trouble-seeking. Shaper ducked, acknowledged nothing, but spent his intelligence trying to figure out why the hands should be wet and slippery, also the toes, and now his back the same. If this kept up, he would need to buy a set of driver-side seat beads. Harvey gave a warning honk good-bye.

What right had Harvey to emit that critical beep? He couldn't know what Shaper intended any more than Shaper did.

Two subsidiary difficulties in Shaper's unformulated program for D'Wayne gave him additional worry. They both involved the German shepherd, D'Wayne's faithful companion. Fella was not an issue between Dan and D'Wayne; yet in case of conflict, a loyal animal would not be an unbiased observer. Dan didn't want to hurt Fella. Even more, he didn't want to be hurt by Fella. Trained to respond to the German command, "Feis!" the dog would leap in defense of its master. Even if D'Wayne postponed asking for teeth-sweeping and flesh-ripping—he might not have the patience—Fella was trained to take the initiative if anyone made sudden movements toward its master. The only argument which would surely stop it was a gunshot to the head. This option gave pain to Dan Shaper.

Yet if he asked D'Wayne to segregate the large faithful companion while they discussed matters, he might stimulate suspicion. This was a case of "A Boy and His Dog" versus "Dan Shaper's Daughter and the Inappropriate Lover."

Deliberations came unsorted in Shaper's head. Wisdom and calm had deserted him. He was distressed and distracted.

While religiously keeping his eye on worldly San Francisco traffic, Shaper prayed to heaven. He feared Jesus would be so preoccupied with making good on His old promise to Gyro that one of the lower angels might be assigned to the Dan Shaper case. He deserved a break. He hadn't bothered heaven in years—maybe the last time he prayed was for solace in Cuernavaca after an experience of unwashed lettuce. It's a law of human nature: we'll deal with any handy religion during a time of raging peristalsis.

As he made his way to the Yerba Buena Foundation, he tried to arrange his procedures in practical order before undertaking this heart-to-heart discussion. Yet in cases of panic and rage—the condition of Dan Shaper at the present time—unsorted elements frequently remained unsorted.

Awareness sometimes helps. He was driving carefully. He parked without causing any accidents. A state of calm panic, placid rage, would have to do.

He had heard someplace that deep breathing eases a troubled spirit. He rubbed his hands against his pant legs. Nothing to do about the damp socks. He stood outside the grand Victorian house on Pine Street and practiced the intake of deep, steady, regular breaths. Okay, let's get to it.

Amanda found D'Wayne before she found her father, and she might have found D'Wayne anyway, or someone like him, or someone worse, if she had had a father to be both bad and good to her, as fathers usually were. The world of Might Have was one of idiot freedom.

Shaper felt an ebbing as D'Wayne and he sat and sighed at each other in deep chairs across the room, stretching their legs, the dog putting its wet muzzle first in one lap and then in the other. The darkness deepened as they sat there without speaking. All there was of the fire between them was one pair of eyes across a room in the dark glowing into another pair of eyes.

Amanda had found D'Wayne herself. Grief puts its arms around grief. There was a silence in D'Wayne to be noted especially when he said nothing. Perhaps D'Wayne's arms wrapped mainly around the griefs of D'Wayne, but wasn't that normal? He had no obligation to proclaim or display his griefs. Amanda had grounds for them; so did D'Wayne. If Dan Shaper had awakened earlier, if something besides Amanda, Gyro, and D'Wayne had awakened him earlier, he might have better noticed his own life.

D'Wayne stared into the dark. Shaper's forehead felt hot. He wanted to consult this stranger about the other stranger, his daughter. Developments were surprising him. He too had griefs.

In his legal-support training, there was no system for getting D'Wayne to do what Shaper wanted D'Wayne to do. He could make all the lists of steps he liked, put them in his pocket or write them on his hands; the results were as unpredictable as what might next come hurtling out the window of the welfare hotel across Ellis; a mattress, a bottle, or a body. The noise below the window was usually a splat sound, only a bottle, but judging by the cries and sobs from the window, it had been one filled with precious fluids for the person who had balanced his supper (dining out tonight) on the windowsill. "Dumb motherfucker!" came the refrain, "dumb motherfucker, dumb motherfucker." The resident either had a clumsy guest for supper or was spurred into a bout of self-criticism. On Ellis, too, folks were known to derogate themselves for their regrets in life.

Shaper was wondering if a threat qualified as an offer.

D'Wayne had all the time in the world. He sat; Shaper sat.

Shaper could walk into the Beirut Brothers convience store at the corner of Leavenworth and Ellis and ask for plain yoghurt just as if he had a right to it—they only carried the sugared, sticky kinds—and a cup of chicken-flavored instant noodles, no actual chicken, but actual chicken flavoring, not actually instant since you had to wait four minutes while the boiling water did its chemistry-aided work. . . . He strolled around his neighborhood, buying dinner on the nights when he had a deposition to study for accurate translation. When he had the time, he gave the four-minute instant noodles an extra minute for that well-done taste.

On Pine, D'Wayne was waiting for developments.

He wanted to communicate a sense of self-confidence to D'Wayne. He feared he was better at telling the convenience store guy, "Brother, you ought to carry the unflavored yo-ghurt for people like me," and listening to the brother from Beirut explain that it would just go sour in the case because he was the only person on the block who didn't like the good, pink, sugared kind.

D'Wayne was sitting there silently, watching nothing un-less he was clairvoyant and watching Shaper's mind wander. D'Wayne was fully occupied with saying nothing about Shaper's knee, D'Wayne's injury.

This negotiation should have made Shaper uneasy, given him aches and pains, such as constriction of chest, wetness under the arms, weakness and fluttering in stomach, a com-bination of all these, and it did. He had left the clamminess of his hands back in the traffic; that was a plus.

For D'Wayne, bargaining over a woman may have been part of the job description in his profession as doorman and bodyguard at the Yerba Buena Foundation. Yet he had diffi-culty meeting Shaper's eyes. He tried and succeeded for a moment, then looked away. The teeth gleamed; the smile was boyish and pure; but it was an act of will, the performer's art. D'Wayne was embarrassed. He seemed nearly confused. Peo-ple were not always what a person expected them to be; that was why crime sometimes paid and sometimes did not, just like right behavior.

Shaper would not let sympathy for D'Wayne interfere with his task. Professionally, interpreting for gangbangers who had forgotten their English language skills when their arrests came along, he tried to keep to a professional standard of no distracting compassion.

The door to the parlor opened and an early evening visitor came strolling through, just as if he had some business here. "Hey, hey!" It was Ferd Conant, wandering around and think-ing this might be the place; Ferd with his last-call eyes and neck corrugations like thoracic smiles, crevices of sub-face mirth above the collar. Ferd, unnecessary Ferd, peeked around in the dark, started dramatically, and peeked some more. His eyes gleamed with the thrill of seeing D'Wayne and Dan together in conversation.

Without a word, Shaper got up. The wet-muzzled dog could stay. Ferd could go. Shaper fitted a winsome smile over his lips (couldn't characterize it for sure without a mirror), then with two hands on Ferd's shoulders, turned him around and headed him out. D'Wayne clasped his own hands together slowly, silently, and awaited further developments.

D'Wayne knew that Shaper was close to letting go. D'Wayne stood up, gave him his back, ambled over and pulled the curtain, let in light from the street, looked out the window as if the traffic on Pine were suddenly of great interest to him. Shaper might let go for the second time since he was an eighteen-year-old in an Army Spanish-language training program, when he broke ranks and leapt on the back of an asshole fellow soldier. . . . D'Wayne couldn't know about that first time; he only knew about the recent second time. But he turned to expose his high tight rump.

No, Shaper would not jump him from behind, so then D'Wayne examined his cuticles. They had been done professionally, it seemed, or maybe by one of the Yerba Buena therapists, planning her retirement career. Bluish and pink half-moons and shiny nails covered with clear polish, a veritable art project in fingernail design. During his entire life, Shaper had never sat still for a manicurist; oh, seen them through windows of the Mary Siam Shoppe on Eddy and elsewhere. D'Wayne smiled at his cuticles, turned his hands this way and that, not looking at Shaper, giving him a good shot. D'Wayne worked his lips. . . . Had Amanda done his nails? D'Wayne worked his lips, pouting, unpouting, eating invisible air, in a way which he knew must be irritating, especially to someone who wanted him disappeared off the earth.

D'Wayne was ready for him.

D'Wayne was teasing him with lazy ambling.

D'Wayne was waiting for Shaper's move.

A bad time for Shaper to make his move.

D'Wayne's low, clicking, tickling laughter, something like embarrassment, more like a private pleasure of the chest, passed the time until Dan Shaper would offer him further entertainment. Black Barbara passed through on her way from the kitchen refrigerator with her container of chocolate milk marked "B's Keep Off!!!"; realized they wouldn't speak until she left—"Parm, guys. Short cut"—and flounced out, her wide soft buttocks flapping unconcernedly. She knew when a girl was unneeded.

Even if Shaper wasn't enjoying this, D'Wayne was. The score was lopsided so far. Next?

D'Wayne seemed to be wearing Gyro's cologne, but the reek of his own body changed the flavor. Shaper wished his nose would mind its own business and not bother him when he was busy with negotiations.

"Yo, kitten got your tongue right there?" D'Wayne suddenly asked.

Shaper wanted to make sure about his options.

"So nothin' make you utter? You so uncool?" D'Wayne inquired. "Hey, you over there?"

He was, and uncool.

"No skin off my butt, man. You somethin', but hey, that's natural, cause Amanda she really somethin' too. One of the thangs about that girl."

Flattery was not D'Wayne's normal practice. He called up

this heavy artillery as a pure exercise in maneuvering. Time to reflect was an element in his favor.

Dan Shaper decided it was time to follow a plan. "Everybody can use a nice vacation," he began. "I'd like to help." This sounded clumsy, so he tried again. "I can find you a deal, you understand what I'm saying?"

It wasn't all that complicated. D'Wayne showed his healthy teeth as if the whole of his life were a vacation. At times D'Wayne had seen people hurt, but he didn't enjoy it— hurting may have been something he had seen himself obliged to do to others. A smile, smoothing things over, was preferable unless rigor mortis took place, in which case even a steady high beam wasn't enough.

"Maybe someplace where you grew up," Shaper said. "Where you could stay awhile, settle, get into some line of work."

D'Wayne was still grinning, not speaking, wondering how this would go. He was already in a line of work.

"Not too late to put down roots there, or someplace else, yours is the choice. We"—who was *We?*—"we could arrange for a guarantee, the ticket, moving costs, and then something for the adjustment—"

D'Wayne broke his silence. "Man, grew up? Grew up right here, man. Cross the Bay, on the old bus line. I was a kid, just stretch out and nap, twenty minutes quick from Oakland, and even I was a kid, nobody standing in that bus say, 'Hey, give some old white lady there a seat.' Know what I mean? Didn't want to say that, man."

"I want you to stay away from my daughter."

"Oh, man, you a *individual.* Oh man, you take being a father to heart, don't you? What I mean, you know, you full of shit?"

So, just as Dan Shaper had suspected, the line of practical

appeal and small sums of money did not offer an immediate solution.

D'Wayne's eyes closed. For a moment his lips hid his teeth, those biting instruments. "You don't understand, mister. How about Mandie and her mother both? You just walked away, am I right? It ain't like that with me and her."

Now was coming the part where he said he was a responsible person. Hardly anyone ever says, *I'm unreliable.*

"You think I don't know how to be. Sometimes *I* think I don't know. I never had a daddy neither, just like she didn't. They all took off. You took off and that was it. She had to find you, man, didn't she? So listen up."

Shaper was listening. The dog's flanks shuddered as it crouched, dozing at D'Wayne's feet. Fella was having a dog dream, thinking a dog idea.

"Mandie and me, Mister?" D'Wayne's lips were moving, practicing what he wanted to say, and then he said it. "Whatever it means, whatever it's good for, I love your daughter, asshole."

Was this the time? No, this was not the right time. How could a person plan the time for this? It must have been the word *love*, or perhaps the linked words *love* and *asshole*, that set the mechanism in motion.

Shaper started at D'Wayne, an abrupt forward jolt, instead of asking (whispering, shouting), What right have you to talk about love? D'Wayne's response was odd. He protected Shaper from a slashing wound. He spoke sharply, "*Stay!*" and grabbed the collar of the dog as it lunged. A greedy burr rolling in its throat, the dog jerked forward, striving against D'Wayne's arm. "Stay! Stay!" D'Wayne shouted. The dog pulling, the collar choking it in D'Wayne's fist, D'Wayne tugged toward the door, opened, dragged it out. He shut the door tight and stood against the furious and bereft barking just outside. D'Wayne said, "Now, man, you gonna get yourself some cuts turn into cute scars like that. If you lucky."

Shaper did not say thank you.

D'Wayne crooked his finger. "I beckon you," he said. "Just don't excite the animal."

Barking, barking, a knot of rage bumping at the door, the dog smelled trouble, its nostrils full of it. D'Wayne smelled no serious trouble for himself. He smelled delight and sniffed the air, as if the sweat that burst off Shaper were a nice spray of cologne he would take joy in walking through.

While Shaper was admiring D'Wayne's sportsmanship, D'Wayne seemed to be unbuttoning his pants. It was not the act of a son-in-law relaxing in the company of his beloved's father. Inside his belt, inside his pants, somehow protected from causing him harm—why not a switchblade?—was a knife. The knife seemed to leap out of D'Wayne's pants and into his hand. The barking outside the door diminished; there was a small deprived mewling. The animal was still objecting to something. The animal seemed to resent that D'Wayne didn't need it for protection. The animal was jealous.

D'Wayne yawned.

Pardon?

D'Wayne yawned, showing bluish soft palate. He held the knife with his eyes squeezed shut while flapping sounds were transmitted from his throat, defenseless, vulnerable, and throbbing with contempt.

"You know, if I could," he said, poking with the point of the knife at his own finger, peering closely for a spot of blood, "I'd prefer to be a thinker, one of those—I don't mean rap or hiphop, that's not my preference, see—a *thinker* type thinker."

Shaper waited for further explanation.

"Ain't no job opportunities in that field," D'Wayne said.

"You can use thinking in a lot of ways—"

"Hey, man—word." He licked the drop of blood. He wasn't suggesting drawing a drop from Shaper's finger, joining like blood brothers, sharing since they already shared. He tasted his own. Since Shaper was studiously not staring at the knife, he wanted to convince him that the point was sharp. D'Wayne was a thinker.

D'Wayne was enjoying the discussion. Objectively speaking, he admired it. He looked ready to stand up and waltz around their words, addressing the ensemble from every angle. He sacrificed this pleasure in order to continue a productive give-and-take. "Alls I'm saying is . . ."

But he had said enough. A good conversationalist has intuitions about when to stop; good conversation was one of D'Wayne's favorite fields of endeavor. "You know?" This was not a request for reassurance. It was more like a command: you *know*.

D'Wayne turned the knife with its grayish blade over in his hands. He licked the nick in his finger, sucking to draw another drop of blood. Then swiftly he lifted the knife— Shaper was ready, but readiness doesn't help with knives— and D'Wayne didn't use the foolish old-movie overhand grip, didn't use the menacing underhand jab against which there is no defense except running away. . . . He flipped the knife into the air at Shaper. Shaper dodged as it landed with an odd heavy thump. He picked it up and D'Wayne was laughing and saying, "April Fool."

The blade, hard rubber, bent in Shaper's fingers.

"Got this little nick in my finger just waiting to show you," D'Wayne said. "Ain't I cute now?"

No wonder Amanda liked him. She didn't have a cute father.

Cute D'Wayne had excluded the dog with its steamy wet muzzle and its mission to rip flesh. He flashed only a rubber knife for protection. He cut Shaper to the quick. The father-in-law equivalent did not wish to be laughed at by the son-in-law equivalent.

So if D'Wayne really cared for Amanda, since he was busy saying he loved Amanda while the asshole father wanted to move his daughter from the wrong place in her life to some better place. . . "How much would it take? Give me a reasonable number."

"Gelt?" D'Wayne asked. "That still your idea?"

"What do you need? Okay, gelt-wise," Shaper said, "how much?"

D'Wayne appreciated the echo. Shaper was paying attention. One courtesy deserved another. "Ain't no cheap pimp," D'Wayne said. "What you got in mind, not knowing your basic means? You tell me."

Finally they were on a track of mutual listening; one said something and the other heard it, responded; the other took it in, chewed it around, transmitted further messages. They proceeded.

Shaper appreciated the distinction D'Wayne insisted on making. He was no cheap pimp, so Shaper asked: "How about the high two figures, say ninety-nine dollars?"

D'Wayne looked peaceful, absent, filled with dreamy calm, close to grace, close to God as if this proximity were a habit.

"Nine-nine," said Shaper, rubbing it in.

It was time for D'Wayne to show what he could do; to reveal hidden talents. He stood up, stretched, and perched on one leg like a stork, a dancer, or a tribesman startled in the forest. Sometimes he liked showing off; it was one of his hobbies. He liked respect and, in a big city careless of its gifted ones, got little unless he stringently demanded it. Others, such as Dan Shaper, would topple if they tried this posture. Dan was no tribesman, dancer, or stork. It wasn't just the age difference. Shaper paid tribute with a respectful nod.

Slowly D'Wayne's foot descended. Invisible choirs applauded. "Wanna try it, or can't?" D'Wayne inquired of Shaper, and followed the question with a sincere shy duck of the head (*Just kidding*).

Folks around here seemed to be good at changing the subject. Shaper said: "I'll raise. An even hundred on the line. Cash."

On two legs D'Wayne moved toward him. He considered it disrespectful to be disrespected. In the closed room, with its dust of life just passing through on a temporary basis, D'Wayne's moving this close brought personal smells nearby, his face so close that purplish nostrils, flaring open for business, displayed their oily wet hairs within. For a moment Shaper regretted his sarcasms. He was startled by abrupt nearness. He butted D'Wayne away with a swift raising of the knee, thrusting it into the crotch, and despite D'Wayne's adeptness at balancing on one leg, he was hit, he cried out in surprise, he stumbled against a chair. Falling, his head struck a table, the lamp spilled, there was the popping noise of a lightbulb shattered and then a long sigh. D'Wayne lay silent, ungainly. Blood oozed from his forehead.

Shaper stood above him. It was an accident even if it was not. If the blood was oozing, it meant he was alive, didn't it? Maybe it didn't.

Shaper must have waited a few seconds, as still in a ready crouch on his two legs as D'Wayne had been on one leg when he showed how it was done.

A bubble of saliva on D'Wayne's lips just stayed there.

Shaper bent to see if he was breathing. Shaper should have done other things, called for help. There was an old Van Morrison wail reverberating through the wooden building. Shaper thought of things to say to the police. He was drugged and fell and hit his head; surely they would find drugs in his blood. He'd pulled a knife, hadn't he? Even if it was rubber. Shaper couldn't be held responsible for a fall, a big man who attacked a smaller older one, fell, struck his head. Even if Shaper had dreamed of murder, he wasn't guilty if his dream came true.

The threat had been real. The knife was gray and ominous in the half-light of drawn curtains. A man has the right to defend himself.

Light glinted from D'Wayne's eyes. Sometimes, watching a woman sleep, Shaper had seen this sign that eyelids never truly closed, the life of dream went on, soul was ready to break through the lashes. The house was shaken by Van Morrison. Barbara liked the old songs, and so did some of her clients, and the deaf ones liked it loud. The dog twitched and quivered, yelped piteously. Fella's sensitive German-shepherd ears were tormented by Van Morrison's Celtic keening. D'Wayne wasn't moving. A man shouldn't curl up and close down like a stepped-on alley creature. His eyes, a yellowish pink, rolled up under ajar eyelids, seemed out of commission. "That getting to be a habit, man?" D'Wayne asked. "Don't you ever learn?"

Shaper bent down and whispered, "I'm sorry, I'm sorry, I'm sorry—"

"You got to learn manners. You got to stop that."

Shaper let D'Wayne have the last word. He opened the door. The women were in their rooms; the dog watched suspiciously; the music reverberated against wood and shingles. Gyro must have been away, looking at automobiles. He liked to browse in used-car lots. Like a good father, he may have taken Shari along for the ride. Someday he wanted a fleet of caravans; everyone had dreams.

Shaper slipped out and the dog whimpered and rubbed a wet muzzle on his leg as he went.

Seventeen

It couldn't have happened; it did happen. He found a traditional remedy to the trouble rolling over him. He lay on his side in bed, curled with his sore hand clasped between his knees in his less sore hand, and he sank—it was like a fall through space—he checked out. He fell asleep and then surely he would wake and this life would have been a dream, someone else's wrong dream.

In this other universe of delightful dreams, he was a clever young man with stylish clothes and a job ("position") as an investment manager and two very pretty girlfriends, one an elegant blonde with a black velvet headband in her shining hair and the other, the other . . . The other really loved sex, loved him, loved lovemaking more with him than with anyone.

Right. In this other world there was no daughter, there was no D'Wayne, but in the world as it existed he wanted the daughter more than anyone, D'Wayne less than anything. So he did not merely sleep and dream of a life he would never have chosen even if the genie MBA recruiting agent had said, Here, go for it. Stuporously he sank into his bed on Ellis.

Amazed and exhausted sleep of panic; sleep of despair; sleep of not knowing what else to do, what more could be done, since he had already succeeded in doing everything wrong.

What kind of a shambling old fart does the same thing wrong *twice?* A man with a daughter can't give up, thinks he can hide in sleep.

A screech and maximum-volume ringing shook him from his bed. The screech came from the person across the street in the welfare Single Room Occupancy (formerly Residence Hotel with rooms by the day, week, month, or if need be, hour, many with running water), the woman with the long gray hair worn to her shoulders like an aware teenager's with hormones erupting—the teenager she must have been when Shaper was an adolescent engrossed in his own stirring. The ringing came from the telephone. He answered with a former-smoker's phlegm still thick in his throat.

The woman with the long gray hair was shrieking from her window at the street below, "Shut-the-fuck-up, shut-the-fuck-up," as was her habit when the noise of the city subsided. She shrieked at silence. When there were brakes grinding, fights for domestic, drug, or alcohol reasons, loud sidewalk negotiations about who suffered more in Vietnam and whether St. Anthony's food was shit while Food Not Bomb's chow was yummy—once a quarrel involving Janey of Janey's Medal of Honor Tavern about whether Janey was a real woman, since she had won her distinguished piece of tin as a Navy man in World War II—when there was appropriate action on the street, the lady with the long gray hair listened, elbows on her windowsill, smiling, nodding, serene, a part of the great chain of being. In the case of Janey, she actually came downstairs to the sidewalk to adjudicate: Janey had now spent most of her life as a woman; ergo, she was a real woman, no matter what President Truman thought when he pinned the piece of tin on her seaman's dress jacket.

Shaper felt a kinship with the lady with the long gray hair. In her own way she responded critically to what went on in the world. She broke into her chant at hiatus, at Tenderloin intermissions. A lull had occurred. She was enraged.

The ringing of the telephone was Amanda calling, wanting him right away; she wouldn't explain; he should drive back to the Yerba Buena Foundation immediately; she wouldn't discuss anything by phone. "Get onto those wheels of yours. Now. I think you've got to."

On the street, a gathering of Vietnamese kids, learning American manners, was trying to flip cigaret butts into the room of the lady with long gray hair. Aerodynamically, a difficult task. They were hip to current street style, but not the American law of gravity. The glowing butts fell short, sparking against the pavement around their dragging jeans. They were wearing last year's fashionable low-crotch diarrhea pants. The lady was beaming benevolently down upon them. Now, with action occurring, she herself could feel free to shut the fuck up.

Shaper was fully awake. He had new respect for the besieged gray-haired lady. In her position he might have been boiling kettles of water and it would be a big, big mistake to do so. He was awake, trying to think straight in the real world. Whatever lay ahead, he wanted to be clean and sweet-smelling for his daughter. He hurried into the shower like a young swain, opening his mouth and shouting against the cold stream. Not sweaty for awhile.

For a lifetime he had let the years happen to him, a pimply kid one day and the very next day a guy with white cheek bristles on weekends when he saw no reason to shave. The Latino crime trade, his vocation and chief distraction, was no fault of his, was it? It was what he knew how to do. Then he found in himself another person whom he never suspected. The angry and anxious father, the doting stingy dad, was no one familiar to him. Watching over Amanda, he was no smarter than D'Wayne's German shepherd. Guard parent was not a good plan. He had never given up the idle dream of finding dearest love, perhaps with violins on the sound track— would she come scampering across a lawn, leaping into his arms? Sometime in the receding future?

It turned out that he found her in the past, in the real world, in the past of which he was ignorant, in this gum-chewer Amanda, this narrow-eyed and suspicious young flesh of his flesh whom he didn't know at all. They had skipped the stage of hair products. He seemed to know Amanda a little less with every encounter. Maybe parents who went through the hair-product period in their daughters' lives also experienced the process of gradually becoming strangers to their children, but Shaper was not other parents.

The telephone was ringing again as he toweled off between his legs. He let the answering machine click on, the volume turned up loud as always, and it was a lawyer about a kid in the usual trouble, driving a vehicle without a license, and also the vehicle wasn't his, and also he had an underage girl— similarly Guatemalan legal resident, similarly inept—and they were just out having fun, but the fun included picking up a big Pepsi, el Pepsi grande, some microwave burritos, and the money in the cash drawer at a convenience store; no weapons, just a knife, just a lot of yelling, raised voices—Korean clerk— not much in the way of firepower. . . . Shaper wasn't picking up messages just now. It could wait or he would lose the job, whatever. The woman across the street, straining toward the maximum volume from his machine, inadequate at her distance, leaned out the window and readied herself for her mantra: *Shut the fuck up.* Shaper stood at the window, half dressed, and shrugged at her. He could do no better with his PhoneMate. He was sorry. She should understand. How about a good neighbor policy?

He retreated from the window and the lady resumed her serenade. As he dressed, checking that he could still lift one leg to slide it into Jockey shorts while standing on the other— not so unbalanced by years that he toppled—he was not one to peer into the mirror and ask mirror questions, Why am I here? Where am I going? Instead, he was one to note that there was a gradual slippage of balance and he had already toppled once or twice. After a few more times, reaching to prop himself against a wall, he would take to putting on his shorts while sitting on the edge of the bed. Not yet; not yet, O Lord. And he needed no mirror to ask these questions and give these answers. No one hanging about with sly questions. No cool eye to behold his old-guy strangeness.

Running shoes. Doubled pair of white socks because he didn't want feet slippery with anxiety. AIDS Benefit tee shirt. Soft tan flannel shirt from L.L. Bean. Street-ready as he was going to be.

The woman across Ellis peered into his apartment. If he pulled the curtain or drew the shade, she might start shrieking again. All things considered, letting her watch him dress was a better solution to the noise-pollution issue on Ellis.

A fellow needs to take a pee before he gets into the resolution of his future. The lady across the street couldn't see into the shadows of his bathroom. As a man who lived alone, Shaper wasn't used to shutting the door of his bathroom, although sometimes he did when sitting in the dark and seeing the lady across the street peeking this way and that. He took the time to appreciate the song of the pee stream, that enamelled tune slamming vigorously against the walls of the toilet bowl, demonstrating the enduring power of his prostate. No dribble, like some he could name. If there was a serious problem about D'Wayne, better empty his bladder fully before heading back into the problem.

Amanda said immediately. There was a creature out there who had the right to make demands of Dan Shaper.

Into the lull of Ellis, the lady in the S.R.O. reuttered her imperative mantra, her version of the Ommm.

Su-James, one of the tall transvestites from the corner, tottered over, clicking like a pony on her heels, stood under the lady's window, cupped her hands, squinted carefully through her mascara in case the lady decided to drop major food or a mattress on her head, and called up, "Honey, I'm making as much noise as I can, but my deep throat's sore tonight—"

Su-James knew the requirements. She asked to be excused.

"—so give us a break, honey, okay?"

"Give you a break," said the gray-haired lady, flinging a cup at the feet of Su-James. It bounced, did not shatter; tacky plastic. Mesh-clad legs splayed, Su-James picked it up. "Really needed that," he/she said. "Don't need your constant whining, girlfriend, so would you kindly go stick your head in the microwave?"

How would she shut the door? thought Dan Shaper.

He finished tying his shoes, his hand aching. How serious was the damage to D'Wayne? His hand was cramped. Insidious old-guy arthritis, was that on the way? The usual bad results of life had been gradual in making their appearance, now were rushing at him. One of his clients, whose English was better than he admitted in court, claimed that he shouldn't be asked to raise his right arm to tell the whole truth because he was afflicted with Arthur-itis.

Shaper's knuckles weren't swollen, but the entire hand hurt. No, yes, the knuckles were swollen a little and it was painful to make a fist. He shouldn't have made a fist at D'Wayne, or kicked, or kneed.

He felt okay, not quite, running down the stairs.

Trash was blowing through the canyons of Ellis, condoms

in the gutter, blood on the curb, whitish sprouts of weed between the cracks, a soothing edge of green moss in places
where the lady across the street had not come out with her
spoon to scrape the walk clean of growing things. She ignored
the styrofoam cups, the condoms, the takeout throwaway cartons, but attacked anything green and growing with a pure
rage like her rage against silence.

A parking ticket flapped in the wind under the eroded
windshield wiper of Shaper's Honda Civic. He didn't look to
see why he was ticketed. He didn't remove the ticket. He
would drive until it blew away, if it blew away, and in time it
would. Didn't matter now.

A-No. 1 Cantonese on the corner had put up a new sign,
suffering from the recent competition from Cambodian, Vietnamese, Hunan, Thai, and just plain McDonald's.

> **GOURMET PRICES: All you can eat plus more**
>
> **(No baggies please.)**

Mr. Wong at A-No. 1 was agitated by competition and perhaps too much MSG. Shaper ducked a little, not wanting Mr.
Wong to notice him, ashamed at having shifted his dining-
out routines in recent times, due to beef-broccoli over rice
fatigue. When he ducked, he caught sight of something in his
side mirror.

A beat-up Buick Skylark was tailgating him down Ellis. The
driver saw the flick of his head as Shaper picked up the tail,
and in a roar of leaky motor, a fume of illegal emission, the
Buick pulled alongside. In his black body shirt, tight around
the muscles, Harvey mouthed *Watch the road*, with a puzzled

stare of: why you wobbling, drinking at this hour? Harvey cruised past in his unmarked car, the usual confiscated vehicle which would go to the police auction next month. The police department had the illusion that the pimps and dealers of Tenderloin Village wouldn't recognize them if they changed vehicles frequently. Maybe they wouldn't if they looked only at the car—today a stupid hood's Buick, tomorrow a tasteful pimp's Volvo—and not at Harvey himself, bluish tight shaving, black muscle shirt, jaw so tight he had to wear a nightguard after the dentist warned him he was loosening his rear teeth. For esthetic reasons, Harvey didn't want to lose those teeth; he liked tucking into steaks at Original Joe's on Taylor. As to the cars he was given, that was mere business, not a matter of status or taste, and didn't affect the general outlines of his cheek and jaw.

Watch the road, Harvey mouthed, and roared past in a cloud of illegal particles.

Lately Shaper was with Harvey in the tooth-grinding, jaw-clenching area. He awakened sometimes with his pillow wet—it wasn't tears leaking out of this grown man, this fully adult confused individual. Even now his mouth tasted of cotton. The grown man was biting his pillow like an angry child, but since it happened in sleep, he couldn't be blamed by anyone but his dentist, couldn't be called an angry child, could he? Not by anyone but himself, the pillow-biter, the fretful cotton-eater with degenerating sleep habits.

Faith was supposed to be the best evidence of things not known, but this didn't apply to the flesh of his flesh. The evidence had to be gathered on earth. For Dan Shaper, the hard part was to bring Amanda to evidence and faith in San Francisco. Love found through an accident of blood and event was awakening him before his life ended. He looked for a chance to prove he was alive and confused, like others. Amanda, she still had many chances, she could think of children to come—to claim, care for, enlist in routines of which Dan Shaper had been ignorant. Amanda was her father's last chance.

He was learning about debts. He owed much to Margaret. He may not have earned the right to tell Margaret and Amanda they owed him something, too. He was more than a cranky Spanish-speaking guy who walked to 850 Bryant from the Tenderloin. He needed to convince them. Youth was gone, but they could still find desire in his eyes if they didn't see only old-guy neediness.

Margaret, I have a secret for you, but I can't tell you, you won't *believe me, I don't dare tell you, it's unjustified, I have no right.* . . . Whatever power there was in the universe, it did not make for righteousness or correct ideas. It only made for what ensued. The motive of power between one stranger and another was this gravity, this embarrassing behavior. He loved his daughter and it changed everything.

He parked in the blue handicapped zone in front of the Yerba Buena Foundation. A man who wanted to kill his daughter's lover, even if it was only manslaughter due to murderous jealousy, shouldn't worry about a parking violation.

He ran up the steps, his feet pattering like a kid's, happy to be home. He stopped at the door. Usually the door was locked, opened by a release from within.

The door was ajar. Someone was expecting someone.

Eighteen

He admitted himself and was greeted by no one. A twenty-four-hour therapy center should have a receptionist on duty at all times, including the twenty-four-hours of the day. Where was everyone?

There was a hospital smell of cleaning powder, something blue-green to be swept up, and also a smell of Mercurochrome, that useless childhood antiseptic which Shaper's mother painted on boo-boos. He headed toward the former maid's room where he heard a stir of voices, a radio playing hiphop, a chair being moved. It was D'Wayne's apartment, the place where D'Wayne and his faithful German shepherd kept their privacy. A woman's voice murmured something and turned down the radio. Shaper recognized the voice. He pushed open the door.

That smell of Mercurochrome, a wad of pinkish bandages in a wastebasket, a litter of Kleenex on the floor, an ashtray with a joint in it, and the clock radio humming on the table alongside the bed. D'Wayne was sitting up, propped against pillows. His skin glowed against the fresh bandage on his head, a becoming whiteness setting off the tawny eyes, one of which had a fine network of broken capillaries. His nurse, Amanda Shaper, glared at her father.

"So," said Shaper.

"I like that, I like that a lot," Amanda said. "*So.* That is one terrific apology."

D'Wayne patted her arm. "Hey, lay off the old guy, okay? He's embarrass. He's sorry, you hear me, Mandie? Get to know the daddy, understand what I'm saying?"

"So," she repeated.

Dan Shaper was at a disadvantage. For one thing, he was outnumbered; also, a sense of moral weakness tended to make his bowels turn flimsy. The bathroom was just down the hall; he could get there in time if need be. Even sprawled and injured, D'Wayne was too big to be called a plucky little fellow with a boo-boo.

Shaper felt old and tongue-tied in these premises. The weak hiphop din from the clock radio jangled his nerves, interfered with hearing things he might not like to hear but needed to hear anyway. He pressed the On-Off button.

D'Wayne nodded stiffly. He approved of a man who reached for what he wanted, in this case, no radio.

"You could have been badly hurt," Shaper said.

"I'm not."

"I didn't try to get help," Shaper said.

"Probably do the same for you."

Shaper appreciated forgiveness, if that's what it was, or understanding, in case that was what D'Wayne intended. Since he used to think he knew himself and it turned out he didn't, there was no reason to think he knew D'Wayne.

"Thing bother me, though, Fella didn't make no move—not enough a one."

"He knows me," Shaper said, finding excuses for the dog. "Wasn't he locked out?"

"Not that tight. Suppose to be man's best friend, not suppose to hang around knowing people, thinking you some kind a buddy. Suppose to be barking, acting bad, jump and scratch on the door, maybe get smart and come through the window take a chunk out of you."

Shaper expressed no satisfaction that Fella failed the test.

"So now we talk business, how's that sound?" D'Wayne asked, squinting under the bundle of wrapping on his head. He seemed to have a headache, but intended to work right through it. There were things on his mind. He gave Shaper a little time to catch up with the program.

Are you the person I thought you were? Shaper wanted to ask. Better not to do so, because D'Wayne preferred to be the person D'Wayne thought he was, not what Shaper decided for him. And it turned out that Dan Shaper was not the person he had thought he was, either, when Amanda came around, bringing D'Wayne with her. Margaret was who she thought she was. Gyro, maybe. And Harvey, Ferd, Shari, those fortunate others who were what they seemed to be or maybe not. How could Dan Shaper ever again be confident in these matters?

He should have been ready for anything, even "checking out," as he liked to name it, since "dying" was too personal, but he had not been ready to become a father. D'Wayne and Amanda were ahead of him in their planning.

While D'Wayne rested against a pillow, Amanda slipped her hand under his head and burned reproachful eyes against Dan Shaper. "Even if I like him," she began, but D'Wayne interrupted: "Mandie!" She rolled her eyes, indulging the cripple, the wounded hero, who wanted to talk first. But didn't give up her place in line. "I got a few things—"

"Mandie!"

"—to tell you," she finished, and grandly shrugged. "I'll wait." She continued her dramatic presentation, thrumming fingers on her knee, meaning, Hurry, get your shit out so I can get on with it. Indulgent impatience was the product she was presently putting on display. "I got all the time in the world, they tell me. That's what they tell me."

D'Wayne called upon the power of remaining silent. It was a skill he had developed as a doorman with difficult visitors. He fit a space of silence around the speech he had prepared. The house was not still; quiet was relative around here. Barbara was singing or making love a few rooms away; Amanda thrumming; laundry machine churning. And that squeal and a faint hot stink . . . No, not, Shaper thought, no one ran over a skunk on the street out there. No, no, no, that acrid skunk smell was something else, antiseptic, bodies, his own anxiety; or maybe a truck ran over a raccoon out foraging with its family.

Time for D'Wayne to attend to business. "I give you credit," he said, "those moves you got, one-two, right with the shove and then the table rear up and crack me upside the head. Lucky I got muscles on my scalp, but then kind of *mis*-lucky—hurts on the outside *and* inside, man."

"Headache bad?" Shaper asked.

"Gyro give me something for it. I got a nice buzz, almost make it worthwhile, that's how good I feel."

"He's rational," Amanda said. "He ought to take that more often, dope that makes him rational. Makes me feel like cuddling. How about you, Dad?"

Her face was sly and catlike. She liked to try things out. She was checking through possibilities.

"Would you like to lie down with me, Dad?"

"Come off it, Amanda."

"Just rest, hey, what a baby does with a daddy, you know, if she has one? Isn't that what they do? Nap time?"

"No."

"Are you nervous, Dad?"

D'Wayne was watching through sleepy slitted eyes because he didn't know everything and here was something to learn. He patted the bed and invited Shaper to relax, have no fear, take a nice seat after his long tiring life. "What I paid for it, this ain't no mattress. I saw this on Home Shopping Network, cable, it's one fuck more'n a mattress—feel! This here is my Personal Contemporary Sleep System I got without giving them no stupid credit-card number—from the outlet store on Potrero, man. This here's a no pee stains, no pecker tracks, no visible flaws mattress, because D'Wayne right here, it's first-class travel all day, all night. Am I right, Mandie?"

"Pig," she answered fondly.

He accepted this in the spirit with which it was offered. "Hey, but sensitive to girl's issues, ain't I, baby?"

"Go to sleep," she said. "I think there's some speed mixed up in that stuff Gyro gave you—"

"Anal-gesic," he said, showing off, finishing her thought for her. He tried to wink at Dan Shaper. He wanted a little gratitude for getting him off the hook in a difficult confrontation with his daughter. D'Wayne sought to be sensitive to a father's issues, too. He couldn't complete the wink, due to facial swelling.

The door opened and uninvited visitors stood there just as if they had been invited. Margaret Torres said mildly, "What the goddamn, D'Wayne, your head looks like—"

Words failed her.

Margaret sank into an overstuffed chair. She wouldn't bother anyone, she would just sit there. After all, she was family, wasn't she? She left Gyro alone in the doorway to decide if he were family, too, although he wasn't.

Arms linked behind his back, surveying his domain, turning his gaze from one to another, from Amanda and D'Wayne to

Margaret and Shaper, scanning the entire picture for his ancestral memory stash, Gyro moved his bulk through the doorway. His checked sports jacket had very wide shoulders. He was dressed for success at Golden Gate Fields, where the horses were running today, but he preferred to preside over this reunion. He appeared ready to offer little glasses of something sweet if somebody would make him feel welcome, but nobody was doing so. Gyro's feelings weren't hurt. "I admire a man who accepts his responsibilities," he said. "Even Jesus—"

"A proven fact of history," Shaper interrupted, unwilling to listen again to the bill of rights of a wandering tribe.

Stirred awake by company, definitely speeding through his analgesic, D'Wayne enjoyed being part of a philosophical discussion. Amanda just accepted being here. Margaret was curious about consequences without needing to mention all the work she had done in raising her child. Shaper could have used the backup of Harvey, stretching and sucking in his gut and not putting up with shit, but perhaps it was for the best to deal with this alone. He definitely enjoyed not seeing Ferd hanging around and making mental notes.

"Dad," said Amanda, "one day soon you and I really got a lot to catch up with."

It was her way of breaking the ice. That day had begun to come, but the ice was not broken, despite Amanda's best efforts. "Something about you all here gets me to thinking," Gyro said.

"Thinking you got other things to do." Shaper's voice was sharp.

Amanda looked startled. She didn't expect Gyro to be spoken to that way. She didn't expect Shaper to be the one to do it. What girl knew her father anyway?

D'Wayne made a face of happy surprise at Shaper. He assented, he spoke agreeably to Gyro. "You got some deal going down somewheres else, don't you, man?" And he grinned at Amanda's father for approval of their united front.

Amanda diddled fingers against knees.

Margaret leaned back to disappear into her chair.

Gyro sensed that his company was not desired, figured it out. He waited for a retraction. None came. He raised the extra shoulders in the extra-broad sports jacket. He wasn't going to make an issue of it.

"Bye, Gyro," said Margaret from the depths of the upholstery, cuddling down to scratch her back.

Gyro opened the door, showed his teeth, showed them his new clothes one more time—not heading for the track at all, heading downtown to argue with a judge about parking tickets—and stated, "You guys. All's I had was nine violations, so then they come at me with the fuckin Denver boot. . . ." No comment from anyone. ". . . Not that I don't love you all, because I dearly do, like my own family."

Shaper emitted the beginnings of pro forma coughing politeness, but Gyro, finicky, elegant, living up to his sports jacket, ran right over him. He seemed a little aggrieved by lack of due honor. "Ignorant Rom people call you guys *gadje*, which doesn't show respect, because it means piece of crap, but when I was in Georgia down there near Florida selling cars—"

"We're busy," said Shaper.

"*I'm* busy," said Gyro, correcting him. Gyro had met confused *gadje* before, people who thought they could do their business better without him, but this didn't mean he felt more kindly about gross error and discourtesy. He left without offering something sweet to drink or saying good-bye.

They listened to the clang of footsteps, sending up sparks. He must have been wearing metal taps on his shoes to impress the parking and traffic judge. Because he cared for the dummies, plus the dog, back there having their summit conference, he sent up a polite double beep of farewell from his Chrysler Imperial in the alleyway. Somehow he had removed the Denver boot, but drove off with the big orange card glued to his windshield: WARNING! DO NOT TRY TO MOVE THIS VEHICLE! He loved that rounded Imperial opulence, like a woman with overflowing breasts, thighs, the rest of it. It was wrong to lock its wheels. Jesus, who died for the sins of others, but lived on for Gyro's, should have anticipated the Denver boot in His all-compassionate soul. They sure messed up the whitewalls, Christ, with their fucking orange trap which didn't match the color scheme at all.

Shaper took a deep breath. Everyone was sighing, even D'Wayne, whose soft palate vibrated slightly in a territory someplace between deep sigh and snore. Gyro tended to suck up the air in a room. They were all needing oxygen, taking in motes of Victorian dust, leftover soft grit after the stir he brought. In due course, Shaper might settle himself about Gyro Brown's presence in the world. Gyro's character got in the way of his personality—that smiley personality, gliding along on wings of song. Shaper had always admired charm, not according it a possibility for himself. Gyro had it. But then there was his character, and wasn't it fitting about the life of a great city in this part of history? If a man had a whole big hunk of quality personality, he didn't need character at all.

Dan Shaper, older guy, new father, hoped his personality and his character might come to coincide. He no longer had all the time in the world. He needed to proceed in the direction of where he needed to go, although events tended to interfere with the important things in life; even Shaper's perpetrator clients pointed this out. (Santos could have made today's fix, a whole week's fix, on this harmless through-the-window daytime home entry, but some stupid *nino* out of school with a runny nose heard Santos break the glass and knew about punching out 911. . . .)

Amanda removed her hand from touching D'Wayne's head. This gesture made Shaper less shy about looking at her. The flanges of her nose were pink. He had never seen her with a cold, and she didn't have one now. What kind of a father has never seen his daughter with a runny nose? He had missed the tantrums of a baby, the sulks of an adolescent; he had missed the child's small hand tucked into his, trusting him. No trust had been stored for future emergencies.

It was easy to be cruel to someone new to loving. All Amanda had to do was not love in return.

Life had happened to Dan Shaper in earlier times; such was his opinion about it. If the rain fell, it wetted, it chilled him; he was not impervious. Now he was part of the rain, he was making happen what was happening—his modified present opinion—by becoming what he was with Amanda. It was no longer merely a possible point of view. Gradual fathers, the usual kind, present at birth and thereafter, experienced this shift into the hope of immortality by proxy almost without noticing, just doing daily what they had to do. Shaper did what he was doing with no preparation in history. He was a father; a fact, not a judgment call. He was stuck with someone. The future was no longer something in which he would not be implicated.

Amanda took his hand, pulled his arm, insistently held his hand, spreading his fingers on the warmth of her belly. She was smiling and watchful. "Hey Dad, cat got your tongue?"

This was highly interesting. It was confusing. The cat had gotten his tongue. Shaper tried to halt his tears, but he failed to do so.

"Even if I start looking kind of funny, my stomach, you'll take me out sometimes like a boyfriend?"

"No, can't do that."

"Cause I'm getting fat?"

"Can't do that like a boyfriend—"

She laid her finger across his mouth. They could agree, their secret, that he almost said *like a dad.*

D'Wayne was confused by what was going on here, but he started work on it in his own way. "You think I like her cause she's white? There's lots of white stuff out there, man. She needs me, thanks to having no daddy. That happen what I need, too—somebody need me. So you gonna hit me again?"

"No."

"I didn't have a daddy neither, you know what I'm saying? Mandie and me, we teaching ourself, man."

I'd like to learn, too, Shaper was thinking.

"Say what?"

"All you were telling me, D'Wayne—"

"Living our lives," Amanda said, "that's what we're studying."

Slumped dramatically in her chair, Margaret expressed herself with the loud sighs of needing notice. Amanda turned to her and said, "It's okay," and waited till Margaret answered: "Yeah. Okay." This was her daughter whose milky burps had stained the terry cloth robe she still sometimes wore. It was the same robe she had worn after a shower with the stranger who had made her a mother and was now no less strange to her than her daughter.

"He must've thought I needed him to get D'Wayne out of my life, that's what he thought," Amanda said. "I'm getting a zit on my chin."

"He's not out," Margaret said. "At this stage you get pimples—the first-trimester zits. They go away."

Amanda touched her belly; today her hand was groping for D'Wayne, for Shaper, for herself. "I feel like a stove in there."

During an event filled with apprehension, a real man gives helpful advice to his significant other. "Lighten up, Mandie," said D'Wayne.

Margaret Torres repeated, "He's not getting out of your life." She knew better than Dan Shaper about D'Wayne. Also she was ready to tell her daughter about nausea, night sweats, and food cravings, and it was still an open question for Margaret—an open-minded person—whether these matters should be blamed on the patriarchy. One thing she knew: first-trimester pimples are not permanent or fatal. Meanwhile, D'Wayne was dealing with the father-daughter section of these events by having a little mother-in-law, inappropriate-son-in-law moment of his own. His aching bandaged head moved slowly from side to side, admitting to any concerned observer, Oh, man, I got to lighten up, too. If D'Wayne had a headache and a bit of confusion, well, that was a normal stage on life's way. Margaret Torres hunkered down in her chair and enjoyed the discomfort of her daughter's man, her daughter's father.

Shaper measured his choices. He could try to figure out everything that was going on or he could live through what was going on and later come to some conclusion or no conclusion at all. He wasn't sure he actually had a choice. As a veteran with much experience in looking after himself, he didn't consider it the end of the line for him. He intended to head back and redo his past, just as if this could be done.

Margaret Torres, still sunk in her chair, silent and alert, had not wanted a father for her daughter, and this not-wanting, this desire for absence, carried both mother and daughter for nearly twenty years. What right had a sturdy young woman, her life mostly still ahead of her, stuffed like a sausage with unknown ingredients, to claim there was a place in her life for this stranger, the court translator? Margaret knew the first answer: none. And then the next: it was up to Amanda.

"Amanda," Shaper asked, "will you let me be your father?"

"She's not a child anymore," Margaret said.

"Amanda?" Shaper repeated.

Amanda sat on the arm of her mother's chair and raked her fingers through Margaret's hair. "Hey mom, I'm not a baby anymore—"

D'Wayne repeated: "Lighten up, man."

"I had another idea," Margaret began, but didn't need to go into it at this time.

"But I'll always be your baby," Amanda said.

Shaper was thinking: She's an interpreter, too, like her old man.

"Hey guys," D'Wayne said, "I don't want a smoke, kind of lost my taste for it, this headache I got, but anybody carrying some stuff? This thing, this thing hurts."

His bandage pulled the skin tight and it was purplish at the taped edge. Amanda picked up a bottle from the floor near the bed. She shook out one pill, two. He didn't reach for them; he opened his mouth like a child. His tongue wet her fingers. She handed him a bottle of Crystal Geyser water. "I'm not sleepy," he stated, although no one had said he was. He lay back, closed his eyes, and waited for the capsules to kick in.

"Amanda—" Shaper began.

"Okay, enough," Margaret said. "You're nagging."

His eyes closed, D'Wayne muttered, "That makes it unanimous."

From his court experience, Shaper knew that unanimous wasn't always the correct judgment. Clever ones could get their way with juries. Once in a while they were innocent;

sometimes even their lawyers were, too. Shaper himself stood on the outside of the crimes he translated. He didn't use the drugs, snatch the purses, break into the cars. Now he was thrust into the midst of the turmoil, not knowing where he was.

Imperative impulses caused the bodies at the Yerba Buena Foundation to knock each other about and keep their souls in privacy. If there was danger in the vicinity, it was silently gliding by as if not in the vicinity. The radios and TVs in separate rooms, the workings of hair driers and plumbing, were muffled for the moment. This family was busy surviving. The capsules Amanda placed on D'Wayne's tongue seemed to put all of them in a better mood. From many rooms away Barbara made her daily triumphal shriek, so much like the joy of love, but in her case just another victory over chronic constipation. The toilet flushed. Her ritual cry went back to some childhood anxiety, or mistrust of her body, or hemorrhoids. Once more she proclaimed victory. The toilet reflushed, gurgling because not finished with its previous exercise. Calm returned.

"Hey Dad? You want to be a happy senior citizen, that's all you want?" Amanda asked. "Yecch, that's so sick."

"You think it's wrong of me?"

She shrugged. "Go right ahead, be my guest." She wrinkled her nose. Some young women expressing loss of interest tended to do that; it was a habit that faded with age. "But I think you listen to your friends too much—Gyro, that lawyer Fred—"

"Ferd."

"—your other buddies. Harvey."

Wrong about that. His daughter was a normal person who didn't know everything. Someday she might learn about matters she thought she already understood but didn't.

Amanda was curious about the tears in the eyes of the man

who used to be a perfect stranger except that he happened to be her father. A little glaucoma problem, a conjunctival irritation, some kind of allergy? She had a California temperament, a survival mind; she observed him, reserving judgment. She preferred not to make errors unless absolutely necessary in the advancement of a woman's life. She gave him a chance to wipe his face while she switched her observation of matters to D'Wayne, who was asleep, or pretending to be asleep, or dreaming he was both asleep and pretending. Eyes politely averted, she reminded Dan Shaper, "You're a persistent bastard, you really insist on things, don't you? Only I'm the one who's the bastard, right, Dad?"

She watched him stand; she watched him wipe his cheeks. Again she turned away out of consideration for any embarrassment in the room. It was confusion, not grief, that was making him so boyish. She had no right to think she caused unmanageable emotions in this person who was still a perfect stranger. He finally said, "I didn't know."

"Nobody did," said Amanda.

"I did," said Margaret.

"I don't know," Shaper said.

"Men don't, how could they?" Margaret asked.

Amanda glared at her mother to tell her to keep her mouth shut. Margaret had practiced the arts of open secrecy for twenty years; it was a course she might as well continue. But not liking the expression on Amanda's face (congested, stubborn, in need of a mother's advice), Margaret said, "Listen, you—"

"Shut up."

"Don't talk to your mom that way," D'Wayne said, "'cause you're keeping me awake." He knocked the pillows with his elbows for emphasis, sank back, and eloquently, dramatically, almost loudly shut his eyes.

"So who am I, Dad?"

292 · H E R B E R T   G O L D

"My daughter."

"Is that all you know?"

"For some reason I care for you a lot."

"Gotta do better than that," said Amanda, but since it had taken him so long already, added kindly: "Mom, you can talk now."

Margaret was clearing her throat for a possible comment and Dan was trying to clear his head for possible listening and learning, and D'Wayne was wondering what he had gotten into, grumbling in family fashion, "Never gonna get no rest around here." That was true, too. When Gyro returned, they would have to listen to the ancient wisdom of a lost, sinning, and forgiven tribe, probably about as satisfying as any other ancient wisdom. "*Never* gonna get no rest," D'Wayne repeated, uttering Shaper's very own thought, with Gyro heading their way in his sharp suit to tell of the rights given by the Son of God (disputed) to wander the earth and make the best of things, provided you were one of the Romany band.

But even they might belong in Gyro's family—what person under Gyro's gaze could be certain of who his father was?

Only by their works shall we know them.

"If you died now," Amanda said, "at least I had a father."

"Daughter mine," Dan Shaper said.